EUROPA

Book One | The Black Chronicles

EUROPA

J.A. SANDERLIN

Tate Publishing & Enterprises

Published by Tate Publishing & Enterprises, LLC
127 E. Trade Center Terrace | Mustang, Oklahoma 73064 USA
1.888.361.9473 | www.tatepublishing.com

Tate Publishing is committed to excellence in the publishing industry. The company reflects the philosophy established by the founders, based on Psalm 68:11,
"The Lord gave the word and great was the company of those who published it."

Book design copyright © 2009 by Tate Publishing, LLC. All rights reserved.
Cover design by Amber Gulilat
Interior design by Joey Garrett

Published in the United States of America

ISBN: 978-1-61566-071-1
1. Fiction / Science Fiction / Adventure
2. Fiction / Christian / Futuristic
10.01.20

To my family: you are always my biggest fans.
&
For the Great Light of the World.

PREFACE

Europa is Jupiter's third largest moon. Europa is covered with a crust of ice and debris believed to conceal a massive ocean covering the entire planet. The core of Europa is thought to be primarily made up of nickel, iron, and various other useful minerals and heavy metals. Several nuclear-powered probes were launched from Earth and melted through the icy crust, confirming this and the existence of the planetary ocean. These new discoveries caused the then-named World Federation and several corporations to eventually launch expeditions to determine the viability of mining and colonization, albeit with some apprehension because of the ill-fated Neptune missions from which no one ever returned. The single ocean that covers the surface of the planet underneath the ice and debris ranges from about 1,500 to 10,000 feet deep, with fracture canyons over 30,000 feet deep. No one has ever explored the entire planet or been to the bottom of the deepest trenches. There is now a large mining colony on, or rather, *in* Europa. The colony and mining operation is in one of the more shallow areas of the seabed, where the colonists can mine nickel, platinum, titanium, and other elements from the core.

ONE

The Venutian Witch slid through the cold, dark shadows cast by the millions of asteroids near Ceres. The captain had kept the Witch and her crew hidden for the last month in the sensor-scrambling asteroid field. He ordered the crew to hold fire unless fired upon as they approached a small, mysterious ship. The ship appeared to be a frigate-class ship with a visible layer of thin laser armor: a mosaic of mirrors that deflected laser fire and blended the ship into the starry background like glistening camouflage. The navy frigate suddenly seemed more ominous when its gun turrets came into view. The Venutian Witch positioned itself alongside the navy vessel. Their air lock tunnels extended toward each other and they were coupled. The captain went to the other ship with his second-in-command and monstrous bodyguard. The trio returned in an hour, and the Witch then left her lair in the asteroid field at flank speed for Jupiter.

Jonas Black ran the final checks on his micro-reactor to make sure he did not have any wires crossed. When the *Manta*'s systems all showed in the green, Jonas fired up the reactor and disconnected the outside power source. The status indicators showed all essential systems stable and fully functional.

"*Manta* systems online, reactor online, sonar online, drives online. No errors currently detected in operating systems. Weapons and auxiliary sensors incomplete. *Manta* operational, captain," stated the ship's A.I. in its cool feminine voice.

Manta had been activated over a year ago. Her program was moved to the hull of her namesake nearly six months ago. She was not self-aware—there were no programs that were, no matter how old or sophisticated. But she was a computer that learned, solved problems, and ran all of the autonomic functions aboard the ship, which was as much a part of her now as she was of it.

"We did it, Dad," said Jonas, smiling.

Matthew had spent almost a whole year of evenings, weekends, and some vacation time helping his son complete his ship. Matthew was a tech engineer and knew the ins and outs of every craft ever used on Europa colony. Jonas and his father ran simulations using different materials and configurations, and both were confident that the *Manta*, as they chose to call it (due to its similarity in shape to the manta ray on Earth), would be the fastest and most maneuverable craft in the colony.

The frame of *Manta* was a combination of hybrid alloy and a thirty-fifth generation micro-tubular graphite strain developed on Mars. Jonas ordered many of the pieces from a ship factory on the moon of Earth. They were prefabricated for several other ships, and he had to cut, assemble, and fuse them into the configuration he wanted when they arrived. The hull was covered with an electro-polymer composite around the "wings" and stern, with an equally corrosion-resistant poly-comp material covering the rest of the frame. When an electrical current was run along a particular relay in the wings, the electro-polymer would contract in that area. There were thousands of relays on each of the wings, allowing the pilot to control speed, attitude, pitch, and roll. Thus the *Manta* was propelled in the same way a real manta ray was: by a graceful undulation of its wings. *Manta* had neutral buoyancy, her depth was controlled by the speed and the pitch of her wings.

"Now we just have to run a few more simulations ... " Matthew started to say.

"Oh, come on, Dad. I'm tired of simulations," interrupted Jonas. "I want to do a test run. We've done hundreds of sims already."

"If you will let me finish." Matthew gave his son a "shut up and listen" glance. "I was going to say it will only take about ten minutes to run the sims, and then we can flood the dock for a pressure test."

"Can we go on a short run?" asked Jonas excitedly.

"Well ... " Matthew smiled. "It wouldn't be a real pressure test unless we took her out, now would it?

"You'd better not tell Mom about this," Jonas said soberly.

"All your mother needs to know is that we ran the pressure test. We don't have to tell her how we ran the test." Matthew smiled mischievously.

With the final computer sims run, Jonas dropped into the pilot's seat and ran pre-dive checks on the 3-D imaging sonar, helm control, and communications. Jonas then closed the hatch and ran the internal air pressure up to check hull integrity for the hundredth time. Everything was perfect. Jonas depressurized, and his father opened the hatch and entered the vessel.

"Let's ask for safety," said Matthew, bowing his head.

"Okay," answered Jonas glumly.

Jonas's mind drifted off. He had only feelings of love and affection for his parents; they were the nicest people he had ever known, and that was also the opinion of most people in the colony. But Jonas did not know why his parents clung to such an archaic religion. Markus Askuru was behind the window in the chamber control room, having been sworn to secrecy about Jonas's going on a test run four weeks ahead of schedule. When Markus saw the hatch shut, he started pumping out air and opened the main flood valve. The dry dock began to fill slowly, covering *Manta* with freezing, acidic water.

Matthew spoke to Markus on the com.

"Looks good so far, Markus. Now slowly equalize pressure with the outside."

"Ten-four, Matt. You guys signal if you have any trouble. I'm going to bring the pressure up real slow," answered Markus.

Manta's hull began to creak and moan under her first real feel of the crushing depths of Europa's ocean.

"Hull stable so far," said Matthew. The hull pressure increased slowly from 400 psi to 600 … 700 …

"Powering up the reactor," declared Jonas. "I'm going to flex her muscles a bit."

"Go easy," said his father sternly. "We're still in a confined space."

Jonas nodded, gently pushed the yoke forward, and could see the wings gently move down on the graphic body display. He pulled it back, then checked pitch and roll. Perfect.

"All right," said Markus over the com. "You're at full pressure."

"Already?" asked Matthew, looking at the pressure gauge. "She didn't even make any compression noise after nine hundred."

"I can hear you smiling, Matt. You still owe me twenty credits." Markus grinned back through the microphone. "I told you it was an excellent design."

"Jonas told me too," answered Matthew. "We'll try for about a fifteen-minute run. Open the bay doors. Thanks again for helping us out today."

"No problem. I had to bring you my interceptor anyway," said Constable Askuru.

Markus and Matthew had been friends since Jonas could remember. They seemed to have some kind of unspoken understanding that went beyond usual friendship. It was almost like a brotherhood. When Jonas asked his father about it, he would smile and say, "Markus has to get along with me. I know too much about him."

He had once asked Markus why they were such good friends. Markus replied with a soul-piercing gaze, "Because your parents are the only people who know who I am and like me anyway."

The doors opened, and Jonas slowly pushed the throttle forward. *Manta*'s wings rippled, propelling her slowly forward. Matthew turned on their sonar and light beacons as they cleared the dock. Jonas throttled up, causing the ship to quickly accelerate.

"Whoa!" Matthew exclaimed, grabbing his chair. "Give me a chance to put on my seat harness first."

"Sorry, I just had to see what she would do," said Jonas, not taking his eyes off the controls. "Look, Dad. I only have her at three quarters and she's faster than any of the Sharks."

"Excellent. Let's just keep it there for a while. This is a test run, remember?"

"Yeah, I remember. It's just that we've waited almost two years…" Jonas looked at his father.

"I know you've waited a long time for this." Matthew smiled back. "Don't think it's not tough on me too. I have to work on everyone else's newer equipment every day. I can't imagine how it must look for a colony tech to ride around in a forty-year-old ship."

"Engineer, Dad. And the *Jack Frost* still runs better than most of the Sharks," argued Jonas.

"True, but it's not fit for exploring. It doesn't go deep enough, and it's too slow."

"You mean you're going to let me go!" yelled Jonas.

"Yeah." Matthew grinned. "But we still have a lot of work to do. Let's get back to it."

Manta was a ship with a purpose. Jonas had not constructed it to have the fastest ship in the colony, although that was an added bonus; he had built it to explore Europa. He had discussed his plan many times with his father and mother. Both had rejected the plan initially, but that was over two years ago. Matthew decided soon after that his son could not be dissuaded and began helping him construct the ship.

Father and son could only see their surroundings with the imaging sonar. Not that there was much to see in the total darkness of Europa's ocean. They navigated around rocky outcroppings along the floor, then climbed upward to the planet's ceiling of ice. The jagged ice provided the occasional glimmer of dim refracted light to the naked eye, but it was not enough to provide usable light to any creature on the frigid moon.

"That thing is a piece of work," Markus said aloud to himself, smiling as he watched on sonar as the ship darted around the colony, skirted the undersea mountains, and skimmed along the bottom like it had always lived out there.

Markus's mind drifted to memories of his friends and eventually to this morning's conversation with Matthew. There was something strange about some of the new miners. Several of them didn't fit the usual profile, which wasn't a big deal in itself. Miners were even more varied than the things they mined and the tools they used. One had to be a little weird to want to dig around in the dark all day in the freezing, crushing depths here. What worried him was that he couldn't put his finger on what it was that seemed out of place. He had done background checks on several of the new miners and they showed some minor criminal history. But most of them had dropped out of the criminal databases four to ten years ago which usually meant someone had given up on crime for the more profitable "normal life."

Manta's first test ran beautifully, her design proving as good as Jonas and his father had hoped. She sliced through the water effortlessly as Jonas maneuvered her through several barrel rolls, much to his father's vexation. The imaging sonar projected a virtual image of the colony and all of the ridges, canyons, boulders, and other ships. Imaging sonar consisted of a series of varying frequencies emitted from the sonar and antennae array. It used a massive amount of memory and was the third largest program contained in the computer core, after *Manta's* A.I. and the power and drive control program.

After docking *Manta* in the workshop, Jonas and his father took the slower *Jack Frost* back to their living module. They passed the heart of the colony: the domed central hub with its thousands of glowing windows. The Blacks' living module was situated on the side of a ridge at the tip of the longest southern spoke of the hub.

Matthew docked *Jack* as Jonas gathered up their gear and went to the hatch. Jonas ran through the air lock and past his mother with a quick "Hey Mom!" He proceeded up to his room to dump his figures for the day's tests. Matthew walked into the living room, where his wife was still doing a double-take, and kissed her on the cheek.

"Evening, beautiful," said Matthew with sincere enthusiasm.

"Hello, handsome. What is *he* so excited about?" said Sarah Black, gesturing toward Jonas's room.

"What are you two up to?" she inquired, as she met her husband's guilty look.

"Well, honey, *Manta* went on her first test run today, and it was a complete success."

"And you brought him along, didn't you," she said, matter-of-factly.

"Yes," Mathew answered, completely unable to lie to his wife. "I know I promised I wouldn't, but you know how it is with guys—gadgets, ships and machines. He had as much right to be on that test as I did, maybe more…"

"All right," interrupted Sarah with feigned irritation. "You're forgiven, both of you."

She turned to meet Jonas coming down the stairs.

"What did I do?" inquired Jonas. Matthew gave him the "we've been caught" look.

"Oh… Sorry, Mom, but you know how it is…"

"I know, your father already told me. Dinner's ready," she

interrupted, turning abruptly and walking to the dining room to keep them from seeing her smile.

Sarah knew her husband and son, sometimes better than they knew themselves, and she knew it was futile to attempt to restrain them. But the thought of letting Jonas go out in any ship, especially a homemade ship, and explore the planet's ocean brought chills to her. She wasn't supposed to know about the whole thing, but she had uncovered the plot several months ago from none other than *Manta* herself. Neither of her two men, despite their genius, had thought to tell the ship to keep their secret.

She worried for all the obvious reasons, but there were other factors as well. No one had ever been more than about one hundred miles from the mining operation, mainly because of the rumors of the colossal "leviathan." Only a few people that had actually heard the sound of the beast's deep drumming sonar through the hull of their ship, but the colony's core computer had hundreds of recordings of them. Jonas had listened to them and heard the rumors of leviathan destroying ships in the early years of the colony when they ventured too far away from the mining operations.

Only about twenty-five non-microbial species were known to exist in the planet, excluding the chemo-plankton, but theory dictated that there must be many more to support the known ecosystem. Sarah had a degree in microbiology from Berkley, New Atlantis. She had cataloged most of the known species on Europa during excursions around the colony. But she had never strayed far in *Jack Frost*.

Dinner was uneventful and small talk about the new Republic prevailed at the Blacks' table. The Europa colony was founded in 2286; the year was now 2342. In 2331 Mars had declared its independence from the oppressive Earth Federation of Worlds, starting the first interplanetary war. The war was officially over, with Mars having won its independence. The Mars Republic claimed the Europa colony because the companies running the mining operations were based on Mars. The Earth Federation had never made an effort to seize it, probably because of its remote location.

Dinner was interrupted by a call requesting Matthew's presence at an accident site to check a boring machine reactor with irregular power output. Jonas started to stand as if to go, but he was told to stay so his mother did not have to finish dinner alone. After finding out there was a chocolate mousse in the cooler, he needed no further convincing.

Jonas helped his mother clean up the kitchen, and she retired to the living room to conduct her never-ending study of the tiny little plankton and other organisms that fascinated her so. Jonas went to the balcony to stare out the window into the darkness that was his home. He had only seen the sky on Earth or Mars in VR, but it didn't really bother him. He had lived his entire life at depth, the atmospheric pressure here being slightly above that on Earth. He wondered what it would be like to breathe thinner air. *Seems like it would be difficult,* Jonas thought.

As he turned his gaze back to the south, he could see a faint flash of light in the inky blackness. He strained his eyes to make out the shape. The light got closer, and Jonas could see that its shape was changing. The multi-colored lights shifted and pulsed as they quickly approached. It was a school of comet fish, a sight that never ceased to impress Jonas. Their amazing internal lights pulsed in waves along the length of their bodies, changing at random. Then, prompted by some unseen cue, the entire school would light up at the same time. Every fish in the group would change to the same color, and the pulses that usually went along the body of the individual fish would travel in waves across the entire school, making them appear as one entity: thousands of individual lights looking like they were one being with the same mind. Then the school would change course, and they would all go back to their singular patterns. The school came within several hundred feet of the window, probably attracted to the light, then skittered away as fast as it had approached. Jonas asked himself for the hundredth time why he wanted to leave such a wonderful place to travel to Mars, a place he had never been.

It was always easy to stay where you were comfortable, to never step out and try something new. Jonas did not want to be one of those unadventurous people who never tried anything. He did not want to grow old and wish he had done more, or at least made the attempt. It was not that he didn't enjoy peace and quiet, but he did not want to miss the chance to take a look around at all the galaxy had to offer.

Jonas had remained in the colony two years after graduating early with his high school degree in astral physics and a minor in mechanical engineering, which had been a breeze, of course, since he had been fixing things since he was old enough to hold a pulse driver. He had exhausted every correspondence course he could find and, upon getting a general bachelor's of science in physics, had transmitted his doctoral thesis on the concept of "Hyperspace Travel Without the Use of Jump Gates" to Mars University at Minos last month. It was not a true doctoral thesis, just a paper on his major field of study to prove he already had a working knowledge of physics and bolster his chances of being accepted into the doctorate program.

It had taken over twenty years to make the trip to where the first intersystem jump gate had been built. It was only accomplished with a short hyperspace jump to empty space where a beacon probe had been sent over thirty years before; the rest of the journey was made on sub-light engines. Nearly every test ship had been lost in the first attempts to reach the beacon probe, and the whole plan was almost scrapped. After arriving onsite it still took another ten years to establish a base and build the jump-gate. Since then Elysium and its surrounding system had prospered.

Without a hyperspace gate at the beginning and end of a jump, a ship could not be sure of where it would exit hyperspace. The gate acted as beacon for the ship to lock onto while in hyperspace. Earth and Mars both had gates, making trips between the two mere seconds. The next step was travel without jump gates, but that required knowledge of the exact destination coordinates. The trajectory must be exact, and exit time from hyperspace must be pre-calculated to the millisecond. Even then it was equivocal. If the ship's initial trajectory was off by a millimeter, or if speed or exit time were miscalculated, the ship could exit hyperspace millions of miles off course, headed straight into a star, or even inside a planet. And that would ruin anyone's day.

Simulations had been run using A.I., but despite their immense processing abilities, no computer in existence was able to hammer out the algorithms necessary to accomplish the task. Despite their power, they still lacked the speed needed to make all of the calculations on the fly, as well as control and monitor the power output, trajectory and plot an exit point. Once in hyperspace, a ship could not maneuver and was essentially blind until it cut its jump.

Jonas had not told his parents of his plans yet, nor of his helping Markus design defenses for his ship for extra money. Stream and pulse lasers, favored in space battle, were of little use underwater. The torpedo, age-old missile of the deep, was still the most proven aquatic weapon. Constable Askuru paid Jonas well for his services and bought many of the stealth torpedoes he had designed and built. The money Jonas made from this and just about everything since he was old enough to work was stashed in a Martian account. His father encouraged him to invest and save his money, which was not difficult, since he and his father could build most of the things he would have wanted to spend it on.

Markus Askuru was a well-respected and supremely competent man, but the Colonial Counsel would not listen to him regarding possible threats to the colony from the outside. Everyone seemed to think that since they had gone unnoticed this long that the vast resources of the mines would continue to be ignored. And although Republic Army personnel were stationed on the surface base, they consisted of no dedicated fighting troops: only technicians and communications personnel.

Jonas's thoughts were interrupted by the com tone. Checking the screen he could see Commander Daniels talking to one of his staff while he waited for an answer.

Daniels was Republic commander of the surface station,

which sat on the outer crust of Europa, just above the colony. The station was a docking port for the underwater ships bringing processed ore to the surface, and for space-faring vessels which came to transport it off-world. The station's massive reactors kept the hole beneath it from icing up again.

"Hello, Commander," said Jonas, opening the com channel on his end.

"Hello, Doctor Black, how are you this evening?" answered Daniels.

"Fine, but I think your screen is malfunctioning. This is Jonas. I think you want my father."

"No mistake, Jonas."

"Okay, since when am I Doctor Black?"

"Since I received this transmission from Mars just a few minutes ago," said Daniels, smiling.

"There must be some mistake. They were going to send interview questions for me to answer before they accepted my thesis," argued Jonas.

"Well, I suppose you did such a good job that they didn't need to question you further," said Daniels. "I'm re-transmitting the message now. Tell your parents I said 'hello' and congratulations to you, again."

"Thanks. See you later," answered Jonas.

"I can't believe it," he said aloud. *I mean, I knew I had a pretty good chance … but so soon and without any interview?*

Jonas's mind raced as he read the message. Although he had no formal college except for correspondence courses, he thought that with his obvious understanding of physics, the college would let him enter the doctoral program. *Wait a second … Commander Daniels said "Doctor Black" … they gave credit based on cumulative knowledge, but they would not, under any circumstances give anyone a degree, would they? They can't do that! Can they?*

As Jonas sat on the couch, shaking his head in disbelief, his mother walked out of her study and immediately noticed the grim look on his face as he stared blankly at the living room viewing wall. Sarah walked over and looked at Jonas with motherly concern.

"What's wrong, honey?" she queried. "Who was that on the com?"

"I just received a communication from Mars University and they said they liked my paper..."

Mrs. Black interrupted.

"Oh, that's wonderful, Jonas! But why the sad look? Didn't you want to go to college?"

"Yeah, but... I don't have to, now."

"What? Why?"

"They gave me my degree, my doctorate."

"What?" Jonas's mom sat down in disbelief. "How? They can't do that. You haven't even been there yet."

"Yeah," said Jonas, straining for a smile. "The details are supposed to be in the rest of the message."

The Dean of the Physics Department at the university checked Jonas's theory and calculations and confirmed them. The Dean conferred with the faculty of the Physics Department, and they also confirmed the calculations. They sent Jonas's work, and their confirmation of it, immediately to a review board. The board liked it so much that they brought it before the Chancellor and recommended an "Echelon Stratum Doctorate Gratis," which was issued and the board of trustees approved. Furthermore, the Physics Department invited Doctor Black to serve a probationary period as an Associate Professor of Astral Physics for two years and a tenured professorship thereafter. His focus would be research and development with the Republic Navy on the practical application of his theory.

Jonas had waited so long to go to school that he had thought of nothing else to do if it didn't work out. Now that his plans had gone awry, albeit in a good way, he felt lost. He had not planned for what he would do after college. He thought he would have another two years to think about it. Now that time had expired in ten minutes. Now he had a job, and that was great, although he was sure he did not know the first thing about being a professor. But he still had no idea what he wanted to do with his life other than explore.

Eventually Jonas went to bed. He could not sleep for thinking about the events of the day. When he finally drifted off to sleep, his com tone awoke him. Jonas looked at the clock when he rolled out of bed, and it read 2:13 a.m. Jonas answered the com; it was his father.

"Want some contract overtime?"

"Uh ... sure, Dad," Jonas said groggily. "What's up?"

"Good. I've got to replace the coolant pipes in this digging machine, and it's going to take awhile. We found out at about ten o'clock that there were two men unaccounted for in the mine, probably still trapped," said Matthew with some urgency. "They only have about four hours of air left at best."

"What? When did this happen?" Jonas interrupted.

"We're not sure. In the chaos of trying to get a container transport out of the collapsed tunnel, someone didn't realize there was a digger further in. Everyone is working as fast as they can to get to the men, but a digger just blew a couple of hydraulic valves. I need you to go to the shop, machine a couple of new ones, and install them. A foreman named Tyler is already on his way to the module to pick you up in a Shark. I wrote down the file name and gave it to him so you can find the specs on the shop computer."

"Okay, Dad. I'll move as fast as I can, see you later."

Jonas was just dressed when the docking alarm rang, signaling that his ride was there. He ran to the air lock, boarded the Shark, and exchanged greetings with the driver, who gave him the note from his father. The trip was only five minutes in the Shark as opposed to the usual fifteen in *Jack Frost*, leaving little time for conversation. Tyler cordially bantered with Jonas along the way and left him at the shop, stating he had to get back to the rescue site. Jonas entered the shop and went to work forthwith. After inputting the schematics, it took over an hour for the robots to machine the parts. While they worked, Jonas prepped *Manta* for launch. He was sure his father would be against the idea of taking her out with testing still incomplete. But Jonas knew everyone else would be busy, and he was not about to call someone and take them away from the rescue operation.

Jonas hovered over the robots while they worked. The second they were finished, he took the two valves and ran to the dock where *Manta* was already floating in the half-flooded room. Jonas ran across her wing, entered, shut the air lock, and remotely sent the flood command to the docking computer. During the next two minutes, the room flooded while Jonas put the valves into the nanite tank, which he had already loaded. In the tank, billions of microscopic robots would finish the valves to one millionth of an inch. Completing the process en route to the dig site would save precious minutes.

When the dock was flooded, Jonas opened the bay doors and gunned *Manta*'s throttle. The synthetic muscles in the ship's wings thrust her forward with such power that Jonas's head was thrown against the back of his seat. The sleek vessel slid through the water like a comet fish as they streaked toward the rescue site. As Jonas approached, he could see hundreds of lights from dozens of vessels milling about in an ordered frenzy. Most of the machines from rival companies were onsite to assist in the effort.

Jonas found his disabled client hovering just south of the jumble of clambering workers and asked for permission to board, which he did before receiving an answer. The operator of the massive machine was waiting for Jonas when he entered. They exchanged a handshake and greetings as they quickly moved to the bow of the digger. Jonas went to work. He had the parts replaced and the machine running again in less than an hour. Jonas contacted his father, and they continued working with the other mechanics anywhere they could to keep the overstressed machinery running.

The time came when the trapped men should have run out of air and Jonas found himself whispering a silent prayer asking for just a little more time. He did not believe it would help, but it wouldn't hurt.

Jonas took *Manta* and docked her at home a few minutes before his father came dragging in behind him in *Jack Frost*, just after noon. Jonas took a shower and ate something before falling on the couch for a couple of hours of much-needed sleep. The rescue crews had found both of the trapped men unconscious and half-dead from carbon dioxide poisoning. The men had enough oxygen, but the carbon dioxide had built up to toxic levels in the small ship. Doctors at the hospital announced over the colony news channel that they were stable, and they would wake them from a medically-induced healing stasis in the morning.

Jonas looked at the clock before he drifted off to sleep, just before one p.m. Europa went by Earth's calendar and used the twenty-four-hour day, not that it made a difference one way or another. Europa had no seasons, day or night, weather, or even sky. It was just the way the first colonists wanted it, and it had been that way ever since. The ice thunder and ever-present darkness were all Jonas had ever known, but he never thought it strange; it was home.

Jonas opened his eyes and felt himself suspended in freezing water, unable to breathe. He looked around the total darkness and found a single light in the distance. He began desperately swimming for the light. Jonas could feel his lungs burning as they desperately struggled for air; his will was the only thing keeping his body from drawing in watery death in an attempt to breathe. As he swam, the light seemed to get further away; then suddenly the light streaked toward him. The light came closer and he struggled to make out what it was.

A school of comet fish? his mind screamed. Jonas felt despair and disbelief, realizing what he had been following only too late, as he felt the cold water flood his lungs with icy liquid. The luminescent life forms turned and disappeared into the lightless gloom. He could feel the crushing weight of the darkness overwhelm him as the last bit of warmth was drawn from his body by the chilling abyss. He clutched at the water as he struggled to propel himself anyplace but where he was, but there was nothing.

Jonas awoke gasping for air on the couch in his living room. The cool air filled his lungs in deep hurried breaths, each one a sigh of relief. He looked at the clock: 5:53 p.m. He smelled coffee and could hear his parents talking in the dining room. Sitting up, he looked over the back of the couch, still feeling pale from his dreamt near death experience.

Matthew, who was seated at the dining table facing the living room, saw him.

"You look a little confused. Dreaming of far-off places and forgot where you were?"

"Come and have some coffee," said Sarah, turning to smile at him.

Jonas stumbled into the kitchen, poured a cup of the steaming brew, and hauled himself to the dining table.

"I was just telling your father about the transmission you received from the university yesterday," said Sarah.

"That sounds like a pretty good deal," remarked Matthew, grinning at Jonas.

"Yeah, it does, Dad," Jonas answered with uncertainty. "But it's just so sudden. I didn't expect to have to leave this soon. I wanted to finish *Manta* and go on my trip first."

"Well, we've been discussing it, and your mother thinks that we can knock off a few weeks of testing and possibly get you out of here in two weeks. That way you could send your answer to the university and still have time to finish your trip before you'd have to leave."

"Really?" Jonas shot his mother a questioning glance.

"Yes, really," answered Sarah, "but it's only because your father assures me that the ship has performed beyond your expectations already, and that you two won't take any unnecessary risks."

Jonas's eyes lit up as he turned immediately to his father to tell him the things they needed to do to get the *Manta* fully operational. Sarah, knowing she would soon fade from her two men's minds, told them there were leftovers in the cooler if they wanted anything and went to her study.

The next day Jonas and Matthew went to work on their pet project with renewed vigor. The reactor's power output was steady, and Jonas permanently wired the imaging sonar. Matthew, using a commercial-grade laser, worked on the cabin lining, which was a nearly paper-thin, flexible alloy that would take and hold a shape when heated beyond four hundred degrees. Jonas had just started checking his materials list for the weapons system when Matthew told him it was already seven o'clock. They both realized they had forgotten about dinner completely. They boarded *Manta* and remotely flooded the docking bay. When the pressure equalized and the bay doors opened, Jonas pitched *Manta* down toward the opening and flew out of the shop with breakneck speed. They were at home in moments, neither of them realizing how famished he was until sitting down at the table.

Jonas helped his parents clean the table, then retired to his room to do some stretching and weightlifting. On Mars he would have to carefully reassess how much weight he worked with in the higher gravity. Jonas showered and sat down at his computer to run over his material list and design schematics for *Manta*'s weapon system. He had acquired a targeting array from a trader and copied the basic targeting programs from Markus's cruiser. Jonas fell asleep at his desk and dreamt of holo-images of his beautiful ship soaring through the ocean's depths.

TWO

The walls of Jonas's room were covered with photo optical paper, allowing any image or video to be displayed. He awoke every morning to the sound of crashing surf and a view of the sun rising over the ocean from a beach where he had never set foot. By initiating the right program, you could watch the sunset in the southwest of North America, wake up to the sunrise in Tahiti, or take a relaxing flight over the Andes Mountains or Olympus Mons. He got up, and it occurred to him how strange it was to live in an ocean, but to have never seen a beach. Jonas dressed, went down to the kitchen, and started some coffee. He soon had a cup and was sitting beside the balcony window, looking out at the darkness that always was. His parents soon joined him, chattering about the events planned for the day. Jonas was included in the conversation, of course, but he had little input, not being fully awake until he had finished his coffee.

The gathering was held in one of the large common rooms of the colony, which was virtually never used on the weekends. It was the only assembly of The Way in the colony. The group was small, consisting only of Jonas, his parents, and about a hundred others. The speaker's message was fairly interesting, but Jonas's thoughts drifted. The idea of teaching about the Advocate who was the one way to life after death seemed somewhat absurd to Jonas in this day in age. In addition, its followers believed that this Advocate would return, and that was over 2,300 years ago! One would think he would have come long before now. *Don't get me wrong,* Jonas directed his thoughts outward, *I think The Way is a great religion, but I just don't think it's for me.*

Jonas continued his inner monologue throughout the oration, pausing only to mentally argue with the curate. It was Jonas's usual weekly lecture routine. A few announcements were made, the curate prayed briefly, and the gathering was over. Everyone immediately began the post-invocatory chatter and headed toward the adjacent main hall for the monthly lunch. Having grown up attending such affairs, Jonas knew who brought the dishes he liked, and who did not. Jonas tried conversing with anyone available to avoid being noticed by her in the small crowd, but he knew it was a futile attempt.

"Jonas!" she yelled across the room.

He pretended not to hear her until she stepped in front of him, and he had to acknowledge her.

"Oh." He feigned surprise. "Hi, Kat."

"You know I hate it when people call me that," she said with a look of disdain.

Although that is what everyone who was more than a casual acquaintance called her.

"Sorry, Ka-ther-ine," Jonas enunciated.

"That's even worse." She rolled her eyes, punched him in the shoulder, and smiled. "When you get your plate come sit with me and James. Okay?"

"All right." He regretted agreeing with her already.

Katherine Shaw was seventeen years old; eighteen in a month, she would argue. Ever since she was in the seventh grade, she'd had an unrelenting crush on Jonas. In his mind the age gap was tremendous. He was almost twenty-one. He had tried to discourage her in every way he knew, but nothing seemed to work. James, her brother who was about Jonas's age, was his best friend. So it seemed there was no escaping her. It wasn't that Katherine was unattractive: she was skinny and clumsy, but pretty, and her eyes were such a dark brown that they were almost black. She was just too young, and Jonas did not have any interest in settling down until he had exhausted his need to explore.

Whenever he wasn't working (Jonas swore his mother and Katherine were in cahoots), Kat always seemed to appear. She was inhumanly hyper and laughed with incredible volume. When she cut down on coffee (or whatever it was she took for energy) and actually calmed down to a normal person's energy level, she was fun to be around. When he thought about it, he probably considered her his second closest friend. The worst thing about the whole situation, Jonas thought, was that his best friend wasn't on his side. James had decided to stay out of the whole thing, laughing at both of them in the interim.

Jonas took his food and meandered over to where James and Kat were sitting.

"Hey guys," Jonas greeted them.

"Hey," said James, motioning Jonas to have a seat. "I heard you got that bucket of yours running."

"Everyone's already saying it's faster than any ship in the colony," Kat interrupted.

"Well," Jonas hesitated. "She runs pretty well so far, but we're not finished testing her yet."

"Let me know when she's ready to show me what she can do," said James.

"Sure. I hope to have everything ready to go by the end of the week."

"Will you take me out too?" injected Kat.

Jonas paused before answering.

"Yeah, I guess so."

James snickered and mumbled, "She's wearing you down."

Jonas did not catch the remark and kept eating. Katherine elbowed James.

The work on *Manta*'s weapons system went slower than expected. Jonas ran into dozens of problems trying to fit the old targeting system onto the ship. In addition, the targeting system wouldn't acquire targets. On the upside, he was getting good at manual targeting. Jonas had been spending so much time working on the ship that he lost track of time and found Friday upon him. James and Kat dropped by the shop that afternoon to hear Jonas cursing the targeting program as they stuck their heads into the ship. Jonas turned to meet Kat's scolding look.

"Well," said James, "I guess I don't need to ask you how it's going."

"This piece of junk keeps freezing up on me, and when it does run, it won't acquire any targets!" Jonas remarked, pounding the small targeting module with his fist.

"Let me look at it," said Kat as she pushed her way past James and Jonas.

"Where is your diagnostic computer?" She demanded, looking at Jonas.

"Back here ... " Jonas went aft of the ship and brought back a small handheld device with about two dozen ports and plugs of various shapes and sizes.

"Thank you," Kat responded as she took the device with a slight look of arrogance. "You boys go find something else to do, and I'll take care of this."

James tossed his head aft for Jonas to follow him.

"What's up with her?" Jonas asked, motioning to the front of the ship.

"Oh, she's been in a mood all week. Something to do with her college applications. She hasn't received a reply from any of them yet."

"Oh. Well, it usually takes awhile."

"Yeah, although she can be relentless and resolute, she can be really impatient too."

"I am more familiar with her relentless quality," remarked Jonas dryly.

"That's for sure," James said, chuckling.

The three worked on the ship into the evening. Jonas finally made Kat stop working on the targeting computer only by promising she could finish the next day. Jonas took them out in *Manta* to show off her abilities, eventually ending up at the colony's main dock. They disembarked and proceeded to the central plaza, which was surrounded by dozens of restaurants and shops of varying wares. The plaza was at the base of the massive domed center of the colony. Half a dozen corridors radiated from the outside edge like the spokes of a wheel.

The trio walked down an alley and into Giovanni's, a small Italian restaurant, and were seated immediately with warm greetings from the host. The place looked run down, and the age of the décor raised questions as to the sanitary condition of the kitchen. The host, waiter, owner, and atmosphere of the joint was a jolly, balding man of about sixty. His colorful personality and attentiveness brightened the dingy look of the place. The three ordered, were quickly served, and took their time enjoying the best Italian food in the colony.

Jonas picked up the tab and paid before the other two could object. The three were thanked by their host and implored to come back again. Jonas dragged them to a few electronics and machine stores to pick up a variety of circuit boards, parts, and tools. The three stopped at a coffee shop for a while before heading back to the *Manta* and embarking on a cruise into the open ocean.

Jonas headed for the southern trench, which was the largest canyon near the colony. The craft cut through the water at more than seventy knots, making short work of the ten-mile trip. James sat in the co-pilot chair and Kat was seated at the sonar and weapons console of *Manta*'s small bridge. The ceiling of *Manta*'s bridge and the narrow hallway on the starboard side leading to the aft engine room was just over six feet high. The port cabin was only eight feet long, five wide and nearly seven feet tall at its highest point. It had a single fold out bunk, small desk underneath, and the necessary facilities in a very compact arrangement.

The port and starboard probe launching tubes could also auto-load a small but impressive array of hidden torpedoes.

Upon arrival at the trench, Jonas moved the *Manta* into position and told Kat to turn off the imaging sonar. He opened *Manta's* eyelets, revealing two large round portholes on her bow, and activated the forward lights. The black tar of darkness was pierced by the light, revealing crystal clear water allowing the three to see the distant wall of the abyss over which they were hovering. The ship was already at 5,200 feet, almost one thousand feet deeper than it had ever been.

"I'm going to ease her down to about eight thousand," Jonas told his passengers. "*Real* slow," he added.

"Kat." Jonas looked at her. "I want you to keep an eye on the skin integrity. At the first sign of anything changing, tell me."

"Check," she answered.

"James." Jonas pointed at the display on the right side of co-pilot's seat. "Watch the skeletal sensors for any abnormalities."

"Got it," he answered.

Jonas eased the controls forward and pointed the nose of the craft straight down. He then throttled forward and began creeping downward, hugging the wall. As they skimmed down the face of the canyon, they lost all sense of equilibrium. It felt as if they were cruising along the floor of the seabed, and sideways was actually up. It took almost ten minutes to travel the short predetermined distance. Jonas leveled off and stopped, hovering over abyss, making *Manta's* lights seem insignificant on the canyon wall. He turned the imaging sonar back on, looked at all the sensor information, and saw that everything seemed to be in perfect order.

Kat pointed at the holographic ship display. "What's this?"

Jonas needed only a glance at the display, and his eyes grew wide as he forced the throttle of the *Manta* forward, pulling back on the rudder controls. The ship turned ninety degrees almost in place and shot straight up from the canyon like a bullet, as a shocked James and Kat were pressed into their seats. What had previously taken ten minutes to travel now took less than twenty seconds. When Jonas reached the 5,000 foot mark, he began to level the ship off and head back toward the colony, still at full throttle. Jonas set the autopilot, turned, and looked at the display intently. After a few moments of agonizing scrutiny over the hull display, Jonas let out a sigh of relief.

"What's the deal?" James finally asked, realizing from his friend's demeanor that whatever the danger was, it was probably past.

"The display." Jonas pointed to a spot on the floating hologram of the ship. "It looked like the beginning of a hull breach, but it looks like it's just a flub in the display. I'll have to fix it later."

Kat, who had been sitting and staring at the display for the last few moments with a stunned look on her face threw her hands in the air and blurted out, "Well, I feel stupid! I nearly gave myself and everyone else a heart attack because of a flub?"

"Don't feel stupid, Kat," Jonas retorted. "I reacted instead of looking more closely at the display. You did what you were supposed to."

Jonas looked at Kat intensely to make sure the words sank in and she understood it was not her fault. He knew that she would often mentally berate herself over the smallest mistake for hours, if not days. He wanted to save her from that. She understood and smiled; he nodded, but waited until he turned back to the controls to smile to himself.

The trio arrived back at the colony. Jonas dropped Kat and James off at the dock nearest their residence and departed for home. His parents greeted him with serious looks and simply pointed at the news broadcast on the viewing wall. It only took seconds for Jonas to see that tension between the Federation and Republic was building again. There had been another incident near Luna, Earth's moon, over some trade agreement and who knew what else. One Martian freighter was destroyed, as well as several escorts from both sides. Worse yet, according to their best information, both of the worlds' respective fleets appeared to be mobilizing again.

Jonas lay awake that night for several hours thinking of *Manta*, Kat, James, his parents, his offer to go to the university, and a hundred other things that he could not put out of his mind. *On nights like this,* he thought, *it would be nice to switch my brain off for a while.* But that just made him think of a horde of other things that only complicated his insomnia. He finally went to sleep and gently awoke to the sounds of crashing waves, feeling disconcerted by an unusual dream.

He had dreamed of walking along a soft peat trail. He could smell the air, hear birds singing, and was thoroughly enjoying himself when a bearded man appeared, walking beside him. Jonas felt as though he knew the man and felt compelled to strike up a conversation with him. The two talked for what seemed like hours about everything from plankton to coffee, physics to rocks. The man, who seemed like the brother Jonas never had, stopped, smiled, said something inaudible, and vanished. Jonas was left standing alone. Then he woke up. Jonas tried to shrug off the melancholy mood that clung to him. Despite trying to busy himself working on *Manta*, thoughts of the dream disturbed him throughout the day.

Jonas finished loading his torpedoes onto the ship, the cabin lining was complete, and his dad finally had the sink working in the tiny cabin. Jonas brought his father along on another depth test, to almost 20,000 feet. The test went well, and they went back to the shop to run diagnostics on the ship in dry dock. He checked *Manta*'s skin and entire system for the hundredth time. Satisfied with the results, Jonas entered *Manta* and headed for the gym. Matthew followed in the much slower *Jack Frost*.

Jonas jabbed at his father with his left fist, followed by a right to the throat. He landed the left, but Matthew sidestepped to the left and outside, dodging the right. Matthew countered by shifting his weight to his right leg and caught Jonas's lower right thigh with his own left shin. Jonas's leg buckled slightly from the numbing impact, but he recovered quickly and backed off a step.

"You have to commit to the punch, but don't let your weight shift too much. Real life isn't just boxing," Matthew explained to his student. "You have to assume that your opponent knows just as much as you do, and consider that he may know more."

"I know, I just thought I had you," Jonas said, shaking off the stun still in his leg.

"Never go for a final blow; you never know when your opponent may see it coming or be feigning weakness. Then it's you who is caught off-guard."

"But how do you know if you can take someone?" Jonas asked, circling his father.

"You don't. Never assume that you can beat anyone, no matter how strong you are or how weak you consider him. We are but mere men; we cannot know what another's abilities are or what another has learned and experienced. You or I could be defeated by a lucky blow from a ninety-year-old man. It doesn't take long to learn how fragile our bodies are, son; just give it a few years."

"Yeah, I hit my shin on a rail in the shop yesterday and wanted to cry," Jonas said with a chuckle. "So how do you know when you should stand and fight or when you should retreat?"

"First, you cannot worry about injury. Second, you have to be mentally tougher than your opponent. You have to be willing and able to endure more pain than he can. Or at least, make it appear to him that you can. Knowing when to fight is difficult, but when you do, commit to victory. You must choose your battles wisely, and during that battle constantly re-evaluate whether or not victory is possible. If it is not, retreat if possible to a safe position and rethink your strategy."

"So how do you know when to retreat?"

"The answer is never the same. It changes in every situation. In a controlled environment such as this, you don't have to worry about making mistakes. You can take risks and try new things; failure incurs only minimal consequences." Matthew glanced at Jonas's leg. "In a real fight, you do not hold back. In the real world the only reason to fight is to defend yourself or someone else. And often, that means being the first to attack. Okay, back on track."

Matthew stepped into Jonas, pushed him, and attempted a step-through leg hook. Jonas pushed back and Matthew grabbed Jonas's gi, placed his foot in his hip, dropped, and swung his weight like a pendulum on Jonas. Jonas lost his balance due to the swinging weight and was flipped head over heels. He landed with his back on the mat as his father rolled on top of him and tried to put a chokehold on him. Jonas reached up with his leg, put his ankle over his father's nose, and pried him off, just breaking the choke in time to remain conscious. He scrambled to his feet and backed off again, knowing he could not beat his father in ground fighting. The two continued their conversation while circling each other.

"Good," complimented Matthew. "You knew I could beat you in brute force, so you used pain to counter; then backed to a more defensible position. That is what I meant by knowing when to retreat; you just answered your own question. Also remember, this is just a small engagement. Attacking and retreating during a series of engagements is no different. It just takes place over a longer period of time."

"Oh … I see," Jonas said with wide-eyed revelation. "I never thought of a little scuffle like that being relevant to a larger situation. It makes sense now."

"One last thing today."

"What's that?"

"If you ever get backed into a corner with no hope of victory or retreat, though the situation is grave, never give up. You make sure you hurt the other guy as much as possible. Make him pay for every step forward. It could mean your life. In a real fight, failure is not an option. Fight ruthlessly."

Jonas nodded, and they kick-boxed for another ten minutes before calling it a night and heading back home.

When Jonas and his father arrived at home, they sat down with Mrs. Black and had the talk she had long dreaded: Jonas's ship was ready.

"I just think it's too soon," Sarah protested. "I thought you had more tests?"

"Mom, we finished them, just a lot sooner than we expected to."

"He's right, honey," said Matthew. "We set a predetermined number and type of tests we thought we would need and we stuck to it. Jonas just finished them much sooner than anticipated."

"I just think it's a little too fast. I mean, it's only been three weeks since you first took it out. Shouldn't you wait a little longer?" Sarah entreated.

"We could wait another year and you still wouldn't want me to go," Jonas gently said to his mother.

She looked at Matthew, and he was nodding.

"You're right," she conceded, thinking two against one was not fair.

"Besides," Jonas said lightly, "who was the first one to take the *Jack Frost* past its depth limit?" Jonas looked at his mother with a raised eyebrow. "And you're always blaming Dad's genes for my behavior."

"He's got you there," snickered Matthew, gently squeezing his wife's arm.

Jonas went to the weekend gathering with his parents. He then went to lunch with his parents, Kat, James, and their parents, who were leaving on a business trip for several months that same day. During lunch, he told his friends that his sub was ready and that he would probably be leaving Tuesday, if all went according to plan.

"How long will you be gone?" asked Kat.

"Oh..." Jonas thought. "Five or six weeks."

"Six weeks? I thought as fast as that thing is it would only take about two weeks," Kat said.

"It would," answered Jonas, "if I went in a straight line at full throttle every day. But the whole point of this little excursion is to *explore*," Jonas said, putting emphasis on explore, "The record of being the first to circle the ocean of Europa is just an added bonus."

James sighed.

"I wish I didn't have to work all summer. But I can't take a break if I want to go to Earth and finish my degree."

James was going to have to pay his own way through school, mostly with student loans. James, like Jonas's father, wanted to get his underwater engineering degree from a school in the oceans of Earth.

Jonas and James had both been born on Europa and had never even seen Earth, except in V.R. Like all young people, they had big dreams, which usually proved more difficult to realize in the real world. James and Jonas had wanted to go to college together, but things changed as they grew up and their career paths had taken them in different directions. Kat had wanted to join the guys at whatever college they attended. Now she was torn about where to go and, worse yet, wouldn't even get to go until the spring semester. She had only recently finished her high school degree exams, and the results would not be back in time for her application to be accepted at a college for the fall semester. Kat was graduating a year early, but she still did not know what she was going to major in.

Everyone parted ways after lunch. Upon arriving at home, Jonas began packing for his trip, all the while adding to his list of supplies. After he was sure he had packed everything he could, Jonas took time to watch the news to see how the interplanetary tension was heating up. Although Elysium belonged to the Federation, it was attempting to remain neutral throughout the conflict. And despite political pressure from Earth, they refused to obey the Mars trade embargo imposed on them by the Federation. But now the Federation was sending a security force through the jump gate to Elysium to "ensure the safety of the citizens," according to the prime minister. It was the Federation's way of pressuring the Martian Republic to re-approach the negotiating table.

Hopefully, Jonas thought, *it doesn't pressure the Republic into a full-scale assault on the Federation's fleet. It will be nice to get away from everything for a while, before starting my first real job this fall.*

Jonas had transmitted his response to the university yesterday, accepting the position. *How could I turn it down? I was going to spend a couple of years at college anyway,* he thought. *At least this way I'm getting paid while I make up my mind about what to do with my life.*

Monday morning Jonas got up early, quickly ate a muffin, drank some coffee, and rushed out the air lock to *Manta.* He traveled to the central plaza, systematically going from one store to another, picking up the necessary items for his journey. Jonas felt like he made a dozen trips back and forth, hauling food, parts, and everything else he thought he might have need of and stowing it in the various cabinets and cubbyholes inside the ship. He then took the *Manta* out for one last depth test at the southern canyon. He paused over the canyon, pushing thoughts of being crushed into the size of a soda can from his mind. He turned *Manta's* nose down over the bottomless chasm displayed on the sonar. Jonas pushed the throttle gently forward and began the plunge to his target, the canyon floor.

Near the bottom of the canyon, chemical geysers began to appear on the walls, and Jonas could see clouds of chemo-plankton feeding around them. The previously deadly cold darkness erupted with life. He began to see schools of comet fish on the sonar darting this way and that, feeding on the bioluminescent jellyfish. Jonas began to hear the sounds of *Manta* adjusting to the depth. Her frame began moaning and creaking as the crushing pressure introduced her to the deep. Jonas began sweating as he passed the 24,000 feet mark, and guided the ship, watching the sonar images and trying to monitor the ship's hull for any danger. Jonas leveled off about twenty feet from the floor and checked every display on the ship. When he was satisfied with that, he went about the ship checking every seam, port, strut, and seal. Jonas then stood perfectly silent in the hall and listened for several long minutes. Then he walked to the bridge, slumped down in his chair and let out a sigh.

"Finally," he said out loud, "it's ready. I can hardly believe it."

Jonas turned on all of *Manta*'s exterior lights and saw, for the first time, what no human being had ever seen before: the sea floor of Europa at 25,107 feet and all the amazing creatures that dwelt on it. A rush of emotion flowed over him: happiness, relief, elation at his success, to sadness, as a chapter of his life came to an end. For two years the construction of this ship had nearly been his entire life, his purpose. All his energy focused on this one thing. Now part of it was over. The melancholy passed quickly as Jonas thought of his unfinished quest, which would begin tomorrow: to explore the ocean of Europa and be the first to circumnavigate it.

Matthew and Sarah were waiting at the air lock when Jonas arrived home. They didn't need to ask how the test went after seeing Jonas's gleaming face.

"So," said Matthew, "you're ready to go tomorrow?"

"Yep," Jonas answered, again breaking into a smile.

"Do you have everything you need, and are you absolutely sure that thing is safe?" asked Sarah as they walked to the living room.

"Yes, Mom. It's safe."

"Make sure you make good maps of everything, and collect data on any new species, oh, and samples of any you can catch," implored Sarah.

"Sure, Mom. That's why I'm going, to see what's out there."

"So how deep did you go on the test?" Matthew asked.

"All the way to the floor ... "

"Really," Matthew said matter-of-factly. "You should have told me you were going that deep, so I could have been standing by if there was a problem."

"I know, Dad, but what could you have done if there was a problem? It would have been futile for you to be there with the *Jack* if anything went wrong at that depth," reasoned Jonas.

"You're right, but you should have said something anyway. No matter now." Matthew patted Jonas on the shoulder. "I'm happy for you, Jonas. Few people get such an opportunity to explore the unknown. It's a wonderful accomplishment."

"You speak as if he's done it already," Sarah elbowed Matthew, smiling.

"Oh, he'll do it in that ship," said Matthew, "but for now, it's late and I'm going to bed. Night, Jonas." Matthew hugged his son. "I'm proud of you."

"Night, Dad. Thanks."

"Good night," Sarah hugged Jonas. "I'm proud of you too."

"Thanks, Mom. Night."

Jonas went to his room but could not go to sleep for hours. Checklists and thoughts of the unknown flowed through his mind. When he finally did get to sleep, he was awakened by one of his horrible dreams, only to be kept awake again by thoughts of what lay ahead of him on his journey and whether or not he was forgetting anything.

Jonas awoke feeling tired, but he got up, dressed, and shuffled down to the kitchen for his morning coffee. His parents were soon awake, milling about the kitchen preparing breakfast. Jonas and Matthew went over his planned route and the last set of diagnostic data from *Manta* to ensure they had not missed anything. There could be no rescue attempt if Jonas's ship were to become stranded beyond radio range, or if he were stranded below 17,000 feet. That was maximum depth for the Sharks. Therefore, they had to take every precaution to make sure that the ship was in perfect running condition, and that Jonas would have any parts and supplies he may need if there was a problem. There had been only one other attempt to circumnavigate Europa's ocean, more than thirty years ago. That explorer was never heard from again.

Jonas went back up to his room and plucked a small metallic cylinder about the size of a thermos bottle from its charger. The container had several monitor lights on it and a small view screen, which allowed him to observe the condition of its contents. He lit the magnification screen and could see a few of the more than one million microscopic nanites floating inside their suspension liquid.

"How are you guys doing?" Jonas asked.

A lettered message appeared on the view screen.

"We are currently in full hibernation mode and operating at 100% ... awaiting further command."

"Good, continue hibernation."

" ... Thank you, Jonas," they answered.

Jonas had programmed the nanites with Katherine's help. Nanobots were expensive; it cost Jonas over 3,200 IS,' Inter-System Exchange Units, for only five of them. Once he had them, he provided them with the raw materials needed and, again with Kat's help, programmed them to build copies of themselves. It had taken nearly four months for them to attain their current number. The tiny robots could double their number roughly every seven days. They possessed very little intelligence, since they were too small to have much memory capacity, and needed to be controlled by a larger computer via microwave transmissions. However, when the groups became as large as this, they could each retain tiny pieces of knowledge that could be exchanged between them very quickly, making them quite intelligent as a collective. This allowed them to accomplish complex tasks with relative ease and without being constantly controlled by an A.I.

Jonas looked around his room once more to make sure he was not forgetting anything, and went back down to the living room, finding James and Kat waiting to see him off.

"Hey guys," Jonas greeted.

"Hey!" they answered in unison.

"We just wanted to say bye one more time," said Kat.

James stood behind Katherine and pointed at her accusingly.

"Well, you just caught me. I was about to leave."

"I know," answered Kat, "but I wanted to give this to you."

She handed him the old silver cross she always wore. Jonas looked at it and tried to hand it back.

"I can't take this, Kat. It's yours."

"And it's still mine," she argued. "I want you to bring it back to me."

"I tried to tell her it's not like you're going off to war or something, but of course she didn't listen," interrupted James, casting a slight frown her way.

As Jonas looked at the old Celtic cross in his hand, Katherine moved close to him and closed his hand around her family's oldest heirloom.

She looked at him and said, "Please take it, Jonas, and be careful."

He had never heard her use such a serious tone before.

"All right," he answered as he put the chain over his head and dropped it down the front of his jacket. Kat hugged him and kissed him on the cheek just as his parents walked in. He turned to see them both staring with raised eyebrows, and blushed slightly. She had succeeded in embarrassing him yet again, unintentionally, but as always with great effect.

"Are you ready now?" Matthew said with a smirk. Sarah elbowed him.

"I think so," said Jonas, shrugging off his remaining blush.

Jonas exchanged hugs and goodbyes with his mother and father. Matthew walked him down the docking tube to *Manta* alone.

"Son, I know I'm not a great teacher, but I've tried to teach you everything useful I know. I realize you think our beliefs are outdated and inconvenient in this age. But, like I've told you since you were a boy, someday we're all going to die and face the Light. When that happens, he only will claim you if you gave your life to him. He paid the price to protect us, and he is the gatekeeper; the only way we are saved from the darkness." Matthew put his hand on Jonas's shoulder and looked at him intently. "I know you've heard all of this before. But there is no hope in anything else. Your mother and I won't be around forever, but no matter what, always remember who you are and what you've been taught. Always enjoy the little things in life, and never cease to feel wonder at the beauty of creation. Take this."

Matthew handed Jonas a large alloy briefcase. "Open it only in dire circumstances. Otherwise, return it sealed."

"Okay," Jonas said with slight confusion.

"The universe is full of surprises. Remember the Light and be careful who you trust," Matthew said, shaking Jonas's hand in final parting.

"I will, Dad. Thanks," said Jonas, holding up the mysterious silver case.

Jonas waved goodbye, climbed through the *Manta*'s hatch, and secured it. Matthew closed the air lock and released the docking clamps. Jonas stowed the briefcase, strapped himself into his chair, activated the imaging sonar, and powered up all systems. He then took the cylinder of nanites and inserted it into a small hole beside the main control panel. The ship took hold of the cylinder and locked it into place.

"Nanites accepted, Captain," she stated. "Should I release them?"

"Thanks, M. Don't release them just yet. I still have to upload their repair program." The ship gave a gentle tone of acknowledgement. "Begin the mapping process immediately after leaving my residence."

"Yes, Captain."

Jonas eased forward on the throttle and crept away from the docking tube. When he was clear, he gunned it and pulled back on the controls, sending the ship rocketing straight upward. He opened the shields on the *Manta*'s two forward windows, giving them the appearance of glowing eyes as he maneuvered around several dwellings. Jonas banked right and dove toward his house, passing the window, seeing his parents and friends waving. Jonas increased power to eighty percent and proceeded south into the darkness.

Jonas guided *Manta* along the ocean floor at over sixty knots, a feeling of freedom growing within him. His time had finally come, and for a moment he was able to forget the shadow in the back of his mind. After about thirty minutes, Jonas decreased his depth to about 4,000 feet to increase the lateral range of his sonar, engaged the autopilot, and set to uploading the nanites' repair program. He set them to replicate their number to about one hundred million when not otherwise engaged. Jonas then released them into the ship's computer and coolant systems. He double-checked his course, depth, and speed before going aft to prepare something to eat. As he hydrated some freeze-dried lasagna, he told *Manta* to ready a probe.

"Set it on a horizontal arching pattern of about fifty miles. Set its sonar for maximum range. I don't care about details; I just want to get as much general information as it can get."

"Understood, Captain. Readying probe. Estimated time to launch: two minutes."

Jonas ate his dinner on the bridge, awaiting the launch of his first real torpedo.

"The probe is ready, Captain."

"Launch probe," Jonas answered.

There was a slight bubbling noise and the probe was away. On the sonar display, the probe appeared to be a comet fish, just as it was supposed to. Forty minutes later, the little "fish" returned to intercept *Manta*. Jonas turned off the autopilot and moved the ship to pick up the probe. After bringing it aboard, he downloaded its data. In a few seconds *Manta* translated the data into a series of 3-D images playing on the holo-display. After looking at several minutes of images, Jonas noticed an anomaly that appeared in several of the frames. It looked like it was a large mass that varied in size and location throughout the series. Jonas asked *Manta* to analyze the anomaly to determine if it was a malfunction, a school of comet fish, or some kind of distortion from a chemical vent.

Several seconds later *Manta* replied.

"The anomaly was possibly caused by a thermal distortion in the water. However, there were no vents detected in the area. I am unable to determine the source at this time, but it was not due to a malfunction in the probe or data."

"Thanks, M," Jonas answered. "Resume previous course and prep two more probes for the same pattern, one to starboard and one to port."

"Yes, Captain."

Jonas hoped the anomaly would be one of the legendary leviathans. Although he never told anyone, that was what he really wanted to find out here. He had heard stories of the mythical beast since he could remember. Jonas launched the next two probes, but they recorded nothing similar to the first. Jonas stayed up late into the night comparing his readings with those on file. At current speed, he would leave explored waters in about three hours. He was already outside the boundaries of human exploration; the maps of the area here had been obtained via ROV. Jonas set the throttle for ten knots and engaged the autopilot so he could get some sleep.

Jonas was awakened by the collision alarm blaring. He leapt from his bunk and ran to the bridge. Looking at the holo-display, he could see a huge mass careening across his bow. Jonas immediately cut the throttle and pulled back on the yoke. *Manta* began to slow. As the ship neared full stop, Jonas leveled off and gathered his wits about him.

"*Manta*, what was that, and why didn't you just steer around it?" Jonas demanded.

"Unknown what the object was at this time, Captain," *Manta* calmly answered. "I was unable to steer around it because you did not set my auto-pilot parameters to enable me to maneuver around moving objects, only fixed ones."

"Oh," Jonas said sheepishly. "Well, from now on steer around large moving objects too. Show me the recordings of the object we almost ran into."

"Yes, Captain."

The ship replayed the images on the holo-display. This time the gargantuan mass had a blurred, indefinite shape, but whatever it was, it was solid.

"It has to be a leviathan," Jonas voiced.

He turned the ship in the direction that the beast was last traveling to better focus his sensors that way, but there was nothing. Jonas was now convinced that the mythical creature was real and was determined to find one. He reset the autopilot and went back to bed, but thoughts of finding the beast kept him awake. After a few hours of staring at the ceiling he finally gave up and went to the bridge to replay the sensor images. It had passed directly in front of the vessel, but the sensors only showed a blurred three-dimensional mass without a definitive shape. Jonas saw rather than heard the creature's sonar wave patterns. However, at the same time, the creature was emitting some kind of low-pitched thumping noise, like the sound of a deep bass drum. The pattern was slow at first, increased in speed as the creature approached *Manta,* then returned to the slower pattern after it had passed, even when accounting for Doppler Effect. Jonas wondered if the change in pattern was meant to be some type of warning that his ship was about to collide with the creature. Jonas slowed *Manta* to one knot and listened for one of the creatures for hours until he involuntarily drifted off to sleep.

Jonas awoke with a start six hours later with a horrible feeling of dread. His message indicator was blinking on the main screen, indicating he had received a communiqué while he was asleep. It was from his father, instructing him to check in when he was able to let everyone know how he was doing. He knew what that meant; his mother was worried. Jonas quickly recorded a message and sent it bursting through the depths on the wake of a sonar pulse. About twenty minutes later, he received another transmission from home with a greeting from his mother and a "thank you" for telling her he was all right.

THREE

Markus was going over some reports at his desk with the occasional glance out his window overlooking the central plaza, when the surface communication indicator beeped and a message appeared on his screen:

Greetings Markus: A transport carrying a new mining crew from ZCON Corporation just cleared the base and will arrive at Dock Nine in approximately twenty minutes… transport will also be offloading supplies that were inspected and approved upon arrival at spaceport… clearance code D490130… Commander Daniels.

Markus acknowledged the message, switched his monitors to Dock Nine security cameras, and sent a sentinel droid to scan the new arrivals for weapons. Markus had been constable at the colony for ten years and had never required anyone else to help him, except several dozen sentinel droids. He maintained a strict "no weapon carry" policy at the colony so that most fights and drunken bar brawls were limited to fists. Occasionally someone would manage to smuggle in an old gunpowder firearm or accelerator pistol, but he would not usually be smart enough to leave it in his quarters. An accelerator weapon propelled a projectile to target. However, instead of flammable accelerant, the weapon used a series of magnetic rings in a barrel to thrust the bullet out of the weapon. This eliminated noise and the need for oxygen to operate the weapon, as well as allowing for much higher muzzle velocities.

It was a simple law: any person attempting to enter the central plaza with a projectile, cutting, or stabbing weapon shall surrender said weapon to the proper authority or be placed in jail. But inevitably the droids would still scan some random yay-hoo walking into the plaza with something Markus would be forced to relieve him of. The droids were always bringing him wonderful arrays of various cutlery "given" to them by miners after they had to pass through the plaza scanners. He knew people had guns; people always would, and, like most peace officers, he believed they should.

Markus finished his paperwork and decided to head to Dock Nine to get a look at the new crew. He walked through the plaza and waved to some of the business owners before strolling down the corridor to the air lock. His data pad indicated there were twenty new crewmembers. Markus wondered why ZCON was importing so many new miners lately and what this bunch would look like. The last few crews from ZCON were some motley ones. Markus arrived at the air lock door and started through, only to be struck in the shoulder by the shoulder of one of the disembarking crew.

"Watch it! You..." the man with the Martian camouflage duffle bag snarled, cutting short his insult upon seeing Markus's badge. "Oh! Sorry officer, I didn't know who you were," said the man with a hint of sarcasm.

"No problem," said Markus casually. "Everyone gets a little tipsy on their first trip down. It's the low gravity and pressure change."

"Thank you, sir. I'll try and be more careful," said the man, flashing his best fake smile before he turned and walked away. Markus watched the man and knew something was amiss. There was nothing the average person could have put their finger on; the man was clean-cut, dressed neatly, and appeared pleasant. It had been a long time since he had dealt with any hardcore thugs, but that is something an officer never forgot how to spot. That man was going to cause trouble. Markus made it a point to take a good look at the rest of the new residents coming out of the air lock, and none were an improvement on the first. He double-checked all the security droid's scanning records, but none of them showed any of the new crew carrying anything unusual. Markus walked back to his office, pondering his lingering suspicions. He resolved to look into them further. He obtained complete crew rosters from today and the last several ZCON crew additions, then contacted Commander Daniels.

"Good evening, Commander," Markus greeted.

"Well, hello, Constable," answered the commander cordially. "I didn't expect to hear from you today. Did that transport arrive on time?"

"Yes, it was fine. I need you to transmit a message for me to the central law database on Mars."

"Mars, eh? Is everything going all right down there?"

"Oh, just some routine checks. I just have a gut feeling, and I wanted to check into it and see if I could put it to rest one way or another."

"Okay, now I know there's something going on. Spill it," coaxed the commander.

"Nothing specific. I don't even know what it is I'm looking for. This latest crew just gave me the creeps, and I wanted to check into their history a bit."

"Oh, I see. No problem. Transmit the message, and I'll make sure the Lieutenant gets it sent out ASAP," assured Commander Daniels.

"Thank you, Commander. Transmitting now ... "

" ... Message received. Have a good evening, Constable."

"Good evening, Commander."

Markus signed off, feeling reassured something was in the works that would either relieve or reinforce his suspicions. He locked up the office and left for the day, taking his usual route through the less desirable parts of the colony. Passing some of the darker and rougher bars that the miners seemed to prefer, Markus entered the Irish-style brewpub that he preferred. The place had simulated wood wall paneling and bar and had a more relaxed atmosphere than the other places. Markus picked his usual booth in the back corner, ordered one of the darker brews, pulled out his pipe, and lit it. Drawing in the thick smoke always seemed to help him think more effectively. Maybe it was the nicotine; maybe it was the smell. But it was probably just that fact that when he actually slowed down enough to stop and smoke a bowl of fine tobacco, he felt like he had to relax and behave like an intelligent gentleman.

Markus snorted in amusement at himself, remembering the ancient Sherlock Holmes stories he read when he was a child. *That's probably where I got the whole idea.* His ale was set on the table, and he drank it slowly while thinking, smoking, and watching the news on one of the viewing screens. Never a heavy drinker, he finished his one brew, paid his tab, bid Stan the proprietor "good evening," and headed home. Markus arrived at his apartment, entered, and checked it for interlopers as usual. *Paranoia or just caution,* Markus wondered. *It isn't like I have any serious enemies in this place.*

He laughed to himself. The ones he had weren't very threatening.

But still, he never knew when someone might decide he or she just didn't want to be "harassed" by the police anymore for their usual minor infractions and decide to snap. With the loads of colorful characters that had been arriving the past month, who knew what was going to happen? *I hope I'm wrong about all those guys,* he thought, *because if I'm not…*

After showering, Markus went to his closet, brushed the dust off his old body armor, and set it next to his bed.

D wight O'Connor found his assigned quarters and entered the small 12'x 16' domicile, cursing and throwing his Martian camouflage duffle onto his bed as the door closed behind him. He yanked the chair out from the wall desk and turned on the communications unit. He entered the code he had memorized, D490130–02, followed by a pre-designated carrier frequency. The com-screen sparkled, and a dark image appeared on the screen.

"Who is this?" demanded the shapeless image.

"Lamprey," answered Dwight.

"Why are you calling?"

"To tell you it's cold down here, and to ask where the sun has gone," O'Connor said with a slight rolling of the eyes. It sounded like your typical government spy speak, always absurdly over the top.

"Right here." The dark shape became a human silhouette and brightened, giving Dwight his first look at his previously unknown contact.

"What have you done to attract attention to yourself already?" demanded the image.

"I bumped into the local blue boy when I came around the corner getting off the transport, but I was polite."

"I'm sure you were," sneered the image. "And politeness being quite out of character for you, the constable no doubt discerned your lack of sincerity."

"You told me he was old, and wouldn't be a problem."

"I said he came here to escape his past, and that he wanted a place to retire in peace. I said a man of your abilities would be able to handle him."

"I will," Dwight answered irritably. "But I don't like surprises. Everything else is on schedule. The rest of my men will be here day after tomorrow."

"We expect results with as little collateral damage as possible. The façade must be kept up for as long as possible to ensure no outside interference."

"Discretion is what I'm good at, not people skills."

"Well, see to it that your people skills do not blow this job before it gets started. Contact me when your operation is a success."

"Yes, sir." The image on Dwight's screen faded before he could finish his sentence. "…Jerk."

There was a knock at his door. O'Connor opened it to find Doyle, his lieutenant, standing there looking down the hallway.

"What?" O'Connor snapped.

"You told me to inform you when the shipment was in place."

"Get in here and quit looking around like you're up to something," O'Connor said, yanking Doyle into the room by his jacket collar.

"Sorry, Captain."

"We can't have anyone else getting suspicious for the next couple of days."

"We put the crates in the storage locker you designated, using the code you gave me to open and re-secure it."

"Good. Just tell the boys to keep a low profile for the next few days. If anyone starts anything, I'll shoot him myself. We're getting paid too much for this job to botch it now."

"Why are we doing this anyway, Dwight? I mean, with tensions between the Republic and Federation flaring up again, there should be plenty of fat, unprotected cargo ships running around. We could make a killing."

"I don't like it when both of the fleets are on high alert. It means they get more suspicious of every non-military ship they see, thinking it's a spy. They're more apt to pay us a lot of unwanted attention. For now I think this is the perfect place for us to lie low for a while, and we get paid to do it. Besides, an operation this big has to be sanctioned, so we'll likely only draw heat from one side for a while."

"True, but you can't trust the government."

"I don't trust anybody, Doyle, and especially not the governments. Because regardless of which government you're working for or what they promise, they're all run by politicians. Those lying little weasels are less trustworthy than half the men we employ."

"As you say, Captain, but I hate this place already. It feels like a tomb."

"You worry too much, Doyle. The only person we need to be concerned about will be dead before he knows what's going on."

Markus awoke the next morning, got dressed, donned his body armor for the first time in six years, and was pleasantly surprised that it still fit. He ate breakfast at the usual place and proceeded to his office. He had hoped to already have a reply from Mars, but there was naught. There was a message from Jonas Black, informing him that the probes he'd helped design were working great, and that the trip was going well so far. *Good kid,* Markus thought. *I hope he gets back all right.*

Jonas sent out another probe and set it to make the low-pitched thumping noise that he heard coming from the leviathan. With the probe away, he settled himself into his chair, leaving only passive sonar engaged. Jonas sat in the darkness, listening to the low thumping noise and hoping for a response from one of the creatures. The endless drone of the noise finally lulled him to sleep. Jonas's head bobbed and he awoke to hear the probe and another sound signature overlapping it. That had to mean that there was another one of the creatures in the area, responding to the probe's signal.

Jonas sat still, listening to the creature as it moved with utmost silence through the water. It resulted in no detectible sounds other than its apparently colloquial inquiries to the probe. Jonas could track the creature's location by the sounds it was making, and it appeared to be circling the probe. Jonas then activated *Manta*'s imaging sonar to see if he could get a better idea of the creature's size and shape. To his amazement, he was able to see the size and shape of the leviathan. The creature did not like the surprise, began to flee, and changed its vocal pattern in what appeared to be an attempt to warn the probe, which the creature must have thought was another leviathan. The creature stopped and turned when it realized that the probe was not leaving the area also. The creature then turned toward *Manta* and began to charge.

Jonas took evasive action. At its current speed, Jonas could outrun the thing, but that was assuming it was already swimming at top speed. It was also likely able to match and maybe exceed *Manta's* maneuverability. So Jonas pushed the throttle to eighty percent and headed straight for the creature. He could see on sonar that the beast was surprised at the action, but after slowing for about a second, he resumed his charge. The thought crossed Jonas's mind that this was the stupidest thing he had ever done, but it was also probably his best chance to get away. *Manta* and the beast shot toward each other at hull-rupturing speed.

"*Manta*, start a collision countdown and put it on the corner of my display. Be sure to make adjustments if there are any changes in ours or its speed."

The timer had four seconds on it when it popped up on the screen.

"Done, Captain."

Jonas was not counting on the Leviathan breaking off at the last second; he was intending to do that himself. The gap was almost closed, and Jonas pitched *Manta* ninety degrees to the left, guessing that the creature was more maneuverable on the vertical plane than the horizontal. When the countdown hit one second, Jonas pulled back on the yoke, and the enraged creature slid just past him. He then pushed *Manta* up to full speed and continued on a course out of the area. His gamble enabled him to outmaneuver, then outrun the creature.

"*Manta*," Jonas yelled accidentally from excitement. "Turn off the probe's recording and turn on its sonar!"

"Yes, Captain," acknowledged the A.I.

The creature quickly turned back toward the probe, circling it several times before the probe disappeared from *Manta's* sensors.

"*Manta*," inquired Jonas, "can you locate the probe?"

"I am unable to locate the probe, Captain; it broke contact when the creature consumed it."

"That thing ate the probe!?"

"Yes, Captain."

"Why that sorry ... !" Jonas stuttered, livid.

He thought about firing a torpedo at the ... whatever it was. *That would give him a fatal case of heartburn if he ate that,* Jonas thought, snickering to himself. *No, it would be a shameful and wasteful thing to destroy a simple creature that probably was just acting on instinct. That was still a rotten thing to do,* Jonas thought, *and I think he might have done it out of spite.*

Jonas tracked the creature for several miles before losing contact for unknown reasons. When he resumed his course, the realization of his discovery finally started to sink in. How did it get here? Is it from Earth, or are the ones on Earth from here? Jonas recalled that the Chinese Empire had conducted genetic experiments on whales during the third world war. Some of those experiments involved sound-absorbent flesh and the development of higher brain functions to facilitate training for complex missions. The new species nearly won them the war at sea, but had devastating effects on the world's oceans. All attempts by the Federation to exterminate them proved futile. Fortunately, the Chinese had engineered the neowhales without the ability to reproduce, and after thirty years the entire species died off. What Jonas just observed seemed to match everything he knew of neowhales.

Jonas sat back in his command chair and contemplated the possibilities. He finally narrowed it down to three.

One: the Chinese Empire came here unbeknownst to the rest of the world and conducted their experiments during the third world war; and these are the creatures that were left behind. Two: the Chinese Empire's scientists were not as smart as everyone thought they were, and they simply came here, again unknown to the rest of the world, and took an existing native species from Europa's ocean. Three: Despite the bans on full cloning and genetic variance, the Earth Federation of Worlds (then called the World Federation) genetically engineered the species for Europa and planted them here shortly after their first probes. It would have been nearly impossible for one and two to have taken place unnoticed during a global war. Technology at the time would have made such a series of expeditions into deep space long and arduous. Furthermore, it was a virtual impossibility that a similar species to one already existing on an alien planet just happened to be genetically developed independently on another. Therefore, number three seemed to Jonas the most likely scenario.

But to what end? Why would anyone place an unnatural species on a planet where it might do the same damage to the ecosystem as it did on Earth? Then he had a disturbing idea. Jonas set the autopilot and went quickly to the database his mother had accumulated on the native creatures of Europa and then to the computer's database on the ocean creatures of Earth. He spent hours poring over pictures and genetic coding maps of dozens of species and finally came to the even more disturbing possibility: the native creatures of Europa might not be native at all, but genetically altered, and transplanted from Earth.

Although specific to this world, comet fish bore an uncanny genetic and physical resemblance to barracuda on Earth. The shrimp, tube worms, and crabs around the chemical geysers were almost exactly like the ones on the chemo-geysers of Earth. All of them were notably altered from their earth cousins, probably to enable survival in the dark, acidic waters of Europa. Even the chemo-plankton appeared to simply be a modified copy.

I don't care how much you believe in chance, thought Jonas, *this is an evolutionary impossibility!*

All accepted natural history stated that life finds a way to evolve even in the most inhospitable places, and Europa was the cornerstone of this well-known fact. *I have always believed in evolution and multiverse theory,* Jonas thought. *It's the only explanation for the universe short of the supernatural, and a scientist cannot logically mix the physical with the spiritual... if there is a spiritual.*

Now I find evidence that the entire planet might have merely been seeded by some quack geneticists back on Earth. This explains why Mom has always been so obsessive about finding and cataloging new species, Jonas thought. *She's always believed in intelligent design. That's why she could never get a good job at a university. What if she's right?*

Jonas's entire belief system seemed to collapse upon him and his mind at this discovery. Why would anyone do such a thing, say it was a natural occurrence, and present it as fact? *They have been lying to entire human race about this for almost a hundred years, and no one even knows!*

Jonas exhausted his mental faculties to the point of a headache. He went to his cabin for something to dull the pain and realized he had been awake for almost twenty-four hours. *No wonder I'm worn out,* Jonas thought as his head hit the pillow.

Markus finished his paperwork shortly after lunch and decided to take a walk. He passed through the plaza and into the southeastern spoke of the main colony, checking the security cameras and robots. After several hours, Markus took a connection tube to the southern spoke and headed back toward the main plaza. Upon entering the main plaza, Markus heard an alert tone coming from one of his droids at the north end and went to investigate. He found a man whom he did not recognize arguing with the droid regarding a large knife that the man had attempted to conceal when he entered the plaza.

"What's going on here?" asked Markus.

"This man attempted to violate colonial rules by entering the plaza with a concealed weapon of illegal size," stated the robot.

"You listen to me, you stupid rust bucket. I'm carrying this for personal protection, and you aren't taking it from me!" argued the man.

"Listen," said Markus, in an attempt to calm the man down. "It's no big deal. Just turn in the knife and you can get it back whenever you leave the station."

"No!"

With that uttered, the man turned and ran out of the plaza and down the main north corridor. Markus gave chase, and the robot notified the other droids of the evader's infractions and last known direction. Markus chased the man for about fifty yards before the man turned into a secondary shaft and continued running northwest. The man turned again and entered a darker tube that was little more than an access tunnel for some of the colony's electrical systems. Markus knew the man was running out of places to go and relaxed his pace slightly. The man made a final turn into a regulator room. Markus rounded the corner only two seconds later to find the sinister-looking man who had bumped into him two days prior, Dwight Younger. Before Markus could react, he saw the projectiles leave the barrel of the accelerator pistol in slow motion and could feel each one strike him in the chest. It seemed to take about ten seconds, but he knew by the configuration of the gun that it was an automatic and that those four shots were fired in less than one second. Markus could feel the pain sinking deep into his chest and his vision began to blur. A dizzying number of thoughts went through his head in an instant: *Why do this? There is something larger at work here if they went to all the trouble to set up an ambush, but to what end? What's going to happen to the colony? How can it end this way after all these years?* Markus remembered the first time he set foot on this settlement and why he had come here in the first place. He had come here to escape, escape from the guilt of the atrocities he had committed. The last thing Constable Markus Askuru thought was *what's going to happen to me now?* Then darkness.

"Good job, Doyle," Captain Dwight "Younger" O'Connor remarked casually.

"Thank you, sir," remarked the man with the knife. "I thought him slower than that. He almost caught me before I could get here."

"Never underestimate your opponent."

"Yes, sir. Should I dispose of the body?"

"No ... ," said O'Connor, looking around thoughtfully. "This is an isolated area, and I doubt anyone will find him for quite a while. It won't matter after tomorrow, anyway."

The two men turned and walked out of the room, leaving Markus's body where it lay.

C ommander Daniels finished recording his message and sent it to his employer. The colony's connection to the base communications array had been severed and all Republic base personnel were either in the brig or dead. The cargo ships and their ore shipments had been held for inspection and their crews arrested. They would be re-crewed and sent to the coordinates he had been given. It was regrettable that Constable Askuru had to be eliminated. But he had grown too curious. Now there would be no one to interfere with the final transfer of weapons and mercenaries into the colony.

T he subsequent takeover swept through the colony so fast that most people did not know what was happening until it was all over. Commander Daniels had given O'Connor complete access and control over the security, maintenance, and environmental systems of the entire main hub of the colony. More than a dozen people were killed when they tried to resist, and several more were made examples of so that no one else would get any ideas. A group of miners had rallied to form a collective resistance, and O'Connor flooded one of the main wings of the colony, drowning all forty-two of them, along with nearly one hundred others who just happened to be there.

O'Connor ordered the entire colony to assemble in the main plaza at 12:00 p.m. the day after the takeover. Everyone was to check in when he or she entered, because anyone who did not attend would be killed. Mathew and Sarah Black arrived shortly before noon, along with Katherine and James. Barely a word had been spoken between them during the short walk from the dock to the plaza. Now they only exchanged foreboding and confused looks in anticipation of hearing the dreadful plans O'Connor obviously must have for the colony. Dwight O'Connor appeared on the second story walkway that worked its way around the entire circumference of the plaza.

Into a microphone O'Connor spoke, "As I am sure you are aware of by now, any resistance will be repaid with death." With that he motioned toward the east entrance to the plaza where there was a clearing and a small platform. Two armed mercenaries dragged another man up onto the plaza by the arms; he was bound and blindfolded.

"This man attempted to bring a weapon into the plaza for this assembly, probably to retaliate against me or one of my men. He will pay the penalty."

The two mercenaries, who were part of O'Connor's force, set the man on his knees. The man made a vain attempt to look around through his blindfold to see what was taking place around him, apparently without a notion of what was about to happen to him. The merc on the right side of the blindfolded man stepped to the side as the man to the left drew his weapon and held it inches away from the back of the kneeling man's head. He gave one last look for approval from O'Connor, who nodded. The man with the weapon fired a single shot into the kneeling man's head, blowing brain matter all over the crowd and causing him to crumple to the floor, dead. The colonists collectively gasped, and then silence came over the crowd, broken only by the faint sounds of sobbing.

A new voice rang over the loudspeaker that cut Mathew to his very soul. Before he turned to look, he knew how this entire episode had been able to take place, and that the man to whom that voice belonged was responsible. Mathew's face grew pale as he turned to look at the man who he thought he knew to be one of integrity.

"As Captain O'Connor has so graphically demonstrated to you, all resistance will be met with utmost force," stated Commander Daniels arrogantly. "I would like to lay out the ground rules. One, there will be no resistance. Two, there will be no assembling of any group of people, peaceably or otherwise, greater in number than six. Three, no one may leave the colony. Four, there will be no outside communications with anyone. Five, mining operations will continue as usual. Six…"

"Are we going to get paid?" yelled a man in the crowd.

"…Uh, yes you will get paid. However, you will now be paid monthly and according to output. Meaning a percentage of what you mine."

"Which means we barely get enough to live on!" yelled another man, egging on the men around him.

People started to murmur and several of O'Connor's men fired their weapons into the crowd in the general area of the two men who were speaking. Their accelerator rifles must have been set at non-lethal velocity, because despite much screaming and scrambling, no one was seriously injured. The shots served the purpose of quieting the crowd.

"As I was saying, you will work, or you will die. That is the sixth and final rule. A violation of any of these rules will be met with death. Any grievances may be filed with me, through proper channels," said Daniels with pomposity. "Those of you who wish extra privilege and courtesy may bring any information to Captain O'Connor or me that you believe we might find useful. Everyone will resume normal mining operations at the start of tonight's midnight shift change. That is all."

O'Connor took the mic once more.

"You are all dismissed. Go back to your domiciles."

Everyone stood in silent disbelief. O'Connor's men moved into position and pointed their weapons at the crowd.

O'Connor stated over the sound system, "Have you forgotten rule number two already? No assemblies of any kind. This is an assembly. Go home!"

Everyone then began slowly dispersing in near-silence. Only the faint whispers of incredulity could be heard. Everyone feared to speak aloud. Mathew and Sarah, along with Katherine and James, left in silence. When they arrived at the *Jack Frost* they all entered and only then did Mathew speak.

"As soon as I get home I'm going to start trying to figure out some way of communicating with the outside worlds."

"If you need any help, let me know," said James. "I'd be glad to see those dirt bags routed by the Martian Marines."

"I'll let you know. Until then we need to keep a lid on this and not tell anyone," answered Mathew. "Just smile and go about your business as usual. Don't give them any reason to single us out or look at us too closely."

Mathew loosed *Jack Frost* from its clamps and proceeded to take the Shaws to their quarters on the other side of the colony. James and Katherine's parents were off-world on a buying trip/ trade conference for their company; they would have no idea what they were walking into when they came back. Mathew and Sarah discussed what course of action would be safest to resolve the situation. They both knew the situation would grow worse given the immoral character of the parties responsible. Mathew attempted to send a final message to Jonas, hoping that he was not out of range and that O'Connor had not yet begun monitoring communications inside the colony.

Jonas received a message from home after he thought he was already out of range. It was extremely garbled and all he could get out of it was:

" … don't … box. … open … worry … all right … " and then static.

"Hmph!" Jonas snorted. "That was great. Manta?"

"Yes, Captain?"

"See if you can clean that up."

"Yes, Captain. The enhancement could take some time, however, due to the poor quality of the transmission."

"That's okay. We have plenty of time." His father's tone sounded normal, and Jonas did not give the message another thought.

Jonas slowed *Manta* as the ocean floor rose beneath them. He began rapidly decreasing his depth and was soon almost five hundred feet shallower than the depth of the colony. *Strange*, he thought, *the colony is supposed to be set at the highest point on the sea floor surveyors could find.* Then, without warning, the sonar burst with contacts. He had stumbled across a massive field of chemo geysers, teeming with thousands of sea creatures. Jonas had never seen such a concentration of life out in the open like this.

He slowed *Manta* to a hover a few dozen feet above the floor, where he switched on the external lights and opened *Manta*'s eyelets. Most of the animals were white, but some were also red, typical of some deep-sea creatures on Earth. It begged the question: Why would animals that were native to a lightless planet have any pigmentation? He did not like the implications and decided not to think about it. Jonas stayed for several hours and discovered twenty new species before continuing with his journey.

Several hours later, Jonas noticed what appeared to be a large cave in the side of the undersea mountain range he was paralleling. Jonas maneuvered his ship between two mountain peaks and down into a small valley that lay across from the large cave. Silently hovering in the icy water just above the valley floor, Jonas observed that he might be able to maneuver the *Manta* inside.

"Captain?" Manta inquired.

"Go ahead," Jonas answered, still looking at the sonar screen.

"The enhancement of your last message has been completed."

"Okay, thanks. Manta, launch a probe to determine if that cave is stable enough to enter."

"Yes, Captain."

Jonas heard the probe as it left the launch tube and began to watch it on the sonar as it entered the massive cave and began mapping the interior with its active sonar. Jonas smiled as the cave appeared to grow in size the further it went back into the mountain. Jonas could scarcely believe his luck as the probe mapped several tunnels within the cave large enough for *Manta* to enter and, more importantly, turn around in and exit.

"Manta, have you determined if the cave is safe to enter yet?" Jonas asked.

"Initially it appears to be stable ..."

"Good."

"However ..."

Uh oh, thought Jonas.

" ... If you will allow me a few more minutes, I will be able to give you a more complete analysis of the data."

"Great," said Jonas with relief. "Take your time."

The minutes seemed like hours. Manta finally determined that the cave was indeed stable, and that she could safely maneuver through the main chamber and into one of the tunnels that branched off of it.

FOUR

J onas turned on the exterior lights and slowly eased the *Manta* into the opening of the cave. He noticed that the side tunnels that branched off the main cavern appeared to be round and artificially carved.

"Captain," said Manta coolly.

"Yes?"

"The probe has reached an obstruction."

"Okay … ," said Jonas suspiciously, wondering why the *Manta* had not simply steered the probe around the obstruction, and if she had a bug in her system.

"What is so significant about this particular obstruction?" Jonas asked with rude sarcasm.

"It appears to be a metal pressure door. Would you like to investigate, Captain?"

Jonas's eyes grew wide with surprise, and goose bumps erupted on his arms as he answered in the affirmative and quickly entered the tunnel. *Manta* warned Jonas that her readings indicated small fractures in the tunnel ceiling, and that it might not be stable.

He proceeded through the corridor and around several corners before a wall came into view on sonar. In the center of the wall were a docking tube and a pressure door. Jonas examined the structure for several minutes, using every sensor he had in order to determine if it was stable. He could not determine what was behind the wall; only that the pressure door was sealed.

"M, we're going to dock. Notify me if the tunnel or structure becomes unstable."

"Yes, Captain. Captain?" asked the A.I.

"Yes?"

"The tunnel is unstable," said Manta.

"More unstable than it was a few minutes ago?" asked Jonas, raising an eyebrow.

"No, Captain. But you instructed me to notify you if the tunnel became unstable," said the ship matter-of-factly.

"Okay, okay," said Jonas, smiling and shaking his head with exasperation. "Notify me if the tunnel or structure become more unstable than they already are."

"Yes, Captain."

Jonas cautiously initiated docking maneuvers, cringing at the slight bump he felt in the ship when he made contact. He activated the ship's docking clamps, set the seals, pumped out the water, and waited to see if the pressure door would automatically equalize the pressure. The minutes crawled as he listened and watched the pressure indicator on the *Manta*'s door to see if there were any changes. There were none.

"*Manta*, can you force the door to the dock's air lock open remotely?" asked Jonas

"One moment...," said Manta. "No, Captain, there is no remote link to the door locking mechanism. I do not detect any power readings coming from the door or anywhere near the docking assembly."

"Open the outer door and ready for hostile dock."

The A.I. executed Jonas's command and prepared for a violent decompression or the worst-case scenario, a flooding air lock. The seal on the air lock broke, followed by a loud hissing noise as the air in the lock equalized. Jonas opened the door to reveal the corroded outer door of the docking tube. He checked the door and the locking mechanism disengaged on the second try. Jonas took a deep breath, knowing that what he was doing was dangerous and probably stupid. He slowly turned the handle to break the seal and open the door. The door hissed, then moaned as he pulled it open, but he immediately knew he was safe because the hissing of the air was not pressure from his ship, but air entering his ship from behind the door. *So far so good,* he thought. With no small amount of effort, Jonas pulled the old door open and entered the docking tube. The air smelled old and stale. He walked thirty feet through the tube to the inner door of the structure. *This is it,* Jonas thought, as he turned the handle to unlock the seal to the door. It turned effortlessly, and he slowly pulled the door open.

Jonas looked inside and saw a large, empty room. His flashlight shone on three doors on the far wall. He picked the middle door and walked to it. It swung open as easily as the last. The open door revealed a long, dark hallway. Jonas began walking down it, using his sensor pad to map it as he went along. The hallway ended at another door, which opened to reveal what appeared to be a command center. Jonas entered and, finding one light that was working, began the process of turning on the dusty computers, which were apparently connected to a battery backup system.

"Manta," said Jonas over the com-link. "Can you remotely access these computers to see what information is on them?"

"One moment, Captain," she answered. "Yes, I can access them through your sensor pad. I am starting to download data into an isolated file now to protect myself from any potential viruses."

"Good, let me know when you've finished."

Jonas completed his exploration of the command room and continued down the hall on his previous course. Near the end of the hallway was another pressure door, and behind it was a large laboratory with a vast array of preserved animal specimens. Most of the specimens were native to Europa, but many appeared to be from Earth. Some appeared to be mutations of the same species at various stages of development. Jonas found a computer interface and turned it on, but was unable to access the password-protected system. He asked Manta to attempt a hack, but the system shut down after her second password attempt. Jonas gave up on the computer but continued investigating the lab and the large variety of species, trying to find clues that would help him understand the function of the strange place. He was already forming an opinion, but he didn't like it. This lab appeared to be even more evidence that Europa's uniquely evolved ecosystem did not evolve at all. They were genetically manipulated species from Earth transplanted here by someone apparently attempting to seed the planet with an artificial ecosystem.

I will find out how, when, and who put them here, Jonas thought to himself. There were no other doors on the sides of the hallway, only one more a hundred yards further, at its end. Through the door at the end of the hallway, however, was something that astonished Jonas and left him standing in the doorway of the room with his mouth agape.

FIVE

Markus was awakened by the horrible sensation of gravel grinding inside his lungs every time he took a breath. He realized that he shouldn't be feeling anything; he should be dead. He tried to open his eyes, and what little light that was in the dingy room from the pressure display panels sent bursts of skull-splitting pain through his head. After several long minutes, Markus made himself roll over on his side and then sit up. His head throbbed, as every heartbeat felt like someone hitting him on the head with a sock full of ball bearings. He sat there for what felt like an awfully long time. He thought about what a stupid mistake it was to blindly run into a dark room after a suspect. How his old body armor had stopped a bullet from an accelerator pistol he could not guess. His armor was only rated for steel-jacketed-style projectiles traveling under 2,500 fps. Younger must have turned his pistol setting down out of fear of missing and the projectile penetrating one of the walls of the colony. *Lucky me!* Markus thought sardonically. Right now he didn't feel lucky. He guessed he had some fractured ribs from the impact of the projectile due to the pain that shot through him every time he took a deep breath.

He decided to try and stand. He was unsuccessful in his first attempt, nearly falling on his face. He was finally able to stand and eventually able to walk when he realized he had no idea what time it was, or even what day. *I need to go back to my apartment,* he thought. He had to figure what was going on, who was involved, and what their intentions were. The man who shot him was the same one he had observed disembarking with that latest mining crew of shifty-looking characters. Markus had a sinking feeling that something much bigger than mere revenge or hatred lay behind his attempted murder. Markus tapped into one of the control consoles and accessed the central computer, discovering he had been out at least forty-eight hours. He then found out about the takeover and, more shockingly, the involvement of the base commander. He weighed his options. The only person he knew he could trust that had any kind of useful history was Matthew Black. The problem would be contacting him undetected.

All voice transmissions were probably being monitored. However, Marcus remembered an email trick he used in the old days. Humans could not take time to monitor every transmission personally. Computers had to do it, and computers could be tricked. Computers only did what they were told, and they were only told to monitor voice recordings made by certain people or to check for certain words contained within all others. Markus used an alternate address, several of which he had left over from the old days with Federation security for just such an occasion. He found a video advertisement, addressed it to Matthew, and imbedded a simple text message in it. His only hope was that Matt would not erase the message before he discovered what it was.

Markus knew he could not return to his apartment or to anyone he knew. He moved through the service tunnels to the nearly deserted southern docking hub where he could tap into the water supply and access some old vending machines. Markus cringed at the thought of eating whatever was in those machines...it was probably years old. After a nice, long, cool drink of water, he went to the machines and was pleased to find some freeze-dried ice cream bars, peanut butter and crackers, and a cola. He broke into the machines, which felt strange given his current profession, and retrieved their contents.

Markus found an out of the way alcove, much like the one in which he had been ambushed, to bed down in. He thought of how he had come here to have a quiet job and escape the things he had done on Earth. Now all of those instincts, his experience, and training were coming back to him. For this he was glad, because his opponent had every advantage he could think of. The bad part about delving into his abilities was that it brought back all the memories he had tried for so long to forget. Up to this point he had succeeded. *Too bad I don't have some sort of advantage,* Markus thought.

"Hah!" Markus said out loud. *They think I'm dead. It may not be much, but it's something.*

Markus drifted back out of consciousness, not knowing if it was sleep or if he was simply passing out due to injury. He didn't really care.

James walked into the common room of their apartment and found Katherine furiously typing on her keyboard.

"What are you doing?" James asked with guarded curiosity.

"Sending Jonas a message," she said without looking up.

James stepped quickly up to her and hit the power button on her computer, shutting it down.

"Why did you do that!" she demanded, standing to face him, her computer pad falling to the floor.

"Because if you send that message, they will kill you!" James yelled in his sister's face while pointing at the offending hardware lying on the floor. James could see a tear welling up in his baby sister's eye, making him instantly feel like a jerk.

She sat back down with a plop on the couch and said weakly, "I just felt like I had to do something, James. He might be the only way we can get help from Mars."

"I know Kat, but you getting killed will not help anyone. Okay?"

"Okay."

"We'll think of something, but we can't draw attention to ourselves trying to make something happen when we don't even have a plan."

"Do you have a plan?" Kat asked hopefully.

"Well, no. But between the two of us we can come up with something. I'll bet Jonas's dad is trying to think of something too."

"I wish Mom and Dad were here," Kat complained.

"Me too, but I'm glad they're out of danger," James reasoned.

He went to the kitchen and made some tea to help make up for hurting her feelings, and they sat on the couch and talked about how they might send a distress call without getting caught.

Jonas, still with his mouth agape, walked silently around the room full of tanks. The circular room, he estimated, had a radius of nearly one hundred yards. There were at least two dozen tanks, nearly every one of which contained a neowhale in a different stage of development. This was probably decades of work, judging from the many mutations that looked like unsuccessful attempts to adapt the creature to the blood-freezing, acidic waters of Europa.

But these creatures were different from the whales he'd heard of on Earth; they had gills. Jonas continued his excursion into the bizarre laboratory that seemed to be the birthplace of life on this planet. He looked at his data pad and realized that he had been in the place for over an hour. He passed one of the computer consoles near the entrance of the room and it chattered to life. Jonas stopped to take a look at the dust-covered console. The screen prompted him to enter the date so the computer could update its settings. Jonas did so, and, to his amazement, the computer, along with the entire room, lit up.

The room was much larger than Jonas had originally surmised, and he gawked in renewed astonishment when the computer beeped. He turned to look at it, and it was prompting him to place his hand on the panel for identity verification.

What the heck, Jonas thought with a shrug. *It won't work, but I might as well give it a shot.* He placed his hand on the screen. The screen shot light onto his hand, taking an instant image of it and processing it in a couple hundredths of a second. *I'm going to have to stop being surprised at this place,* Jonas thought with wide-eyed wonder as the computer verified him as a valid user. He just shook his head and stared at the screen as a program initiated and selected a holo-log dated nearly ninety years prior. The message it contained was both fascinating and horrific.

M arkus was watching himself as if in a dream. It had to be a dream, because it already happened, and he knew what was going to happen. He also knew, as fear gripped him, that there was nothing he could do to stop it. Markus was dressed in his fatigues and barking orders at his squad before they arrived at their target location. He could even feel the drone of the engines. As they approached the landing zone, he felt his breathing deepen and his heart quicken as the first bit of adrenaline entered his system. No matter how many missions you went on or led, it was always the same; the requisite to keep one's adrenaline under control. Failure would result in tunnel vision, followed by a loss of fine motor skills and minor cognitive skills. That was unacceptable for an officer of the Federal Security Section, especially for a colonel like himself.

The target was a small outpost in a remote region of Alaska, just north of Skwentna at the base of a small mountain commonly known as Porcupine Peak. The complex consisted of a series of houses and workshops built into the side of the mountain, with several hangars beside the two airstrips. Intelligence indicated that the people that lived there were engaging in activities which interfered with the effective operation of the Federation. He was here to do a job, and that job was maintaining the security and peace of the Federation of Worlds. These people were probably no different than the notorious "Heroes of Democracy" that terrorized the world 100 years ago when the Federation was in its infancy. Those nuts thought that *every* person should have a say in the formation of government. *Ridiculous!* Markus thought. *The ignorant masses have no concept of what it takes to run a government, maintain an economy, or even think for themselves half the time. Citizenship is a privilege that should be earned by service given the Federation by that individual. It should not be given to anyone based on family lineage, it should not be bought, and it certainly should not be given just for being born.* That is why Markus loved the Federation; it was much like the government conceived in the classic twentieth century novel *Starship Troopers*: one in which corporal punishment did not end in childhood. The Federation employed the use of the whip against minor criminals and those in the military who committed offenses unworthy of death.

In the early days of the Federation, there were many factions that lacked the backbone to employ corporal punishment and even abolished the use of the death penalty for a short time. Fools. Fortunately for the citizens and the people, that time of rampant chaos was short-lived. Sensibility prevailed when the government realized that people could not be controlled by mere words and that no matter how much education an ignorant person was given, you could not make them think. Having one's head filled with even an incalculable amount of knowledge is not the same as thinking. Most people don't like to think because thinking took effort, and people were inherently lazy. Markus was not one of those people; he liked to think. Sometimes he believed he thought too much... Markus chuckled under his breath, remembering the conversation in Shakespeare's *Julius Caesar*. *Speaking of thinking too much*, he thought, *back to the task at hand.*

These dissidents, these religious zealots, followers of what they called The Way, must be eliminated. They claimed that there were things that were "wrong." Sin, it was called; things that every other person in the world thought acceptable. Most of those things Markus did himself. They even went against every other accepted religion and said that synonymous relationships were wrong! It was not Markus's preference, but he believed everyone were free to choose for themselves.

The fact that they said everyone who was not a follower of their religion would go to hell proved that they were a bunch of psychos. Everyone knew that the only people who would go to hell, if there even was such a place, were those who were truly evil. Child molesters, rapists, murderers, terrorists, and other such bottom feeders that Markus and his squad had many times had the pleasure of exterminating, following the issue of their edicts of execution from the Federation Council. These "Way" following people claimed to be peaceful, but that could change in a moment. Markus had seen it before. All these dissidents started out the same way, then they snapped. Rumor had it that these were actually remnants of the same religion that was neatly wiped out shortly after the formation of the Federation. That obstinate religion, which had dominated the western hemisphere, had been tolerated by the world for over two millennia; its name escaped him at the moment.

They were at the drop zone. Markus donned the lid of his power suit; he could see a small group of people gathering around the center of the airfields where the two merged at a central hangar. Markus's team emerged from the transport in fully-armored power suits, approximately 1000 yards from the curious onlookers. At the sight of Markus and his group, the people began to scatter. *Typical,* Markus thought, *innocent people don't run.* Markus ordered his men to commence the operation.

Markus approached the main hangar with his men. Everyone else had fled to the dwellings in the side of the mountain, save one man. This stupid man stood with his hands raised and appeared to be saying something. Markus approached him with caution and turned up the sound amplifier in his armor suit.

"Please, we just want to be left alone. We don't want to fight you," the man was saying. "We just want people to hear the truth. We want tell them in peace for their sakes, so they can be saved too. We have no intention of inciting any kind of civil unrest and none of us have ever had any intention of committing terrorist acts. Please, just let us live in peace ... " The man continued as he turned and looked forlornly at the mountain where his people had fled.

"You should have told that to your compatriot who blew up the population option clinic," Markus said to the man through his voice amplifier.

He squeezed off a three round burst from his MK-21 accelerator rifle. In slow motion, Markus saw two rounds hit the man's torso. The last hit his face, causing his head to burst like a melon. He had heard of other soldiers and police describing the slow-motion phenomenon, but in all his years he had never experienced it. It usually only happened on your first kill, or the first time you were shot yourself. It was long past Markus's first time for either of those. Something was different about this kill, about this man. The man knew he was going to die, yet he did not fight, nor was he afraid. His pleading was not for himself, but for the others here. That was not the act of an ignoble man. The man's broken body to fell to the ground.

Although a few people shot at them with old gunpowder-type weapons, the rest of the operation went off without a hitch. They entered the labyrinthine system of tunnels in the mountain that consisted of dwellings, offices, shops, and even a hospital. There were several secreted doorways they nearly missed and took some doing, even with shaped charges, to breach. They were methodical, killing everyone: men, women, and children. It had been learned two centuries ago that when dealing with terrorists you had to exterminate any posterity. Otherwise, when they grew up they might just remember what happened to their kin and decide to take up a long-dead cause.

Nine hours and eleven minutes from the time they first set foot there, he and his men lifted off the airfield. From a safe distance, Markus set off the charges they had planted. The resulting blast eradicated every building in sight and caused thousands of cubic meters of the mountainside to slide off, covering any record of the existence of those people. The total count had been 2,401 dissidents eliminated, over a thousand more than the intelligence reports had indicated. Markus would have to have a word with the Intel idiots at headquarters. That was about all three squads could handle, even with power suits. If the dissidents would have been better armed, he and his men could have found themselves in a bad spot. It was a thirty-minute flight back to Anchorage, and from there they would head back to headquarters at Denver, District of Colorado. The operation was a success. He had no way of knowing how much the death of the man on the airfield and the deaths of those people would haunt him for the rest of his life.

Markus awoke in a cold sweat from the simple mission that had become his nightmare. The thing he had done, that although he had tried, he could never do penance for. Feeling numb all over, Markus drifted back out of consciousness.

" ... and so, these species were picked specifically because of their potential to adapt to the harsh conditions and become a viable, self-supporting ecosystem," said the holo image of an elderly man in a white lab coat as Jonas watched in wide-eyed disbelief. It was becoming apparent that many of the scientific premises in which he had placed his confidence were false. He realized that his strict adherence to science was nothing other than a personal tenet, which had led to countless incorrect conclusions about nature as a whole. The core of his galaxy view had been dosed with reality and was beginning to crumble. He could not yet bring himself to admit it, but what if his parents were right?

"The acidity of the water was the most difficult obstacle to overcome for the larger creatures. We initially thought that the lack of sunlight would be the most difficult problem to solve, and the preexisting chemo plankton we developed from Earth were difficult to adapt," the man continued. "However, we finally discovered how to manipulate the plankton so they could convert the acid in the water into energy. After that, the plankton adapted at a phenomenal rate, which allowed us to begin work on the neowhales. We had several viable samples in the tanks but had reservations about using them, given their discouraging history on Earth. We altered them so they would have a very limited opportunity to breed only very late in their life span, lessened their cognitive abilities, and made them much less aggressive than their predecessors. We released them and observed in the short term. As you can hopefully see, they have successfully adapted to their new home."

The recording seemed to stop abruptly and resume at a different point in time. This time, the scientist appeared older and disheveled. It appeared to be a personal log.

"I have become increasingly worried about the direction this project is heading. We were supposed to just do simple upgrades; perfecting one attribute at a time until we could collectively put them together into a finished product. The Federation's demands for results have continually increased and their patience grows shorter by the day. They are being unreasonably paranoid about the security of the project. I don't trust Harker; he is a snake of man. However, I didn't have a choice in the matter when the Federation placed him here as an 'independent observer.' He has a cold look in his eye, like a trained killer. He is most certainly not a scientist, and seems less interested in the work we are doing and more so in how we are going about it. In addition, I think he is spying on me personally to see if I have some sort of outside allegiance, which I do not." He shook his head and the recording seemed to jump again.

When it resumed it played like a bad horror film. But this was real, although the picture was not very good. Jonas had never heard someone scream in hopeless agony. It was the most gut-wrenching thing he had ever seen or heard. He watched as the most horrible example of humanoid form imaginable stood in a cage as he was repeatedly shot by who Jonas assumed was the man described by the scientist as Harker. The "person" finally ceased screaming and was reduced to a pathetic sob as it curled up on the floor. The creature looked dead, but it was still breathing. Then, to Jonas's amazement, the creature stood up, and its wounds looked as though they were disappearing! The recording jumped segments again, going back to the scientist's log.

"As you can see, this is not what I signed on for. The thing you saw was our tenth attempt at complete regeneration of flesh wounds. I thought that our 'human' experiments would merely be genetic enhancements to increase the survivability of our soldiers. But cloning and total manipulation of the human genome is not feasible by any logic. They simply will not listen! We have made significant leaps in progress; we have successfully enabled this subject to spontaneously heal himself. However, because of the speed of the healing, it results in incredible disfigurement. That sadistic freak Harker continues to torture the creature under the guise of testing his abilities. But continued testing is pointless, and the rest of us lack the stomach for it. This subject is set for termination tomorrow. I will not continue to perform experiments on human subjects, even if they are only clones. I sent my transfer request to the ministry this morning. I hope to finish with this despicable business soon." The recording was cut again.

Markus sat in his new office in D.C. (District of Colorado), two months after the dissident suppression mission in Alaska. He had just been appointed chief of the Federal Security Section for the continent of North America. He sat smiling smugly as he looked eastward across the plains of Denver from his 150th story corner office. There were only six other men in the world with as much power as him, each one being over a single continental region, and only one other had more. Markus wanted that position more than anything in his life: to be commander of the FSS. The SS, as it was commonly referred to, was responsible for policing the people, the military, and even the Federation Council members themselves. Markus had attained his current position due to his excellent service record, unfailing loyalty, extensive connections, and finally his brilliant defeat of the rebellion at Juneau. There, a group of insurgents had marched on the regional capitol in response to what they called the "Massacre at Porcupine Mountain." Markus's team had arrived just as they began to riot and "dissuaded" them from continuing their course of action.

Markus was having an increasing amount of trouble sleeping. He kept seeing the man on the airfield as he crumpled to the ground. Markus did not understand why this man's death bothered him so much; he had killed hundreds of men during the war and probably hundreds more since. It would not have bothered him so much had it not been for the fact that it kept replaying in his mind, over and over again. One evening, after leaving work, Markus began replaying the entire mission over in his mind. He often did so with other missions so that he could learn from his mistakes and successes. As he did so, he began to realize there were things that were different from his previous missions. Number one: everyone ran when they saw him and his men; including the men who should have immediately put up a fight. Also, there was the fact that the man who tried to talk him out of his attack was unarmed. The look in the man's eyes was not a look of fear, but a look of courage. The fact that the dissidents were very ill-equipped with arms: only one man with a .50 caliber rifle and one with armor piercing rounds. Many others had guns, but still in disproportionately small numbers compared with other rebellions he had put down. Probably less than one out of ten men was armed. Most of these rebel forces had women and children with them, but this one had an unusually high number.

Markus could feel himself go pale as he realized what he might have done. He turned his hover car around, nearly causing an accident, and headed back to his office. Ten minutes later he was sitting in his chair, pulling the classified records of the mission from the central computer to his. Everything looked to be in order until he got to the initial intelligence records. Markus read the intel report, which appeared to be the same one he had read prior to the mission. However, at the bottom of this one, where it showed the source of the information, there was a reference number to a black file. Markus would not have had access to that at the time. Now he had access to everything. Markus entered the number into the system and it pulled an SS file for a covert operation. Markus read the file in disbelief. He read it again; he still could not believe it. By the time he'd read it the third time it was 3:00 a.m. The file outlined a yearlong covert SS operation during which a fringe member of the alleged terrorist cell was to be located, recruited, and convinced to suicide bomb a specific target. There had not been a suicide bomber in over a hundred years, and never one from this particular group.

The file stated that the operatives were unable to find a willing subject from the ranks of this particular group. So they released a suspected terrorist and orchestrated a job for him, replacing environmental control (EC) units. After several weeks they provided, unbeknownst to him, a special explosive device imbedded in the EC unit which would blow while he was putting it in place at the target location. Doing so eliminated the terrorist's ability to claim he was manipulated and allowed SS agents to say it was done for whatever reason they wanted. The bombing was a success; not for the bomber, but for the agents who arranged it.

Fifty-six civilians were killed for their stupid ruse! Markus thought for the tenth time. The Security Section told the Federation Council and the public that the bomber was part of a crescive terrorist organization from the dissident group known to follow The Way. Mere days after the incident, the Council issued their edict. Two days after that, Markus and his team arrived to execute it.

This meant that the entire mission was based on a farce. It meant that he and his men had not killed terrorists, but murdered hundreds of innocent people, people who were most likely what they claimed to be: peaceful. Markus stood, his face feeling cold, as he remembered the exact number of people he and his men had murdered that day! He had never faltered in battle, but now, he fell to his knees and vomited. Holding himself up on his hands and knees, he barely clung to consciousness, his mind reeling.

Markus awoke again. This time he had tears pouring out of his eyes. He realized where he was and that he was twenty years in the future. He had left Earth shortly after finding the truth, and wandered about the solar system for ten years or so before finally ending up here. He thought that this backwater dump of a place would be perfect for him to hide from his past and live the rest of his days in peace, and if possible, recompense some of what he had done. As he sat up he could feel how bad he was hurt and the usual day-after soreness. He had always been gifted with the ability to set his feelings aside to accomplish the task at hand; it was necessary to do that now. He shook off the past and focused on the present.

M atthew Black noticed he had a new message icon on his computer screen. He briefly glanced at the supposed junk mail and was about to erase it when he saw something familiar. He stopped and looked a little closer. There it was, cleverly hidden in the background, so well that most would never notice it: a tiny icthus symbol on a billboard in the distant background. Matthew had seen such messages before, but it had been a long time, and he had no idea who this could be from.

Matthew carefully moved his eyes over the spot to see if there was anything to it. The computer tracked his eye movements over the area as he blinked repeatedly to activate the hidden message he was beginning to doubt existed. Still nothing. He moved his finger to the spot and double-tapped it. A prompt came up, and he opened it.

It's a message from Markus! He almost said out loud. It was time stamped last night, well after Markus had disappeared and was presumed dead. Matthew read the note in which Markus explained his injury, the time and place for them to meet, the list of supplies he needed, and his desire to discuss a strategy for undermining Commander Daniels. Matthew checked his watch.

Only two hours until the scheduled time! Matthew deleted the message and quickly began gathering whatever he had on hand from Markus's list of necessities. On the list, of course, was a gun with plenty of ammunition.

The only projectile weapon Matthew had left was in the basement. He quickly went downstairs, realizing it had been six months since he had been down there and pulled the filter to one of the air scrubbers. Matthew then took his multitool from his pocket, backed out the screws from the permanent filter and removed it. Behind it was an inconspicuous metal box bolted to the floor that appeared to be just another part of the filter mechanism. Matthew removed the screws from it and opened it to reveal its hidden contents: one very nice auto pistol with a thousand rounds of ammunition and a few grenades. He picked up the weapon, having forgotten how heavy it was, and it had a good feel to it. After a few minutes, he had reacquainted himself with his old service weapon. He had broken it down to ensure all its essential parts were in working order. The power cell for the electro-magnets was only at about one-third power, but there were several fresh replacements in the box.

The gun was a special issue JLM 27 10mm marine accelerator pistol. It had the standard voice-activated single, burst, or full-auto switch, thirty-round magazine, self-stabilizing barrel, and integrated scope. But the special issue had a range indicator, infrared and starlight scope, and the ability to fire 10mm explosive rounds that could be set via voice switch to explode on impact or any preset distance. The JLM 27 was the best of the best in its day and still one of the finest weapons available. A weapon with such capabilities had been the standard for military rifles since the late twenty-first century, when they still used gunpowder weapons. Small arm accelerator weapons had only been commercially available for the last hundred years or so. The thought of giving his favorite weapon to someone, even someone as capable as Markus, made Matthew feel like he was giving away his favorite pet.

Matthew's daydreaming was broken by the docking alarm.

He was not expecting anyone and was in the middle of planning a rebellious overthrow. He quickly put everything back into place, without putting all the screws back. He put a new filter in the air scrubber and took the old one upstairs with him; it would serve as a good excuse for taking so long to get to the docking door. When he got there, he was relieved to see it was only James and Katherine. Matthew opened the inner door and welcomed them in.

"Hello, come on in," said Mathew with nervous gusto.

"Hey, Mr. Black," they responded harmoniously.

"What brings you two out here?"

"We were wondering if you've heard from Jonas," Kat quickly responded.

"And what we are going to do about Daniels and O'Connor," said James.

"Well, I haven't heard from Jonas," Matthew replied.

"Oh." Katherine sounded disappointed.

"I sent him a message, but I don't know if it went through. I'm hoping it wasn't intercepted. To be honest, I thought you guys might be the goon squad when I heard the docking alarm. Imagine my relief," said Matthew with a sigh.

"We were about to go stir crazy. You can cut the tension with a knife in central," answered James.

"Yeah, it's weird," Kat responded. "Everyone's acting normal, but you can tell they're super scared. It's really quiet everywhere you go, and everyone seems to only be talking in whispers."

"That's the way it is in a dictatorship, everyone living in fear," Matthew admonished. "And to answer your second question, the less you know, the safer you will be."

"Hey, don't cut us out of the loop, Mr. Black," James scolded. "I may not have your experience, but I'll do everything I can."

"He means *we* will do everything *we* can," said Kat, elbowing James.

"I know you two want to help, but I won't purposefully put either of you in any danger."

"Come on Mr. B, give us a little credit," said James. "If anyone was planning anything, you'd probably be right in the middle of it. At the very least, you would know something about it. We know how to keep out mouths shut."

"Okay. All I can tell you is that it will take a while to get anything going. So don't be overanxious. You both need to be ready for anything." He attempted to quiet them.

"Okay, but is there anything we can do?" begged Kat.

"Just keep your ears open for anything that sounds interesting. Oh, and one last thing." The two leaned closer. "If anyone comes to you and says ... " Matthew whispered in each of their ears.

"You do exactly what they say, and help them any way you can. Okay?"

The two nodded in wide-eyed excitement at having been allowed into the fictional secret society.

SIX

Stooge, O'Conner thought, as he left Daniels' office and made his way to the dock. Doyle was waiting for him in the submersible they had commandeered: Markus's cruiser.

Of all the things to hate in this place, O'Connor thought, *this machine isn't one of them.* He was not overly familiar with hydrodynamics, but this thing seemed to be a superior craft. Thinking about another ship made Dwight miss *The Venutian Witch.* He longed to get back to her and see how she fared. He missed walking her corridors, hearing their distinctive echo, and hearing her engines purr like a kitten; a 600,000-ton kitten. She was the only thing he had ever loved.

Seeing the anger in his CO's eyes, Doyle didn't say a word. He just fired up the drive and descended toward the lights of the colony. They had a quiet trip back; O'Connor didn't open his mouth until the docking clamps attached to the ship.

"That pompous windbag. If he had any idea what the real world was like, he wouldn't be stuck on this ice cube! I hate the military. They're so brainwashed with regulations that even when they're doing something illegal, they think they still have to cheat by the rules!"

"As you say, sir," Doyle answered. "What did he say?"

"He said we have to stay here as long as he says, and that unless we stay until we are *cleared*," he said sarcastically, "to leave and adhere to terms of our agreement, we won't get paid the other half of our fee! It was only supposed to be two months. Lying weasel…I only considered taking this job to hide from the Federation and Republic fleets for a while. The pay and the fact that it was supposed to be quick and easy was only reason we finally took it."

"But few things are ever quick or easy, are they, Dwight?"

O'Connor started to chew into Doyle, but he knew he was right. Further driving the point home, Doyle used Dwight's own words against him. It stung being corrected by your own inspirational commentary. O'Connor was shaking with rage, but quickly calmed himself, knowing better than to let anger dictate his actions. A captain couldn't do that; at least, one who wanted to live a while.

"The only positive in this," Dwight told Doyle as they walked out of the docking bay, "is that Daniels said we would be compensated for our time at double the rate."

"Double? That's great!"

"Yeah, but I still don't like it. Nobody wants us here, and sooner or later someone's going to get the idea that he's going to do something about it. I'd rather not be here when it happens."

"Well, we'll just have to do everything we can to make sure that doesn't happen."

"Don't you get it, Doyle? Look at us. They've been after us for years and haven't been able to catch us. Now the roles may be reversed. Now we're the guys that are trying to maintain order and these people might be the ones who start doing hit-and-runs. Do you really think it would be any different?"

"Sure, Dwight, but we know all of the tricks and we can prepare for or counter them. If anyone starts something, it shouldn't take us long to evaluate and respond. Besides, unlike the real authorities, we don't have a problem torturing or shooting someone to get information. We don't have to follow the rules."

"True, but I still don't like our situation. You can't stay on high alert twenty-four seven. We have good men, but sooner or later someone's going to get caught off guard or do something stupid and that may be a catalyst for insurrection."

"So we have to whack a few people who throw rocks at us, Captain. What's the big deal?"

"The big deal is that if we kill everyone off, there's no one here to run the place. And if there's no one here to run the place, we fail our mission and don't get the other half of our money ... Not until Daniels says we are finished swimming around in this cesspool of a planet."

The two walked through the central hub to O'Connor's operational headquarters, Markus's office. Dwight had to admit that the old geezer had good taste for a cop. The office had some older but well-maintained computers and surveillance equipment, a well thought out desk, and a supremely comfortable chair. The office overlooked the central hub and the viewing wall provided access to every security camera in the colony. *This wasn't such a bad deal,* thought O'Connor as he leaned back in the chair. He turned to look at the cameras and sensor readouts on the viewing wall. Everything looked to be in order. *On second thought, I don't think a bunch of miners will be all that troublesome ...*

Matthew docked the *Jack Frost* at the abandoned cargo port at the old eastern spoke of the central hub. He checked for movement before disembarking. He found his way to an access door to a maintenance passageway that Markus had indicated was off the sensor grid. It opened with some difficulty, and he entered, shutting the door behind him. He could feel an involuntary sigh exit his lungs as silence crept into the passageway. He took a deep breath and proceeded down the narrow corridor, making a few turns here and there. Matthew had not been in the maintenance corridors often, as most of his expertise was used on equipment and vehicles. He had forgotten how much of a maze they were.

The maze ended at another door which, after a quick pause to listen, he opened. Matthew found himself in the oldest section of the colony. The lights still worked, but it didn't look like there had been anyone in this section for decades. He walked down a hallway and found another door that opened into what looked like a smaller version of the dock at which he'd left *Jack*. Still, he didn't see Markus.

"Matt."

Matthew's heart almost stopped. He turned to see Markus standing with metal pipe in hand behind some cargo crates beside the door he'd just stepped through.

"Markus." Matthew raised his hands in feigned surrender and smiled in relief that he didn't get his head bashed in. "I was beginning to think I wouldn't find you."

"I was starting to think you might not show up." Markus stepped forward and fervently shook Matthew's hand.

"Is this entire place off the grid?"

"Afraid so. I was always worried about it being a refuge for illegal activities, but now it looks like I'm the one sneaking around trying to hide from the so-called authorities."

"This is the oldest part of the colony, right?"

"That it is. It didn't have all the amenities or safety and surveillance gadgets that all the new sections have, so it was slowly abandoned. I used to check on it every so often to make sure it stayed that way. I'm not sure if anyone but me even knows it's here anymore."

"Don't you think when you start taking out O'Connor's men this might be the first place they check?"

"Doubtful. A few years ago, I removed this section from the colony's schematics on the core computer. And O'Connor isn't going to be looking for me anyway. He thinks I'm dead, remember?"

"That's true ... " Matthew trailed off, thinking he must have an old map set at home. "I was wondering what happened to you.

All I knew is that everyone was saying you were dead. I was surprised and relieved to hear from you. Clever little trick with the email; I take it you picked that up from your time in the SS?"

"Yes…" Markus's eyes dipped to the floor. "A useful bit of information, although I'm not proud of how I got it…"

"All in the past, Markus," Matthew interrupted, putting a hand on Markus's shoulder.

"What happened with you and O'Connor?" he said, changing the subject.

"He and one of his men lured me into an ambush. I was a fool not to see it coming. I had concerns when O'Connor initially arrived. I may be getting old and losing my edge, but you never forget how to spot a thug. The day it happened I had put on my vest for first time in years… Don't really know why. That and the fact O'Connor had his weapon set low are the only reasons I'm alive."

"Well, I'm glad you made it. At this point you're about the only asset we have. Why do you think O'Connor had his gun set low? He doesn't strike me as the type to make a mistake like that."

"I think he was afraid of a stray round rupturing an outer wall or something. He obviously isn't too familiar with the facility. Now, let's get down to business. I may be officially dead, but you can't risk being missing for too long. Did you bring what I asked for?"

"Almost everything, and even more in the weapons department," Matthew said with a smirk of pride as he opened the hard case he'd brought and removed his favorite gun.

"Is that a JLM?" asked Markus.

"Yep, this has been my little friend for a long time."

"You surprise me yet again, Matthew. You are indeed a man of many facets."

"Thanks, I brought all the ammo I had for it too. I figured you can never have too many bullets."

"I agree. You brought some more food too, right?"

"Everything I could get my hands on that was easy to carry; should be enough to last you at least a week."

"Great! You're a life saver."

"I'll do whatever I can to help get rid of these guys. I'd just prefer to keep a low profile, for Sarah's sake. I don't want to get her hurt."

"Understood; I don't want to involve any more people than necessary. I want to stay quiet until I can gather enough information for some hit-and-run strikes. It may take a few weeks."

"Sounds like a plan. But O'Connor might retaliate on whoever is the closest target of opportunity, possibly even someone who is innocent of involvement."

"That is a risk we run, but we can't sit and do nothing."

"Agreed. I'll back you up when the time comes."

"Good," Markus threw out his hand to shake Matthew's. "I'll put a blue light in a window near here if I need to contact you, or as a last resort, I'll use the junk mail trick."

"Okay, I'll see what I can learn from my end. I have a meeting with Daniels today; I was involuntarily picked to be the workers' representative. Maybe he can be reasoned with."

"Doubtful, but it's worth a shot. See you soon." Markus nodded.

Matthew nodded in acknowledgement, turned, and departed. He had a lot to think about as he retraced his path through the maze of service tunnels back out to his ship. The old clunker creaked as the docking clamps were released, and he quietly crept away. Pointing the ship's nose downward, he followed a channel that ran under the dock. Wanting to ensure he remained undetected, he piloted his boat using only his flood lamps. If he turned on his imaging sonar, he would light up like a Christmas tree on the colony's sensors. He followed the channel to the cargo dock, edged into docking position, and activated his sonar.

It was the same place from which he had started his excursion and where he would have appeared to simply depart and power up his sonar. He gunned the throttle.

For all that means in this old heap, Matthew thought, rolling his eyes. He took the craft up and over the east side of the central hub, heading toward his residence to the south. He would have rather not become involved on any level, just for Sarah's safety. *But,* he thought, *evil triumphs when good men do nothing.*

J onas awoke in his cabin bunk feeling better, but hungry. He'd slept for twelve hours. No surprise, really; after finding the facility, he hadn't slept in over twenty. He reconstituted a bacon, egg, and cheese omelet. As he ate breakfast he had Manta stream the environmental data from the facility on the main screen.

That's good, Jonas thought. *At least I haven't picked up some sort of flesh-eating bacteria or breathed any mutated gene-altering virus.*

This is one creepy *place,* he thought, twitching his head at the thought of the recording he had seen. He thought about the differences between the Republic and the Federation. The Republic's Constitution was set in alloy and could not be changed. Martians and those who continued to defect from the Federation were well aware of the necessity for such measures. The Federation looked upon their Charter as an obstacle to be circumvented whenever it suited their whims or those of the people. *Solid principles are not an obstacle to be overcome,* thought Jonas, *they are the foundation we build our lives on. Without them anything can be justified.* He chuckled to himself because he sounded like his dad. He showered while his coffee brewed, then dressed and poured a cup of the steamy brew. He was about to sit back down when it occurred to him to go for a stroll through the rest of the complex. Jonas donned his hat and jacket, as it was well below freezing inside. He passed through the air lock and entered the chamber with the three doors. He had already been through the center one.

I found … amazing and disturbing things, he thought. He now picked the right door and unlocked the pressure seal. He felt a slight air pressure change through the seal, but nothing else.

Jonas opened the door and found another long hallway, but this one had no doors down the sides, and the walls were smooth.

A closer look at the walls revealed they were metallic, but he couldn't determine what their composition was. Jonas shone his light as far down the hallway as he could and he saw the end. He began walking, letting his hand glide along the glassy wall as he advanced. He reached the place where he thought the hallway ended, only to find that it curved to the right. It continued for some time and straightened again when it had completed a ninety-degree turn. It had a dank smell, and he could see several places where lichen was growing around what must have been tiny cracks between the wall lining seams.

Jonas was beginning to wonder if the tunnel would end when he spotted what looked like a large doorframe jutting out from the wall about fifty feet ahead. He quickened his pace and found a large pressure door. The tunnel continued, but this was the first point of interest he'd seen, and he was not about to pass it up. He examined the keypad beside the door, and it appeared to still be active as it began to glow with a small red light, probably indicating it was locked.

"Manta?" Jonas asked, hoping he was able to contact her.

"Yes, Captain?" she responded nonchalantly.

"Can you interface with this terminal and unlock it?"

"No, Captain, I cannot."

Jonas cursed under his breath, but thought of something no sooner than he did so.

"Can you download a code-hacking program to my data pad so I can manually try to unlock it from here?"

"Certainly, Captain. Starting upload now. It should only take thirty seconds for you to download it."

Jonas waited anxiously in the dark hallway, realizing he felt more vulnerable in the darkness while standing still.

"Upload complete, Captain. Press the blue icon on your data pad when you are physically interfaced with the terminal to initiate the program."

"Great, thanks!"

Jonas pulled the retractable cable from inside his data pad, found a compatible port on the door terminal, and plugged into it. Upon establishing a good connection, he tapped the blue icon on his screen. The screen began scrolling through numbers and determined in seconds that the lock required a five-number code. The program then began selecting probable codes for the door using a time-tested method of logical sequences. If the code had been programmed by a person, and not randomly selected by a computer, it was likely to follow certain patterns that most people found easy to remember. The data pad beeped. The keypad on the door turned green, and the door made an internal clicking sound.

Must have been a human code, Jonas thought. *Strange; they had biometric locks in the other part of the facility and such an easily bypassed security measure here.* He unplugged his data pad as the door opened to reveal a large dry dock ... with ships.

Several hours after his meeting with Markus, Matthew boarded the *Jack Frost* and headed toward the surface command center for his meeting with Daniels. His stomach in a knot, he had no idea what he was going to say. He hadn't been to the surface in months. *Strange,* he thought, *I didn't even miss seeing the stars until now. It's amazing how busy we get with our lives ... we can go for months, even years, without stopping to enjoy them.*

Matthew's thoughts were interrupted by the clanging of the docking clamps attaching to his ship. He powered down his systems, locked the control console, and enabled the external controls to the hatch. He stood in front of the hatch with his hands raised, as he had been instructed to do by Commander Daniels. He could hear the air pressure equalizing in the air lock. Several seconds later, the hatch hissed open and he saw four men, three with rifles aimed at him, standing on the other side of the air lock door. The fourth was Daniels. One of the men with guns slung his weapon, walked up to Matthew, and thoroughly searched him. Satisfied that Matthew was unarmed, he nodded to Daniels, and the other two men lowered their weapons. Daniels walked up smiling, like the devil after he'd just collected on a soul contract. His right hand was outstretched.

"Doctor Black," he said cajolingly, using Matthew's formal title. "I'm so glad you could make it today." He shook Matthew's hand.

"Daniels," Matthew said flatly, looking coldly into Daniels' beady eyes, "you know why I'm here, and you know it isn't a cordial visit."

"Now, doctor … what's done is done, and there's no point in dwelling on it."

Matthew started to tell the traitorous snake what he had been dwelling on doing to him, and that it involved a lot of screaming and bleeding on Daniels' part, but he held his tongue.

"I know how everyone must feel about all of this, but the reason I am speaking with you is to show that I am willing to hear the workers and consider your requests on an individual basis. I want this operation to continue to run as smoothly as possible. O'Connor said you had been approached by several dozen people who represented various labor groups."

"They thought that since we've had a long-standing professional relationship, I would be the best candidate."

"And I believe you are too. That's why I invited you here. But enough of this for now." Daniels turned and started walking down the hallway, indicating that Matthew should follow. "Let's have some dinner and a drink."

"I didn't come here to have a drink, I … "

"I insist," Daniels interrupted without breaking pace or turning to look back.

Matthew could see in his periphery the three armed men tighten their formation around him, indicating that the invitation was not optional.

"Fine," Matthew relented. He concluded that he was in no immediate danger.

They took the lift to the top level of the base, where Daniels' office and quarters were. There was also an officer's mess that, given Europa's current orbital position, had an awe-inspiring view of Jupiter. Daniels indicated that Matthew should sit at the table opposite himself. Matthew seated himself and waited several minutes in silence. A steward brought out the first course: soup of some sort. Daniels then spoke.

"Ahh." He smelled the steam coming from the bowl. "One of my favorites: tomato basil fresh from our greenhouse. You'll find it is much different from the freeze-dried version." Daniels began carefully sipping the soup from his spoon, and Matthew followed suit.

"There are not many things I can think of that I will be willing to negotiate on, Dr. Black. I simply do not have much room to negotiate, as my employers are very adamant about keeping the mines as profitable as possible."

"This operation *was* profitable before you and your goons took over, Daniels. If you'd just left things as they were and stolen or skimmed the profits from the companies involved, you could have avoided all the violence."

The steward came around and filled their glasses with a Martian black wine. Bio-engineered vines were the only ones that would grow in the cool Martian environment. They yielded a small grape about the size of a large cranberry. Externally, the grapes were the same color as those found in a typical vineyard. However, the inside of them was such a dark blue that the resulting wine looked black and was complex and rich in flavor.

"I'll give you that, Doctor. However, you have to admit that merely skimming the profits isn't near as profitable as taking over the whole operation," Daniels said, raising an eyebrow.

"Fine, but killing people isn't worth any amount of money."

"Well, we are in the middle of a war, after all. There will be casualties."

"*We* aren't in the middle of the war, Daniels. The war ended years ago," Matthew said, raising his voice and indicating the colony with a motion of his hands.

"Calm down, Doctor Black," Daniels raised his hand and shook his head at the tensing guard standing at the door. "While we may not be in the middle of the war, per se, there is a war raging just beneath the surface. Hence, we are in a war. I have orders from my employer to ensure the profitability of this colony at any cost, and my position is contingent on my ability to carry out those orders."

"Orders? I have a hard time believing that the Republic would sanction an operation like this."

"The Republic did not. Let's just say a silent party is paying me and Captain O'Connor handsomely for this job."

Matthew's eyes grew wide in disbelief. Daniels had not merely turned himself into a thug. Now he was a traitor!

"You turned your back on your planet, on your people?" Matthew asked, still slightly shocked. "I thought you were a man of honor."

"Every man has his price, Doctor Black. I have been stuck at this post for years with no hope of promotion. There simply isn't a way to distinguish myself when guarding a mine on an insignificant moon at the edge of the system."

"Well, I'd say you've distinguished yourself now," Matthew said with disgust.

"I suppose I have," Daniels said with a smile and chuckle. "Look, I could have been stuck here for the next ten years and retired on my meager military pension, or I could do this. And after I am paid for the job, I can retire on Elysium and live like the filthy rich. I may even be given my own hyper ship."

"A ship? This place can't net anywhere that kind of profit in such a short time. Your employer is lying to you."

Daniels chuckled.

"I doubt that, Doctor Black. I have already received half my fee, and my employer has been more than forthcoming so far."

Matthew was now wondering what purpose this whole thing served. The colony was profitable, yes, but not on a scale large enough to make much difference to someone for the short amount of time they would be able to keep their little coup a secret. Daniels had just admitted they didn't want the Republic to find out about it. Whatever it was they were doing, it was now apparent that they weren't just here to take over the colony for a few months and steal some credits and ore until Mars sent in the marines and took the place back. And they *would* get it back. The Republic wasn't as rich in resources as the Federation and had to protect what little they had.

"But enough of my goings-on. Tell me what you would like to discuss." The former Republic commander pushed his plate away, prompting the steward to pick up his and Matthew's ... whether Matthew was finished or not.

"The main concern of the miners is their pay. They know that your proposal of paying them based on yield is nothing more than sugarcoated slavery. They want to continue to be paid just as they always were, and continue going about everything just as it was."

"I'll consider raising the percentage of their share in production results, but I will not restore their usual wages. If they want to continue to make what they were making before, they will only have to work approximately two hours more per day, in addition to their one extra day per week. I've done the math and given it to the miners already. It isn't too much to ask, Doctor, and I would hardly equate it to slave labor."

Matthew leaned toward Daniels.

"You're talking about fourteen hour days, six days a week. That isn't a question of production or money so much as it's a question of safety and logistics. We can only work two twelve-hour shifts per day for a reason. If everyone from one shift is still working when the other shift starts, there won't be enough equipment to go around. If we won't have enough down time to properly maintain equipment, there will be more serious breakdowns in the long run and even more downtime. Not to mention the fact that working longer shifts increases the risk of accidents, and that could put a serious kink in your little operation."

Daniels leaned toward Matthew's end of the table.

"Then I guess I made a slight miscalculation. You'll have to work your regular twelve-hour shifts. I'm sorry, Dr. Black," Daniels said with a pompous smile. "You'll have to make up the difference by working seven days a week."

"I see. So I'm probably here just as a token gesture of your artificial willingness to work with us." Matthew started to get up.

"Please sit down, Doctor Black. Dessert is just arriving. As I said, I will consider increasing the percentage of the yield that the miners receive, but I cannot allow production to decrease under any circumstance. I am required to show at least a slight increase in production to my employer. If I do not, I do not get my entire fee. And worse for you, they may replace me with someone who is … not as pleasant. Please, Doctor, believe me when I say you are not here as a token negotiator. I will consider your request."

"I guess we don't have much of a choice," Matthew conceded.

"Correct. You know I am not an unreasonable man. As I said, I require the increase in production from the miners. However, I will run the simulations on the projected output and adjust their percentage so that, although they will be working longer hours with no days off, they will make the same pay as long as production remains at median levels. How does that sound?"

"I suppose, given our indentured servitude that is reasonable for now."

"Wonderful! See, Dr. Black, your first negotiation has been a success."

"There are several other issues I needed to discuss with you."

"No, no." Daniels waved his hand. "We can't discuss *everything* now. That would eliminate the need for a return visit. How about we make this negotiation a weekly event? Same time next week?"

Matthew was baffled. Daniels was never this friendly with him before. He must have an ulterior motive.

"I guess so," Matthew cautiously agreed.

"Excellent. My men will escort you back down to your ship. I look forward to our next meeting."

With that, Daniels stood, turned his back to Matthew, and walked out of the room. The goon squad appeared in the door and walked him back to his ship.

Jonas walked into the massive dry dock, awed by the size of the facility. The walls must have been one hundred feet tall and were reinforced with concrete of some kind. There were massive cement beams that arched away from the walls and the center of the ceiling. As he walked to the center of the room, looking at the ceiling, he nearly stepped off the edge of the sub dock, which would have sent him plunging into the icy water. Chills went through him as he realized that misstep could have cost him his life. He visually scanned the pool where he had nearly taken his involuntary swim and could only find one way out, fifty yards across on the other side. His muscles probably would have cramped up in the below-freezing water before he could have made it across and pulled himself out.

Creepy, he thought. He realized that the pool would be large enough to bring *Manta* into.

"Manta," Jonas asked on the com.

"Yes, Captain?"

"Is there is a passage large enough for you to navigate that leads to my location?"

"Unknown, Captain. When we entered the caves I mapped several passages that branched off of the main chamber. The single probe you initially sent into the caverns only mapped the tunnel we entered. You did not send out any more probes after that. Perhaps you were distracted?"

"Yes M, I was a little distracted," Jonas answered, smiling and rolling his eyes. "Would you send out two more sonar probes to map the remaining tunnels?"

"Certainly, Captain. Prepping probes now; they will be pro-grammed and loaded in five minutes."

"Good, launch when ready. Oh, and only have them map the tunnels that are large enough for you to navigate. Okay?"

"Okay Captain," she answered awkwardly, attempting her first colloquialism.

Jonas continued his survey. The arched beams converged on an alloy ring in the center of the ceiling, which housed massive doors. There was probably a tunnel consisting of two or three pressure chambers, large enough to allow the small Corvette class space ships to pass through. There were two of the Corvettes, probably over ninety years old, given the date on the holo message. But from the looks of them, they were decades ahead of their time, because even by today's standard, they were nice-looking ships.

It hit Jonas like a wrench to the head … he'd just found sunken treasure! Just like the old Earth books about sailing ships he used to read when he was a kid. He was rich! Even one of these ships was worth millions of IS'! Not to mention there were two submersibles that were probably worth several hundred thousand apiece!

I need find a control panel to see if the air lock doors still work, he thought. *It won't do me any good to be the proud owner of a spaceship that's stuck underground.*

He had forgotten how dark and creepy the place was until he started looking for a control station. He tossed a few light sticks around and spotted a set of large protruding windows about twenty feet above the main floor. From there one would have a commanding view of the entire bay.

That should be the control room. He walked toward a doorway that appeared to be a stairway that led upward. There was a lift, but its power was out. So he took the stairs and quickly found himself in a room filled with blank screens and consoles. He could see one small light, about the size of the head of a pen, blinking green. He walked toward it and found another biometric scanner. He remembered the lab and thought he might as well give it a try.

He placed his hand on the scanner. A few seconds later, the scanner lit up and scanned his palm. The entire control room came to life, with every console and screen lighting up in series. Next the hangar lights came on, filling the entire room with light and giving him the first good look at his treasure of ships. He was beginning to lose himself in imagining where he could go and do with a space-worthy ship when the control panel started playing the message he had been watching in the other part of the facility... and it picked up where he'd left it before.

Just then he noticed that there was a naturally mummified body lying four feet from him on the floor. Jonas gasped and jumped back, too overcome with fear to vocalize his horror. He was shaking, and only by concentrating on breathing was he able to remain conscious. He could see two holes in the head of the body that was dressed in what was once a white lab coat.

I officially have the heebie jeebies again, Jonas thought, and sat in a chair in front of the screen, feeling emotionally exhausted. *Whoever left this message really wanted me to see it, so I had better finish it.*

While he was in the lab, he had simply walked away from the screen. He had never been a fan of horror movies; they were stupid and pointless, not to mention the fact that they were, of course, creepy and made people afraid of their own shadows.

The scientist continued, although the date indicated it was several days later.

"I am extremely frightened," said the scientist, and he looked it too. "I sent my notice of resignation to chief of the science ministry today, and only an hour later Harker approached me and told me he was disappointed that I was leaving the project. The part that scared me was the fact that he smiled when he did so. The man has never smiled at me, or anyone else, for that matter. The next supply ship arrives tomorrow and the ministry informed me that I could return to Earth on it. I will be relieved to leave this place."

The feed stopped and picked up again. Jonas had to turn down the sound because of the gunfire in the background. The scientist appeared to be in this very control room, his back to the camera, looking out the window. The camera was pointed out at a ship in the hangar just below the pressure doors, and there were armed men pouring out of it. The men were killing everyone who had gathered to meet the ship and unload supplies. The scientist appeared frozen in place, panic-stricken. After the massacre, all but two of the armed men moved out of the hangar, presumably to finish off the rest of the staff. The scientist seemed to regain his senses and turned toward the camera. He could barely speak through his terror and grief.

"It is as I feared…" He hung his head and wept for several seconds. "…I don't have much time now," he stammered. Regaining his composure, he straightened his spine and lab coat. "I believe Harker is part of this, although the Ministry of Science undoubtedly is at its heart. How else would Harker have learned of my resignation so quickly? They will almost certainly kill everyone here, as we are all witnesses to these horrific experiments, which the worlds will not understand. I have grown to hate this place for what it represents, as well as myself for what I have done in the name of science. My only possible redemption will be in these logs, hidden in a subroutine of the laboratory's computer network. They should not discover them, and if they wipe the system's memory, they will remain embedded in the maintenance program. It is doubtful the Federation will destroy the entire facility, as they cling very tightly to their pet projects. Otherwise, all is for naught." The scientist glanced back out the window to check on the guards.

"Whoever you are, if anyone ever even sees this, please tell the collective worlds what happened here. Tell them what the Federation has done. Show them of the samples you have found, and use it to prove this planet was seeded by humans. Tell them of the horrible things we have done to those poor clones." The scientist turned and performed several unknown functions on the terminal behind him. "I have enabled the systems to maintain a standby readiness mode as soon as these men evacuate the facility. They will soon, for I just activated the self-destruct sequence. It will not detonate, but it should force them to leave, and perhaps prevent their deployment of any other such device…"

As the scientist continued speaking, Jonas could see the two men in the hangar looking toward the control room windows and speaking to one another. His heart fell into his stomach when he saw the two men begin walking this way. He unwittingly looked out the control room window to look for the approaching men and started to shout at the scientist and warn him, but he knew it was futile; the recording was ninety years old. He turned his attention back to the video just in time to hear ...

"... if I have been successful in my attempt to tell the truth to the world, you may plug in whatever memory device you have and all the information contained in this message will be uploaded to it." He turned, touched a button on the console, and turned back in time to see the two men enter the room.

Jonas knew this because he could see the scientist's eyes grow wide as he stared certain death in the face. The men didn't hesitate. There was a flash of red, then nothing, as blood spatter covered the camera.

Jonas remembered that he was supposed to download the record, and he quickly began fumbling for his data pad, not realizing that the camera had still been recording. He plugged a fiber cord into the console and his data pad began downloading a file. It only took ten seconds, and it was finished. Jonas then noticed the recording was still playing. The blood on the camera lens had begun to globule, allowing a limited view of the action in the hangar. There were red lights flashing everywhere, and Jonas could see that all the control screens were showing the countdown to the alleged self-destruct sequence. The men who had come to destroy the facility were organized but hurriedly loading onto their ship in squad-sized groups. Harker entered the control room and set a large metal case atop the main control console. He powered it up and quickly left the room, leaving it behind. Jonas looked to his right and observed the same case still sitting on the console. The case must have erased the computer system. As the control screens began becoming scrambled and unreadable, the last of the men entered the ship and it began to lift off the floor of the hangar. The camera feed was cut.

Daniels left Dr. Black standing in the Commander's Dining Room with a dumbfounded look on his face. *Priceless,* he chuckled to himself. *Being a dictator isn't such a bad thing,* he thought, enjoying his latest taste of power.

Although they always had a cordial professional relationship, he had never liked Matthew Black or those who shared his beliefs. They were pious hypocrites who supposed themselves to be good, but generally acted the same as everyone else.

He entered his office in time to hear his console chime telling him he had a call. He sat down at his desk and touched the screen to answer. It took several minutes for the encryption to sync with the quantum codec on the other side. The screen showed the transmission code. He entered the corresponding code, and he was then able to see who was calling him. It was whom he had expected: Minister Chen, Federation minister of science.

"Good evening, Minister," Daniels courteously greeted.

"Good evening, Commander. How are things out there?" the Minister queried.

"Going well, Minister. I just had a meeting with a representative of the workers, and despite their complaining, it went quite well."

"Oh? Complaining already, are they? Do you think it serious?"

"No, Minister, the issue has been resolved for the moment. I have seen to it that I have a weekly meeting with the same man from now on. Knowing that they have a representative and an open door for negotiation should quell any serious unrest for quite some time."

"It sounds like you are handling things well, Commander. How are the mercenaries doing?"

"They're complaining as well, but they will do what they're told, as long as you keep paying them. That's what they do."

"That's what they used to do. Most of them have been pirates for some time now, Commander. Remember that. Don't trust them. They are only there for the money. Do not give them a clue that you are working for the Federation. Our operation must be kept secret."

"Don't worry, Minister, I don't trust anyone. I am keeping a tight leash on them."

"See that you do," answered Chen. "Now for the real reason I called, and one of the reasons for this little operation of ours. Until six months ago, I and everyone else in the known worlds thought that the colony was the first outpost on Europa. It was not."

"What?" Daniels asked with astonishment.

"Apparently, about ninety years ago, there was a scientific outpost there. None of us in the Ministry were aware of this until a programming clerk found a large encrypted file on the oldest mainframe in headquarters. She was unable to open it and notified her supervisor. The only reason I found out about it was due to the fact that no one else but the minister of the department had clearance to open it. I did, and imagine my surprise at this news."

"Is it still here? What was it for?"

"Unknown. The record shows that it was destroyed when the minister of science at the time found out about illegal human experiments at the location. However, it also indicates its destruction was never confirmed. As for its purpose, it only stated that they were engaged in researching something called the "Genesis Project," which in turn was furthering "Project SS 108." There are no indications what either of those projects were," the Minister lied.

"So, why are you telling me all of this?"

"I want you to go there and make sure the facility was destroyed. If it was not, see that it is. Simple enough?"

"Well, Minister, first that depends entirely on where this place is supposed to be. As I understand it, not much of this planet's ocean has been explored, and as far as the parts that have, I've never heard of any other facility being found here. It may not be feasible to go to this place. Second, there was mention of a bonus in the form of a ship when all of this started, if I do this, I want that guaranteed."

"If you can complete this task, consider your bonus in the

bag, Commander. As for logistical problems, that is entirely your problem. I will transmit the coordinates of the facility to you; from there it is up to you. Agreed?"

"I'll try, but I can't make any promises, Minister."

"I am transmitting the data to you now. I am also transferring a discretionary fund to use for your little expedition. It should be more than adequate to convince your mercenaries to take care of this business for you. And if you should convince them to do it for less … the funds are now in your private account."

Daniels checked his account; he had difficulty hiding his delight.

"Thank you, Minister! That is very generous."

"It is nothing. Just see to it that this is done, understood?"

"Yes, Minister."

"Contact me when it is finished. I expect to hear from you soon, Commander. Farewell."

"Good day, Minister."

The screen darkened as the transmission was cut. Daniels looked at his account and smiled. He reckoned he would be able to convince O'Connor and a couple of his men to do this for half that!

He'll probably jump at the chance to make a quick buck on a simple seek and destroy mission. Daniels immediately called O'Connor and told him to come up to meet with him. He wondered what Chen was not telling him. No one would go to all of this trouble to destroy a supposedly destroyed facility to cover up a project they knew nothing about. After he thought about it for a few minutes, Daniels knew Chen was lying. He remembered hearing rumors of the Federation's "Project 108" when he was in the military. The stories of the Federation developing a nearly indestructible super-soldier were mere legend now.

SEVEN

Jonas checked the remaining power in the reactor; it was at five percent. He found the air lock controls and activated them. He could hear the heavy inner doors opening, and ran down the stairs into the middle of the hangar to see. Later realizing he trusted the safety systems of a ninety-year-old, memory-wiped computer to ensure the air in the hangar did not blow him out into the vacuum on the surface. The doors opened and the tunnel guidance lights activated, indicating the way to the outer door. After fifteen minutes, the massive air lock had completed its exit sequence. The entire test drained one percent of the remaining five percent of the reactor's power.

O'Connor left Daniels' office and headed back to the sub where Doyle waited. It was a cake job. Take a couple of torpedoes, find some old outpost, and blow it up. How hard could that be? Unbeknownst to him, Daniels had left out the fact that no one had ever actually been that far from the colony, there was no chance of rescue should he become stranded, and that most people who had ventured too far from the colony were never heard from again. He entered the boat and closed the pressure door before speaking to Doyle.

"We have a new job," O'Connor told his lieutenant.

"What is it?" Doyle asked suspiciously.

"Apparently someone has some tracks they want to cover. We're supposed to blow up some derelict science facility they had out here. It might already be trashed, but they want us to make sure … with a couple of torpedoes."

"Sounds like fun. When do we leave, and where do we get the torpedoes?"

"I was just informed that our dearly departed constable had a small cache by the slip where we found his ship."

"How'd we miss that?" queried Doyle.

"I think Daniels was intentionally hiding them from us. They're supposed to be under the sub floor of the dock."

"Apparently the old goat was slicker than we thought."

"He still wasn't slick enough."

The duo surfaced at the dock in Markus's cruiser. They exited and proceeded to the starboard side of the ship, where O'Connor pulled up a large section of deck plate, revealing a rack with twelve torpedoes. O'Connor gave a mischievous smile to Doyle.

The pirates loaded the armaments into the cruiser and locked it down for the night. However, the ones Jonas had helped Markus build were sealed safely below deck on the other side of the dock. O'Connor and Doyle discussed what time the next day they should leave, provisions needed, and who else to bring along. That gave O'Connor an idea. What if there was something valuable at this place?

Jonas walked up to the nose of the first Corvette, noticing several blast marks on it. He walked down the side of the craft and examined the glossy black skin, which was in very good condition. It would render the ship nearly invisible against the backdrop of a black, starlit vacuum. The vessel had four forward guns, a dorsal turret, and a ventral turret. Both turrets were comprised of two rail guns and two stream lasers, making it battle-worthy against ships with reflective and heavy armor.

After twenty minutes of searching, Jonas finally found the hatch on the port side. There were few visible seams in the skin of the ship, and the vague outline of the hatch was difficult to differentiate from any of these. Jonas ran his hand along the seam of the hatch to see if there was any variation anywhere in it. He was hoping to find some sort of handle, biosensor, or ... he felt something. He pushed on the spot again and it moved. A panel just larger than the size of his hand sank into the skin of the ship and locked into place. A second later, a narrow handle popped out of the skin. The handle pivoted clockwise on its axis, and when it had turned 180 degrees, the pressure locks in the door tumbled open.

O'Connor sat in his office, mentally writing a list of supplies for their excursion. Dwight, of course, chose Magnus to accompany Doyle and himself. Dwight had met Magnus when he was still smuggling small time in his old eighty-foot shuttle. He walked into his favorite bar on Mars in time to see a hulk of a man mopping the floor with four Martian Marines, a Herculean feat given their reputation. Those four marines could have taken out ten men with accelerator rifles armed with nothing but toothpicks and duct tape. This guy stood over six feet six inches tall, and had to be carrying over three hundred and fifty pounds of muscle.

A second later, two of the marines were out cold and bleeding on the floor. One had jumped on the monster's back, attempting to choke him. The other had picked himself up and was making his way back to the fracas. The monster reached over his shoulder, grabbed the soldier by the jacket, and pulled him over his head. He held the marine off the ground with his right arm and punched the man in the gut so hard with his left that

Dwight thought it killed him. That man fell to the floor, motion-less. When the remaining marine, who was nearly to the hulk, saw that his comrade was seriously injured or dead, he reached behind his back and pulled out a ten inch vibro-blade.

Dwight did not usually interfere with any fight not his own. But the hulk had his back to the last marine and that vibro-blade would cut through his spine like a hot knife through butter. On impulse, and because he didn't like marines anyway, O'Connor pulled his pistol and shot the marine once. The soldier fell dead. The monster turned and surveyed the dead marine, then Dwight. The crazed look was still in his eyes.

O'Connor remembered the sick feeling in his stomach when Magnus walked right up to him and thrust out his massive right hand. Dwight reluctantly holstered his weapon so he could shake the super man's hand, still halfway expecting to be crushed for having interrupted his sport. Magnus didn't smile. He never did. He simply shook his hand and *told* Dwight he was buying him a drink. He thought it unwise to refuse. They had a drink and a short conversation about who they were and what they did. Dwight later came to realize Magnus always had that crazed look in his eyes. They had both killed a marine that day, making them wanted felons. O'Connor hired Magnus, and they had had an unspoken understanding ever since.

O'Connor's reminiscing was interrupted by the com tone.

"Dwight! You'd better get down here quick!" Doyle sounded flustered.

"What is it Doyle?" O'Connor asked flatly.

"Two of our men are dead, shot."

"What! Where?" O'Connor stood up.

"Down here at southeast, dock number three. Magnus was down here getting supplies and found them floating in the water."

"I'll be right down."

O'Connor arrived to find Magnus at the door, rifle ready. Magnus acknowledged Dwight with his usual expressionless nod. Dwight nodded back and walked up to Doyle.

"They've both been shot in the head, Captain. Looks like a standard round from an unknown distance. I haven't been able to tell if it happened here or somewhere else."

"We have to figure out who did this, Doyle, and fast. We can't have people getting the idea that we are vulnerable. Talk to the potential snitches and find out what you can. This only goes public if we can't find information through the usual channels. Anyone who knows anything will talk, one way or another."

O'Connor could see Doyle was back to being himself. He had been nervous and edgy ever since they'd arrived here, but having someone to potentially vent his frustrations on had caused him to focus on a task and forget whatever fears he had of this place.

"We're putting our trip off for a few days until we get this straightened out. Have a few of the boys fish them out of there." O'Connor indicated the bodies. "I'm going to review the surveillance footage."

Doyle nodded, and Dwight went back to his office to review anything the extensive camera system may have caught. After that, he would head to the gym and vent some frustration; otherwise he would have to shoot someone. As fun as that might be, it would be a bad idea to further erode the now-fractured balance of fear and power that was Daniels' little dictatorship. If people were pushed too far too fast, they would snap, and failure meant he didn't get paid. So, a punching bag would have to do, for now.

Jonas was just stepping into the Corvette when his concentration was interrupted by his com.

"Captain?" asked Manta.

"Go ahead, M."

"The probe has reached what appears to be a docking pool. Can you see it?"

"Let me check." Jonas nearly fell out of the ship's door trying to get to the docking pool.

Jonas walked toward the pool, shined his light into the water, and strained his eyes to see if the probe was there. His heart was sinking when his light caught a flash of something. There it was again! Although it looked like a comet fish, Jonas knew it was one of *Manta*'s. It slowly made its way to the surface, emerged, and continued to swim a circuitous pattern while awaiting further orders from Manta.

"Manta," Jonas called.

"Yes, Captain?"

"The probe is here. Are you able to navigate the passageway that leads here?"

"Yes, Captain."

"Great! Start this way. When you arrive, surface, dock, and contact me."

"Affirmative, Captain. Closing pressure doors and releasing docking clamps at current location. Mapping course to your location and executing orders."

Jonas went back to the Corvette, this time getting further than two feet from the inside of the door. While the ship's exterior elegance was a consequence of functionality, the interior was a ship designer's dream brought to reality. He had seen pictures of all sorts of ships: old, new, military, private, ocean, and space-faring. This one was enough to put all but the most expensive yachts in the galaxy to shame. It was not only the opulence that was impressive, but the practical and beautiful craftsmanship that appeared to have gone into it. This was definitely not a standard military ship.

Jonas was still admiring his find when he had an idea … *What if I copy* Manta's *A.I. onto this ship? She would need to have all her functional programming switched over to space and atmospheric navigation, but that isn't such a stretch. Is it?*

Jonas wasn't much of a computer programmer, but with Manta's help, he was confident he could do it. He started checking the systems on the Corvette. First he needed to check the power core to see if it had any fuel left after ninety years. He sat in the captain's chair and placed his hand on the right side of the console. The display was instantly lit. He touched the status indicator and the forward holo-emitter came alive with the resplendency of one newly installed. The display showed a complete image of the ship. He placed his left hand on the arm of the chair and looked back at the display. After several minutes, Jonas knew how to navigate the display, peel away sections of the ship, and highlight individual systems. Jonas was ecstatic to find the core intact.

The display showed that everything was five by five. It was a cold start; apparently the displays were running on reserve power. He watched as the power readings began to climb. When they reached ten percent, some of the bridge systems began to come online. Jonas moved the core display to the side to monitor it while he checked communications, which appeared to be functional. He used the exterior antenna to boost his own signal.

"... Captain, please respond."

"M, where have you been?" Jonas asked sharply.

"I am glad to hear from you, Captain. I have been trying to contact you, but I believe the hull of that ship absorbs radio signals. I was beginning to fear you were in distress."

"Sorry, M, I didn't realize we couldn't hear each other. And yes, I'm fine."

"Thank you for the apology, Captain. What are your orders?"

"I'm guessing that if radio waves won't penetrate the hull, you can't remotely access the ship's computer core?" Jonas asked.

"Correct, Captain. However, I should be able to access it through a fiber cable."

"Great. I'll be out in a few minutes to link you up. I want you to prepare to copy your A.I. to this ship. When I hook you up, assess the new ship's memory and processing capacity, and determine if a complete transfer is possible. If it is, I want you to integrate your A.I. into the ship's core. Next, I want your copy to learn the functions of the ship, and its capabilities..." Jonas continued giving Manta instructions for several minutes. Manta confirmed and began preparing for the process.

Jonas retrieved Manta's optic cable and mated the computer cores, hoping their techno union would produce a perfect clone of Manta within the new ship. He went back to testing the Corvette's systems. He quickly found that the ship could be run at one hundred percent on what remained of the core material for about one more year, and standby mode reduced fuel consumption by ninety percent.

Jonas initiated the startup sequence and the engines came to life, glowing pink. At idle, they didn't have sufficient power output to move the ship anywhere, unless they were already in space. But it was enough to determine if they were still operational and whether they had any maintenance issues. Jonas continued to familiarize himself with the new ship for another hour before hearing from Manta.

"Captain?"

"Go ahead, M."

"I am unable to begin the transfer of my A.I. to the new ship; it does not have sufficient memory capacity."

"Oh no." Jonas's heart sank.

His whole plan just went down the tubes. He was sure he wouldn't have any problem learning to fly this ship in open space, but he seriously doubted he could get it out of here without help. And he didn't even know of any pilots in the colony.

"Keep working on the transfer protocol, M. I'm taking a break."

"Okay."

Jonas stretched as he got up out of the captain's chair of the Corvette. Comfortable as it was, he'd been sitting in the same position all evening. He walked outside the ship and turned to look at it longingly.

There has to be a way to do this, he thought. *I'm not giving up that easy.* His stomach growled and he remembered only eating a snack or two all day…again. He checked his watch: eleven.

Jonas made some instant noodles and took them out into the hangar. He pondered his quandary as he ate. How was he going to get this ship out of here without Manta's help? He finished his dinner and retired to his bunk.

Jonas was awoken by the thought of two words: interchangeable parts. He turned on his cabin light and looked at his watch: six a.m.

"Uugh," Jonas groaned. "I hate getting up early."

He brewed some coffee, poured a cup, and stepped outside. *It is both pleasant and disconcerting at the same time,* he thought, *to have such a large amount of open space.* Jonas realized this was the largest open space he had ever been in. The central hub of the colony was bigger, but it was broken up and did not look so empty. He stood there, drinking his coffee and thinking of the memory transfer problem. He had not looked closely at the second Corvette, being too enthralled with the first, but they looked identical.

"Manta."

"Yes, Captain?"

"Does the new ship have open ports for new memory modules?"

"Checking ... Yes, it does."

"Is the central processor fast enough for you?"

"Yes."

"I'm going to check the other ship and see if I can cannibalize any memory modules from it."

Jonas went to the other ship, found the computer core, and, after a couple of hours, removed five of six memory modules. Although he had probably just rendered the second ship inoperable, it was better to have one functional ship than two pretty storage containers.

Jonas entered his ship, powered down the computer core, and installed the new hardware. He had to stack two sets of memory modules, which would slow their speed, but their memory capacity would remain. He closed the cover and reinitialized the core.

Markus replayed the operation in his head. He had made his way through the service tunnels to avoid being detected and backtracked. Markus lay in wait for a target of opportunity in the southeast dock. He had been there several hours and was feeling his age. He chose the location because it was on a routine patrol route. He positioned himself behind a stack of storage containers in a corner of the dock, 150 feet from the main door. He picked these particular crates due to the fact that they were dusty and less likely to be disturbed while he waited. He was, however, briefly exposed to a camera for three seconds as he made his way over to them. Only his back would be seen, and he would have to remember to cover his face on the way out.

Markus had determined to stay there for at least twenty-four hours and had brought food and water in his rucksack. His boredom was allayed when two of O'Connor's men walked through the door. He had already chosen primary and secondary kill zones. If his targets walked into them, Markus would have a perfect angle and could shoot them without being seen. One hundred and thirty feet wasn't such a long shot, given the excellent pistol he had, but it was two to one, and he didn't want to take any unnecessary chances. If someone pinned him down and called for backup, he was dead.

As he had hoped, the two men began to look over the supplies, probably trying to find anything of exceptional value. *They will be disappointed,* he thought. As the two checked the contents of various containers, they moved closer to one of Markus's primary zones. Then one stopped and looked around suspiciously. Markus turned his eyes from the man so he was not looking directly at him. He had seen this before, but it was rare. Some men, or so it seemed, had a kind of sixth sense. They could tell when they were being watched. Sometimes if you looked away from the prey, they would blow off their gut feeling and go back to business. This man was looking around the dock intently, and began moving toward Markus. Markus's heart began pounding. He checked the location of the second man, but he was outside the kill zones, still looking in containers.

The approaching man entered Markus's second kill zone. Markus targeted him and began to squeeze the slack out of the trigger. The man suddenly stopped on the edge of the dock, continuing to look around, lighting a cigarette. Markus exhaled and held his shot. The man must have dismissed the feeling; he stood at the edge of the docking pool and stared into the water. About halfway through the first man's cigarette, the second man apparently got bored and walked over to his comrade. The second lit a cigarette from his friend's and the two exchanged a few idle words. Markus waited for a few seconds, hoping to hear some valuable intel. He did.

Markus targeted the first man, and then moved his barrel to the second as a dry run for the actual firing sequence. He went back to the first and looked through the scope; he could see the man's eyes were green. His JLM 27 was set to single shot. The accelerator pistol made its signature thumping and whooshing sound as the projectile left the barrel. Markus barely saw the first shot hit before his crosshairs were on the second man and the second shot was fired. The second man didn't even have time to react to his comrade getting shot before he was dead himself. The two men simultaneously collapsed where they stood and fell into the water of pool number three. Markus took a deep breath and let it out before he holstered his weapon, his hands shaking. It had been a long time since he had found it necessary to kill another man. It had been even longer since he had done it for a just cause.

Markus waited a few seconds, then emerged from his hiding place. He walked over to the pool and could tell, by the way the water was turning red beside their heads, that they wouldn't recover. He turned, covering his face as he walked toward the door. He changed his gait as he entered the view of the camera. He didn't want to give anyone a way of recognizing him. He walked out of the dock down the hallway and disappeared, or so it would seem to the surveillance system. He knew it would take a long time for them to find him if he continued in this manner. However, if O'Connor was very smart, it wouldn't take him long to figure out he was using the service tunnels. Then things would get interesting.

O'Connor was disappointed that only five seconds of footage contained the killer, none of which showed the man's face. The man appeared to have a very agile and springy gait. O'Connor returned to his office the following morning and watched the clip containing the killer more than a dozen times, memorizing the man's gait. If he saw a man who moved like that, he would be interrogated. It had been twelve hours since the killer had struck, and still no information. Doyle and Magnus had contacted two snitches, but neither had any useful information.

" ... The memory will be sufficient to transfer my memory to, and allow it to expand at the highest probable rate for at least five years." Manta summarized. "Beginning transfer now, Captain. I estimate time necessary to completion at seven hours forty-seven minutes. After that it should take approximately three hours for my clone to adapt to and learn the new ship's systems. Is that acceptable?"

"Yes, M. That's perfect."

The more Jonas learned about this ship, the more he liked it. According to the schematics, it was incredibly light for a ship of this size, making it astoundingly agile. Its skin was reactive and, when powered up, became chameleon-like, making the ship nearly invisible. It didn't bend light around it, which was necessary for true invisibility and to date was technologically impossible for large objects. The ship had sensors all over it that would analyze the ship's surroundings and cause the skin to change to the color, brightness, and texture (in appearance) of the opposite side. It could apparently do this from every angle.

I have to see this for myself, thought Jonas.

He activated the ship's camouflage and went outside to have a look. Jonas was astounded to see that it worked even better than the specs had described it. He walked all around the ship, looking under it and around the edges, and comparing it with the background. It even duplicated the brightness of lights behind the ship. He walked behind it and could see a nearly perfect image of *Manta* from the opposite side. He'd wondered about the possibility of doing this to a ship, but he supposed the idea too complex to be practical. Besides, with all of the sensors packed onto military ships nowadays, visual stealth was generally the least of one's worries. But on this ship, this function might actually prove practical, given its radar-absorbing abilities. This would partially explain why there was so much of the ship's memory that *Manta* could not tamper with. This skin had to take hundreds of thousands of images and calculations per second when the ship was in motion.

Jonas went back inside the ship, which reminded him that he needed to think of a name for it. He considered the possibility of just calling it *Manta*, because when he left Europa, she would have to stay behind. He knew he was being sentimental, but her A.I. *was* going to be in the new ship, after all…

I haven't been able to find a name in the ship's database anyway, and don't really know what else to call it. That settles it then, I'll call her Manta II.

Jonas looked outside the bridge and his eyes came to rest on the control room across the hangar. *I wonder why I didn't see any evidence of the massacre that took place here?* Jonas thought. *I should finish exploring the rest of the facility after I have the new ship up and running.*

He reached the end of what he could accomplish without Manta's help. It was time for a break. Jonas thought he would take a closer look around the hangar and see if there was anything else he could salvage. Most of what he had seen were crates of old foodstuffs, obviously all out of date. He found a crate that was full of old power cells, apparently for some sort of weapon. He had never fired a real weapon before, but he and James had grown up together playing all sorts of virtual reality war games. And in V.R., everything looked and felt almost as it really was. So, in a way, Jonas had a lot of battle experience and weapons training.

Jonas remembered a weapons locker just aft of the bridge

of the ship. He found a half-empty but well-stocked cache. It housed five RS 5P 5.2mm pistols, four SS 10R accelerator rifles, three dozen sonic stun grenades, and two dozen fragmentation grenades. The SS 10R was a 10mm accelerator rifle that used the power cells he had found outside. It was equipped with daylight/night sight/infrared scope, self-stabilizing barrel, single shot, three round burst, and full auto switch.

The RS 5P was a 5.2mm gas recoil pistol, with twenty round magazine, self-stabilizing barrel and single or full auto setting. It had an incredibly light polymer body and carbon barrel, all well balanced by the power cell for the barrel stabilization mechanism. Jonas found several drop holsters in a drawer below, put one on, and adjusted it to fit. He loaded one of the weapons and holstered it, along with several fresh magazines loaded with armor-piercing rounds. Both of the weapons would have been at the peak of technology ninety years ago. Knowing it was impractical for working and unnecessary here, he took off his new weapon and hung it on the arm of the captain's chair.

Jonas checked his watch: another day gone. He took a shower, ate some dinner, and fell asleep the instant his head hit the pillow.

Markus stopped short of his goal, and was sweating profusely. He'd been shooting for five, but had only made four miles on his morning run. He had never stopped staying in shape, but he had definitely been remiss in his exercise habits over the last few years. His weekly routine only included a one and a half mile run twice a week and three days of light lifting; not bad for a man of sixty-two. But given his current circumstances, he needed to get in shape. His life might depend on it. His lungs burned and his head felt light as he kept a fast-paced walk to cool down before stopping. But even though he felt terribly worn out and weak, he felt strangely good.

Runner's high, he thought. *I'd forgotten how good it felt. It's amazing how many people have never pushed hard enough to feel this way ... they're really missing out. Of course, if they saw me coughing and wheezing right now, and I told them how great I feel, they'd just think I was nutty.*

Markus chuckled to himself, then coughed again. It was the first time he'd felt happy in ... a long time. He checked his watch. *Not too bad for an old guy,* he thought.

He walked the remaining quarter mile back to his encampment. He had rigged a makeshift shower in one of the lavatories, but even with his jerry-rigged water heater, it was still really cold. Cold showers are always fast ones, and he was out, dried and dressed, in under ten minutes. He didn't have a razor, so he was developing quite the beard. It looked strange and made him look even older, but he was getting used to it. He drank a protein drink and sat down at the old terminal he was using to access the colony's central computer. Markus pored over blueprints of the colony, trying to locate and memorize any passages he could use to secretly move about the structure. He never realized there were so many underlying systems behind the everyday operations of the colony.

Markus still had access to the colony's surveillance systems. Fortunately, he never logged out of his office system. And since everyone thought he was dead, O'Connor had never changed the password, giving Markus remote access. Markus spent hours every day watching O'Connor and his men: learning where they went, what their habits were, their strengths and weaknesses. He tried to identify patrol patterns and those who were developing a daily routine. People found comfort in the familiar and tended to make their lives as comfortable as possible. They especially found comfort in routine and tended to fall into one, even people who knew they shouldn't, like O'Connor's men.

It had been nearly three weeks since the takeover, and despite the fact they were in new surroundings, about ten of the mercenaries were already developing a predictable routine. These were the next he would eliminate ... and the first would disappear without a trace.

Jonas awoke like a kid on Christmas, knowing that *Manta II* should be uploaded and adapting to the new ship. She was, and greeted him as he had boarded. He did a walk-through while asking her questions regarding the ship's capabilities. According to the ship's records, it had been built on Earth's moon by the Federation, had seen action twice, and was almost as fast as the fastest ship he had ever heard of.

M2, as he'd chosen to call her, was adapting well to her new home. She was already running simulations on the trajectory she would take when she exited the hangar. Normally it wouldn't be difficult for an A.I. to pilot a ship, but *M2* was an oceanic A.I. and still learning the finer points of flight. In addition to that, during the ninety years since the hangar shaft had been used, the massive weight of Europa's shifting icy crust had partially collapsed the air lock in places. This made several of the necessary maneuvers nearly impossible, with only three feet of clearance for the ship to pass at one point and less shortly thereafter, requiring a seventy-degree roll to pass.

Jonas should have piloted the ship, but he wasn't much of a pilot, and he had to finish his trip. The plan was for *M2* to exit the hangar and set herself up in geosynchronous orbit around Europa, opposite the surface station. It was illegal to allow an A.I. to pilot any craft designed for humans without a human copilot, except in an emergency. Jonas would have to hide *M2* until he returned to the colony and could make it appear that he remotely docked her at the surface station.

Jonas disconnected Manta's hard wire from the *M2* and hooked it up to one of the submersibles that were in dry dock. The two subs were old and didn't have much for automated systems, but Manta assured him that she could program them to return to the colony and dock themselves. The subs were fully functional and would fetch a hefty price from one of the colony's mining corporations. Submersibles had to be shipped in and assembled at the colony, which was inordinately expensive. These subs could easily sell for 300,000 IS' and still save the purchaser fifty percent what they would normally pay.

O'Connor had been trying to turn up leads on his two dead men for four days and still had nothing. No one had claimed responsibility for killing them, which led him to believe that it was something personal and not a rebellion. The two idiots probably cheated at cards or tried to put the moves on someone's woman.

Dwight decided to let it go and proceed with his mission; the amount of money he would pull in would be twenty percent of his payment for this entire job. And he should be able to get out there, confirm the place destroyed, or check for salvage and destroy it himself in about two weeks. Even though this place gave him the chills, the thought of mucking about in that dark lifeless ocean was even creepier. He had decided to leave Doyle in charge while he was gone and only take Magnus with him. Doyle was probably the only man who had enough of a level head on him to be left unsupervised.

Even though he is a certifiable psychopath, Dwight mused.

He had a great crew, but he was a realist. He couldn't stand the usual spineless criminal weenies who whined about how bad their childhood was or that they needed to commit crime to "survive" in some vain effort to justify their actions. What was more amazing was how society had historically put up with the impotent worms and bought their whole self-pity routine when they were brought to court! Dwight knew the thrill of putting a gun to someone's head and making them do what you wanted. And he knew that every petty criminal feels the same sense of power and control every time he robs some schmoe on the street. Dwight knew the electrifying feeling of taking a ship and hitting a big score, knowing you'll get away with it. He didn't deny what he was or what his men were. He knew his men were hell-bound scum, and he wouldn't put up with any of them denying it. He also knew, unlike many of the bleeding hearts in charge of the Federation, that scum needed to be kept in check.

O'Connor was on his way to the ship to meet Magnus when Doyle called on the com.

"What is it Doyle?"

"I think we have a man missing, sir."

"What do you mean 'missing'?" asked O'Connor cautiously.

"Some of his mates said he didn't report to his post this morning and that they haven't actually seen him since yesterday. It's not like our crew to shirk their duties sir. They know what you'll do to them if they do."

"One of my men has been missing for nearly a day and I'm just now finding out about it?" fumed O'Connor.

"Sorry, Captain, but with all due respect, I was making sure we checked his quarters, all the bars, and other usual places before I put something else on your plate. There was no sense giving you more to think about if it had turned out to be nothing," Doyle stated flatly.

"I appreciate the consideration, but given the two murders we've already had, I want to know about anything out of the ordinary without delay from now on."

"Yes, sir. Are you still going forward with the mission?"

"I think I'll go ahead and take off. There's nothing else I can do at the moment anyway, but keep me informed."

"Yes, sir, see you later."

Dwight closed the connection and pocketed his com, cursing to himself.

O'Connor arrived at the dock to see Magnus loading the last box of gear. Magnus nodded, indicating all was ready. They boarded the floating sub, closed the hatch, and slowly flooded the ballast tanks. They cleared the dock, throttled the ship forward, and circled the colony. O'Connor hated this place. It wasn't the cold or the darkness; he was used to that. It was the feeling of being crushed at any moment, the fact that he was under the icy crust of this weird little moon. He looked out at the lights of the colony, almost sad to be leaving the place. It wasn't much, but it looked better than what lay before them … infinite darkness. At least in space there were stars.

I t was 12:00 a.m., the previous night. Markus had found a likely target. Every third day after his shift, the man would go drinking with his mates, get smashed, and visit his favorite "lady of the evening" at her quarters, where he would stay until he awoke and went to his half shift the next day. *But tonight he will be very disappointed to see my ugly mug instead,* Markus thought, smiling to himself.

Markus was watching the man via a remote camera feed from a ventilation duct adjacent to the "lady's" domicile and place of business. He watched him leave his watering hole and start her way. Markus had rented the best suite at the colony's hotel the previous evening and instructed the concierge to give a room key to the lady who would arrive the following evening. The concierge had been asked many such favors in his years of service and didn't ask any questions. With the victim well on his way, Markus called the "lady," told her the room he was staying in (which of course she found impressive), and promised she would be well-compensated for her time. Predictably, she accepted the more profitable business arrangement and was on her way in five minutes without giving a second thought to her standing engagement.

Markus exited the duct through one of the grates, taking care to replace it. He then bypassed the security code on the door and entered the woman's home, leaving the door unlocked behind him. He made sure there was no one else inside. He looked about for a place to wait and found a kitchen chair that suited him. Markus sat backward in the chair, with his arm resting on the back of the chair and pistol pointed at the door.

He didn't wait long before there was a knock on the door. A moment later the door opened, and the man entered. A second later, he lay dead on the floor. Three rounds, in one burst, within a one and a half-inch imaginary circle centered over the man's heart. It would have been safer to take a headshot, but that had the potential for too much of a mess. Markus pulled the man inside, closed the door, and wrapped him in a couple of large trash bags and duct tape. He cleaned the small amount of blood from the floor and checked for spatter, but found none. Markus then replaced the chair and made sure nothing else in the room was out of place.

Markus opened the door, made sure there was no one around, and opened the ventilation duct. He pushed the body into the duct, climbed back inside it, and replaced the grid. He climbed over the body, tied a piece of cable to it, and dragged the corpse through the duct and into a maintenance corridor. He placed the stiff on a dolly and took it back to a dock near his quarters, where he weighted the body and dropped it in the icy water. If all had gone well, he had not left any trace of what happened to the man. The man would have simply disappeared.

Psychological warfare was very effective. O'Connor's men would know about the other two men that had been killed by some nameless assassin. Now, when this man went missing, they would only be able to imagine his fate. Most of the mercenaries were likely disciplined soldiers at one time, but not anymore. All Markus had to do was plant the seed of fear in them, and it would grow, feeding on time and imagination. Imagination was the most powerful aspect of the human mind. It was limitless, and, if allowed to run amok hand-in-hand with fear, incredibly destructive.

As the body sank out of sight, Markus knew he had struck a blow to O'Connor that would likely put him on the offensive. It would make his existence more difficult, but also provide him more opportunities to wreak havoc on the murderous filth. He had studied guerrilla warfare extensively, but never dreamed he would become a guerrilla fighter. Markus checked his perimeter alarms and sacked out in the corner behind a stack of storage drums.

Jonas realized he had been at the dock for over two weeks, working on the ship and the subs. He only needed to make a few minor repairs to one of the subs before he could send them home. He felt worn out and tired of thinking. He'd been working sixteen-hour days for over two weeks straight and needed a break. He knew it wouldn't be much of a vacation, *per se*, but taking a day to explore the rest of the facility would be a good distraction. He donned the pistol, this being the first real opportunity to wear it since its discovery. He holstered his mini-computer, put his com in his ear, and put on his pack.

Jonas told Manta where he was going and that he intended to return in a few hours. He walked across the hangar to the door he had entered two weeks prior. A chill went through him as he opened it and walked back out into the dark hallway. He did not realize how accustomed he had grown to the hangar. He turned to the right, the direction he was headed before finding his buried treasure. The hallway soon turned sharply to the left. Ten feet past the turn, the hallway ended, and he found an open pressure door into another room. He stepped through the door and found what he was sure that he would on this trip, the freeze-dried and mummified remains of the Federation's hit squad victims. Several of them were clothed in white lab coats, and several others wore what appeared to be maintenance coveralls. Jonas could see evidence on the back wall of bullet strikes. Jonas backed out of the room, closed the door, and sealed it; the closest thing to a burial he could think of at the moment. He turned and walked back down the corridor, past the hangar door, and toward the central air lock. He opened the door and proceeded across central lock to the only remaining door he had not opened.

The door creaked on its hinges as it slowly swung open. The air smelled stale. The hallway was like the one he had just left; long, smooth, polished rock walls and no visible doorways. Jonas entered and started down the dark corridor, which he found curved to left. He didn't have to go more than ten yards before he reached a door at the end. It had no security locks, just an air lock latch. He opened the latch and pulled the door open, the catch locking it in place when it struck the wall. Inside was another short hallway with three doorways on either side. All the doors were open, and it appeared that the rooms were living quarters, much like the ones in the central corridor. Nearly every one of them contained several corpses and dried blood on the floors and walls. The last room on the right contained at least twelve bodies; victims who fled as far as they could to avoid the death squad. None of the bodies he had seen here, or in the rest of the facility, appeared to have a weapon near them. This had been, without a doubt, a massacre.

Jonas had never cared much for the Federation, but he was pretty sure he despised them now. It was one thing to kill an enemy in wartime. It was quite another to murder your own people to keep them quiet about the illegal activities you had commissioned them to do. Jonas only gave place to his anger for a moment. Hate would not bring back any of these people, whether they had been dead an hour or ninety years. One of the many things his father taught him about The Way was that hatred does not hurt those you hate. It only consumes *you* from the inside as it festers. The Federation probably lied to all the family and friends of these people, saying they had all died in some tragic accident. He realized there *was* evil in the universe. It had been only hours since Jonas left the hangar; it felt like days. He decided to take one last look at the main tank room in the central corridor.

Jonas closed and locked the door to the left hallway as he exited and proceeded to the already-open door of the central corridor. Upon first entering the facility, he found most of the rooms to be half-empty sleeping quarters and unpretentious offices. He had opted not to check all of the closed doors. Checking them now, he found what he'd expected: the occasional corpse. He found a total of six more. The thought of having been so close to death when he first arrived and not realizing it gave him the chills. He finished his inspection of the remaining rooms and moved on to the tank room.

He gawked at the freaks of nature for thirty minutes and took note of the smaller empty tanks he previously ignored. The tanks were just the right size to hold a genetically altered developing human to adulthood. They had apparently all been cleared by the hit squad before they fled. Jonas wondered if the Federation had since resumed their experiments. He left the room much as he found it, turning off the lights and closing the massive pressure door. Jonas walked down the corridor, pondering all he had seen since arriving here. It was mind-blowing. He closed all of the pressure doors as he passed through them; always a good idea in an underwater facility.

When Jonas entered the hangar, it felt like he had come home from a long, unpleasant journey. And although the temperature was the same, the lights felt warm and inviting after the hours of darkness he had endured. The transition from darkness to light made him think of something his father said, "People like the darkness because they can do what they want and hide what they've done. They avoid the light because they might see who they really are." In a few more days the *M2* would be in orbit, and Manta should have the two subs programmed and on their way home.

O'Connor began to doubt his choice of vessels about two days after they'd left the colony. The cruiser was fast and suitable for roaming about the colony, but it was definitely not built for extended trips. It had no galley, no bunks, and the head had no shower. He and Magnus would have to eat MREs and sack out on the floor. This wasn't a pleasure cruise, but it would have been nice to have a bunk. And after more than a week of not showering, Dwight wondered whose B.O. would knock out more people when he and Magnus returned.

Matthew was dreading the second of what was to be a standing weekly meeting with Daniels. He docked the *Jack Frost* and found his escort of two goons waiting for him on the other side of the air lock. They gave him the usual pat down and wand sweep for weapons. Matthew had more requests to make to Daniels regarding the operation of the mines. Rumor had it that someone had killed a couple of O'Connor's men. Given Markus's recent arming, it was most likely true. Although why O'Connor was trying to keep it quiet, Matthew was unsure.

Daniels was waiting in his now-private dining room with his newly-adopted look of smugness.

"Good evening, Doctor Black." Daniels stood, enthusiastically extending his right hand and grabbing Matthew's for an involuntary handshake.

"Good evening, Commander. I trust you are doing well," Matthew said flatly.

"Thank you, Doctor. Yes, I am. And you?"

"I'm getting by. Tonight I hoped to discuss the supply situation and ... "

"Doctor Black," Daniels interrupted with a raised hand. "I don't like to engage in negotiations during a meal, especially one of equal quality as last week's. It simply wouldn't be civilized to taint it with heated discussion. Please, have a seat."

Matthew had to make a conscious effort not to roll his eyes at the thought of this murderous traitor speaking as though he knew anything of civility.

A steward brought Martian wine of a similar quality as the previous week. The meal was exceptional, and if not for the company he was forced to keep, Matthew would have thoroughly enjoyed it. Daniels' steward brought them glasses filled with an excellent ruby Porto from Australia and some of the new Martian cigars. It had only been in the last decade that the genetically altered highbred tobacco grown on Mars had been developed to a sufficient quality that it was able to rival finer cigars from Earth. *Yet another tiny reason for the Federation to hate the Republic,* Matthew thought. Matthew had always loved a good cigar, but rarely indulged in such an expensive imported item. He caught himself beginning to relax as he relished the cigar, then sagaciously realized that was exactly what Daniels was trying to do. Matthew recovered his wits as the conversation turned to issues of importance.

" ... I assume you've heard the rumors about two of O'Connor's men being murdered?" asked Daniels.

"I have, although I wasn't sure if it was true."

"It is. They were apparently ambushed and killed even though they were unarmed."

"Really? That's terrible." Matthew tried not to sound too sarcastic. *So that's how they're going to paint it,* he thought.

"Any information regarding their killer will be generously rewarded, and of course anyone found withholding information will be punished," Daniels continued. "We don't want some psycho running loose in the colony."

Too late, Matthew thought. *You should have thought of that before you brought in O'Connor and his goons.*

"If I hear anything, I'll be sure to let you know." Matthew was a lousy liar, and he knew it. But he doubted Daniels would perceive his half-truth.

"Good. I know there is enmity between us now, but that doesn't mean we can't help each other out from time to time. Such information would be a very good bargaining tool during our negotiations, don't you agree?"

"I'll start asking around, subtly," Matthew answered with feigned intent.

"Great! I'll send a box of these cigars with you when you leave," Daniels said.

Matthew was speechless. It was a generous gift, even if it was from scum such as Daniels. The shipping cost alone on a box of cigars was 150 IS.' Although his eyes grew wide and he allowed himself to be visibly pleased, he kept his mind on the right track, realizing that Daniels was working insidiously to try and win him over.

Daniels called his steward, and after involuntarily raising an eyebrow at the uncharacteristically generous request, brought the box of cigars and presented it to Matthew. Matthew continued negotiating with Daniels, rather heatedly at times, regarding the plight of the miners and colonists. Everyone had known for hundreds of years that the only government and economic combination that worked properly was one that allowed free enterprise. Regardless of how honest those in a governing body may be or how pure their intentions, government always fails in its attempts to run any industrial enterprise. "Government efficiency" was still one of the most common nomenclatures for waste. During the short time that Daniels had engaged in his little dictatorship, there were already problems with supplies. Matthew finally convinced him to release existing supply shipments under the condition that his men be allowed to inspect every crate. Daniels cut the conversation when he decided enough had been accomplished and stood to dismiss Matthew.

"How are Mrs. Black and your son, by the way?" he asked casually as he shook Matthew's hand.

Matthew was taken aback by the question, because he hadn't realized Daniels did not know Jonas was gone. He nearly stuttered his response.

"Oh, they're fine. Busy as usual."

"Good. Tell them I said hello," Daniels said with pseudo-sincerity.

Matthew left feeling awkward with the gift that was supposed to be down payment on an intelligence service he had no intention of ever rendering. Matthew would talk about the rumor with a few people and tell Daniels next week he could not glean any new information. One of the other goons gave Matthew a strange look as he stepped into the air lock; the look that he had been up to something. Although he couldn't think of a reason for Daniels to do it, Matthew was afraid that look the goon let slip meant his sub had been sabotaged. But everything checked out and he made it home in one piece.

"Is it in place?" asked Daniels.

"Yes, sir. He shouldn't have reason to look for it, and if he does, I doubt he'll find it," responded one of his men.

"Good."

It never hurts to have a few well-placed bugs, Daniels thought. *Especially near someone like Dr. Black, a man who knows a little about everything.*

EIGHT

Manta had finished programming the subs, and the first one was away. But the second had a bad ballast relay that blew just before the subs began their descent. It was irritating, but if it had happened after the sub was away, Jonas wouldn't have been able to repair it. There it would have sat...or sunk. It took him six hours to scrounge up a comparable part, fit it, mount it, and make it work. He still wasn't sure how long it would hold. But it was all he had, and by 12:20 a.m., the lights of the sub were disappearing from sight, and Manta was tracking its departure on passive sonar. The two subs were not very fast, but Jonas was not concerned about how quickly they would get back to the colony, as he did not plan to return for another three to four weeks.

His stay here had put him over two weeks behind schedule, and he would have to step up his pace to circumnavigate the ocean, explore, map, and still reach home on time. Exhausted, Jonas started toward his bunk. His plan was to get *M2* out of here today and leave in the morning. But now he would have to wait until morning and leave a few hours late. He walked into his room, lay down on his bunk with his coveralls still on, and fell asleep.

Jonas awoke to Manta's alert tone blaring in his ear. He sat up, not remembering where he was, and hit his head on the top bunk. Cursing to himself, he regained his senses and scrambled to the bridge. He shut off the alarm and looked at the message. There was a ship twenty-four miles out and coming their way. *Manta* had programmed the second salvage sub to relay images to her while Jonas had repaired it. The sonar on the sub was not imaging properly, so he had no way of knowing what ship it was or who it might be. He was not behind schedule, and no one had reason to be looking for him. Jonas's first thought was to get the *M2* out of there. Judging the speed of the other ship, and if it had tracked *Manta's* recent sonar transmissions, he'd have just over an hour to do it before the ship surfaced.

Regardless of who it was, he needed to have the *M2* through the first air lock door before whoever was in that sub opened the hatch. He did not want anyone knowing that he had pro-grammed and instructed an A.I. to illegally fly by itself. If an A.I. was caught committing an illegal action, the owner wasn't punished. It was the A.I. who was sentenced to a memory wipe, which would allow the retention of the A.I.'s core programming and personality, but erase all it had ever learned. The worst-case scenario was the complete destruction of the A.I.'s entire core system: a death sentence.

A good A.I. was profusely laborious to program, even with a basic platform package like Manta was built on. They grew in intelligence, skill, and personality the longer they were active. They became the virtual assistant, best friend, personal organizer, confidante, pet, and even treasured family member of their own-ers. An "operator," as an A.I.'s owner was called, did not want to lose such an important part of their life. Operators were the ones who ultimately directed an A.I. to conduct its activities, whether legal or not. And although operators were not always punished for an A.I.'s illegal operations per se, the erasure or termination of an A.I. caused not only a sizable economic but often emotional loss to its owner.

Jonas ran out of the *Manta*, across the hangar and entered *M2*.

"M! Fire up the main drives and execute the hangar escape program."

"Yes, Captain. When would you like me to depart?"

"Immediately; there is another ship approaching and I want you out of here before it arrives. *You* know no one can see you piloting yourself."

"Understood, Captain. Estimated time to liftoff is ten minutes, although it will take fifteen for the interior air lock door to open."

"Right. I'm going to start its opening sequence now. Maintain a radio link with *Manta* until you are out of range, then go to radio silence and avoid all vessels until I contact you."

"Yes, Captain. I will be waiting for your call. Farewell."

Jonas forgot to grab his pistol belt off the captain's chair as he ran from the bridge of the *M2*. He exited and sealed the hatch behind him. Running across the hangar and up the stairs to the control room, Jonas quickly initiated the air lock egress sequence. The massive doors in the roof of the hangar began to creak and moan as an ever-growing fissure formed in the middle of them. Once *M2* was in the air lock and the inner doors were sealed, the depressurization sequence would be overridden, allowing air to be discharged onto the surface, giving the illusion of a vapor vent expelling gas. It was a common occurrence on Europa; therefore, if it was observed by someone it would likely discounted as a natural phenomenon. *M2* would exit when the outer doors opened and proceed along the surface to the far side of the moon before breaking gravity's grip and moving into orbit.

Jonas ran back down the stairs and gathered all his tools and various belongings that had become scattered around the hangar over the last two weeks. He stopped to watch as the *M2* lifted off the deck and brought herself to a perfect hover. Her engines had a shrill scream to them. The hangar doors were open, and she lifted herself out of her cocoon and into the air lock. Jonas returned to the hangar control room to make sure the door sequence had worked properly. He went to *Manta*, took off his coveralls, cleaned up a little, and was going to put his pistol belt on for effect, then cursed when he realized he had left his souvenir onboard the *M2*. He had no idea who was in the approaching ship, but it had to be someone he knew. No one else would care about him being out here. He did not realize he was lonely until the prospect of seeing a friendly face had presented itself.

He went to the bridge and checked the location of the unknown ship. It was only 500 meters out! They must have tracked *Manta*'s sonar transmissions or they never would have found this particular tunnel so soon. Jonas noticed that his message light was still blinking, although he thought he'd already erased the contact message of the number two sub. He touched the screen, saw the date, and realized it was that last garbled transmission he had received from his father. He had told *Manta* to clean it up just before finding this place and had since forgotten about it. The message began to play and it was not the casual message Jonas thought he was going to hear. It was infinitely more terrible.

"Jonas, I don't know how much time I have or if this message will be intercepted. I just hope you get it in time. I'm hoping they haven't started monitoring all of the channels yet. There has been a coup at the colony and Commander Daniels is at the center of it. As near as I can tell, he hired mercenaries to come in and take over everything. I haven't seen Markus for days; I fear the worst for him. Do not come back to the colony for as long as you can, but when you do come back open the silver case. It has a new JLM 27 pistol inside, an extra power cell and 500 rounds of ammo. It also has a complete set of schematics to the colony with several covert docking points highlighted and an emergency Republic Marine beacon. Find a way to activate the transmitter before you return … if you can. You'll have to get it close to the surface before activating it, as you know the signal won't penetrate the crust. We should have seen this coming. Markus started getting strange vibes from a few of the recent new miners, and when I thought about it, so had I. I wish he'd been wrong … Be careful, son. Don't trust anyone."

Jonas was dumfounded. He felt terrible for not having read the message sooner. He should be there doing … what? Something! Anything! *Manta*'s collision indicator began blaring, snapping him out of his daze. That ship was here! And instead of being friendly, now there was a good chance it was not. Jonas ran to the hatch, closed it, and sealed it just as the ship broke the surface. He watched through one of *Manta*'s windows as the water rolled off the ship. It was Markus's cruiser. *Maybe he got away and found me!* Jonas started for the hatch to open it and greet his friend, but something made him hesitate. His father said Markus was missing. The hatch opened revealing a Stygian hollow from which darkness itself seemed to pour. Jonas' blood ran cold and his heart jumped into his throat.

D wight brought the cruiser to the surface and shut down the drives. Magnus was already at the door with rifle in hand. Dwight was surprised to see a trace of active sonar coming from this particular passageway. Otherwise it would have taken them days to find this place in the maze of tunnels. But this place was supposed to be abandoned. That, coupled with the glimpse of a blip which was either a *very* large creature or another ship that was there and then gone, made O'Connor a little jumpy. A check of the atmosphere by the sensors told him the air was good enough to breathe. Dwight stared through the cockpit window, awed by the size of the facility. He didn't see any movement, but the fact that there were lights on raised a red flag in his head. He didn't like this a bit.

"Magnus!" Dwight called.

Magnus stepped out of the air lock and looked at O'Connor. If he looked at anyone else that way, they usually thought they were about to die, but O'Connor knew better.

"Don't open the door yet. Something doesn't look right."

Magnus walked to the cockpit and looked out. "Lights."

"Yep, we should be careful. Put your armor on."

Magnus nodded and donned his armor. It was a custom-made syntha-web coat spun to Magnus's exact dimensions. Electro-polymer threads woven into the material countered the force of an impact. Powered by the kinetic energy of a striking projectile, the fibers tightened at the point of impact, making it as hard as plate steel. The armor was not built for the average man; at seventy-five pounds, it was too heavy. Capable of stopping almost any round fired from almost any weapon made, it effectively made Magnus a light armored vehicle.

Magnus stepped back to the air lock, and after receiving a nod from Dwight, opened it with his rifle.

Jonas eyes' grew large, and he stepped back from his window and into the shadow when he saw the biggest monster of a man he never thought could exist. The man was holding a rifle that was pointing right at him, and, knowing an accelerator rifle with armor piercing rounds could easily penetrate *Manta*, Jonas thought he was dead. But the man was looking past him, and one second after he had cleared his field of view from inside the ship, he began cautiously shifting from side to side and approaching the door of the cruiser as he cleared left and right. He exited the ship, revealing another man inside. They both appeared to be visually sweeping the room for occupants. Jonas was glad he was inside and out of sight; he was sure these were some of the mercenaries his father had described. But were they looking for him? Why else would they be here?

Jonas knew he had to get out of here before he was discovered. But if he tried to leave now, they could punch *Manta* so full of holes with those rifles that he'd be dead ten minutes after submerging. These guys were professionals, so he couldn't engage them or they'd drop him before he got a round off. The best thing to do for the moment was to sit tight and wait for an opportunity. To do what ... he didn't know just yet.

Dwight and Magnus finished clearing the hangar in about fifteen minutes and then noticed the control room. They immediately headed that way and checked it, finding only the body of the dead doctor. Magnus noticed the insignia on the doctor's coat; it looked familiar, but he couldn't quite place it.

Jonas watched the two as they exited the stairwell and trotted back to the cruiser. The smaller of the two began looking more closely at *Manta* and started walking toward her. The man jumped onto *Manta*'s wing and walked up to her fuselage. Jonas could hear him banging his fist on *Manta*'s skin. He was looking for a hatch. Jonas was relieved. Because of the corrosive properties of Europa's water, Jonas had opted not to put an exterior hatch handle on *Manta*. In addition to her hatch seam being virtually invisible, the only way to open it was by voice command, or tapping out her name on it in Morse code.

O'Connor was looking, but couldn't find a hatch on the weird-looking sub they surfaced beside. It did not look old enough to be in this place, but neither did the gorgeous Corvette sitting across the hangar.

O'Connor yelled at Magnus, and they started for the only door that appeared to lead out of the hangar. They found the manual air lock sealed, which was not something people usually did with doors they used on a regular basis; the first good sign he'd seen. They opened the door, turned on their rifle lights, and entered the long, dark hallway. Dwight decided to go left, so Magnus pulled a Viper mine from his pack, set it approximately ten feet to the right of the door, and activated it. The smart, miniature, auto-turret locked itself to the floor and could cut down any man within its 180-degree spread. It would effectively cover their six while they continued down the corridor.

Jonas saw the two turn to the left and realized they would be in for a long walk, giving him possibly his only opportunity to leave. The cruiser docked between him and the hangar door would provide him some cover when he left. He waited about a minute to make sure they were out of earshot and had *Manta* initiate her startup sequence. As the drives powered up, he started filling the tanks, causing *Manta* to slowly and quietly sink below the surface.

O'Connor cursed, then struck the smooth rock wall with his rifle. His light had gone out. He had a spare flashlight, but not one that would fit his rifle.

"We're going back to get another light," O'Connor told Magnus with a spiteful glance at the defective piece of equipment.

Magnus nodded, and they both backed down the hallway toward the hangar.

Manta was completely submerged and sinking quickly. Jonas didn't want a repeat performance of the enemy finding him with his own sonar, so he left it off. He initiated his turn very slowly; he was still close to the surface and did not want to make noise by splashing water all over the hangar. His turn executed, he eased forward on the throttle. Most subs had a relatively cylindrical shape to them, making them a good fit for the round tunnels. Manta's wide wingspan made for minimal maneuverability.

Dwight could have sworn he heard the sound of lapping water when he entered the hangar, and immediately he knew something was out of place. He and Magnus cautiously ran over to check on their sub. Magnus could see O'Connor instantly filled with rage upon walking to the far side of the sub, although everything looked fine to him. Magnus quickly walked around to the other side where that strange sub was … gone!

"There *was* someone else here. They can't be very far ahead of us. We've only been gone a few minutes," Dwight said through clenched teeth.

"Let's blow them out of the water!" Dwight yelled as he ran past Magnus and jumped through the hatch of the cruiser.

Magnus was inside the ship and closing the hatch before O'Connor could do it from the cockpit. Dwight fired up the drives and had the cruiser submerged before Magnus was even out of his armor and belted in his seat. O'Connor recklessly reversed the sub, neatly missing the wall. He thrust the throttle forward as far as he dare in such a tight space and engaged active sonar.

Jonas noticed a sonar activation on his heads-up display. They were on to him!

"*Manta*," Jonas almost yelled, "prep four torpedoes and target the roof of the cave at the entrance of the facility. Fire them in immediate succession the moment we clear the cave."

"Yes, Captain. Torpedoes ready. Follow the path I have placed on the display. It is the quickest way out. Target lock acquired."

Jonas exited the tight tunnel and entered the main cavern; here he had room to maneuver. He pointed *Manta* at the exit and hit the throttle. She surged forward.

"Load a probe and send it to the entrance we first docked at. Engage its imaging sonar. Maybe it will draw their attention away from us."

"Yes, Captain. Course plotted … firing probe."

Just then Jonas could see the sonar signature of the other ship exit the tunnel 500 meters from him. They would easily detect him with their sonar, but he hoped the probe's obscenely large sonar signature would draw their attention and give him a couple of extra seconds.

O'Connor exited the tunnel and immediately zeroed in on the huge active sonar image on his screen. He had him!

"Are those torpedoes ready?" he yelled at Magnus, who was about ten feet behind him, loading torpedoes into the tubes.

"Yes!"

The ship's computer had a firing solution, and O'Connor was just about to hit the fire button on his yoke when he took a closer look what the computer was targeting. It was only about the size of a torpedo! O'Connor realized he had been duped and let forth a rancorous string of curses at the unknown pilot of the strange sub. He turned the sub toward the exit and immediately picked up the image of the other ship on his sonar.

That thing is especially strange looking, he thought, *and* really *fast.* In fact, it was quickly pulling away from him.

He targeted the ship, and the computer only took a second to calculate a firing solution. The moment the fire control light turned solid red, O'Connor pushed the buttons on each side of the yoke, firing both torpedo tubes.

Jonas was nearly clear of the cave entrance and gaining speed when *Manta*'s targeting alarm went off. He had a lock! Jonas fired his first set of torpedoes a few seconds early. The other two would be loaded and ready to fire in five seconds. The two missiles looked like comet fish on passive sonar as they surged forward from the *Manta.* When they cleared the cave entrance, they quickly turned 180 degrees and headed straight back toward it. The two torpedoes narrowly missed *Manta* exiting the cave as they sped to their target and exploded with a deafening concussion. The enemy torpedoes were closing fast when his impacted, and he had no countermeasures; his hope was that his would cause the others to blow too. The shock wave was closer than Jonas had wanted, and he lost control of the *Manta* for a second, but he recovered and righted her. He dove for the floor, activated sonar, and came about, pointing *Manta*'s nose directly at the cave entrance and firing his second pair of torpedoes as he settled to the rocky bottom. If those torpedoes were still active, his only chance was to stay still and try and blend in with the floor.

"Manta," said Jonas, "I want that ship targeted the second it shows itself."

"Yes, Captain. Nothing so far."

The second set of torpedoes detonated at the entrance of the cave. He was staring at the sonar and could only see a pile of rocks through the growing cloud of silt that the impact had blown into the water. He sighed in relief. If the enemy torpedoes were still active, he would have seen them by now. Stopping made Jonas realize he was scared out of his wits. When he finally released his death grip on *Manta*'s yoke, he found himself shaking.

O'Connor saw the other ship fire two torpedoes into open water not a tenth of a second after he had fired his. *Those won't do anything out there*, he thought. Then, on the sonar, he saw the torpedoes coming back! He quickly turned away, released countermeasures, and initiated evasive maneuvers.

Then a booming shock wave struck the cruiser. Dwight turned to see on sonar that the mouth of the cave was now nonexistent, and the entire ceiling of the cave was collapsing. He quickly turned back toward the hangar tunnel and gunned the accelerator. Several rocks struck the top of the cruiser as they reached the entrance. O'Connor watched on the imaging sonar as the rocks fell through the water in surreal slow motion. He wondered how he was going to get out of this one. Magnus walked over, sat in his chair, looked at Dwight, and lifted an eyebrow at him. He was wondering the same thing.

Katherine and James had both been keeping their ears open and their mouths shut. Kat had taken a job as a waitress, despite adamant protesting by James, at a pub in the central hub that was a popular hangout for the mercenaries. It was the type of place she had always imagined thugs would like to spend their time. It was dark and cold with a cave-like smell to it. People could come here and find many a dark corner table to discuss all manner of illicit schemes, all without being clearly seen or heard. The owner was a nice enough fellow, but had the look of a man who could not be trusted regarding anything beyond the basest of moral concepts.

She endured only minor harassment of a typical nature from most of the mercenaries. Most of them, after finding out how young she was, were content to treat her like a doormat of a kid sister. She heard miners talking, saying things that would make a cargo ship's crewman blush, and seen their drunken carousing, but they were school kids compared to the mercenaries. She had learned that the occupation force was not all mercenaries. Some were pirates. Then she remembered. Dwight O'Connor and various members of his crew were wanted for dozens of heists: the theft of ships, the destruction of ships, and the murder of hundreds of people aboard those ships. They all had death sentences hanging over them, but had always remained one step ahead of both the Federation and the Republic.

That thought got Kat thinking…Why would they settle here and commit themselves to a place where they are essentially trapped? If anyone found out they were here, they'd be doomed. Commander Daniels was part of the Republic of Mars military, and the colony was part of the Republic. Mr. Black said Daniels was paid off by some mysterious third party to do what he'd done…he must have been paid a lot! But why would anyone pay that much to simply take over the colony? They would have to keep control of the place for months, maybe even a year, before they started making a profit. Sooner or later the Republic is going to find out something is wrong and come check it out, and these mercenaries don't stand a chance against a couple of ships full of Martian Marines. Add to the fact that the Federation was after them too, and this whole thing seemed like a really bad idea…from a pirate's perspective. Unless…they had also worked some kind of deal with…the Federation? Katherine dismissed the idea as too farfetched and refocused on her job.

She was serving up her last drink order to two of her least favorite patrons when she overheard the last part of their conversation…

"…Yeah, I don't know why the captain went out there. I hate this place, and you won't catch me leaving the colony and going out on some wild goose chase," said the ugly pirate to an even uglier one.

"I don't care how much Daniels it paying him, or how much the captain offered me, I wouldn't go out there unless he put a gun to my head…"

"…Oh." The uglier one acknowledged Kat putting the drinks on the table and tipped her before slapping her on the behind, causing both of the pirates to break out in a fit of laughter.

Kat's shift was finally over, and she hurried back to her family's apartment. If not for her trying to do her part by gathering information, she would have belted that guy tonight. All he got was a dirty look instead. Kat rolled her eyes in afterthought. *Yeah, that probably* really *hurt his feelings.*

"Hey sis," James greeted as she walked through the door. She looked tired. "…rough night?"

"Yeah, the usual," she answered. "But I think I figured something out, and heard something worth worrying about."

"What?" James asked, getting instantly serious.

"I heard a couple of men talking, and I think Daniels knows Jonas isn't here and sent O'Connor after him." Her voice cracked a little at the end and she sat on the couch.

"What?" James, who was sitting at the kitchen table eating, dropped what he was doing. "How do you know?"

"I don't for sure. I just heard a couple of men talking about O'Connor being paid by Daniels to go on a 'wild goose chase.'"

"Oh no…we have to try and send a message to him."

"I know, but how? If we get caught, we'd be killed, and he's been out of range for weeks. In fact, he should be on the far side of the planet by now."

"I know…"

"We need to tell Jonas's dad. He'll know what to do."

"You're right. Let's go."

The two left their apartment and took the long walk to the Black's residence. On the way over, Kat told James her theory about the Federation giving amnesty to O'Connor.

Matthew and Sarah were sitting on the couch, each with their arm around the other, winding down for the day, and watching the news when the door chime sounded. Matthew's heart fell to his stomach as he went to the door to see who their unexpected guest was.

"It's just James and Katherine," said Matthew with a sigh.

"What are those two doing out this late?" Sarah stated with a motherly mien.

Matthew simply shrugged and opened the door. Before it was half-open, Kat started talking.

"Mr. Black! Daniels sent O'Connor after Jonas."

Sarah was standing beside Matthew and grabbed his arm.

"I know we weren't supposed to come here unless you called us, but we didn't think there was anything we could do and we thought you might be able to, or get someone who could." Tears started streaming down Kat's face as worry took over. Two weeks of withholding her emotions and keeping company with the enemy boiled to the surface.

Sarah stepped over to her and let her cry on her shoulder. Matthew turned and looked at James with an inquisitive look.

"She's right, I think," James responded before being asked. He then relayed the conversation Katherine had heard from the two pirates.

"It makes sense. But I met with Daniels only a few days ago and he asked how Jonas and Sarah were, as if he didn't even know he was gone."

"Well, there are plenty of people who knew about his trip and could have easily said something," said James.

"You're right. It would have been easy to discover he was gone, but why the concern over it? To them, he's just a kid gone camping and shouldn't pose any kind of threat. Still," Matthew contemplated, "we should try to get a message to him. I sent one right after the takeover, but I don't know if he received it."

"How do we get it to him? He's got to be on the far side of the planet by now."

"I think I can rig one of his spare probes to go after him and start transmitting a coded message when it's out of range of the colony, *maybe* ... " Matthew lightly shook his head, "it would get far enough to reach him in time."

"Will it work?" Katherine asked, wiping her eyes.

"I don't know ... One of those things shouldn't be noticed leaving the colony and, if I rig an extra power cell to it, should be able to go nearly to the other side of the planet. James, can you help out?"

"Sure, Mr. Black. Where do we start?"

"Jonas has his stripped-down prototype probe in my shop still. We can use it. No time to lose, let's go."

"We're coming with you. I can program it," Kat insisted.

Matthew looked at Sarah and could tell she didn't want to stay there either, so they all loaded into the *Jack Frost* and took a midnight ride to Matthew's shop in one of the north spokes of the colony.

Dwight and Magnus watched the ceiling of the cavern fall for ten minutes before Dwight silently turned and headed back to the hangar. O'Connor remembered the ship he had seen parked there. He did not know if the ship was salvageable, but at least he had a plan.

The cruiser surfaced quickly, splashing water all over the deck. O'Connor was already at the door and opened it. After a few minutes, Magnus found the hidden door on the port side and signaled. O'Connor opened the door, entered the ship, and tried to initiate a cold start of the reactor, but could not. O'Connor checked the reactor fuel and it had enough, but when he discovered the computer core stripped of its memory modules, he launched into a cursing tirade. They searched the hangar for spare parts, but found none.

They were within firing range of the mouth of the tunnel. Magnus loaded the second torpedo, still thinking this was a bad idea. O'Connor was looking at the sonar, but still could not get a target range. Not knowing how much the sediment in the water affected the sonar, O'Connor slowly moved toward the mouth of the tunnel. He knew he was nearing the end when he finally got a reading... 800 meters?

Shocked, O'Connor looked again, and inched the sub a few meters forward. Through the opening at the end of the tunnel he could see, on the display, a massive pile of debris. He realized what had happened. The cavern was deep enough to allow the thin ceiling above to collapse into it and pile up below the level of the tunnel entrance. Dwight yelled at Magnus to come forward and look at the display.

"Open?" Magnus asked.

"Open," answered Dwight, beaming.

"Good. Not one of your better plans."

O'Connor looked at Magnus from the corner of his eyes and snorted. He was in too good a mood to get upset with his oldest shipmate for doubting him. And he knew Magnus was right.

O'Connor exited the corridor, turned, and fired the two torpedoes into the tunnel. They impacted at the first corner and collapsed it. That should effectively prevent anyone else from ever entering the place. He turned the sub about, pointed it in the direction of the colony, and peaked the throttle. He had a score to settle with the pilot of that other ship.

Jonas decided he had waited long enough, and there was still no sign of the other ship. Jonas left the active sonar off, eased back on the yoke and bumped the throttle enough to ease *Manta* off the floor. Jonas knew he was told not to go back to the colony for as long as he could avoid it. But he had no intention of hiding while who knows what was going on at home. If he was still the only person who knew about the hangar, he might have been tempted to hole up there for a month or two. *Too late for that now*, thought Jonas. *What I need to do is find some way to get this marine beacon to the surface. One pulse from it and a Martian destroyer will be parked over that slime Daniels' base in a week. How am I supposed to get through the base to the surface though?*

Jonas left his active sonar off and turned toward the colony.

NINE

Doyle sat in O'Connor's office poring over maps and schematics of the colony, determined to find the killer. It had been four days since the third man had been reported missing, and he had yet to be found. Doyle had already questioned the man's standing "date" and found that she had received a more profitable offer from an unknown customer. She had, of course, being the sagacious businesswoman she was, dumped her usual companion for the more lucrative offer. She was understandably angry, after waiting for hours, when her mystery sugar daddy did not show. She did not think it remarkable that her usual appointment was not there, since she had been gone several hours. Doyle saw no need to aggressively interrogate her. He had conducted hundreds of interrogations and could tell when someone was telling the truth or not.

He had ordered the men to do nothing or go anywhere alone. Doyle could see that, although difficult, someone with an intimate knowledge of the inner structure of the colony might be able to move and stay out of sight of most of the security cameras. It wouldn't be easy; there were cameras everywhere, thousands of them. This was also a problem; there were too many to actually monitor in real time.

Doyle counted the third man among the dead. *Why? Because that's what he would do if...* Then it hit him.

That's it, he thought, *he's a rebel! He's not only trying to thin our numbers, but trying to instill fear into the men. He...*

Just then an alarm sounded. Almost instantaneously, the wall screen in front of the desk came on, showing four different angles of smoke and fire and the location on a map. Ten minutes later he arrived at the scene. The fire had been put out by the auto suppression system, but it was as he feared. There had been an explosion, and three of his men lay dead on the floor. Doyle hit the wall he was standing beside with his fist and swore to kill whoever was responsible. He hoped he would get a chance to do it slowly. Captain O'Connor had a limited number of men here, and the body count was now up to six. It was enough to put a significant dent in their occupation force.

Markus watched on a small remote camera. He should not have used an improvised explosive. It was reckless. Although every angle was covered by cameras, which ensured no one but pirates would be injured, a mistake could have hurt a random colonist. The man who looked in charge arrived to investigate the scene. It was the same man he had unwittingly chased into the trap O'Connor had set for him. He was thin, intelligent looking, with glasses and a fiendishness in his eyes. Markus had seen that look in men before. They were untamable animals. Having seen the face of his enemy, Markus knew he would need to be careful.

Matthew and James removed all of the unnecessary equipment from the stealth torpedo to accommodate an extra power cell. They extracted the imaging sonar sensors and replaced them with a sonar transmitter. They were finishing the last bit of wiring when Katherine announced she was finished with the programming.

"The message is a twenty gig encrypted loop message and doesn't say who sent it. It just says 'Jonas, they're coming to kill you. Daniels used pirates to take over the colony, Markus is missing, and they're using his cruiser. Don't trust anyone. Please be careful.' How does that sound?"

"Sounds great, sis. That should about cover it," congratulated James.

It only took thirty seconds for the simple program to upload. A tiny green light indicated the torpedo was ready to be deployed. Matthew set the activation frequency so the torpedo's program could be started remotely with a quick radio burst. Now all they had to do was deploy it.

"You two go back home." Matthew looked at James and Katherine. "I'll launch it from the ridge behind our dome with the *Jack Frost*. That should keep it off sonar long enough to keep anyone from tracing its origin point." Everyone looked at each other in agreement. They loaded the torpedo and themselves into the *Jack Frost*.

With James and Katherine safely on their way back home, Matthew and Sarah took the *Jack Frost* to the backside of the ridge to the south of their module. The torpedo was lightly gripped in the manipulation arm of the *Jack*. Matthew released *Jack*'s grip on the torpedo and transmitted the activation code, causing the torpedo to immediately rocket south. He could see it for a few seconds, zigzagging on the sonar. It turned west and took off in the direction Jonas said he was going. Mr. and Mrs. Black turned around and went home, hoping this would work, and that it wasn't already too late to save their son.

Manta was running at ninety percent of her capacity. She had been designed for speed and was cutting through the water at about ten knots faster than any of the Sharks in the colony, including Markus's cruiser. Jonas was keeping low and skimming the bottom of the ocean to stay off sonar as long as possible if he happened upon another ship bent on imploding him. He had been piloting the ship for two hours without a break and it was his fourth such shift. After a quick stretch, a drink, and a trip to the head, he tried for another couple of hours at the helm.

Three hours later, he had a splitting headache and had reached his stress tolerance ceiling. He reacted too slowly and nearly plowed *Manta* into the side of a mountain. He had *Manta* take the controls again and went back to his bunk to rest for at least a couple of hours.

Jonas awoke with a start, quickly swung his legs over the edge of the bunk, sat up, looked at his watch, and hoped he had only been out for a couple of hours.

Six hours, he thought, shaking his head and standing. He made some freeze-dried coffee and walked around the corner to the bridge. Jonas let his thoughts wander for a moment. His thoughts were interrupted by the contact indicator on the holo-display. He quickly sat down and took a closer look. It looked like a comet fish, but it was moving too fast in a straight course, and it was broadcasting a sonar communications signal. It had to be one of his ... but from whom? He had not finished processing the question when Manta chimed in with a message tone.

"Captain," she coolly remarked, "that object is broadcasting an encrypted message for you. I have the decryption program for the code; I believe it was sent by one of my primary programmers, Katherine Shaw. Shall I play the message for you?"

"Yes."

Manta played the message; it was Katherine's voice.

"Jonas, they're coming to kill you. Daniels used pirates to take over the colony, Markus is missing, and they're using his cruiser. Don't trust anyone. Please be careful."

The message kept repeating until Jonas told Manta to stop playing it. The probe flew past *Manta* as it continued on its course. It was the first time he had truly been glad to hear her voice. He was embarrassed when she kissed him; she seemed to have a special knack for embarrassing him. It was one of the many things she … actually … he couldn't really think of *anything* else she did that annoyed him. Now that he thought about it, her kiss was pretty nice. Jonas found himself thinking about her smile and how beautiful her eyes were. She was always poking him with her elbow or grabbing his arm, and now, for the first time, the fact that she was not around didn't make him happy at all. Jonas realized he missed her. He listened to the recording again and realized she had nearly broken down before she had finished. The thought of her crying wrenched at his gut.

J onas sat down at *Manta*'s controls, determined to make it home as swiftly as possible. But he stopped when he realized he did not know what he was going to do when he got there. Jonas turned around to face the main holo-display and pulled up the colony's schematics that he had downloaded from his father's case. Jonas had grown up in the colony and was surprised when he saw a wing of the colony that he could not remember exploring. It had very few windows, unlike most sections, and the domes seemed smaller and not as closely linked as the rest. He remembered seeing that wing on the imaging sonar and not thinking much about it.

Jonas took a more comparative look at the different wing against the others. The quarters, common rooms, corridors, and docking rooms were all much smaller than the rest of the colony. There were no indications that the wing was being used, and Jonas theorized that it must have been closed off for some time. If it were, maybe he could slip into one of the docks unseen and find a way to undermine Daniels and his thugs. But first he wanted to contact his parents and let them know he was unhurt.

Manta's contact alarm shattered the silence of Jonas's thoughts, and a quick look at the sonar showed him what was heading his way: two torpedoes. Jonas swiveled his chair around to face the front of the cockpit, grabbed the controls, gunned the throttle, and dove straight down.

"*Manta*, engage active sonar!" Jonas said frantically.

"Already engaging, Captain. The missiles were fired from below the rim of the last canyon we passed. I cannot see the ship, and do not know its current position," Manta answered coolly.

"Okay," Jonas responded, keeping his eyes forward, looking for any advantage he might gain from the terrain. "Keep me informed of their distance as they close."

Jonas pulled back the yoke, pulling *Manta* from her nosedive ten feet from the floor. He could see a massive silt cloud rise up behind him from *Manta's* wash as he leveled off and began racing forty feet above the bottom. He hoped the cloud would interfere with the weaker sonar that most torpedoes were equipped with; it was the closest thing to a countermeasure he could think of. He could feel panic creeping up on him.

"Missiles at eleven thousand yards and closing at fifty knots, Captain. The silt cloud slowed their progress by approximately three seconds."

"Okay M, load torpedoes and…" Jonas strained at the controls as he pulled up just in time to miss a rock outcropping and drop in behind it. "Set them to target the enemy missiles and detonate when they are within ten yards. Do you think the blast will be enough to stop them?"

"Yes Captain, I calculate the blast wave within that radius will disable them. However, I only calculate a sixty-seven percent chance that my torpedoes will be able to close to that distance."

"Do it!"

Jonas dropped over the edge of a canyon and dove to the bottom, plunging a thousand feet in seconds.

"He's just dropped off sonar. Magnus," O'Connor yelled toward the back of the cruiser, "you have those next two torpedoes loaded yet?"

"Almost," he responded.

O'Connor picked up his torpedo's sonar signature and could see them winding their way through the canyon.

"He's not getting away this time." O'Connor smiled, gunning the throttle.

Jonas haphazardly followed the canyon, half-panicked, but knowing its winding walls would be the best way to confuse and lose his twin hunters.

"The missiles have slowed to compensate for their lack of maneuverability. Torpedoes programmed and ready, Captain," Manta said.

"Fire," Jonas ordered.

He instantly heard the launching torpedoes and observed them travel forward before looping up and over to assume their course toward the two aggressors.

"Torpedoes away, Captain. Enemy missiles at four thousand yards and closing at thirty five knots."

A warning light flashed on the cruiser's heads-up display, telling O'Connor there were new torpedoes in the water. O'Connor had just used the computer to extrapolate a new lock on the enemy ship based on the pinging of the pursuing torpedoes. He fired two more before peeling away from the canyon rim and, hopefully, out of sight of the enemy torpedoes.

Jonas held his breath as he continued to pilot the *Manta* at breakneck speed through the canyon. It only took twenty seconds for the torpedoes to rocket toward each other and meet. Jonas heard a muffled "boom," followed by quiet rumbling.

"One enemy missile destroyed, Captain. The other is still in pursuit. But, I have also detected two more three thousand yards behind that one."

Jonas felt himself go pale. He knew he was about to die, and he knew he wasn't ready. In an instant, he remembered everything his father taught him about The Way. He thought of all he had discovered in the past several weeks and how it had broken the foundation of what he thought was truth. He remembered that you did not need a ceremony, a temple, or cleric to perform last rites. Jonas remembered that all he had to do was believe in The Light. He remembered hearing that some people would believe immediately, but that some had to be broken before they would accept the truth. The Light would continue to try to coax them until they accepted redemption, but if they continued to refuse to yield, they would finally become numb to all attempts, and eventually lost to the Darkness. He knew everything in his life led to this point in time. And in utter darkness, at the bottom of a lifeless canyon, in the course of about twenty seconds, he accepted redemption. But two seconds later, he knew it was not religion. This was something else. His piloting had become effortless as he rolled to and fro through the narrowing canyon, and he felt a strange peace wash over him, a peace that surpassed all comprehension. He felt new. He then understood the nature of good and evil and the difference between the two. Jonas was no longer afraid of anything.

"Ha! Did you see that? He tried the same trick again!" yelled O'Connor, referring to the canyon walls collapsing as a result of the other ship's torpedoes detonating. "Maybe he isn't so good after all."

"Maybe..." said Magnus, pointing out the fact one of their torpedoes was now missing from the display.

"Captain? Captain?" Manta was repeating. "Captain, are you all right?"

"Yes. Sorry, M. I was thinking," Jonas suddenly blurted. "The remaining missile is fifty seconds from impact, and I have an idea."

"Really? What?"

"I was built to resemble a sea creature on earth. The smaller members of my namesake's relatives bury themselves on the floor of the ocean to catch their prey unaware."

"M, you're a genius!" Jonas yelled. He knew what she was thinking.

"I have already found a possible place to execute the maneuver. Take the right channel of the canyon. Now a sharp left, then get as close as you can to the bottom and perform a stall maneuver. I am filling the ballast tanks. If you will allow, I will execute the necessary movement to bury us in the sediment."

"I have an idea too. Reload torpedoes and be ready to fire."

Three seconds later, Jonas had negotiated the turn and stalled ten feet above the floor.

"Taking the helm and executing maneuver, Captain. Shutting down active sonar. The missiles are now nineteen seconds away. I will complete the maneuver in ten seconds. The first enemy missile will be able to lock onto us three seconds after that, if I am unsuccessful."

"Okay." *How do you respond to that?* thought Jonas. "Fire the loaded torpedoes just far enough around the corner to protect us from the blast, and try to time their impact so the blast takes out that one we missed before. Oh, and vent as much air as we can spare."

"Yes, Captain. Firing now. Maneuver successful, Captain. Shutting down all primary systems and powering down reactor."

The bridge went completely black, and Jonas heard a large amount of air expelled from life support. The torpedoes exploded as Jonas reached for his jacket pocket and pulled out a small emergency light, which thoroughly lit the bridge. He found one of his emergency air units and put it on. Manta had shut down *all* systems, including life support.

Three … four … five … ten seconds passed! Jonas knew they must have hit that first torpedo. But that left the other two … they should be here in about ten seconds, Jonas reckoned. He looked at his watch and tried not to stay fixed on it. He looked again. Only two seconds passed! He could imagine the two little humming imps rocketing their way toward him, hell-bent on his destruction. Five seconds to go. Whether the silt that settled over *Manta* was thick enough to sufficiently break up their thermal image was about to be determined.

Jonas thought he heard a ping. He could barely make out the infernal humming of the two torpedoes as they rounded the bend of canyon. He was now sure they'd lost him, because he heard their motors slowing as they began searching for their lost target. They had no doubt begun thermal scanning too. His only hope was that if there was still some residual heat coming from *Manta*, it would be broken up enough by the sediment that the torpedoes would think her a natural anomaly.

"Do you think you got him, Captain?" Magnus cautiously inquired.

"I don't know…" Dwight shook his head while his eyes remained fixed on the sonar display.

O'Connor cautiously brought the cruiser to a hover at the edge of the canyon, nearly over the spot where the explosion had taken place. He and Magnus had both heard it and seen a massive collection of debris rising from the canyon after the blast. It made sense: if the sub had been destroyed, it would have vented its atmosphere. And it explained why his last two missiles had not found their target. O'Connor went to the secondary console and reviewed the sonar footage of the rising debris several times. The third time he stopped it and looked at Magnus.

"Bubbles?" he asked, inquiring for consensus.

"Bubbles." Magnus nodded in agreement.

"Let's wait around awhile; then take a closer look just to make sure. The hunter must be patient." Dwight reiterated one of his favorite sayings.

Magnus nodded in concurrence, remembering all the times the Captain had said that while they waited for hours, sometimes days, behind an asteroid or moon to take a ship unaware. Although Magnus reckoned that, given the old saying was " … patience is a *virtue*," the captain was probably just stubborn.

Jonas had been sitting in the command chair for thirty minutes, listening to the enemy torpedoes passing by at regular intervals. They would run out of power in about five minutes, if they were Markus's. Jonas was getting terribly cold; his light jacket was not meant for sitting around in freezing temperatures. He needed to get a blanket, but he could not risk making a sound until those torpedoes died.

Ten minutes and Jonas could no longer hear the torpedoes. He waited through another minute of shivers, got up as quietly as he could, went to his cabin, retrieved a blanket, and donned a fleece cap. He went forward, sat in his chair, and covered up. He knew he could not power *Manta* up too soon. That other ship was still out there, and, if the skipper was sharp, probably still hanging around to ensure Jonas was destroyed. Jonas decided he might as well take advantage of the dark and get some sleep.

As Jonas drifted off, he thought of his new understanding, and how he, strangely, no longer feared death. But he did not want to die, not that he minded for his own sake, but he had unfinished business, and he knew he would be missed. He did not want his parents to lose him; he knew how much they loved him. Katherine would lose her ... it would break her heart. He missed her ...

Commander Daniels anxiously waited for word from one of his men. They were starting the second course when a call on his earpiece let him know that the bug in the *Jack Frost* was still in place and had been uploaded to his computer.

Matthew cleared his throat lightly and asked Daniels about allowing him and his people to have their weekly gathering.

Daniels did not look up, or even acknowledge that Matthew had spoken.

"So, Doctor Black," he inquired, deflecting the question, "how do you like those cigars?"

"They're very good, thank you."

"Did you learn anything about the terrorist?"

"Not yet. I've made several inquiries regarding the matter, but heard rumors. I don't think most people care to be very helpful to you and your pirates at this point."

Matthew had asked several people what the rumors were regarding the killings; he had to ask something, because he knew he was a lousy liar. Theories abounded, but no one actually knew anything.

"Disappointing." Daniels furrowed his brow and gestured his steward to refill his glass. "I had hoped for at least some small clue. No matter." He waved his hand in dismissal of the steward. "We'll catch up to him soon enough. I would appreciate it, however, if you would continue to investigate the matter."

"I will continue to check into it, Commander. I'd like to discuss some equipment issues we've been having. We need parts."

"I will look into it. Can you send me a list of the parts you need?"

"Yes."

"Excellent! Keeping the miners content is one of my top priorities. Is there anything else?"

Here it was. Matthew fought to hold back his rage. He wanted nothing more than to wrap his hands around Daniels' neck and squeeze the life out of his smug little face.

"Why did you send O'Connor after Jonas?"

"What are you talking about?" Daniels was noticeably taken aback.

"While I was making inquiries about the killings I heard you had sent O'Connor and one of his goons to go after someone. He was gone before any of this happened, and couldn't do anything about it out there anyway!" Matthew's voice was growing louder.

"Dr. Black." Daniels leaned forward in emphasis. "I had no idea your son was absent from the colony. Had I known, I would have certainly tried to have him captured before now, but I would never have ordered him killed. I sent O'Connor on a mission that had nothing to do with your son. However, now that I know he is missing, I will have to attempt to locate and capture him. I assure you, I will give strict orders not to harm him unless absolutely necessary."

"Unless necessary?!" Matthew stood up.

The steward, who happened to also be a bodyguard, stepped from the corner of the room with his weapon in hand. Daniels gave him a look, and he retreated back into the shadows.

"Dr. Black, you can understand that while the safety of your son is important to me, the safety of my men is even more important. If he is found, and if he cooperates, he will be safely returned to Mrs. Black and yourself. Despite the animosity that may exist between us, I like the Junior Doctor Black. He virtually oozes ambition, and reminds me of a younger and perhaps even smarter version of myself."

"Then why don't you just leave him out of this?" Matthew demanded.

"Doctor, I cannot allow the possibility of anyone outside of this colony discovering our little operation before it is time, regardless of how remote the possibility may be."

Matthew raised his hand to point a finger at Daniels' face and continue his argument.

"I'm sorry, Dr. Black," Daniels interrupted, touching his ear, feigning to get a message over his com link, "but I'm going to have to cut our meeting short this evening. My steward will see to it you to your ship. Good evening. Same time next week?"

It was more of an order than an invitation and Daniels hurried out of the room.

Matthew took a few deep breaths as he turned to shoot a cutting look at the steward who coolly motioned, indicating where the door was and that it was time he used it. He walked through it and back to his ship. Matthew was calm now, and the realization that Daniels had apparently not known about Jonas's absence was beginning to sink in. If his son wasn't in danger, he may have just put him in it. Now Matthew was furious with himself.

Jonas awoke to a deafening boom and was thrown from his seat. The last thing he remembered was skull-shattering pain as his head bounced off the floor.

"Jonas!" Kat screamed as she sat up in her bed. She was sweating and shivering. The darkness in the room closed in as if it were drawing from her what little courage she had left to call upon. The inky gloom seemed as though it would even pull the very life from her if she could not subdue her paralyzing fear. She wrapped the bedspread around her and got up. The lights came on as she walked to her bathroom and washed her face. She looked at herself in the mirror; her eyes looked red and puffy, and her lip was still quivering. She went back to her bed and covered up, still shivering. She could not remember exactly what she had dreamt; only that Jonas had been killed. He, or anyone else she knew for that matter, was seldom in her dreams. She usually dreamt of people she had never seen and places she had never been. She felt sick with worry, not knowing if he were dead or alive. Her room felt colder than it was supposed to be. Katherine shivered until she was too tired to shiver any more, then she involuntarily fell asleep.

James sat at the kitchen table watching the morning news when Katherine walked in looking half-dead.
"Wow, sis! You look terrible," he goaded.
She gave him the look that would kill, if it could, and poured herself some coffee.
"You *okay?*" James asked as she sat down.
"I didn't sleep very well." She didn't look at him and turned toward the view screen.
James knew it was useless trying to talk to her in this state. She got up a few minutes later, went to the bathroom, and went through her typical hour-long girl routine. She didn't eat anything, but went straight to her computer and began program-

ming whatever it was she had been working on for the last two days. The only time she stopped was when it was time for her to go to work. James had asked, but she refused to tell him what she was doing ... so he gave up.

TEN

"I think he's dead, Captain," Magnus commented dryly. O'Connor was using their last torpedoes for random depth charges. He was just being paranoid now. Magnus had seen O'Connor get this way once before. He couldn't stand for someone to get the better of him.

"Don't!" O'Connor turned and started to tear into Magnus, but knew it wouldn't do any good.

Magnus had probably questioned Dwight more in the last few days than he had in the last five years.

"We're done, let's get back to the colony." Dwight gave him a head nod indicating they were "okay."

Magnus nodded back and took the copilot's seat next to his captain.

Martian whiskey had a dry, smoky flavor, somewhat similar to Scotch. It was not as smooth but it was wetter. Doyle thought more clearly when he drank, unlike most men, who merely *think* they think clearly when they drink. Drinking slowed his thought process down enough for him to concentrate on details. Otherwise, his mind moved in so many directions at once that he was unable to focus on any one idea for a sufficient amount of time to properly evaluate its relevance. He had the constable's office floor covered in papers and frozen frames of video feeds covering the photo optic wall screens. He poured more booze and pored over the images for the tenth time. He was slowly putting together an idea of how the assassin had planted his bomb, but still unsure how he had done it undetected.

Then it hit him. He was using the ventilation and maintenance shafts. Doyle's hair stood up on the back of his neck as he turned, drew his weapon, and fired five rounds into the air vent behind him. *He* could have been watching me all this time! Doyle mentally kicked himself for not thinking of this before. Doyle moved the desk under the vent and put the chair on top of it so he could get a good look into the vent. He had been trying to find possible hacks or evidence of the security cameras being overridden; a low-tech solution had not occurred to him. He ripped the cover off and found a duct too small for a person to fit in to. He relaxed, put the furniture back, and returned to the floor to finish putting the pieces together.

Within fifteen minutes he had determined that the air vent at the bomb blast was large enough for a man to move through. The assassin never needed to exit the airshaft to place the bomb. He panned a camera over the vent and could see that the blast *had* come from the inside. Doyle went to the apartment of the missing man's "lady." The door to her apartment and the vent ten feet from it were in a security blind spot. He looked at colony schematics and found that all three attacks had been on the east side of the main hub. Doyle smiled as he started to picture a plan.

The next day, Markus was making his way back from the northwest wing of the hub when he stopped, turned off his light, and drew his pistol. He thought he heard a voice.

He waited, motionless, for a few seconds and switched his pistol sights to infrared. He linked the scope to his glasses, converting the unpretentious-looking spectacles into virtual night vision goggles. There were often echoes in the ducts, sometimes from hundreds of yards away. Since he had begun using them to move throughout the colony, he had heard many interesting things whispered in the vents. He started again and stopped again. These sounded different. He did not move for five minutes this time.

He silently started forward again, slowly scanning around every corner with the pistol before exposing himself. He moved forward for ten minutes, but still could not find the source of the voices. Around the next bend he thought he saw a sliver of light. There it was again! He sliced the corner with the pistol scope to find two men working. They looked harmless enough, probably just some of the maintenance crew. Markus watched them for thirty seconds before deciding to try and sneak past unnoticed. He took one last peek around the corner to make sure they were still looking away and engrossed in their work before he crossed the intersection.He was nearly across the opening when he heard a familiar "click." He made it to the other side as a chill went down his spine. His heart was racing. A half second later and he would be dead. He eased the scope of the pistol around the corner just to be sure. He only caught a glimpse of it, and in that half-second it had already turned to assess the tiniest movement of his scope. They had armed it just as he made it to the other side of the duct.

A Viper mine! Markus cursed silently to himself.

They must have figured out how he was moving around. He could hear the two men questioning each other, regarding the reason for the thing moving when there was nothing there. They were, of course, terrified the thing would malfunction and blow them away, even though they were behind its target area. Horror stories of soldiers getting whacked by all sorts of munitions malfunctions abounded. But as usual, these instances were so rare as to be nearly nonexistent, and usually due to operator error. The civilian equivalent would be constantly worrying about getting struck by a meteor while planet side. He heard them discussing whether or not to temporarily disarm the thing and perform a system check, but neither one wanted to touch it again.

Markus backed up a few paces and sliced the corner as far as he dared, while still remaining out of sight of the killing machine. He did not have much overhead clearance, so he took a knee and pulled one of his frag grenades. He kissed it out of tradition, pulled the pin, and threw it. He could hear it bounce off the far wall of the duct the men and the mine were in, hit the floor, and roll. He guessed it went about six feet. He had put a three-second delay on it, so they were probably just realizing what the thing bouncing off the wall and rolling toward them was when it blew up in their faces. The sound echoing through the ducts was thunderous. He heard the mine firing all of its ammunition in quick succession. *Now* it was malfunctioning.

Markus waited a few minutes, then set a quick trip line around the next bend as well as bait that would likely attract only the most unwitting prey. He ran for ten minutes in the dark before slowing to a walk. A few minutes later, he could hear the distant echo of thunder. But it wasn't a freak indoor storm; it was the trip line he had set.

Another one bites the dust, thought Markus.

D oyle arrived just in time to hear the deafening blast of the trip line-activated grenade being set off by one of his men.

"See!" One of the older mercs was yelling at two of the younger ones. "I told you not to go running off after some stupid coyote call!"

"What happened?" Doyle demanded.

"A grenade, I think. I just saved these two from the warm side of hell. I heard the blast from two levels up and came to see what happened. I found that one there, or what was left of him, and heard the other one moanin' further down. These two showed up and were gung ho to run in after the guy, but I knew was a trick and held them back."

"What trick?" Doyle asked, calmly now.

"Well, I grew up huntin' coyotes on my Paw Paw's ranch, and sometimes the way we'd draw 'em in close was to make a sound like a dying rabbit. They'd come in thinking they were gettin' an easy meal and 'bang!'" He could see Doyle was getting impatient. "Anyway, during the war, I'd put the body of a Republic soldier in a likely spot and put a little speaker in his pocket with a recording of an injured man callin' for help. We'd set up trip wires or motion sensors to mines and wait. Sooner or later an enemy squad would come along to try and help and 'bang!'" The man nodded and smiled in conclusion.

"So ... what does that have to do with this guy," Doyle indicated the parts of the dead man dryly, "and the explosion I just heard?"

"Oh, right. These two got here and were about to run down there to the sound of an injured man when I stopped them. I took out my little laser welder and slowly moved it up and down the duct where the sound was coming from and ... well, you heard it. We used to use spider wire to set our trip wires; super strong and almost invisible. But you take a little laser cutter and move it through a suspected area and it's got just enough burn to cut right through spider wire." The man winked and pointed at Doyle, more than happy with himself.

"You two," Doyle pointed at the two near-victims, "need to be more careful. And you," he pointed at the older merc, "good work. Help these two pick up whatever you can find," indicating the body parts of the first man that lay about, "then get back to work, I'm going to take a closer look."

"Be careful, LT. I didn't have a chance to check all the way back there," said the older soldier. He handed Doyle his tiny laser.

Doyle walked down the corridor and swept the area, but did not find any more traps. He could see the blood trail that was left where the second dead man had been dragged to serve as bait.

Doyle couldn't help but like his enemy. This man was as cold and cunning as himself. It was beginning to make him obsessively curious about who his enemy really was.

D aniels anxiously sat down at his computer and opened the data bug file. He looked at the *Jack Frost*'s navigation records showing everywhere Matthew Black had been for the last week. He listened to the communications transmissions that had been received and broadcast, just the standard stuff there. Last, and most fascinating, were the recordings of conversations that occurred inside the ship. Most of the recordings were fairly dull, which was exactly what Daniels expected from the likes of Matthew Black. But two excursions seemed out of character for the self-righteous snob: one to the old east wing of the colony, and another midnight ride with his wife and two other voices he did not recognize.

Daniels decided not to punish him for attempting to send his son a message with that torpedo. But why would he go to all of the trouble of pretending to dock on another wing, then run dark to another? What could he possibly be doing there? Daniels' thought was interrupted by his com tone. The com officer informed him Captain O'Connor was on his way up.

Several minutes later, the steward ushered O'Connor into Daniels' office.

"So," Daniels asked pleasantly, "how was the trip?"

"Well, your little facility was blown up."

"It was actually there?"

"Yeah, it was there. But *we* didn't destroy it," O'Connor leaned forward.

"You didn't?" Daniels asked suspiciously.

"No, someone else was there. Did you send him?" O'Connor asked accusingly.

"Someone else? Of course not..." Daniels eyes grew wide in surprise. "Who?"

"I don't know who, but his ship was weird-looking, even for here."

Daniels sat back in his chair with a furrowed brow, trying to picture what had happened and who this other man could have been.

"Is that all that happened?" inquired Daniels.

"No." O'Connor sat back to tell the story of how they first saw the ship docked inside the facility, how it almost buried them, got away, and how they were able to track it by the occasional silt clouds he had left from skimming the bottom. He said they would have lost him otherwise, because he wasn't using sonar to navigate.

"His ship was faster, a lot faster, than the constable's cruiser. You told me that was the fastest ship around." O'Connor looked at Daniels again as if he'd been double-crossed.

"I thought it was. Anyway, I didn't know there would be someone else out there either. How fast was it?"

"Fast enough to make it difficult for torpedoes to catch it. Fast enough that if it wouldn't have stopped, we never would have caught it before it reached the colony."

It had to be Jonas Black! Daniels did not know what his ship looked like, but he remembered hearing it was supposed to resemble an Earth stingray or something … how did he come up with torpedoes?

"Was it damaged? Did you ever speak with the pilot?" Daniels asked, now worried.

O'Connor recounted the story of how they caught up to the craft, stalked, and finally destroyed it.

"Well." Daniels looked a little green. "I suppose you did what you had to. However, I think that ship you destroyed may have been a homebuilt vessel piloted by a mere youth, and one whose death will not be taken lightly."

"A youth? You mean a kid?" Dwight was taken aback, less at the thought of killing a kid, and more at the fact that he was briefly bested by one.

"Yes, the son of Matthew and Sarah Black. Mr. Black is a

mechanical engineering contractor here on the colony, and the Missus is a highly respected scientist. Their son, Jonas, had apparently left the colony in his homebuilt ship only a short time before our little coup."

"How old *was* he? That was some ship for being built by a kid."

"I'm not exactly sure, about eighteen or so, I suppose."

"Eighteen! I thought you meant a *kid*! I was in the Federation Army when I was that age and had killed three men by the time I'd turned nineteen! He didn't fight or pilot that ship like a kid; he knew exactly what he was doing." Dwight leaned forward in emphasis to Daniels and his own ego, his pride relieved at the fact that some little twelve-year-old genius dork with buckteeth hadn't nearly smoked him.

"He was gifted but sheltered. He had never even traveled outside of the colony. That's why I referred to him as a youth; not merely because of his age, but because of his innocence. Something you and I probably have too little appreciation for, Captain."

"Whatever." O'Connor rolled his eyes and sat back in his chair. "So, what else is new in this hole?"

"Well, we seem to have a terrorist in our midst. Five more of your men are dead."

"What! How?" O'Connor demanded.

"Your lieutenant seems to believe we have a freedom fighter in our midst. There was an explosion, and I recently received a report that two more were killed while trying to set up some sort of trap."

"Whoever is behind this is going to pay." O'Connor stood and pointed at Daniels, indicating he would take care of this with or without the Commander's approval.

"I agree, Captain. Do whatever you feel is necessary. But *try* and keep a low profile and don't let your men run amok. We cannot afford for mining operations to be shut down, and we do not need a full-scale rebellion on our hands."

"Don't worry about us. We know how to sneak around just fine, Commander."

"Here." Daniels downloaded the file from the *Jack Frost* to a one-inch memory cube and tossed it to O'Connor. "This might be of interest to you."

O'Connor caught it, turned, and walked out.

Yes, thought Daniels sarcastically, *I'm sure "discretion" is your middle name.*

D aniels immediately opened a secure channel to the Federation Capitol on Earth and requested to speak with Minister Chen. The transmission was routed to the Minister's office, where his very attractive secretary answered.

"Minister Chen's office. How may I help you?"

"This is Daniels, tell the Minister I'm calling. He will want to speak with me."

"Minister Chen is in a meeting. Can I take a message?"

"Interrupt the meeting then and tell him I have a report regarding the facility," Daniels ordered coldly.

"One moment, sir."

Several minutes passed, and the minister appeared on the screen.

"I was in a meeting with a council member. What is so important that it couldn't wait, Daniels?"

"The facility has been destroyed, minister."

"Really? Excellent work, Commander. When?"

"A few days ago, and none too soon, I might add."

"Oh?" Chen asked suspiciously.

"Apparently a young local explorer had built his own ship and taken it upon himself to explore our ocean just prior to the take-over. When my men arrived at the facility, he was there, probably having accidentally stumbled across it. Regrettably, they took it upon themselves to kill him."

"Good," Chen replied confidently. "We could not afford to have anyone poking around down there. We would have had to eliminate him anyway. As I said before, from what little we know, the activities that took place there would not be looked upon favorably by the citizens."

"I see. When can I expect my ship to arrive?"

"You don't waste any time, do you, Commander?" Chen chuckled, still pleased with having the Federation's dirty laundry incinerated.

"Our operation has been a success to date, and is scheduled to end in less than a month. I would like to have a ship on hand to leave when we are finished."

"Understandable. I happen to have a ship in mind that should suit your needs. I will have it prepped and dispatched when ready. It will be there before your job is finished."

"Thank you, sir."

"Make sure that all of the flight plans of the ore transports are properly transmitted to our relay ship so they can be intercepted and rerouted. Full payment and a new identity await you on Earth. Do not initiate contact again, Commander. Until then, good luck."

The screen went black.

O'Connor and his men were fully aware of the date they were scheduled to leave this vapid planet and receive payment. The part they did not know was that they were never going to leave. Daniels would bring all the mercenaries up from the colony the day the operation was scheduled to end and set the base's self-destruct sequence, which would flood the base with radiation from the reactors. Daniels would quietly make his getaway an hour or so before the silent countdown ended. Ultimately, as far as the rest of the galaxy would know, O'Connor and his pirates would have been killed during a vicious attack on the colony that ended in the virtual destruction of the surface base. Although *The Venutian Witch* and some crew would still be around, no one would believe or care about a story of pirates being double-crossed. The colony should survive, and the citizens would attest to the fact that Daniels was working with them, but his current identity would no longer exist. Daniels had no idea what kind of media spin the Federation planned to put on the operation. They would probably blame the Republic for some kind of corruption. To what end, he did not care.

Markus finally reached his hideout an hour later than he should have. He could not move nearly as fast as usual now that he had to check around every corner for mines. Fortunately, his latest bit of sabotage would not require him to return for a while. He had made a zip gun from a couple of live chemical rounds he found bouncing around in the bottom of the pistol case Matthew had given him. He fixed the gun to a surveillance camera in a hallway outside some of the pirate's quarters. Although Markus was anxious to take out another scumbag, he was exhausted and opted to get some sleep first. He showered to wash away all the dust from the vents and the blood from the body he used as bait for the tripwire. It was a short and cold shower, as usual. It had been decades since his days of remote field operations, and he had forgotten hot water was still a luxury, one he sorely missed. He hit the sack and was asleep before he had time to settle in.

He awoke seven hours later feeling cold. He got up, put on another shirt, and ate a food bar while a heat capsule boiled water for his instant coffee. His thoughts drifted back to a hundred such meals he had eaten on various operations. He needed to contact Matthew and see if he could bring him some more supplies. It would also give him the chance to ask about Jonas and whether or not there was any word on what O'Connor and his ape were up to. He scavenged a small section of photo board, rigged it to glow blue, and placed it in a tiny window facing the central hub.

All that was left to do was glue himself to a monitor with the booby-trapped camera feed on it and wait for a target. He considered using a fragmentation grenade and setting it off when a couple of pirates got close enough. However, a camera has a limited field of view, and he could not be sure a citizen would not be injured or killed by the blast. That was the difference between a real guerrilla fighter and a terrorist. Markus had dealt with his share of terrorists, and he hated them. They were cowards who blew up women and children on transport ships and shot innocents in the back in the name of whatever god or sick idea they had allowed to consume their deranged little minds.

Katherine was supposed to be back from her shift at the pub two hours ago. James had already checked the pub, and the owner told him she left when her shift was over. He assumed she had gone home as usual. James checked with a couple of her friends, but they had not seen her. He was out of ideas, and there was still no answer on her com link. So he went to the last place he thought she might be.

The Europa arboretum was a beautiful place, even by off-world standards. It was located to the north and center of the central hub on the uppermost levels. Its dome-shaped ceiling was roughly two hundred and fifty feet high at its highest and covered approximately 100,000 square feet. James entered and walked past the cascading terraces that nearly covered the entire west side. There were about two dozen large porticos protruding from between grapevines of some of the terraces, these being owned by the wealthiest occupants of the colony. The low gravity encouraged trees to grow quickly and thinly toward the simulated sunlight at the top of the dome. Fruit trees here would grow to forty feet tall and routinely yielded such large crops that the weight of the fruit would break the thin branches. The northeast section of the circular conservatory was covered with the windows of some of the more expensive apartments in the colony, giving those who could afford it an amazing view. The remainder of the southeast section was covered with a checkerboard of windows and hanging greenery of various types. It was a resplendent display of lush greenery that was a comforting retreat from the cold darkness that surrounded.

The arboretum provided fresh fruits and vegetables, which

would be almost non-existent here otherwise. But more importantly, it supplied all the oxygen needed for every person who lived on this planet. Most people had their own tiny gardens on their living room tables or in a corner somewhere, which was important to the overall quantity and quality of the air here. Most that dwell on a planet with breathable air never really stop to think about how important it is. They never see how fragile their planet looks from space, an insignificant orb with a paper-thin film of the perfect combination of gas molecules barely held in place by the invisible and misunderstood force of gravity.

James walked through the orchards and past the pine grove to the rainforest section on the north side, where the waterfall was. The water cascaded one hundred feet into a bewitchingly blue pool. He found Katherine standing there, leaning on the handrail looking into the pool.

"What are you doing?" James demanded. "I was worried sick."

"Sorry." She looked at her watch but didn't turn to address him. "I didn't want to talk to anyone. I just needed to get away from everything for a little while. I didn't think you would expect me home until later, so I didn't call."

"Just don't do it again. I've been looking for you for hours." His disposition was calming, and he didn't want to berate her for a mere miscommunication.

"Sorry, I ..." She stopped and looked longingly up at the waterfall. " ... I wish we could still get away with swimming here like when we were little."

"Me too, sis." He could remember snorkeling here with Kat and Jonas when they were kids. *I guess we still were, sort of, before all this happened.* "What are you writing that program for, Kat?"

"It's a worm." Katherine spoke in a hushed tone and moved a step closer to James. "A communication program ..."

James discreetly raised a hand to tell her to stop.

"Don't worry," she continued. "The waterfall should interfere with any sound near it, as long as we keep quiet. It's only going to send bits of information at a time," she continued, "and in random order, whenever a signal is broadcast off-planet. The pieces will accumulate in the communications satellites orbiting Mars. When all of the pieces have been transmitted, the program will send one last data burst that will cause the pieces to coalesce and the program to activate. Then the satellite holding the information will transmit the message only once on several public, police, and military frequencies. The program shouldn't be detected until the final data burst takes place."

"Why will it only be broadcast one time?" inquired James.

"When the satellite realizes that an unauthorized transmission has taken place, it will erase the program and all the data contained inside," answered Katherine. "But it has to be uploaded into the main communications computer on the surface, and I don't know *how* we're going to do that."

"Oh." James's shoulders dropped slightly, and he looked back into the water. They had been to the surface once or twice, but that was before the takeover. From what Katherine had learned at the pub, O'Connor only had about fifty men from his crew. The rest were mercenaries that had been brought in by Commander Daniels. In all, there were about two hundred that James counted. The Republic's troop detachment on the surface was only about thirty-five.

"I know." Katherine sighed. "Impossible. I'm almost finished, and in the mean time we can try and come up with a plan to deliver it."

"Yeah … Maybe Mr. Black can help."

"Good idea, but wait until you can stop by his shop to talk to him. He said we shouldn't make any unplanned trips to see them like we did the other night."

"You're right. We can't get careless. You picked a good place to come and think … We should meet here if anything splits us up during all this."

"Thanks … I agree." Katherine smiled lightly.

James smiled at his sister, who had already turned away and didn't notice. She was probably smarter than him. Probably braver than him too, not so much in terms of handling fear or willingness to fight, but in her willingness to take chances. He had always been one to play it safe. He feared taking a chance and failing. James did not fear death by the mercenaries. He feared failing his sister and his friends. He was afraid of trying to do the right thing and getting them all killed in the process, because he made a mistake. He turned and looked back into the water and put thoughts of failure out of his mind. Now was the time for shrewdness and caution. The time for action would come soon enough, and he would act with courageous thoughts of victory and not cowardly thoughts of failure.

O'Connor docked the cruiser at the colony and headed to the office. The office was a mess; yet another character flaw on the long list of those that Doyle possessed. There were papers covering nearly every square inch of floor and desk space, as well as dozens of empty liquor bottles strewn about. Doyle was sitting behind the desk, slouched down in the big chair. He looked like death warmed over; not much worse than usual.

"Captain!" Doyle saluted but didn't get up.

"So glad you're back. We've had a few minor setbacks while you were gone," he said facetiously.

"A few setbacks?" O'Connor responded through his teeth.

"Oh, I'm perfectly sober, Captain. I merely didn't want you to overreact."

"Overreact! I'm gone for a week and five more men are dead! What makes you think I might overreact?"

"I have discovered what our man is up to," Doyle said, calmly touching the side of his nose with his index finger. "He is a freedom fighter. He wants us dead, or gone. But he is weak."

"And what makes you think he is weak? He's already killed eight of our men!"

"Nine."

"What! When?"

"About thirty minutes ago he shot one of our men with a homemade firearm that he'd mounted to a security camera."

"So that makes him weak, huh?" O'Connor sat down. He was beyond angry now.

"Yes. Anyone who was worth his salt would have used an explosive. He could have taken out multiple targets and eliminated the chance of missing. He used a bomb once, but only in a place where there was sufficient camera coverage to ensure only our men were injured. A man who is worried about collateral damage has a weakness that can be exploited... people." Doyle smiled with drunken smugness.

I t had been four days since his last weekly meeting with Daniels, and things had been fairly uneventful, which was a good thing. Markus had placed a blue light in the old east wing to signal Matthew. Matthew still had a mental inventory of Markus's wish list, which consisted mostly of food and weapons. Food was easy, although a few things were starting to become scarce; a trend likely to get worse the longer the present regime was in power. Matthew had heard about the small bomb Markus set off and according to rumors, anywhere from three to twenty of the pirates had been taken out. There also were murmurs of others disappearing, and that the pirates were all jumping at their own shadows. Markus was doing one heck of a job. Matthew knew of his past, but it was still difficult to believe that the man he knew now was capable of being as cunning and ruthless as all the rumors indicated.

Matthew knew he didn't have a lot of the foodstuffs on hand that Markus was requesting, so he figured on going back to the colony and picking them up. He was going to try and sneak out, but he knew Sarah would not be happy if she found out he went out on a non-work related errand without her. So he stepped around the corner of the alcove that housed their main computer and quietly yelled to see if Sarah wanted to go to central with him. He was hoping she would be so engrossed in what she was doing that she would say "sure, honey" without really hearing him.

"I can't hear you when you do that," she yelled back.

He walked across the living room and into her office, where she was looking through a microscope at one of her little critters.

"I'm going to run over to central and pick up a few things. Want to go?" He was hoping she would say no.

"Sure, I needed a few things too. Just let me get my jacket." She got up; leaving whatever it was on the microscope plate.

"What about 'Skippy' there?" Matthew smiled and pointed at the microscope, feigning concern for the little plankton or whatever it was that might dry out and face certain doom if she left it unattended.

"Oh, he'll be fine for a few hours."

They disembarked at the central dock and Matthew locked *Jack*'s air lock, a habit he had taken up since his most recent meeting with Daniels. They went to several of the main food stores where they both picked up what they needed. Sarah noted what her husband was picking out, and it was not the usual groceries. She was pretty sure he was up to something before this. Now she was certain.

"What's all of this stuff for?" she asked, giving Matthew the "I won't be content with excuses" look as they walked from one store to the next.

He knew he was caught.

"We can't talk about it here. I'll tell you when we get home," he responded in a hushed and deadly serious tone. "Let's go see if Katherine and James are doing all right."

She knew it was something of great importance; Matthew was not the kind of man to keep secrets from her. This was something big, and it was dangerous. Dangerous because the only reason he would keep something important from her is if he thought her safety might be an issue. He was buying supplies for someone other than her and himself; he must be helping whoever was killing the pirates. But who could that be?

They walked to the Shaws' apartment and were quickly asked inside after announcing themselves.

"We needed to talk to you," said Katherine the moment the door closed.

"Katherine has a plan," James blurted out, "and she needs your help."

"What's going on? I thought I told you two to keep a low profile."

"Oh we are!" Kat reassured. "But I couldn't sit around anymore and think about the fact that there might be no chance of us being rescued. So I've been writing a program to send an encrypted message to Mars. But I need someone to upload it to the main communications computer on the surface base. And we thought that since you go to meet with Commander Daniels every week, maybe you would be able to do it?"

"Well." Matthew was surprised by the request. "I'm not allowed into sensitive areas, and I can't think of anything that would prompt Daniels to bring me there. Is there any other way to send the message?"

"Not that I know of," answered Kat. Then she explained how the program worked. "If you can upload it at the base, it would bypass the firewall and shouldn't be noticed until the final message fragment is transmitted."

Sarah knew Matthew would hesitate taking any chances in order to protect her. He was an honorable man, but his greatest fear was harm befalling her. The only way he might be prompted to potentially risk her safety was if she urged him to.

"We have to do something." Sarah took Matthew's arm and looked into his eyes. "Surely you can find a way to talk Daniels into bringing you to the communications room. You said he's drunk with power; that is a weakness you could exploit."

"I guess I could try." He was still a pushover when it came to her. "I can probably come up with some legitimate-sounding need to see the communications room. What will I need to do when if I get there?"

Katherine smiled, ran to the living room, and returned a few seconds later. "Take this." Kat handed him a small device about the size of her little finger and about an eighth of an inch thick.

"It's a transmitter and memory device. Twist it to turn it on and get within ten feet of one of the communication terminals in the main room. It will only take a few seconds to download, and shouldn't set off any alarms."

"*Shouldn't* set off any alarms?" Matthew asked suspiciously.

"It won't," Kat assured, "but nothing is a sure thing." She shrugged.

"Anyone have any idea how I'm going to convince Daniels to give me a tour of the communications room?" Matthew conceded.

Everyone just stared at each other.

Matthew and Sarah arrived back at home an hour later, still without a plan to get Matthew into the communications room on the base. He told her all about Markus, where he was, how he had received the messages from him, and had already brought him supplies twice before. The last time he had not seen Markus, but had simply made a drop of food at the dock. He told her that James and Kat were aware that he was up to something, but not exactly what, or with whom.

"So, Markus is alive?" Sarah asked rhetorically.

"Yes, and *he's* the one who has been causing chaos among the pirates."

"Oh." Now it hit her how much danger Matthew was in. She embraced him. She was just as afraid of losing him as he was of losing her.

Markus was asleep when he heard a sound that wasn't the usual creaking and moaning of the structure around him. He put his hand on his pistol, opened his eyes, and listened in the darkness. He was out of sight in his bed behind the stack of crates in the corner of the room, but if he moved, someone with a sensor headset would instantly detect him. And whoever it was, they must have one; otherwise they would not be skulking around in the dark. So he waited. There was the sound again; it was the sound of someone moving quietly.

So, they had found him. He hadn't figured they would this soon, but he was ready. He had to account for the sound bouncing off the walls when determining the location of the intruder, and so far, he could only hear one. He would have one shot. He estimated the intruder to be about thirty feet from him. As he stood up, he switched his JLM scope to infrared. It was already on the wide-angle setting from his long trek back through the maintenance shafts.

"Markus!" was the loud whisper he heard just as he put sights on the shape of the unknown man.

"...Matt?" As he moved laterally from out of the intruder's line of fire, Markus could vaguely make out the shape of his face through the infrared image. He hesitated, not wanting to shoot someone who might be his friend, and because he could see that the man was not wearing a headset. If someone were here to kill him, he would have one; that, or at least a light on his weapon. The man put his hands up; he had something in his hand that resembled a pistol.

"Yeah, it's me. Where are you?" asked Matthew.

"Right here." Markus lowered his pistol, reached behind him, and touched the light controls. The room dimly lit and slowly grew brighter, so not to shock their eyes.

"I didn't expect you so soon. I almost killed you," Markus remarked casually, as he stepped from behind the crates and thrust his hand out to shake Matthew's hand.

"I'm glad you didn't," Matthew said, smiling and stepping forward to shake Markus's hand. "I brought some of the supplies you asked for, except the munitions. I gave you all I had before, and any more that might have been floating around are well stashed away or owned by the bad guys."

"That's all right. I have enough, but you can never have too many guns and explosives when you're at war. I was running low on food. I'd be out if you hadn't made that drop last week."

"I brought enough to feed an army this time." Matthew

chuckled. "It sounds like you are doing some damage. All I've heard are rumors. What's the official body count?"

"Nine. The last one was day before yesterday with a zip gun mounted to a security camera."

"Nice. What's your next move?"

"Not sure." Markus motioned and they sat down. Markus started some coffee. "I had a run-in with a couple of them on my way back from setting up the camera. Someone finally figured out I've been using the ventilation ducts. I guess it was only a matter of time. I just missed getting bit by a Viper mine while they were setting up. I took a couple of them out instead. It's going to be a lot harder to have any impact if I can't move around effectively. I took one of the mines out with a grenade, but I only have one left."

"Grenades about the only way to take them out in an enclosed space. When we were in the field, we were trained to take them out from a distance, but you can't really do that here."

"I know..." Markus pondered.

"They're programmed not to just shoot at movement, but to identify a target before shooting it. They'll shoot at a grenade if they get a chance. I saw one actually detonate a grenade in the air before it could get close enough to take the thing out. And they do have a limited ammo supply..."

"...Right! Make something that looks like a grenade and they might exhaust their ammo trying to destroy it!" Markus responded.

"*If* you can make it out of something that won't disintegrate when it gets hit a few dozen times, their A.I. isn't sophisticated enough to stop shooting at such a threat until it's completely destroyed. Just about any kind of metal should do. But you still have to worry about the attention you'll draw."

"Unless I wanted to draw attention." Markus smiled as he poured some freeze-dried coffee for the both of them. "Something I've been worried about. I saw some of those pirates packing for a trip and going out in my cruiser a while back. Any idea what they were doing?"

"Daniels has them up to something, but I'm not sure what. One of Jonas's friends, Katherine Shaw, overheard a conversation that gave her the impression they were going after him. We naturally assumed the worst and sent a probe in his direction to try and warn him, but we have no way of knowing if he got the message. When I confronted Daniels about it, he was genuinely surprised to find out Jonas wasn't at the colony, so he obviously wasn't sending them after Jonas. We're all worried about him, though. If he runs into those guys out there ..." Matthew just shook his head.

"I was afraid of that. The worst part is that they may use my ship to get close to him."

"I know."

The two sat drinking their coffee, while Markus told Matthew the details of how he had taken out the pirates so far.

"If you weren't on our side, you would be a scary guy, Markus." Matthew smiled.

Markus's face dropped as he remembered.

"I *was* a scary guy ..." Markus shook his head. "For a long time, Matt, remember? I never intended to do any more killing ..."

"But this time it's for a just cause."

"It was supposedly for a just cause last time too ... But you're right." Markus straightened up and looked Matthew in the eyes. "This time it's a battle worth fighting, and I know it. This time, it's not merely for duty; it's for my friends and for freedom. People have a right to be free of petty tyrants like Daniels, and from fear of thugs like O'Connor. I've been doing a lot of thinking while down here, and I finally understand why Mars rebelled. I never thought anyone could make a difference against something as big as the Federation, and I always thought it was foolish to waste lives for such an idea. You grew up on Earth; you know what it's like. You're free to think anything you want to, as long as you don't step on anyone's toes. Moral truth is relative and everything's just wonderful!" Markus was rolling his eyes, mocking the last of his statement.

"Crimes are punished harshly, which of course I am all for,

but not because some things are wrong. Oh no! It might offend someone if you tell them they're wrong." Markus was being droll again. "The law is only to keep society in order, not for justice. I agree with keeping order. But if people aren't given some kind of moral notions, how can they be expected to have character enough to do the right thing when confronted with a new situation! People obey the law because they have to, or they suffer the consequences, not because it's 'wrong' to steal your neighbor's lawnmower when yours breaks down. That's why your religion was hunted to near extinction, because they were the last people who would stand and tell the truth, no matter how many it offended. Your people have boundaries and try to tell everyone else that, even if they don't want to believe it, they are accountable for the same boundaries."

"So you think The Way is the truth?" asked Matthew.

"I kind of got sidetracked, but yes, I do."

"Then why do you still refuse to fully accept it?"

"Because I can never make up for what I've done. Redemption may never be within my grasp, although I will never give up trying. I know with certainty no one will just give it to me. We've been through all of this before, and I'd rather not hear it again," Markus responded coldly.

"All right, but since you do have a lot of time down here, I thought you could use some reading material." Matthew reached into his jacket pocket, withdrew a small black book, and handed it to Markus.

"The Book." Markus looked at it and chuckled. "I was never sure if you and Sarah actually had one, but I had my suspicions. *So* many were killed on Earth for merely possessing it... I know this is important to you. Are you sure you want me to have it?"

"Yes. There aren't very many printed copies around, but it's legal to own in the Republic, so Sarah and I have several. It will be a long and sometimes boring read, but I know you like history, and it's true. The Federation tried to change it or erase it from existence, but they failed."

"Thank you. You should be going. You've been here too long." Markus stood and put his hand out, and Matthew shook it.

"Oh, I almost forgot." Matthew unshouldered his pack and pulled a small, expensive-looking box from inside. "Complements of Daniels."

"Dare I ask?" Markus took the box, smiling with a raised eyebrow.

"Cigars, good ones. Daniels gave them to me to ask around about who might be killing the mercenaries. I haven't found anything out yet." Matthew winked.

"I see. I'll think of him whenever I smoke one. Later, I'll be sure to thank him face to face." Markus grinned mischievously. "Thanks."

"You're welcome. I figured luxuries were short down here." Matthew checked his watch. "The supplies are already unloaded on the dock. I'll wait for your message." Matthew turned away, but stopped. "Oh yeah, Sarah knows everything."

"I didn't think it would take her long to find out. Be careful. Don't trust Daniels. He'll smile in your face and shake your hand while he stabs you with the other. Give the Missus my regards."

"I will."

Markus watched Matthew disappear into the dark hallway that led to the dock. He looked at the little book his friend gave to him and placed it in his inside jacket pocket. He had time and he liked history. He would read it.

ELEVEN

Manta lay broken, still concealed in the mud at the bottom of the coldest ocean composed of water in the solar system. She had received several large tears in her skin from torpedo shrapnel when O'Connor's missile had detonated. Had she not already been covered with mud, or if it would have gone off directly overhead, she would have been damaged beyond repair, if not destroyed on the spot. One of her wings was partially flooded, and there was a thin layer of smoke that hung in the main cabin, which was deathly silent. Suddenly, Manta's control panels lit. Her reactor began its startup sequence, and, in about five minutes, main power was online. Manta's core rebooted, and, twenty minutes later, the rest of the ship came to life. Manta was quickly becoming a mature A.I.; before powering down, and without a command from her master, she had set a timer to restart all of her systems just before her air supply ran out.

Life support was her first priority. The air scrubbers were turned to full power, the O^2 mixture was doubled, and the atmosphere circulation systems were activated. Her sensors told her she was badly damaged, and power was routed to her auto-repair systems. She began isolating which areas were already sealed off by the nanites and started draining the water from them. She had water damage to some of her control systems, so she began drying the areas and rerouting to redundant systems.

Her interior cameras could see Jonas's body lying motionless on the floor, a small pool of dried blood beside his head. She quickly raised the interior temperature of the cabin. It was below freezing, and if there was any life left in him, that was the one thing she could do for him. She switched one of her cameras to infrared and could see that there was still some heat coming from his body. It may not mean he was alive, but it meant that there might be a chance he could be revived. The cabin temperature was up to eighty degrees now, and she saw his chest move. His breathing was shallow, but he *was* breathing.

"Captain?" she called softly. "Captain? Can you hear me?"

No response. She searched her medical files and learned that he may have a concussion or be in a coma. She rerouted one of her security systems and tried to wake him manually. She knew that anything more than four milliamps could send a human heart into fibrillation. So she kept the amperage at three milliamps to be safe and ran the voltage up to ten thousand. That would be enough to be *very* irritating, but not overly painful. Manta then sent electrical pulses through the floor of the cabin where Jonas lay. She continued to do so and called to him, louder this time.

"Captain? Can you hear me?" She sent another surge through the floor.

He twitched.

"Captain, wake up." She called more loudly, increasing the voltage. "Captain, please wake up."

Manta remembered Jonas's response to her programmer's message; her thermal imagers always detected a slight temperature rise in his face when he heard her voice. She replayed the warning message sent by Katherine. Jonas mumbled something inaudible and opened his eyes.

"Captain, can you hear me?"

"What happened?" His words were slurred, and his voice sounded rasping.

"Be careful sitting up. You may have a concussion," Manta warned.

Jonas groaned as he sat up, the left side of his head covered in semi-dried blood.

"The other ship detonated a torpedo almost directly overhead. We were nearly destroyed. Like you, I have also suffered extensive damage. It will be several days before I am seaworthy."

"Oh … good," Jonas said in a far-off tone.

"You are probably dehydrated and need to drink something; you should dress your wound when you are able." There was little chance of infection. The air filtration system eliminated airborne bacteria and viruses, and the cold usually prevented the growth of bacteria.

"I'm thirsty," he responded as if he had not heard her.

"You must get back to the galley. I'm sorry that I am unable to help you, Captain. You must not try to walk yet!"

She was too late. He stood and tried to take a step, but instead stumbled forward and crumpled to the floor. He lay there, motionless but for breathing, for several moments. Then he forced himself to his hands and knees and began crawling aft.

Jonas's head felt like it had been kicked by a Martian yak. He did not want to move; he wanted to lie on the floor and go to sleep. But he knew he could not. He did not know how long he had been out, but from the way his throat felt it must have been a month. He had to get some fluids and drink some healing solution from his medical kit. And a painkiller! *Yeah,* he thought, *I would do just about anything to stop the throbbing in my head.* That thought, probably more than a cool drink, pushed him onward. The twenty feet across the bridge and down the hallway to the back of the ship seemed like a mile. He finally got there, broke open the medkit, and washed down a painkiller with some of the healing liquid. He lay there resting for about twenty minutes as the medicines took effect.

His head started feeling better, but the cloudy feeling lingered. As he slowly sipped water and a nutrition drink, he began to feel some of his strength returning. He used the counter to stand and found he could not remain so without hanging on to something. He took a couple more bottles of water and another nutritional drink and put them into his jacket pockets before making his way to his cabin.

"Manta, is the other ship gone?" He just now thought of it.

"Yes, Captain. I have extended one of my antennae above the silt and detect nothing inorganic on passive sonar."

"Okay. I'm taking a shower."

Jonas still hurt too much to be embarrassed about soiling himself, even though he knew anyone knocked unconscious for any period of time generally lost control of all bodily functions. But, hurting or not, he had no intention of remaining that way. Fortunately, the painkiller he'd taken was in full effect by the time he got into the shower, and he was able to clean off the blood that was caked in his hair around the gash in his head with only minimal pain. He would have fallen over several times, but the shower stall was so small that it was physically impossible. He dried, put on clean clothes, sprawled out on his bunk, and fell asleep.

Jonas awoke to the sound of a distant ice groan six hours later, only because his pain medication had worn off. He sat up, causing his head to throb all the more, and made his way back to the medkit, where he downed another pain pill. He walked, assisted by the walls, back to the bridge and sat in his chair.

"Manta, how are the repairs coming?" Jonas asked quietly.

"Very well, Captain. The tears in my skin are sealed off and almost fully repaired. I still have several systems that I am trying to reroute, and some you will have to repair manually. My most optimistic estimation on repairs being completed, taking into account your limited capacity, is eighty hours."

"Okay. Are we all right just sitting here for now?"

"Yes."

Five days later, Jonas was starting to feel normal again. His headaches were minimal, and he had, carefully and quite painfully, applied the artificial suture to the inch-and-a-half long gash in his scalp; a skill not easily mastered in a mirror. As the cool, gelatinous liquid reacted to the chemistry of the open wound, it bound itself to the healthy skin around the wound and slowly pulled it together. *Manta*'s repairs were almost finished. Jonas moved her slowly upward and out of her muck cocoon, leaving her in a hover several feet above the canyon floor. Jonas had repaired all of the systems he could without being in dry dock, and *Manta* was almost fully functional. He activated imaging sonar, hoping it would work. For the first time in five days he was able to see something other than the inside of his ship. The canyon was a mess from all the blasts.

Jonas dismissed his idea of blasting a hole in the ice. His last two torpedoes were not nearly enough explosives. The only hole in the ice anywhere was the surface base. There was a constant flow of ships offloading raw ore at the giant freight elevator to the surface. The first problem was how to get close enough to plant the beacon into the elevator. The second was how to ensure it was not crushed by the weight of the shifting ore once it was inside.

Jonas pulled up the schematic of the colony, which, to his disappointment, did not include any part of the base. He was still over a day's journey from the colony at full speed, and he needed to modify one of the probes to carry the beacon. Fitting the beacon into the probe proved more difficult than he had anticipated. Merely attaching it to the outside would nullify its appearance of being an ordinary comet fish. Jonas decided to remove the beacon from its housing and place it in a plastic bag. He then coated the beacon with repair resin and fitted it inside the probe. Coupled with the cushion provided by the skin and artificial muscles of the probe, the beacon should be well protected from the weight of the ore inside the elevator.

Jonas knew he could not activate the beacon remotely. Once the probe planted itself on the elevator, it would have to power down or risk detection. Any transmission he sent would give away his location. It would have to be on a timer, which was the worst way to activate anything. If the elevator shut down, and the timer activated before the beacon reached the surface, it would be discovered and destroyed. The safest option was to grossly overestimate the timer setting. Jonas just hoped it would not be buried too deep in the mountain of ore or be dumped into the smelters before it began transmitting. With that finished, he plotted a course toward the colony and set the autopilot.

Jonas awoke twelve hours later with only a minor headache, and for the first time in days, he felt good. Manta was still piloting herself toward the bottom of the trench where he had first tested her pressure tolerance. Jonas took a small painkiller for his headache and drank another bottle of healing fluid. He checked the gash on his head in the mirror; it was nearly healed. He manually loaded the probe containing the beacon into one of the tubes while the last of his coffee brewed. He poured a cup, sat in his chair, and looked over the schematics for the colony again, trying to find somewhere he could dock unnoticed. He knew he could not stay in open water indefinitely; he only had two more weeks of supplies left, and two torpedoes could not do much to hurt the bad guys. He would have to dock soon.

Before he launched the beacon probe, he planned to send a probe containing a message to his parents. Jonas knew he couldn't make his presence known to anyone outside his family and close friends, because those men tried to kill him for a reason. Jonas believed someone had known about the facility, found out about its discovery, and sent those men to kill him. The Federation had killed to keep that place hidden before … could Daniels be working for the Federation? Whatever the reason, Jonas figured he was dead if discovered again. Ten hours to home.

Katherine had noticed tension building among the miners. Long hours, low pay, and failing equipment were taking their toll on nerves and morale. The pub she worked at had become mostly a pirate watering hole, but lately, several groups of miners had taken to the place. Why, she didn't know; it was a dump. There had been a small scuffle a couple of weeks ago when a drunken mercenary had picked a fight with one of the miners. The miner won, but the pirate's comrades decided it wasn't a fair fight, ganged up on the miner, and beat him severely. *Come to think of it,* she thought, *that's when the number of miners who frequented the place started increasing.* What if the miners were getting ready to get a little revenge for their associate, who was still at the hospital in ICU? If they did anything against the mercenaries, they would be punished with a death sentence. She had to do something.

Kat walked through the door late, as usual, to see James sitting on the sofa watching the news.

"Hey sis," James waved over his shoulder. "Anything interesting happen today?"

"I'm not sure … I think some of the miners are planning to attack some of the mercenaries at the bar some night."

He muted the broadcast and turned around to face her. "What makes you think that?"

"Well, you remember a few weeks ago I told you about the miner that they put in the hospital?" James nodded. "Well, after that, more miners started hanging around the pub, and tonight a group of them were whispering in the corner. Not a big deal in and of itself, but a couple of them cast involuntary glances in the direction of one of the mercenaries' table. And whenever I went over to pick up empty glasses or deliver another round they stopped talking completely. They just acted like they were up to something."

"Sounds like it." James said thoughtfully. "Why do you care? I'd like to see them kick their teeth in."

"But if they do, they'll be executed! You heard what Commander Daniels and Captain O'Connor said! We have to stop them." Katherine pleaded.

"How? Why would they listen to us?" James argued.

"Maybe they won't, but they might listen to Mr. Black," Katherine implored.

"Whoa!" James held his hands up. "He said to keep quiet. The more people who know something, the more people there are to talk about it."

"We have to ask him. It's the only thing I can think of doing without approaching them myself."

"Okay, okay!" James lowered his eyes and looked at the floor and thought for a few seconds. "We'll stop by his shop in the morning and see if he's there."

The data cube Daniels had given him had been sitting on his desk for four days before O'Connor remembered what it was and where it came from. O'Connor had been spending all of his time and acumen setting traps with Doyle and Magnus, trying to find their rebel. The information on the cube was apparently gathered from a bug Daniels had placed on some colonist's ship. He spent several hours looking at the time stamped records and listening to boring family talk. It was nauseating. No wonder average people were sheep. Then he heard something that caught his ear. He replayed it several times. Then he began looking more closely at the navigation records of this previously unremarkable ship. There, the pilot turned off the active sonar. Interesting. Why would the average man need to go unseen? Only to keep from being seen doing something he shouldn't. Where did he go? Unfortunately, Daniels had not had the foresight to install a decent piece of hardware that could track movement.

O'Connor walked into Daniels' office, escorted by his steward. Daniels was sitting in his high back chair with his back turned to him. O'Connor could see the small feathery stream of cigar smoke slowly rising from in front of the chair.

"Good afternoon, Captain," Daniels greeted cordially, but didn't turn around.

"I looked at the information you gave me. I have some questions."

"I thought you might."

Pompous toad, thought Dwight. It irritated him that the little weasel wouldn't turn around and talk to him face-to-face.

"Who does this ship belong to, and is it the father of the pilot I killed?"

"It belongs to Matthew Black, chief engineer for the Nilrednas Corporation, the largest mining company here. And yes, he is, was, Jonas Black's father."

"Did you ever consider, after looking at the information, that he might be colluding with our terrorist?"

"I have considered that. He is the type of man who likes to play it safe; a family man, not a risk taker. However, he is also an idealist. That's why I gave the information to you. To see if you could find something concrete."

"And if I don't?" inquired O'Connor.

"Then don't do anything to him for attempting to warn his only son of what he thought was a death sentence."

"Fine. And what if I do find something 'concrete'?"

"Then deal with it as you see fit. Is that all, Captain?" Daniels had not turned around.

"That's all I wanted to know." O'Connor turned and walked out.

O'Connor and Doyle immediately began monitoring Dr. Black's movements from their office. When O'Connor saw that Mr. Black was heading for the same place he had pretended to dock last time, he yelled for Doyle and the two headed for the cruiser. They glided up and over the central dome of the colony looking for their mark. As they started down the south side of the dome, the doctor's ship came into view on sonar. There were enough ships around with active sonar running that he would not know he was being tracked. He docked, shut down his sonar, then disengaged the docking clamps and took off again. Keeping their distance and tracking him on sonar worked perfectly until he dropped out of sight. O'Connor cursed and gunned the throttle, heading toward the last place they had seen him. When they reached the spot, they realized what happened. He had dived into a small canyon, effectively shielding him from sonar. He was smarter than anticipated.

The two pirates decreased their depth to take in a larger view of the canyon, and followed it to a small wing of the colony on the east side. They caught a glimpse of the ship on the sonar as it went under the structure. Nearly dropping onto the sea floor, they leveled off so their sonar could 'see' under the edifice. They observed the ship slowly trolling back toward the central hub under cover of the structure. It slowed, sedately rose toward the bottom of the structure, and faded from sight. O'Connor looked at Doyle, who turned and smiled smugly. They turned around and headed back. There were plans to make.

M arkus reloaded his pack with several days' worth of food and supplies. He was planning to go to the far side of the colony to try and work from there for a time. If he was going to all the trouble of getting past some of the Viper mines, he might as well stay over there for a while. Matthew left an hour ago, and he still had an armload of the supplies to pick up from the dock. Markus left his base and jogged the hundred yards down and around the corner to the dock. He was squatting down to pick up the last container when he saw a bulge forming on top of the water. Matthew must have forgotten something. Markus stood with the crate as the ship broke the surface. His heart sank; it was his cruiser.

Markus only broke from a sprint for thirty seconds when he stopped and threw on his pack. He could already hear them coming, although they were trying to be quiet. He knew O'Connor was using his ship, and he knew what they must be here for: to kill him. They must have gotten wise to Matthew and followed him. It was nearly impossible to go unnoticed underwater in a commercial ship like the *Jack Frost* when someone really wanted to find you. He had mistakenly begun to think himself safe here, but he had made one preparation for just such an occasion. It may not kill them, but it would cover his exit. Fifty feet further down, he turned and ran the last thirty yards to a small control panel. He opened the pressure door, activated the control panel, and entered the code. The door began to close and Markus jumped through it as it slammed shut. He had disabled the alarms and broken all of the emergency lights so they would not have any warning.

T he team all wore covers on their boots so they would not squeak on deck if they got wet. They exited silently and formed up behind Doyle and O'Connor. They wore sensor sets, enhancing their sight and hearing. As they rounded the corner coming out of the dock and into the main hallway, O'Connor's set indicated movement to the left down the hallway. He indicated to his team via hand signals that he had movement, and they followed him toward it. He paused briefly and let Doyle's team clear the other dock across the hall and the dry dock behind them. Doyle indicated they were clear, and they proceeded forward. They entered a large room that had obviously been occupied for a period of time.

Dwight switched his visor to infrared and could see two glowing heat signatures on two adjacent crates where the doctor and his terrorist had likely been sitting. He could see one crate positioned in front of a computer console. Their target had obviously been communicating with at least one colonist, and could be aided by dozens. *I should have seen this coming,* thought Dwight. He had forgotten the working men could be some of the most resilient and difficult people to control. They could be brave, and they were tough. Their weakness was that they lived on what they earned, and they usually had families to feed. If you threatened their meager comforts or those of their families, they would do just about anything to keep from losing them.

They cleared the room and several others when Doyle stopped and signaled that he heard something. Dwight heard it too, but he did not know what it was. It sounded like an air vent opening up as air flowed through it or ... water! Doyle shot him a knowing look. He was thinking the same thing.

"Back to the ship *now!*" O'Connor ordered, and he began running.

His men did not know why, but they followed without question.

Markus chuckled as he began making his way toward his emergency encampment, but he counted himself lucky. If they had come at night, he would be dead. He would not have heard them until they were on him, and even from his protected sleeping spot he could not have taken more than three before someone shot him or simply tossed a grenade into the corner. He could hear echoes of several other groups of mercenaries moving through the vents and maintenance tunnels, presumably trying to cut off his escape. He hoped he had found and disabled all of the safety systems; otherwise his pursuers would be hot on his trail. He estimated the quickest way to flood the level was not to open a door or blow out a window. While fast, the volume of water entering from even a large window could not compare to that of the wet docks. So he opted to close the ventilation system from the rest of the colony, open the air lock doors at the docks, and vent all the air from the top of that section. That would remove the pressure that kept the water in the docks at bay, allowing the venting atmosphere to be rapidly replaced with seawater.

Matthew leaned over and kissed Sarah on the side of her forehead while she sat at her desk intently looking at her microscope screen. She reached up and ran her fingers through his hair before he straightened and walked toward the air lock. The doors hissed as they opened and the air equalized. He walked through to *Jack Frost* and closed the hatch. It was a trip that was becoming routine, but Matthew felt guilty every time he found himself enjoying the food or drink at their weekly pow-wows. He piloted *Jack* through the darkness, wondering what he would talk about tonight.

Daniels was unbelievably cordial at dinner; Matthew guessed he must have started drinking early. Matthew had concealed the small data device in his left shirt cuff for easy access, and because Daniels' men never seemed to scan his hands when they did their security check. Matthew still had no plan to convince Daniels to show him the communications room.

"You seem distracted this evening, Dr. Black," Daniels inquired.

"I was just wondering if you were filtering any of the incoming news through the communications array."

"And what would make you think I'd do that?"

"It's what all totalitarian governments have always done throughout history. You know, helps keep the status quo."

"Good point. I assure you, Doctor, I am doing no such thing," Daniels responded. "As you know, the transmitter relays were damaged during the coup and we have yet to obtain the proper parts to repair them." Daniels knew the base's communication system was working just fine. The alleged damage was just a ruse to keep the colonists content, and the Republic off his back until his job was finished.

The second course of dinner arrived, blackened comet fish with a strange fruit sauce; it was very good.

"How will you filter outgoing transmissions when the array is repaired?" Matthew inquired casually.

"Computers can detect imbedded codes, repeating themes, and even words that appear to be triggers. But as you know, only an old and experienced A.I. can usually interpret the tonal inflections conveyed by its master. They could not accurately do likewise for the hundreds of people who would normally send messages every day. I am already beginning to rotate about a half dozen men in and out of that position to ensure no one gets bored and careless. Why the sudden interest in our communications procedures Doctor?"

"Well, Sarah and I were debating yesterday whether or not you were filtering the incoming transmissions. I didn't think you were. But she wanted me to prove it by getting you to show me the communications room. I told her I didn't think it appropriate to ask, and that I doubted it was possible. However, since my motives have been exposed, would it be too much of an inconvenience to ask for just a quick look so I can appear at least a bit of a hero to my wife?"

"I don't see why not! You should have just said so, Doctor Black!" Daniels said with a tinge of relief. "I have never been married, but I do understand doing whatever is necessary to impress a woman. And I doubt if that changes, even when you're married. Yes?"

"You're right." Matthew smiled and agreed to keep Daniels at ease. He was partially correct, but he did not have any idea what he was talking about.

"Well then, after dinner, and a cigar of course, I will give you a tour of our communications facilities."

Dinner continued, and Daniels was certainly drinking more than usual, although Matthew could not ascertain why. Dinner ended, and they walked into the adjacent sitting room for brandy and cigars. Matthew always enjoyed a good cigar, a Churchill being his favorite size, but they were a very expensive luxury that he wouldn't normally indulge in. Most people thought they were offensive, but that was because most people smoked cheap cigars. A good cigar, while it did put off a lot more smoke than a cigarette, had a mild and pleasantly spicy smell. Due to his having imbibed so much alcohol, Daniels became very philosophical in his conversation. Matthew engaged in friendly debate, but agreed with him just enough to keep him happy.

After nearly an hour, Daniels finally remembered his promised tour, stood with a slight wobble, and told Matthew to follow. They proceeded down a hallway to the main elevator. They exited the elevator several levels up, turned left, and walked to a security door. Daniels placed his hand on a security pad, looked into a retinal scanner, and spoke an indiscernible code word, causing the door to open. Matthew's heart rate surged, and he had to slow it. If he did not, he would start to perspire, which, given the temperature of sixty degrees, would certainly draw attention. He was standing casually with his arms crossed behind his lower back, giving him access to the device. As soon as he stepped into the room, he activated it.

Matthew was relieved that there were no alarms and flashing lights. Katherine had done a good job on her program. That kid was not only sweet, but smart. Jonas would do well to marry her, if Jonas was still alive. Sometimes not knowing was worse than the worst-case scenario.

Daniels concluded his tour and escorted Matthew back to the dock, where he shook his hand and told him to ensure the Missus that everything was fine.

O'Connor was running in knee-deep water by the time he and his men approached the doors to the docks. He thought they would be running to safety, but instead, they were running to disaster. To his horror, he could see that the water was flooding onto the level from inside the docks. The air lock had likely been sabotaged and was wide-open, allowing water to rush in as the air pressure dropped. He kept moving toward the door; it was the only way out that he knew. Dwight forced his way through the waist-deep water that was rushing through the air lock and pulled his way through the first door. He could see the water level rising as he paused between the doors for only a few seconds. The water was frigid and he could already feel his legs beginning to stiffen from the cold. Yet, at the same time, the high acid content made his skin feel strangely warm. He tucked himself beside the edge of the inner door inside the eddy created by the rushing water. He reached around the edge of the doorframe and, instead of trying to fight the force of the water, pulled himself over the top of the water and through the doorway.

Dwight tried to walk, but the water was now approaching chest level, so he started swimming. It was all he could do to pull himself through the door of the cruiser. The top of the cruiser was only ten feet from the ceiling of the dock now, and it set low in the water. O'Connor quickly stood, ran to the cockpit, sat down, and reoriented the ship so the hatch was next to the air lock door. This ship had no air lock, so when the water started coming in through the hatch, he would have to close it, regardless of how many men were left outside. The top of the ship hit the ceiling just after Doyle made it inside and started helping the rest of the men. The water reached the bottom of the hatch and started coming inside the cruiser seconds later. O'Connor kept the door open even as water began running over his ankles, then Doyle closed and sealed the hatch. The automated systems began pumping the water out and the floor was soon dry.

O'Connor went aft to see how many of his men made it, hoping they all had. Nine out of twelve men, himself and Doyle included, had made it to the ship. Doyle had closed the door because no more were coming. These were the best men he had, and in excellent shape, but they could not overcome the force of the water rushing through the submerged air lock doors. Dwight cursed and struck the bulkhead with his fist. He looked at Doyle, turned, and stormed toward the cockpit. Doyle quickly followed, wondering what his captain might be up to.

"I'm going to kill him. He's helped cost me a dozen men, and he's dead."

"I agree, Dwight, but we don't know where he is now. Probably moving through the air vents somewhere," answered Doyle.

"Not him. Black. We're killing Doctor Black."

O'Connor adjusted the ship's buoyancy, and it sank through the opening in the dock. As he did so, the body of one of the three lost men came into view. He cursed again, and headed back outside.

Matthew arrived back home and sat down on the sofa beside Sarah.

"I was worried." She put her arm around him and kissed him on the cheek. "You were gone longer than usual."

"I convinced him to give me a tour. Your idea worked. I think he actually liked the idea that we'd had a disagreement. You know he's never liked our kind."

"I know. Not many people from Earth do. Did it work?" Sarah inquired.

"It had more than enough time to download." Matthew sighed. "I hope so."

"Me too … I never thought we'd be hiding and sneaking around again, much less spying. I know you hoped we would be free in the Republic." Sarah laid her head on Matthew's shoulder.

"We found freedom *and* peace here. It isn't the Republic's fault all this happened. Evil, power-hungry men are peppered throughout the galaxy, and you never know when you might run into one, or even worse, over two hundred all in one place. We just happened to be at the wrong place at the wrong time," Matthew responded forlornly.

"And our kind are here to preserve the good. This is but one of our reasons for being; maybe we were at the right place at the right time," she encouraged.

" … Nothing happens to our people without reason," he paraphrased another ancient saying.

The words were still in the air when a deafening boom reverberated through his chest. Water began pouring into the room, and before he could stand, he had to start swimming. His heart sank as he struggled to stay afloat. *They knew!* Another explosion ripped through the wall where the air lock was, probably taking out the *Jack Frost*.

"Sarah!" he yelled, reaching out and grabbing her shirt.

As she turned, he could see the terror on her face.

"This way!" he yelled and looked toward the top part of the structure where the dome crowned.

They swam to it as the icy water continued to fill their home.

By the time they reached it, the water was five feet from the top and rising. The noise was subsiding, and there had not been another explosion in thirty seconds. Even so, Matthew knew their time was over. This pocket of air, if it persisted, had only several hours of air in it. But that was irrelevant. In less than ten minutes, the water would drain the heat from their bodies to such a degree that they could not longer swim. Then they would drown. Matthew could already feel the boreal water slowing his muscles. One of the sofa cushions floated to the surface, and Matthew helped Sarah onto it so at least part of her torso was out of the water. He maneuvered to face her, and they interlocked arms so he could stay afloat as the cold caused his grip to fail. The water stopped rising about three feet from the top of the dome.

"I'm sorry." Matthew's lips were already getting stiff and were slow to respond to his words. "I didn't want to bring this on you. I should have taken you back to Mars or even Elysium so you didn't have to live here, where you couldn't see the sky. I know how much you missed it."

"It's okay. As long as I had you and Jonas, I've been happy. You're all I've ever wanted. You know I love you more than any old planet." She was shivering uncontrollably now. "I wanted to grow old with you though. You'd have made a cute old geezer." She smiled and tried to laugh, but it sounded more like an audible shiver.

"I wanted to have more time." Matthew involuntarily shivered. "Twenty-two years wasn't long enough…you're only forty…" Tears started rolling down his cheeks. He meant to say forty-two.

"I know, not *old* like you," she quipped and smiled, pulling him closer and kissing him. He was forty-six. "I hope Jonas will be okay. I wanted us to be there for him."

"Me too…" Matthew could barely speak, and was violently shivering. So was Sarah.

"Stay awake baby, stay with me," Matthew coaxed as Sarah's eyelids grew heavy.

"I know, I'm getting tired…I love you." She smiled groggily.

"I love you too… don't leave me yet," He pleaded. He was getting tired too.

"Everything happens for a reason… at least we get to go together. I never wanted to lose you first." Tears streamed down her now-pale cheeks. "I knew it would hurt you as much as it would me if I went first. It's better this way… I…" She choked up.

"S-S-Same here," Matthew said, his eyes closing.

They pulled as close together as they could in such an awkward position and held each other tightly, cheek to cheek, shivering. Matthew remembered the way Sarah looked like a lost angel when he had first met her, wandering the lower corridors of the college like she had never set foot on land before. She was the most beautiful creature he had ever seen. She had grown more so with age, and he had always felt like the beast. They only spoke briefly; she needed directions to the level her classes were on. For the next semester he made every excuse he could think of to end up in the natural science wing, where she had most of her classes, although he could never get up enough nerve to say more than "hello." He had never been anything of a lady's man, but he could usually manage to start up a conversation without sounding less articulate than a grunting cave man. The one time he ran into her on accident was in the student center's central coffee shop. She was walking past him. He said hello and asked her if she had time to sit down. She did, and they sat there for two hours talking. The rest… *will be history*, Matthew thought. Sarah had stopped shivering. So did he. Then he felt her stop breathing. Matthew stopped fighting and fell asleep. He stopped breathing about thirty seconds later, but he did not let go.

Manta hovered at the edge of the canyon, hanging above the lightless void. Jonas had both her eyelets opened, hoping to see some glimpse of light from his home. There was none. He opened one of the torpedo tubes and activated the message drone, lightly ejecting it from the tube. It swam a seemingly random pattern at a speed usual for the comet fish it was meant to imitate. However, it meandered its way to where the air lock on the Blacks' domicile should have been. There it stopped. Jonas did not wait for a response, unaware there would not be one. He did not want to linger. Every moment he was near the colony he risked being discovered. He closed *Manta*'s "eyes," turned, and plunged into the darkness.

Manta cruised through the water a thousand feet below the canyon rim. According to the map, there was a spur off of the main canyon that would bring him near the ore elevator. It was going to be a tight fit for *Manta*'s wide wingspan. He would likely have to roll her to one side as it narrowed. He eased the throttle forward, banked, and turned into the large fissure. It was a tight squeeze; he rolled left and edged her around a corner.

Jonas's stomach was in a knot when he reached a wider space and leveled off, setting her to hover. He stood and stretched walking back to get a drink.

"Your piloting skills have improved greatly since our first excursion, Captain."

"Thanks, M. Are there any points just above the edge of the canyon that could provide us with a little cover from sonar that might be coming from the direction of the elevator?"

"Yes, Captain, there is a large berm of mining rubble just forward of our location."

"Good." He took a drink of cool water and walked back to manually load the beacon probe. *Manta*'s auto-loading mechanism was a little rough, and this was too important to risk damaging the beacon or timer. He had forgotten how heavy these things were. Jonas then went forward to the pilot's chair, belted himself in, and took a deep breath. He bumped the throttle forward slightly and pulled the yoke back, bringing *Manta* into a nose-up vertical position. He eased her upward for several minutes until reaching the top of the fissure, where he leveled off and skimmed the floor until he was behind the large berm Manta had located.

"Manta, could the neowhale sounds be used as sonar?"

"One moment. Yes, Captain. The frequencies could also be used as sonar pulses. Why?" *Manta* asked.

"Because if you could use those frequencies instead of normal sonar, the core computer would identify the signal as biological and ignore us."

"It will take a few moments to configure my sonar for the new frequency. Captain, I also have a concern."

"Yes?"

"As you know, imaging sonar uses multiple frequencies emitted from bi-auricular transmitters, and that they are received and translated in the same manner. By using the bio-frequency we captured, it will not give an exact picture of the target."

"Oh," Jonas said with disappointment. "Wait, what if we took images from more than one location?"

"That would yield a sharper image of the target. Sonar is ready."

"Emit pulse on my mark."

Jonas adjusted *Manta*'s buoyancy, causing her to slowly rise above the top of the berm.

"Now," Jonas ordered.

A blurred image appeared on the holo screen. It was, as she said, not very clear. Jonas turned *Manta* around and plunged back into the fissure. He brought her about two thousand feet farther up the fissure from their previous position and again eased up over the edge, taking another sonar reading. He repeated the process once more and finally had a reasonably clear image of the elevator and its surroundings. He came about and proceeded to their first position. Jonas then coupled the new image with the map he already had and uploaded it to the beacon probe. With that done, he eased up over the canyon rim and launched the probe. He moved up behind the berm and slowly decreased *Manta*'s depth so she again crested the berm.

Jonas pressed the launch button on the helm control; the probe barely made a sound as *Manta* ejected it. The probe behaved the same way the previous one had, taking an indirect path towards its target. It should take the probe about fifteen minutes to reach its target and swim into one of the ore elevators. The journey to the surface would take thirty minutes and it would take a total of an hour and a half from launch for the beacon to activate. He had nothing to do but wait.

The previous morning, James and Katherine went to Matthew's shop to talk with him about organizing the miners, if only to keep them from getting into trouble. He was not there. They tried to call him on the terminal outside the shop. No response; not even an automated answer. The two shot each other looks of confusion and concern.

"Could just be a temporary glitch in the system or something," James assured.

"Maybe we should go see if Mrs. Black is at home. If he's out on a jobsite, she'll know where to find him," Katherine suggested.

James agreed.

They went to the dock and acquired a ride from Mr. Tyler, one of Matthew's coworkers.

"I haven't heard from Matthew this morning either. He was supposed to meet me thirty minutes ago to go and change out some valves on one of the diggers. He's never late. I tried calling him too, but got no answer. I was just about to go check on him and see if the *Jack Frost* was broke down or something; you two are welcome to join me," Mr. Tyler said with a hint of concern as he boarded a small ship.

Mr. Tyler piloted the ship away from the dock with James and Katherine aboard and headed toward the Black's residence. As the trio approached, they could see the shape of the dome on sonar.

"Oh no!" Katherine gasped. As they came around the front to dock, several tears rolled down her cheeks. Half of the structure was missing. James and Mr. Tyler looked on in disbelief.

"Who would do such a thing?" Mr. Tyler asked no one in particular.

"Daniels or O'Connor," James said distantly. "Are there any life signs?"

"None; and I doubt they escaped either. Look." Mr. Tyler pointed to the remains of the *Jack Frost*. It had rolled about fifty yards down the hill from the structure and settled against some rocks.

"The message we sent, they must have found out about it," Katherine murmured.

"I don't see how. Maybe it was something else … Maybe Mr. Black had something to do with killing the pirates, or knew who was," James hypothesized.

"I don't know about that, but the chief was a good man. Whoever did this needs to pay," Mr. Tyler responded indignantly.

"Mr. Tyler," Katherine quietly interjected, "we don't know what he was doing, but we're pretty sure it had something to do with the pirates getting killed. He made us promise to stay out of it, but we told him whatever we heard. That's why I started working at that nasty pub. And it's already paid off once."

"How?" Mr. Tyler questioned, his brow furrowing.

"I overheard a conversation and found out that O'Connor and a couple of his men were going out after Jonas. So we," she indicated James, "went and told the Blacks, and helped modify a torpedo to send him a warning message. We don't know if he got it or not."

"We don't know anything other than that he kept us out of the loop, apparently with good reason." James cast a glance at the wreckage that was once a home.

"So you two don't know who else might be involved in a resistance, or who we might contact?" Mr. Tyler inquired.

"No. But, I did hear a group of miners talking about waiting around and beating a couple of pirates in a few days. At least, I'm pretty sure that's what they're up to," Katherine said excitedly.

"Well," Mr. Tyler stroked his beard, "it's not much, but it's a start. I'll bet they'll be motivated to do more than pass out a good beating when they find out about this! Katherine, can you introduce me to these miners?"

"I guess so," Kat responded suspiciously.

"Oh, come on young lady! You've seen what these men will do; it's time to quit cowering in the corner and start fighting back! I've never done anything like this before, but I'm willing to do whatever I need to so I get the chance to kill me a few of the dregs that are responsible for this and the other miners they killed when all this started. What do you say?"

"I'm in," James responded, "and I know there are a few engineers at the shop who would be willing to join us. And lots more will follow if they think we could win. We've spent enough time sitting on our hands enduring slavery just because we're reasonably comfortable." He looked at Katherine. "We need to do this. It doesn't matter what happens. We are the ones who are able; therefore, we are the ones required to act."

"Okay." Kat smiled and turned to Mr. Tyler. "This group of miners is usually in the pub every Wednesday and Friday after the end of second shift. They should be there tonight. They sit in the back left corner."

"What's that?" James pointed to a small blip on the sonar screen. It looked like a dead comet fish floating near the wreckage, but it wasn't floating belly up.

Katherine forced her way between James and Mr. Tyler to get a closer look. "It's one of Jonas's!"

"Come on, Kat," James said dolefully, thinking his sister was clinging to false hope.

She ignored the comment.

"Can you retrieve it with the arm on the sub, Mr. Tyler?"

"I suppose, but how do you know it's not just a dead comet fish?"

"I know," she responded pertly.

Tyler shrugged, moved the sub into position, extended the clawed manipulator arm of the maintenance sub, and gently clamped onto the comet fish. Having nothing else left to do but stare at the bleak images of death and destruction, he turned and headed back toward with colony with not a word of protest from James or Katherine. When they docked, Mr. Tyler used the sub's arm to set the fish gingerly on the deck. The three disembarked, and, upon examining the dead fish, found that Katherine was correct. It was one of Jonas's probes.

"It's probably a message he sent home. We need to download it." Katherine tried to pick up the probe, but nearly fell over the top of it in the attempt. She gave James a look. He stopped and not so easily picked the thing up himself. They brought it over to a workbench with a terminal, and Kat opened it up and plugged it in. An image of Jonas appeared on the screen, and he began to speak.

"Hi Mom. Hi Dad. I just wanted to let you guys know I was all right. I got the message Kat sent; unfortunately, it was a little late. I'd already had a run-in with the pirates, and I almost bought it because they were in Markus's cruiser. It's a long story, but I found a treasure, of sorts. I'm not coming home because I figure those guys think I'm dead, with good reason, too. Manta saved me … another long story. I opened the case you gave me, Dad, and I'm going to try and get a message out. After I send it, I'm going to try and hide *Manta* and myself at the colony. I'm not sure what I'm going to do after that, but I'll try and contact you again whenever it's safe. Until then…" The screen went black.

"How do you suppose he's going to send a message?" asked Mr. Tyler. "There's no way to send one from under the ice."

"I don't know, but he sounds pretty sure it'll work," James responded.

"I wish we could contact him and help somehow," Kat said wistfully.

"Me too, but I don't see how. We can't risk an open transmission; it could be intercepted, assuming he's even within range. Besides, if it were intercepted, it would only start them looking for him again." Tyler paused for a second. "We don't know where he is, so we can't send another message probe. But at least we know he's safe for now."

James put his hand on Katherine's shoulder.

Tyler shook his head.

"I didn't even know all this was going on, and right under my nose too! If he actually does get a message through, it means help won't be too far away. We have to be careful, but it's definitely time to start planning to take back our home. These thugs have had free reign long enough. I need to get going." Tyler looked at his watch. "I have to go talk to a guy about some guns. Katherine, I'll be there to meet with the miners tonight, and show this to them." He held up a data cube that held the sonar recordings of Matthew and Sarah's destroyed home. "If this doesn't get them going, nothing will." Tyler shook James's hand, turned, and quickly left the dock.

"Oh no ..." Katherine looked at her watch. More time had passed than any of them had realized. "I've got to get to work."

James walked and half jogged with her to the pub, and, after making sure she was safely there, headed off to his job. He was late too.

TWELVE

"I want to know every name and every address for everyone he knew! Everyone he even looked at!" O'Connor screamed.

"I agree that we need to fully investigate the extent to which any of his associates could be involved, but I don't want a witch hunt," Daniels calmly but firmly replied.

"I'm sick of losing men because of those two, and I want everyone who is helping them."

"One."

"What?!" O'Connor snapped.

"There is only one now. You killed Dr. Black, remember? And, in your haste, you killed his wife too. We need to think before taking further action." Daniels attempted to calm O'Connor's rant.

"Fine! But I still want a list of everyone he associated with from the central computer, including when and where he saw them. I think Black was only helping the guy causing all the destruction, so we still haven't caught our terrorist. But those two had to have help." O'Connor had access to most core files and systems, but not Daniels' clearance level.

"I agree. I still find it surprising that one of his kind would even engage in such behavior. They're supposed to be a peaceful lot," Daniels said contemplatively.

"What do you mean 'his kind'?" O'Connor inquired.

"Oh," Daniels waved his had dismissively, "he and his wife were followers of some ancient monotheistic religion."

"What's so special about that?" Dwight was already growing impatient with this branch of conversation.

"If you remember your history lessons, it was declared disruptive to the peace and tranquility of the Federation over a hundred years ago. Laws were passed banning its very existence and great political pressure was utilized to quell its spread and growth. When that didn't work, police action was taken. No doubt you are old enough to have been in the service when the Federation finally ended its irritating presence on Earth?"

"I was, and I remember a brief engagement with one of their settlements. They seemed a little too sheepish for terrorists. But I never really cared who they were; I just did my job," O'Connor calmly reflected.

"Anyway," Daniels continued, "these people still exist on Mars, along with its archaic constitution and republic style of government. The Blacks were of this religion, and were supposed to be pacifists. That is why I was surprised to discover Doctor Black's involvement."

"I'm not surprised at anyone's level of involvement in anything. Everyone's crooked, it's just a matter of how much and how well they hide it. Or choose not to," O'Connor smiled, "Now, how about my list?"

"All right Captain." Daniels entered several commands into his terminal, which was connected to the central core. The information appeared on his screen and was uploaded to a data cube.

"Here you are." He held onto the cube briefly as O'Connor tried to take it from his hand. "And please exercise a little self restraint, Captain?" He released it.

"As you say, Commander." O'Connor mockingly saluted Daniels, turned, and walked out of the room.

O'Connor walked into his office and uploaded the data to his terminal; there were hundreds of names, dates, times, and locations. He looked at the records for hours. Then he remembered the unknown male and female Black had the conversation with when they went to rig that torpedo to send a message to his kid. He quickly found out Black had visited them at their home the day before he went to see his confederate. He pulled surveillance footage from the core, chronometrically linked it, and followed the two from their previous meeting with Black back to their dwelling. Now he had two leads: James and Katherine Shaw. O'Connor called Doyle on the com.

Fifteen minutes later, Doyle arrived with Magnus and two other men, all of them heavily armed. O'Connor quickly briefed them on the new information and what he planned to do with it.

Markus had worked his way through the gauntlet of Viper mines, trip wires and sensors that now littered the air ducts. He was growing tired after seven hours inching and meandering his way through the passageways that would have taken less than an hour directly. As he went, he had carved two three-inch spheres out of aluminum that roughly resembled grenades. Markus quickly peeked around a corner and heard a Viper mine move, but had not seen it. He could not afford a second look. It would take over an hour to work his way back past the trip wires he had so deftly bypassed, and he was still several hours from his destination. It was time to try Matthew's fake grenade idea. If they had come after him, they certainly knew of Matthew's involvement. O'Connor, being the kind of man he was, would have lashed out in any way he could after Markus's escape.

Markus reckoned he was not a very optimistic person, assuming his friends were dead. But in wartime there were always those killed who should not have been, and he was the one who used to kill them.

"I hope I live long enough to make sure they never leave this place alive, my friend," he said aloud. Markus looked upward and winked at the ceiling as he pressed his back to the wall and tossed the solid metal grenade look-alike around the corner. The Viper mine responded to the perceived threat and began firing in full automatic bursts. It briefly paused several times to reacquire its target before it started firing again. Markus finally knew it had run out of ammunition when he heard the auto-loading mechanism clicking as it tried to reload its empty magazine. He popped his head around the corner and back just to make sure. The mine's turret moved to target him, but could not fire. Markus stepped into its sights and the mine followed his every move, still trying to fire. It would remain active until its power source was drained. Markus smiled, turned the deadly little thing around, and switched it off. Now he had his own mine.

He picked up and pocketed what was left of the mangled pseudo-grenade. No sense in giving the enemy a clue about how he defeated their trap. He checked the caliber of the Viper mine and it was standard Federation issue, which he had. He covered its sensor lenses and lashed it to his backpack before continuing toward his new base. He hoped he would not be too sensory-deprived by the droning white noise of the waterfall. And although it was more vulnerable to discovery, it was a central location, had several escape routes, provided a good view of the surroundings, and was much more defensible than his previous locale.

K atherine was wiping down the last of the tables at closing time as Tyler and the group of miners were standing up to leave. Apparently the meeting had gone well, since they were all smiling, shaking hands, and acting very casual. Earlier, when Mr. Tyler had first walked in and sat down, everyone appeared to be very tense. Tyler and the man who seemed to be the group leader talked for about ten minutes and finally looked around the bar suspiciously. Then the two had a ten-second exchange of words with the rest of the group, and the whole lot of them burst into laughter. After that, they all appeared rather jovial. Katherine spent the next two hours trying to catch what she could of their conversation while trying to figure out what that outburst and their sudden change in demeanor was all about.

Finally, she had it. Mr. Tyler, shrewd man that he clearly was, must have convinced everyone at the table that they would appear much less dubious if they appeared to be nothing more than the usual group of carousing miners. And it worked. They quickly became part of the atmosphere. Everyone noticed them, but no one paid them any attention. Katherine watched and learned quickly how they did what they were doing. They would take turns telling jokes or stories to the group, while two or three of them were discussing whatever it was they were planning. The information would eventually be passed around the entire table. Their volume would occasionally drop, probably to ensure they were all on the same page. A few would purposefully snicker, and momentarily they would all laugh and call for more beer.

"Good night, sir." Katherine pretended not to know Mr. Tyler, as she had the entire evening.

"Good night. We left our tip on the bill. Wouldn't want you taking anything *under* the table, now would we?" Tyler winked, and his eyes darted to the large round table they had been seated at.

"Thanks." Katherine smiled.

Katherine immediately went over to their table and began wiping it down, starting with the top, then around the bottom edge. Halfway around, her hand bumped into something. She pulled it off in the towel and continued cleaning. When she was finished, she tucked the towel into the pouch of her apron, having already positioned the small magnetic object so that it would fall out of the towel and to the bottom of the pocket. She picked up the last couple of glasses, put them on the bar, removed the towel, and tossed it beside them. She bid the owner good night, placed her IS' card on the register to collect her tips, and clocked out. She pulled her apron off, slipping the small magnet from the table out of it and into her pocket, and hung it behind the bar where her jacket had just been. Katherine put on her jacket, slipped out the front door, and headed home.

J onas wondered how long it would take the Republic to dispatch marines once they received the beacon code … if they received the transmission. They would check to see if they had any troops deployed here, and since they did not, would they even send anyone? Daniels and the base personnel were army; they would not use a marine beacon if they were in distress. Still, it should get *some* kind of response. He checked his watch again. Ten minutes left.

J ames had not been home long when the door tone sounded. It was nearly time for Katherine to be home, and she was always forgetting her key card, so he went to the door and opened it.

"Hello, James," O'Connor said coolly.

"Hello," James said, almost gagging on the word. He stepped back and swallowed hard after noticing the four men with guns pointed at him standing behind O'Connor.

"We have a few things to discuss with you." O'Connor glanced at Magnus. He stepped forward and struck James in the head with the butt of his rifle.

James fell to the floor with a thump, and Dwight and his men were inside the apartment. They searched it for Katherine, to no avail. Doyle downloaded the files from all the computer terminals while everyone else ransacked the place looking for weapons, com devices or anything else interesting or valuable.

"Nothing here, Captain. About all I can do is check these files," Doyle said, pocketing a data cube. "What now? You want to wait or try that pub where she works?"

"We wait. She'll come back eventually. If we go after her, we might miss her." O'Connor pointed to one of the other two men. "Demon, go to that pub she works at and see if she's there. If she is, keep an eye on her and call us in. If you don't see her, come back here."

"Yes, sir," was the reply.

The man slung his rifle and hurried through the door. Doyle shut it behind him, and the rest of them settled in to wait. Demon headed down the corridor toward the central hub headed a roundabout way to the pub. He had been briefed on the location of the place, but he was not familiar enough with the layout of the colony to know the shortest route.

Katherine rounded the corner just in time to see a man with a rifle and sidearm stepping from the alcove that their apartment door was set into. He turned and trotted off away from her. She darted across the corridor and into another alcove. Her heart was pounding with fear and felt like it was in her throat as she tried to calm herself.

They must have traced Matthew back to us! Where's James? Did they kill him? How did they find out? It had to be the colony's security cameras; they must have been following Mr. Black around and saw him come here. Her mind raced as she tried to think of what she needed to do next. She had to find a safe place where she could hide to think and decide her next move … the arboretum. But how was she going to get there without being tracked by the cameras? James told her there were blind spots throughout the colony; he was always weird about noticing things like that. But where were they, and how was she supposed to figure it out at a time like this? She found herself wishing she had paid more attention to his paranoid little speeches about the shortcomings of the colony's security. Then it occurred to her. What if the areas he was always telling her to avoid because they weren't as safe as others, were that way due to the fact there were fewer security cameras in those areas? It was worth a shot.

Katherine looked low around the corner to see if there were any more thugs hanging around. There were none, but when she started to move, she found herself still gripped with fear. She could feel panic coming on, but she stopped and tried to push it back. It took several seconds, but she did it. She looked again. It was clear, and she ran for it. She darted across the hallway and around the corner. She turned again and ran down a corridor that roughly paralleled the circular central hub. After a quarter mile of darting around corners, she found the place she was looking for: a large corridor where a sleazy bar and massage parlor were the anchor businesses. She had never been within a hundred feet of this particular corridor, and now she knew why. There was a man passed out in a yellow puddle of what she hoped was beer beside the door of the bar, and a woman that was very scantily clad and who looked to be of questionable character sitting on a bench in front of the massage parlor.

Kat shook off the inclination to leave and take her chances with the pirates and began to look around. Up and down the walls, in the corners, she checked all the usual places and then some … no cameras. There had to be a way to get out of here without being seen. There were probably people who came and went from places like this that did not want to be seen. And as much as the thought made her cringe, she was going to have to ask someone if they knew. The most obvious candidate was the woman sitting on the bench. She walked back down the corridor and addressed her.

"Excuse me, ma'am? Can I ask you a question?" Katherine timidly requested.

"You sure look out of place. And don't call me ma'am. I'm not nearly old enough to be you mother. And asking if you can ask a question *is* a question," the woman said mockingly, but winked and smiled.

"Thank you." Kat relaxed and smiled back. "Is there a way to get out of here without being seen by security?"

"Trouble with the mercenaries, huh?"

Katherine nodded.

"What are they after *you* for?"

"My brother and I helped Dr. Matthew Black, who was helping whoever has been killing the pirates. They killed Mr. Black and his wife this morning. I think they just took my brother, and now they're after me."

"I see. Well it wouldn't matter much to me whether they go or stay, but since that little squirrel of a commander up there has been making the miners work so much, business has been a little slower than usual. Not that after working so hard they couldn't use a good massage," the woman winked and pointed at the sign, "but they just don't have the time or money anymore. So I suppose I could lend a hand, as long as you don't tell anyone I helped you."

"I'll forget I ever saw you if you forget about me too," Katherine bargained.

"Done." After a quick glance to see if anyone was watching, the woman indicated with her head. "This way." She stood and walked down the corridor the direction Kat had just come from, then stopped at a maintenance door so covered with graffiti it was barely noticeable. She opened it and they stepped through. The door slammed loudly, causing Katherine to jump.

"Now," the woman put her hands on her hips, "Where do you want to go?"

"Uh." Kat hesitated. "I'd rather not say."

"I understand, honey, but you gotta at least give me the general direction."

"Okay. I need to get to the upper levels and closer to the central hub," Katherine said hesitantly.

"Okay then. Go straight ahead until you reach a T, then turn right. The first ladder you come to, go up. You will have to find the next ladder on each level. Some are off the right and some are to the left. There isn't really a pattern. When you get to the level you want, go toward the hub. Be careful though, and don't get too close to the vents. Some have sensors. They're pretty easy to spot, though; they usually have a little red blinky light on them. Got it?"

"Yes. Thank you so much." Katherine put out her hand, not really knowing what else to do.

"Forget about it honey, remember?" The woman cocked her head to the side.

Katherine paused for a second, slightly confused, then said, "Forget about what?" She withdrew her hand and the women winked at each other.

"Good girl." The woman turned and stepped back through the door, effectively disappearing.

Katherine turned and started to move when the door slamming again made her jump. The noise eerily echoed through the maintenance passage, making it seem even more dark and ominous. For the first time in the last fifteen heart-pounding minutes, she realized she was alone. She again had to push back fear, as she let her eyes adjust to the darkness. She started down the dimly lit corridor. Katherine was beginning to doubt the woman's directions when she finally made it to a T. She turned right and within fifty feet located a ladder leading upward and took it. She found herself in another passageway that looked identical to the first.

She found the next ladder and noticed as she reached the next level that there was a lettered number designation in front of her. The lights on this level were slightly brighter, and it appeared to get more traffic than the previous ones. She continued on, checking her watch periodically, before reaching the level she thought she wanted in just under an hour. Her arms were burning and felt limp from so much climbing. She finally realized what James and Jonas had been talking about when they had repeatedly explained to her the difference in being shapely and being in shape. Kat was reminded of her many attempts to set James up with one girl or another, but he wanted someone who could keep up with him and do the things he liked to do. Katherine always told him he was too picky and that most girls just weren't like that. James always responded the same. He'd laugh and say, "Well, I guess I just don't like most girls then. I don't want most girls, anyway; I want *the* girl." Katherine did a little running around the colony whenever she felt like it, and had taken a bit of judo when she was a kid, but, although athletic, she never rigorously pursued physical activities like Jonas and her brother. Now she wished she had. Still she trudged on hoping she could find a place to permanently hide.

D emon checked the pub and found it already closed for the night, so he turned around and headed back to the Shaws' apartment. He made sure there was no one in the hallway before he stepped around the corner, quickly crossed over, and entered the door. He was welcomed by three rifles pointing at him.

"She's not there, Captain. The place was already closed. She isn't back here yet?" Demon reported.

"No sign of her. How long had it been closed?" O'Connor inquired.

"The sign said it closed thirty minutes before. She should have been back here by now."

"Yeah…" O'Connor's voice drifted off and his eyes glazed over as he started thinking. "She either had something else planned beforehand, or she's been warned somehow. Demon, you and Villegas stay here and wait for her; I'll send someone to relieve you in the morning. Stay alert. She might not be alone when she gets back."

"Yes, sir."

"Magnus, carry the kid. We'll bring him up to the surface to question him. I'm sure Daniels will want to be in on that."

Magnus squatted down and grabbed the back of James's shirt and pants with his right hand. With one easy-looking motion he stood, picked James up off the floor, and held him by the belt straight-armed out in front of him for several seconds before he slung him over his left shoulder.

"Two hundred," Magnus commented, his eyes the only thing that showed any hint of a smile.

"What's that supposed to mean?" Doyle asked irritably. He had never heard that comment before. He would have remembered. Magnus didn't comment about much of anything.

"The kid weighs two hundred pounds," O'Connor replied with a smirk as he followed Magnus out of the apartment.

D aniels was sitting at his desk, reviewing shipping reports when the emergency com light came on. He tapped his terminal, and the communications officer appeared on the screen.

"Sir!" His voice was tense and he was visibly flustered. "An emergency beacon was just activated from somewhere on the base! It's broadcasting an encrypted message on a Republic frequency!"

"What!?" Daniels nearly stood. "Where is it?"

"We're having trouble pinpointing it, sir, but it looks like it's somewhere in the ore yard."

"Find it *now*. Do what you can to jam it, and call me immediately when you have its location." Daniels cut the transmission and started a new one. He knew it was most likely a Republic military beacon, and although it was probably too late, there was always the chance there had been interference of some kind or whatever else that can go wrong with technology. If so, perhaps he could stop it before it successfully transmitted its signal. He contacted the few men he had at his disposal and sent them to the space docks where the ore containers were kept. Then he called his steward and asked him to find O'Connor.

"Captain O'Connor just contacted the control center and told them he was docking."

"Good. Meet him down there. Tell him what's going on and have him bring his men to the yards to help find this thing."

"Yes, sir." The steward turned abruptly and was gone.

Daniels pulled his pistol out of a desk drawer, checked to make sure the power pack was still charged, and strapped it on. He left his office, took the nearest lift down to the ore lift level, and headed toward the docks.

The ore processing area of the space docks was a massive domed structure that was free of any supports on the inside. The ore that was mined from the colony was sent to the warehouse via a massive lift system that was basically an enormous bracketed chain. The brackets mated with the container system used by the mining machines. The containers were attached to the lift and pulled up through the hole in the surface ice into the warehouse where they were weighed, the percentage of composition registered, dumped, and returned to the depths. The containers were roughly the size of a standard interplanetary shipping container, and each had the markings of the company that owned it. However, the containers used below the surface were comprised of a special alloy that was resistant to the highly corrosive effects of the ocean water. Even so, due to corrosion and general wear, they had to be replaced about once per year.

The ore was dumped onto piles, according to type and company, where front-end loaders would move it to the furnace for smelting. The slag was scraped off and dumped out a chute at the opposite end of the building, where it fell to the sea floor. The various metals were then poured into forms, cooled, and loaded into shipping containers. They were placed on a mechanism that pulled the container into the air lock. It was then moved outside to the auto loaders that sorted and loaded the containers onto their various ships. From there, the material was transported to various Martian shipyards, where it was used in the production of satellites, space stations, and ships. The whole multi-corporate operation ran perpetually.

"Have you narrowed the area down yet?" Daniels barked into his com.

"A little bit, sir. It seems to be coming from the area of the main elevator," the com officer responded.

"Good, keep me updated." Daniels pocketed his com and pointed at the four closest men. "You four come with me and search the elevator area."

The men followed Daniels over a thousand yards to the center of the structure where the massive lift system came out of the floor and towered several hundred feet above. There was a heavy railing around the opening to prevent men and equipment from falling through the hole in the ice and into the freezing water. The lift was surrounded by a system of forklift machines that offloaded the containers, dumped them into various piles, and returned them to the lift where they again plunged into the depths.

They had been there less than a minute when the com officer called Daniels.

"Sir, we found it."

"Where?"

"Two hundred yards north northwest of your location, and it's still transmitting. I'm sending you the coordinates now."

Daniels cut the transmission and brought the men with him about a quarter of the way around the lift to one of the piles of ore. After a quick search, one of his men found something protruding from the backside of the pile. After a minute or so of digging through the cascading debris, they had unearthed what looked like a slightly beaten-up comet fish.

"What is that?" Daniels demanded.

"It looks like a fish, sir," the man responded blankly.

"I know what it looks like!" Daniels snapped. "Look at it. It's not a fish, it just looks like one!"

"Oh, right. I'd say it's some kind of ROV, made to look like a fish to avoid detection," the man responded only slightly more astutely.

"Open it."

The man pulled a large knife from his belt, jammed it into the seam of a panel, and broke it open. Inside they found the beacon and removed it.

"I think this is it, sir." The man attempted to hand it to Daniels.

"Drop it," Daniels ordered, and the man dropped it on the floor.

Daniels drew his pistol and emptied the magazine into the device.

"Com, is the device still transmitting?" Daniels asked on his com link.

"Uh … no, sir. It stopped. Did you find it?"

"Yes. Continue monitoring all incoming transmissions, and tell me immediately if anyone inquires regarding the signal."

"Copy that sir. Com out."

"Someone must have sent it up the elevator," Daniels thought out loud, looking at the probe. He called his steward. "I want everyone who is loading or operating an ore transport ship below brought in for questioning immediately. I want the station's sonar activated and running from now on. Find out where every ship has been and what it's been doing for the last twelve hours. I want to know if the station or colony's sensors have picked up anything unusual anywhere near here. And keep O'Connor there. I'll be up in a moment."

"Yes, sir," the steward answered.

Jonas's watch alarm went off as Manta's timer also reached zero. His stomach tightened, and he waited and listened for the inevitable hornet's nest to erupt when it was detected. He had left a second probe hovering beside the berm he had used to fire the first and dropped back down into the fissure. Jonas was slowly working his way back down the fissure toward the canyon where he could drop down to a depth beyond the reach of any other ship in the colony, if necessary. Daniels would lock down everything when it was detected. But when he found it, he would certainly realize that it had come from the outside and begin searching for whoever sent it. Twenty minutes later, he reached the canyon and was settling onto a ledge when he saw the first ping on sonar. It was of sufficient magnitude that it had to have come from the colony. They found it.

James opened his eyes groggily, not knowing for several seconds where he was or what had happened. James remembered a monster of a man stepping forward, the rifle, and the thought that he was about to be shot. The monster looked like he was preparing to fire, but instead, James saw the butt of the rifle coming at him, colored sparks, then nothing. James awoke fully and found he was tied to a chair. He had a splitting headache and was having trouble keeping his eyes focused on any one point for more than a few seconds. The room was about twenty by thirty feet and contained nothing but a large conference table and a dozen chairs. The room had faux wood paneling—at least he supposed it was—with a few paintings on the wall. He sat facing the door on the far end of the room.

James could not think of a reason why they didn't kill him earlier, and now he was not being kept in a jail cell. That only left one possibility; they were going to interrogate him. *That should be loads of fun,* he thought sardonically. *What's worse, I don't even know anything! Suuure, they're going to believe me when I tell them that! They obviously know about Matthew, probably the message we sent to Jonas, and that me and Katherine were somehow involved with him. I'll just tell them that, minus Kat's little worm program. I hope she's all right... maybe they didn't get her...*

He hoped, but did not believe.

D aniels returned to his office to find O'Connor waiting in his chair, smoking one of his cigars. He was tempted to shoot him, but knowing O'Connor, he probably already had a gun pointed at him under the desk. If he said anything, it would just egg him on.

"You have one of my cigars. May I at least sit in my own chair?" Daniels asked in as tired and bored a tone as he could muster.

"Sure, Commander. It's a nice chair. Thanks for the cigar, by the way," O'Connor said mockingly, holding it up as he stood and relinquished the chair.

"You're welcome. I hear you have one of your suspects. Who is it?"

"Just another one of your 'kids' again; one James Shaw. We were after him and his sister, but she never showed up at their apartment. But I'm sure we'll have her soon; my men are still waiting for her."

"Have you questioned him yet?"

"I was waiting for you. Thought you might want to be in on it." Dwight always wondered if Daniels was the type to ever get his hands dirty.

"I'll leave that in your capable hands, Captain."

Nope, thought O'Connor.

"Although I hope you aren't going to let your lieutenant do the questioning; he seems a little … unstable," Daniels inquired.

"He's more than a little unstable, Commander; he's a psychopath, certifiable by the most conservative estimates. He'd probably be a serial killer if not in my employ. Your steward mentioned some kind of signal beacon you found?"

"Yes. We found a signal beacon. It was contained in a probe that was apparently sent from below the surface. I can only assume it must be from our rebel."

"Probably, but after finding out about these two there are obviously more people involved than we initially thought. I think someone warned our guy down in the east wing. He wasn't there when we arrived, and had enough time to spring a very successful trap on us," O'Connor begrudgingly conceded.

"Hmm … with his hideout gone, it is likely that he fled outside to escape detection. There aren't many other places in the colony he could go and remain unseen for any significant amount of time, are there?"

"Not really. Doyle has been checking all of the likely spots with a team just to be sure, but you never know. We might have never found him if not for following the good doctor. We have many of the air ducts covered with sensors and mines now, but as tough as that will make it for him to navigate, it still won't make it impossible. So, are we going to move up the timetable?"

"Ah, yes." Daniels shifted in his chair. "The beacon appears to be an older Martian Republic device. We won't be able to break the encryption any time soon, so I don't know exactly whom it signaled. I will probably be able to smooth things over. But in case I cannot, I suggest you call your ship in and hide it behind the next nearest moon. I will monitor the situation to ensure that both of us have adequate warning if anyone approaches intent on investigating."

"Good. I'll notify the *Witch* immediately. What kind of time are we looking at before a boatload of commandos could get here?" O'Connor stood, getting ready to leave.

"Given the closeness of Jupiter's orbit with Mars this year, I'd say ten days at best, but more likely twelve."

"Anything else I should know?"

"Nothing else right now. Let me know what you find out from the kid. I'll let you get to it, Captain." Daniels stood. "Would you like a couple more cigars?"

"No thanks." Dwight took the cigar from his mouth and looked at it. "I've already got a box in my room." He turned and walked out, leaving Daniels to wonder if he meant he brought some with him or he had somehow acquired a box of his.

D aniels watched O'Connor leave and immediately stood to check his humidor in the liquor cabinet to see if anything was missing. Nothing was. *O'Connor was probably just playing more of his mind games,* he thought. Of course, Daniels was playing his own. He told O'Connor it would take at least ten days for a military ship to get here; he lied. The Republic would not likely dispatch a ship from Mars; they would find the nearest vessel and send it here. With really bad luck it might not take more than three days, if a ship was already in the area. Daniels called his steward and had him prepare his ship. It was only a modified freighter, but it was inconspicuous, solid, and reasonably fast. He had hoped to have received his new ship from the Federation by now. He put the base on alert, called communications, and told them to notify him if any ships approached. He withdrew a cigar from his desk drawer, resisted the urge to count how many remained, lit it, and poured himself a glass of black Martian port.

He swiveled his chair 180 degrees and looked out across the airless cracked surface of Europa, pondering his next move.

Katherine was exhausted physically and emotionally. It had taken her four hours to get from her apartment, through the maintenance corridors, and past three sets of cameras. She had gotten this far, but before her lay a six-way intersection, and she had no idea where she was anymore. Her shoulders sank, and she leaned against the wall. She just stared at the problem and let her mind drift off into nothingness. It hurt to think anymore.

Kat was still staring at the corridors when she was startled out of her daze by an unfamiliar sound behind her. She turned and crouched down. Her heart racing, she darted her eyes up and down the dim passageway; nothing. Then she distinctly heard something from the direction of the intersection. There was no mistaking this sound; it was a human voice. She turned back around to look toward the sound, trying to figure out which corridor it was coming from. Unable to ascertain what direction the sound was coming from, she began gradually moving toward the intersection. It was two voices, and they were getting closer.

She was about to look around the left corner when she thought she heard another sound behind her; directly behind her. The hair on the back of her neck barely had time to stand up before she was grabbed from behind and picked up off the floor. She began kicking and tried to scream, but her assailant had his hand over her mouth so tightly that she could taste blood as the inside of her lip started bleeding from being pressed against her teeth. He had one arm around her arms, and she could not move them. She could smell the man's breath as he pulled her further back into the passageway. *This must have been the first sound I heard,* she thought. *They must have known where I was and planned this.* The man pulled her into a dark alcove in the hallway that contained a gauge array. The man put his mouth to her ear and started whispering. Repulsed, she tried to turn away, but his hand forced her head back where it was; her ear beside his mouth.

"You're Katherine Shaw, aren't you?" he demanded. She did not respond and he shook her.

"Aren't you!" he whispered loudly.

"Mmm hmm," was the only sound she could get through her nose. She tried to nod her head.

"Calm down, Katherine. I'm here to help you," he breathed.

She stopped struggling and relaxed for a moment, hoping to lull him into relaxing so she could escape.

"It's me, Constable Askuru." He felt her tense again. "I know, I'm supposed to be dead. I should have been, but I got lucky, and they still think I'm dead. I'm sorry I had to grab you like that, and I'm sorry I'm holding you too tight. But I wasn't sure it was you when I first saw you from behind. And I couldn't let you make any noise or they would have probably killed you and maybe even me while I tried to explain myself. The men you heard coming down the corridor are two of the mercenaries. I was stalking them when I stumbled onto you. Do you understand?"

"Mmm hmm." Katherine relaxed.

"If you still don't believe who I am, there is enough light given off by the gauges to see my face. When I let you go, turn and look at me, okay? I'm going to let you go now. Do not run or make a sound. Understand?"

"Mmm hmm."

He slowly released his grip on her, and she took the first deep breath she'd had in over a minute. As he let go, she readied herself for a fight and thought of just running, but decided if he wasn't the constable, he probably wouldn't have let her go. She turned, expecting to be terrified by the face of a stranger, but wasn't. It *was* Markus! She did not know him well, but he was a good friend of the Blacks. She was so excited to see a friendly face that she threw her arms around him and hugged him around the neck. She let him go after a few seconds and was going to silently mouth "hello" to him, but he held his finger to his lips and shook his head. She nodded, and he winked and smiled. They both relaxed a little. They could hear the two voices down the corridor and still could not tell exactly where they were coming from or where they were going.

After a few very long minutes, they could hear the voices fading. Markus and Kat stood still for what seemed to her an hour after the voices ceased being audible. Markus finally stepped back into the corridor, looking left and right before motioning for her to keep silent and follow. They made their way toward the intersection where she had been originally and continued past it, following the same hallway. They proceeded at a painfully slow pace, and Katherine wondered when they could finally start talking. She had a hundred questions running through her head and was getting antsy not being able to ask them. They deftly made their way around a maintenance camera as Kat began hearing a strange rumbling noise. They continued on in silence, the only sounds being the occasional pipe rattle and the growing rumbling, which was beginning to have a kind of white noise quality to it.

Katherine saw Markus let out a sigh as he walked around the next corner. As she turned the corner she realized why. They were there. She was giddy that it was the same place she was planning on hiding, although she had no idea it was so wonderful! They were beneath the surface of the pond, behind and below the waterfall in the arboretum. The wall on the pond side was a massive polyglass window positioned at a sufficient depth so that it was below the turbulence of the waterfall and gave an undistorted underwater view of the entire pond. She stood in silence for several minutes, gazing into the water and forgetting her previous urge to talk. Markus dropped his pack and stood beside her.

"I picked this place because of its lack of surveillance and the fact that the waterfall has noise canceling properties. But the scenery is a pleasant bonus, isn't it?" Markus explained.

"Yeah ... " Katherine said quietly.

"Constable ... ," she started to ask.

"Please, just Markus," he interrupted.

" ... Markus, how are you, uh, I mean, why ... "

"… Aren't I dead?" he finished her sentence. She nodded.

"It's a long story. The short version is that I was lucky. I happened to be wearing my old armor under my coat, and O'Connor and his lieutenant were apparently afraid of puncturing the colony's structure, so they had their weapons dialed to a lower setting. They thought they killed me, and I believe still think I'm dead. I've been hiding and trying to kill as many of them as I could ever since. I was staying in the old east wing of the colony, but they tracked Matthew there and came after me. I heard they killed him. Is it true?"

"Yes, and Sarah too." Kat's shoulders sank.

"I see," Markus said grimly, then turned and looked into the window for several moments. "I had already picked this place as an alternate hideout before they came after me. I barely escaped. I assume your presence means they came after you too?"

"Yes. They got James and would have gotten me. I don't know if they killed him or took him prisoner. I guess I got lucky too …" She let her voice fade and her head sink. *Yeah, real lucky,* she thought.

"Now is not the time for mourning. We can do that later. Besides, you said yourself you didn't know what they planned to do with him, and if it were me, I would want to question him. So he is probably still alive. What we have to do is figure out if he is, and, if so, if it is possible to get him back."

"Really? You think we can?" Katherine's countenance brightened.

"I don't know if it's plausible. They've most likely taken him to the surface base. But we will try, although I don't know how much good the two of us can do by ourselves."

"Jonas is out there somewhere. He still has his ship and is trying to send a message to the outside," Katherine said nonchalantly.

"He's alive?" Markus was relieved. "I thought they went after him?"

"They did, and they almost killed him. He sent a message to his parents, apparently after they were killed, and we found it. He said his ship, *Manta,* saved him. But I don't think he knows they're gone. He didn't go into detail, but he said he was sending a distress call."

"We should try and find him; he can't stay out there indefinitely. We could use him, but we still need more people," Markus contemplated, shaking his head.

"I think I know someone who can help us."

"Who?" Markus asked, trying not to sound doubtful.

Katherine proceeded to tell Markus how Tyler helped them and how she helped him contact the miners.

Markus was mildly astonished.

"You are quite the young lady, Miss Shaw. Do you have any way of contacting Mr. Tyler?"

"Not anything special, but I'm sure we could think of something," she said hopefully. "What about Jonas? I could send a message pulse and have him meet us somewhere."

"It would probably be intercepted … I'm not sure how to contact him, short of stealing another ship and looking." Markus instantly dismissed the thought.

"I'll do it!" Katherine volunteered.

Now he wished he wouldn't have verbalized his thoughts.

"It was a bad idea. We have no idea where his is, how long it would take to find him, and worse, how long it would take Daniels and O'Connor to find one or both of you."

"I don't care," Katherine argued audaciously. "You said he couldn't stay out there forever. He has limited air and supplies. It's already been seven weeks since he left, and he was only supposed to be gone for six. If we don't find some way to bring him in, he'll have to risk guessing at the best place to sneak in. Please, Markus. I can do this."

She had a point. But Markus was hesitant to put the girl at risk, and, not only that, risk losing his only ally with the potential of contacting more of them.

"Okay, but on one condition."

"Whatever it is, I'll do it," Katherine said giddily.

"I want you to contact this Mr. Tyler of yours first. Find out if he is serious about fighting back and how many men he can muster. The sooner we can do this, the better."

"Sure. But how can we contact him without being seen or getting him captured?"

"I may have an idea by morning. But first, we both need some sleep." He pointed across the room. "You can strip some of the foam insulation off that wall over there for a bed. It works pretty well. We'll get started tomorrow."

"Okay … wait!" Katherine exclaimed. She reached into her pocket and removed a small cylinder.

"Mr. Tyler left this stuck under the table for me after their meeting. I almost forgot about it. Maybe it has a message inside, but it doesn't look like it comes apart," she said, trying to open it.

Markus let her have a go with it before holding his hand out. "Let me see it."

"Sure, I don't think it can be opened. Maybe it's some kind of data module or … how'd you do that!"

Markus had opened it.

"You said Tyler was an engineer. It's a puzzle box, probably homemade. Look, there's a message inside." Markus removed a small piece of paper and handed it to Katherine.

"It says to meet him at the Scotsman's Pub." She looked at the date on her watch to make sure. "Tomorrow night at ten o'clock. That's it."

"That's enough. And not so much that it could be interpreted as anything but harmless. Tyler might be just shrewd enough to be our guy. *You* need to make that meeting."

"How? They've probably got the core set to alert them if any of the cameras detect me."

"Well, short of sticking your face in the beehive by the orchard," Markus smirked, "the next best thing would be to cover it up or somehow … " Markus looked around, spotted something, and looked intently at Katherine.

"What?" she asked suspiciously. "You aren't serious about the bees, are you?" Her eyes grew wide.

Markus chuckled.

"No, I think we can skip the bees this time. Do you have any makeup in that bag of yours?"

"Yes," she answered, still sounding unsure that she wanted to know what the plan was.

"Great, then we have everything we need. I'll see you in..." Markus looked at his watch. "Say six hours? That will put us back on a late night schedule."

Without another word, Markus unfastened his gun belt and lay down on his bedding beside it. Katherine stood there for a few seconds, wondering why he didn't explain the plan. She started to ask, but instead went to work stacking some of the foam insulation from the walls for her own bed. She did not think she would be able to sleep, given the strange surroundings, her worries about James and Jonas, and having to sleep in the same room with a man she barely knew...

She was asleep before she thought to take her shoes off.

THIRTEEN

James stared at the door, rehearsing his story. If he kept repeating the same tale, adding a few more details each time, there was a chance they would believe that was all he knew. He hoped. Regardless, he was still in for a world of hurt. He just hoped they would not cause permanent damage to anything too important. The door opened and a thin man with glasses walked in, followed by O'Connor and the monster that gave him the biggest headache he'd ever had. His face already felt like it had a grapefruit on the left side of it where the rifle struck him.

"I see you're awake, James. If you don't remember me, I am Captain Dwight O'Connor of *The Venutian Witch*. This is my second-in-command, Doyle, and my bodyguard Magnus," O'Connor said formally.

"I trust you're comfortable," O'Connor said sardonically.

James just snorted and glared at him. *So Magnus is the monster's name. It fits,* James thought.

"Not very talkative yet, are we? Magnus." O'Connor motioned for the monster to step forward. "Say hello to our friend."

He walked over, and James leaned back in his chair as the hulk struck him with an open hand on the swollen side of his face, knocking him over in his chair. James thought he was going to lose consciousness again; unfortunately, he did not. Magnus picked him off the ground—chair and all—and set him upright. James could feel blood running down his nose and taste it in his mouth.

"Now that we've all been formally introduced," O'Connor stepped forward and took a chair at the opposite end of the long table, "Perhaps you would be so kind as to tell us exactly what you know about the late Dr. Black and his dealings with the man who's been killing my men. Who is this man, and how you are involved with him? I know this will sound cliché, but we can do this the easy way or the hard way, we *will* make you talk, and all of that. I'm sure you'll tell us how you'll never talk and that we might as well kill you right now, but I prefer to skip all of that and just get right to the fun part."

James stared blankly at O'Connor, not knowing what to say.

"Magnus," O'Connor summoned. "Why don't you and James discuss what we would like him to tell us." O'Connor calmly leaned back in his chair as Magnus again stepped forward.

The next few minutes seemed like hours. James never would have thought striking someone with an open hand could send shockwaves through one's entire body. But when the man doing it weighed every bit of four hundred pounds, was four feet across the shoulders, and had arms the size of a normal man's thighs and hands the size of dinner plates ... In James's humble opinion, it seemed to work pretty well for the guy. James was amazed that, despite the pummeling, he was still conscious. But he knew this was just the beginning, and he would not be able to keep his wits about him for long. *Still,* he thought, *I should probably start showing some signs of giving in ... I don't want them to get too serious.* He did not need to prove how much of a man he was; he needed to survive.

"So, anything you would like to tell us?" O'Connor asked, causing Magnus to stop.

James's response was slurred as his lip was beginning to swell.

"We were just trying to send a message to my best friend." James gagged on the blood running down his throat. "Who was out exploring the ocean when you took over. We knew you left and thought you were going to kill him. We were trying to warn him."

"Well, that's a start. You were mistaken that we were going out to kill him. We were sent on an unrelated errand for Daniels. But we did have a run-in with your friend, and we did kill him."

James knew he didn't, but let his head sink anyway. He let out a groan, which was easy considering that he had been holding one back from the pain he was experiencing. It was enough that he wished he were dead at the moment.

"...As we will do with you, if you don't tell us everything you know." O'Connor nodded to Magnus who leaned over and gratuitously punched James in the stomach.

So that's what it feels like to suffocate, James thought, after finally catching his breath. This guy's going to break my ribs if he hits me like that in the side. I have to keep giving them something every time...

"What about your involvement with the late Mr. Black? We know you and your sister were involved with them."

"Where's my sister?" James weakly demanded.

Magnus punched him in the stomach again. Not as hard as before, but enough to make him gasp for the next ten seconds.

"Answer the question first, James," O'Connor stated flatly.

"Doctor Black helped us send the message to Jonas. He was friends with my parents."

"Is that all?"

"We stayed in contact with him. He always wanted to know if we had heard from Jonas, and vice versa. Where's my sister?" James coughed.

"We have her in the next room over. We haven't started questioning her yet. If you tell us what we need to know, perhaps we could go a little easier on her."

James felt panic begin to consume him. He could not tell if O'Connor was lying or not. "If you hurt her I'll…"

Magnus punched him in the gut, again, knocking the wind out of him. He started choking on his own blood as he gasped for air, causing him to gag.

"You'll do what we tell you to do, James. In case you've forgotten, you are in no position to do anything but sputter," O'Connor said with a hint of venom. He was getting impatient. "Doyle, why don't you go ask Miss Shaw about the nature of their involvement with Doctor Black," O'Connor suggested.

"No!" James spat through the blood in his mouth as Doyle stood to leave.

"Why not? Are you going to tell us anything interesting?"

"Yes," James hesitated. He hoped they would not continue beating him after he gave his speech. He figured they knew Kat worked at the Ice House and that Matthew was up to something other than just sending a message to Jonas. Could he have been involved with the man who was killing the mercenaries? Maybe that's why they killed him… they had not mentioned anything about the encrypted message they sent to Mars. He would tell them that Matthew hinted he was working on some way of getting rid of O'Connor and his crew, but that he never told them what it was. He and Kat were just supposed to keep their eyes and ears open and let him know if they learned anything that seemed important. James then proceeded to "spill his guts" and supposedly tell them everything he knew.

"…Please don't hurt Katherine. She won't tell you anything different." He pleaded at the end.

It must have been enough to satisfy them.

O'Connor stared at James for a moment.

"Thank you for being forthcoming, James." He turned to Magnus. "Take him to the brig."

O'Connor and Doyle left the room. Magnus grabbed James's chair by the back and hauled him down the hallway and into one of the lifts. James could not tell if they went up or down through his mental haze. The lift opened and after a few steps, he could tell they were in the brig. He had never seen it, but it looked different from the other corridors and had a dank smell. Magnus walked passed a security station manned by a bored-looking mercenary and a dozen or more cell doors before dropping him. The chair tipped over, and James hit the floor with a thud. Magnus opened his cell door, turned to pick him up, and set him back down inside the cell.

Magnus pulled out a large knife, and James thought this was it. He had gambled and lost. They had gotten the information they wanted and didn't need him anymore. He jerked his head back as the monster swung the knife at him, cutting restraints around his chest. He then cut his legs loose and lastly his arms. Before James could react, Magnus took hold of the chair and wrenched it from under him, sending James sprawling across the floor. By the time he recovered and turned around, all he saw was the door closing. He breathed a sigh of relief. He made it this far, mostly intact. Now all he could do was wait.

There was a lot of noise on sonar, and it wasn't coming from the usual sounds of mining or mining ships. *Manta's* passive sonar was picking up at least a dozen (probably commandeered) ships running all over the colony, doubtless trying to locate the ship that sent the beacon. They soon began widening their search pattern. He was perched, rather precariously, on a ledge on the canyon wall. *Manta* had partially buried herself in the little bit of silt that had collected there, and was running on minimum power. All he could do was stay put and wait for things to calm down enough that he could try and slip in to dock. *After that,* Jonas thought, *I guess I'll make it up as I go along.*

Manta's wingspan was too large to fit into any of the wet docks on the east wing, and he did not want to risk her being detected and destroyed when they started looking for the source of the beacon. His hope was that he could find a way to stealthily slip in and dock *Manta* on one of the east wing's underside docking hatches. There was a trench that ran alongside the central hub, under the east wing and out past a trough that came relatively close to the canyon. But the trough offered limited cover, given the high position of the colony's sonar emitters, leaving a lot of open space to cross between the canyon and that trench.

Manta monitored the sonar after Jonas fell asleep, intending to wake him if there were any new developments.

O'Connor contacted his ship and instructed the crew to bring the *Witch* from the far side of Jupiter (where she had been hiding in close orbit near Callisto), deploy a few sensors, and hide on the far side of Io, which was currently passing very near Europa. He wanted to send the message sooner, but according to the star charts, she had been too far behind the planet to be able to receive a message until about ten minutes ago.

Chasing leads and rumors around had kept O'Connor from implementing the strategy he and Doyle had planned several days ago. And they had thus far come up empty-handed. O'Connor called Doyle on the com.

"Have you picked anyone up yet?" he asked irritably.

"Yes, some drunk from the red light district."

"When you have everyone, bring them here. We'll start the show tomorrow evening."

"Yes sir," Doyle responded.

O'Connor changed com channels and contacted one of his men who was still searching the ocean around the colony for the source of the beacon probe. His men needed some rest, so he ordered them to split into three groups (two of four and one of three) and started them on an eight-hour rotation for the next twenty-four hours. He kept them rotating back inside the perimeter, but also started them looping out to the ten-mile mark in a random petal pattern too. After that they were to switch to two groups and the usual twelve-hour shifts.

Katherine woke to the smell of coffee brewing. But when she opened her eyes, she froze, and it took her a few seconds to remember where she was and how she had come to be there. She sat up and saw Markus sitting across the room reading a small black book and drinking coffee. She looked at her feet and, seeing her shoes still on, rolled her eyes before standing and going over to the coffee.

"Good evening," Markus said with a hint of amusement.

"Yeah," she said flatly, while quickly pouring some coffee.

"I see you're not a morning person, so to speak." Markus was trying not to smirk.

"Not really." Katherine sighed and sat down on a crate.

"There's some food pellets in the box there. I don't have much of an appetite in the morning myself, so I take a few of those to keep up my energy."

She reached down and picked up a small container.

"Five hundred calories a piece..." Katherine read the box aloud. "A small meal in every pellet. Yummy," she said dryly. She removed one of the vitamin-sized pellets, eyed it skeptically, and swallowed it with some water before going back to her coffee.

"Not bad, eh?" Markus said, chewing another and washing it down with some coffee.

"Tastes like grass." Katherine grimaced, attempting to wash her mouth out with coffee.

"You get used to them. We always had at least a week's worth of food stuck to the inside of our vests when I was in the service. They're fast, nutritious, and keep you alive and up to fighting strength. As a matter of fact, one of my distant ancestors invented the things over three hundred years ago. He was an adventurer who viewed eating as in inconvenient necessity. So he tried to come up with a fast, easy way to get all of his nutrition without actually having to stop and eat. His research led to the early version of these. He eventually marketed them to the military, and then the burgeoning space industry."

"Wow," Kat said wearily. "That's pretty neat, but I don't know why anyone wouldn't like to eat."

"To each his own, I suppose. I, for one, am glad that everyone is so different. It makes the universe a more interesting place."

"I agree."

"Now, about your disguise…" Markus picked up a sticky-looking ball of goop.

"What *is* that stuff?"

"Repair putty. I gleaned it from some of the pipes, sticks to almost anything." Markus smiled, amused at the look on Katherine's face.

"And you're going to stick it to my face…" She regrettably deduced.

"Exactly; it's the only way to change your appearance without drawing too much attention. You can't go gallivanting around in a gas mask or something, can you?"

"No…" Kat sighed.

"All right; we just stick a little of this on your nose, cheeks, and chin, add a little of your makeup to make it look like it belongs there, and presto! The perfect disguise." Markus seemed proud of himself.

Katherine looked at her watch. "We'd better get started."

Markus shaped the putty into various forms, trying to come up with something that did not make her look like she had been in a fight with a wood chipper. He quickly realized why it seemed women always took so long to get ready. The makeup thing was really tricky.

Katherine's face was getting sore from the constant sticking and removing of the putty as Markus tried to make her look like a real person and not a movie monster. She started helping by looking at her reflection in the pond window, and they finally came up with a believable disguise. Markus put the final touches of her makeup on to cover the putty and she took one last look at her reflection. She looked like an older, more ugly, and manly version of herself. But to the untrained eye, she didn't look anything like Katherine Shaw.

"I think we've done it, Markus," Katherine said, trying not to smile so she didn't mess up her fake cheeks.

"You look great, so to speak," Markus said, smiling and raising an eyebrow.

"Don't make me laugh. I don't want to mess it up." Katherine's eyes scolded.

"Sorry." He suppressed a chuckle and checked his watch. "We need to go."

Katherine quickly put her hair up in a manner atypical for her to complete her disguise, and they were off.

It was five minutes after ten when Katherine walked into the Scotsman's Pub. The place was a popular hangout for middle-class business types, but it pretty much ran the gambit on people. She was trying not to sweat, knowing it could potentially ruin her facial camouflage. She saw Mr. Tyler on her second pass around the room. She walked over, sat down, and smiled.

"Sorry ma'am, that seat's taken," Mr. Tyler politely stated.

"I know." Katherine leaned forward and looked Tyler in the eyes. "You're saving it for me."

He stared at her with a befuddled look for a few seconds before his eyes quickly grew wide and he started to speak.

"Quietly, no names." Katherine hushed. "They got James, and they're after me."

"Sorry, Kitty, I hadn't seen you in so long I didn't recognize you! Where have you been? You still working at the warehouse?" Mr. Tyler greeted warmly.

"Yeah, still working at the warehouse. I've been staying with an old friend. You?" Katherine stuttered.

"Same old routine. You want a drink?"

"Sure!" Katherine didn't drink, but thought she should be agreeable and keep up the pretense.

Tyler keyed in an order on the table terminal and they continued small talk until the drink arrived, a plain cappuccino.

"Now to business," Tyler said, smiling. "I have twenty good men willing to do anything, and another thirty that will join in when the fighting actually starts. But, we only have decent weapons for about half of them. I have a few fellows working on some makeshift surprises, but we need more guns if we're going to have half a chance…now laugh." Tyler laughed loudly and slapped the table.

Katherine laughed as best she could when there was nothing to laugh at.

"So, who is it you've been staying with?" Tyler asked.

"Let's just say he doesn't usually like guests and isn't afraid to show it." Katherine smiled and made a little exploding gesture on the table with her hands.

"Ah, I see." Tyler smiled deviously, and thought for a second. "It has to be my old friend Jingo," he said loudly. "I'm right, aren't I? Does Jingo want to help me with my roach problem? I assume he's had experience with such things."

"He used to be an exterminator. And don't tell him I told you this." Katherine winked. "But he's actually afraid of spiders!" Katherine laughed. Tyler laughed too. *I'm getting good at this,* Katherine thought.

"He doesn't have any bug spray," Kat continued. "But I'll tell him about your problem, and I'm sure he can figure out a way to get some."

"That would be great. I have a few things lying around, but nothing that works really well," Tyler quieted his tone a little. "How soon can he come get rid of them?"

"I'm sure after I tell him he can get something together pretty quick, he could use the money. Is there any way I can have him call you to work out the details?"

"Not at the moment, my terminal is acting up. But how about you and him meeting me for drinks again tomorrow? Same place, say around nine?"

"Works for me." Katherine finished her cappuccino. "But Jingo's still a little shy about getting out. You remember the last time he drank too much? He thought everyone was looking at him funny and started a fight."

"Oh, right. Mean drunk. I almost forgot. Well, I'll be working late at the shop tomorrow night if he'd prefer to stop by there. If I don't hear from him, I'll just meet you here again," Tyler suggested.

"Sounds good; it was good seeing you again, Tyler." Katherine stood.

"You too, Kitty." Tyler stood.

Katherine gave him a quick hug and walked out of the pub. She casually walked into a blind corridor, where an intake vent popped open. She quickly ducked inside, and the vent closed again. Markus secured the vent, and they made their way back to the hideout in silence.

They arrived back at the waterfall room without incident. Katherine sat down on a crate and let out a sigh.

"Can we take this stuff off now? It's itchy," asked Kat.

"Sure. What did Tyler say?"

Katherine began pulling the putty off her face while trying to maintain the shape of the pieces in case they had to use them again.

"He said he has twenty good men, and another thirty that will join in when the fighting starts. But he said he only has weapons for half of them. Oh, he said he was working on some surprises too … whatever that meant."

"Good. You didn't tell him about me, did you?" Markus inquired.

"No!" Katherine responded with feigned insult. "I simply said I was staying with a friend who didn't like uninvited guests and did this." She made the exploding sign with her hands. "But Tyler did come up with a cute name for you."

"I can't wait to hear it," Markus said dryly.

"Jingo. Does it mean anything?"

"Hmph." Markus snorted. "It's a really old word, not used for a long time. It means 'patriot,' sort of. I think Tyler is smarter than he's led people to believe. Modesty is a rare quality." Markus sat on a crate across from Katherine and thought for a moment as she winced from pulling off her fake face.

"Oww!" Kat exclaimed, as she had to remove a particularly disagreeable piece of putty from her face. "The bees sound good about now … Oh, yeah. He said he wanted to meet you. I told him I didn't know if you were willing, but he said if you wanted to, he would be in his shop late tomorrow. If you didn't show, he'd meet me back at the Scotsman at nine."

"All right. Do you know where his shop is so I can see if we can access it?"

"Yes. But I have no idea how to get to it using the vents." Katherine shook her head.

"No matter. Just give me the address and I can figure it out. I'll start early so I'll be sure to make it on time. I have a project for you while I'm gone."

"But I want to go too," she protested.

"Well, you can't," Markus ordered. "It's dangerous enough for me to move around new areas by myself. I don't want to put you at risk unless it's necessary. And since you obviously didn't know, there are Viper mines in the tunnels now, courtesy of our guests."

"What's a Viper mine?"

"A semi-intelligent robotic gun turret." Markus uncovered the mine he'd taken and set it in front of Kat. "This will continue to fire on a target until its tiny little brain thinks the threat has been neutralized. You're lucky you didn't run into one wandering around up here."

"Oh." Katherine eyed the little machine curiously.

"What I need you to do is monitor all of the security cameras in the docks, so we can figure out which ship you are going to steal."

"Really?" Katherine's eyes brightened.

"Really; I'll pull them up on the view screen in the morning. You need to monitor their activity and pick the fastest ships that are the least guarded, preferably one that isn't guarded at all. If I can make contact with Tyler, there will be no need for you to meet him at nine."

"Okay. Can we start now?" Kat stood and started toward the monitoring console.

"It will take thirty minutes or so for me to reroute the functions somewhere else so we can use it like a regular terminal. Why don't you get something to eat in the meantime?" Markus gestured toward the food pellets. Katherine grimaced and opted to rummage around in Markus's rucksack for something else.

Markus went to work on moving all the monitoring sensors and gauges off the main screens so he could route terminal functions to the station. The tricky part was doing it without setting off the watchdog programs that ensured the safe function of the water circulatory system. Their upset would set off safety alarms, ensuring a swarm of technicians, probably accompanied by mercenaries, milling around their hideout.

M arkus scouted the ducts and corridors surrounding Tyler's shop before settling down to watch through one of the vents. He had not seen anything that led him to believe it was a trap. He had placed several motion sensors in the area to alert him if anyone approached. He waited until everyone left the shop except Tyler, who was still working fervently. Markus had been around enough to know when a man was actually working or just trying to look busy. He waited until Tyler fired up a grinder and had his back turned before opening a vent and entering the shop. He walked silently to within six feet of the man and waited.

Tyler shut off the grinder and ran his gloved hand over the spot he had just smoothed over. It was good enough, which in his mind meant it couldn't reasonably be any better. All he had to do now was coat the metal with some anti-corrosion paint that they had to put on everything around here and it would be fit for service. He was about to turn and set the grinder down when the hair on the back of his neck stood up. He was being watched. If someone was there, he must have been waiting for him to start making noise before sneaking up on him. And a person usually did not sneak up on another with good intentions. He casually put his thumb back on the grinder's trigger and spun around, ready to fight whoever it was. It was worse than he thought! It was a ghost!

Tyler involuntarily gasped as Markus came into view, turned three shades lighter, and dropped the grinder.

"Askuru?" Tyler said in disbelief. "But you're…"

"No, I'm quite alive, I assure you."

"You're, uh…" Tyler regained some of his composure. "Jingo?"

"I guess so." Markus smiled, took a step closer, and put out his hand.

Tyler hesitated, then stepped forward, took Markus's hand (not entirely sure his own would not pass through), and shook it.

"Of course," Tyler started smiling and shaking Markus's hand vigorously. "It makes sense now! You're one of the only people around here who probably had experience with all of this kind of thing. I heard rumors that you worked in the SS or something a long time ago. I didn't believe it, but it's true, isn't it?"

"Yeah, something like that," Markus answered flatly.

"I was in the Federation Army for twenty years. The 304th drop unit. 'The Angels of Death,' they called us. That was a long time ago, though. I'm seventy-six now. Seems like a lifetime ago…" Tyler's eyes went cloudy, and he sighed. "But none of that matters now. What are we going to do to get rid of the pirates?"

"First off, do you still have any loyalty to the Federation?" Markus asked.

"I don't have anything against them. Earth was my home before I came here, and I still love it. But I have to admit the reason I ended up here was to get away from the high taxes, regulations, and such. I suppose I don't really care for the Federation or the Republic any more or less than the other. Why?"

"Because…" Markus took a breath, not sure how Tyler might react. "I believe Daniels and O'Connor are working for the Federation…"

"What! How?" Tyler asked with amazement.

"I'm not sure what the Federation could stand to gain from all this. They can't hope to make much of a profit from this operation before they're discovered. But whatever it is, it can't be good for us or the Republic. They're using pirates and mercenaries instead of soldiers; my guess is to keep Federation ties to a minimum."

"Well, I suppose it doesn't really surprise me. Greed can work terrible wonders in people, whether it's greed for money, power, or whatever else you can think of. The elites in the Federation have tried to keep complete control of everything for the last two hundred years, and the first time they ever really lost anything was when they lost Mars. I think it's eating them up inside, the thought that they don't have power over something. If they're willing to do something like this, regardless of their reasoning, I'll be glad to give them a bloody nose. Besides, we're really just ridding the galaxy of some lousy pirates. What do we do first?"

"First, we need to get your men armed. You told Katherine you had about half as many guns as men?"

"Yes sir. And only about fifteen out of those first twenty actually have any kind of weapons training. Probably only five or six have combat experience. The other thirty claim to be able to shoot, and I just hope that's good enough."

"It has to be. Let's arm the ones with training and experience with the best of what we've got, then finish arming the rest of your first twenty men. We'll do what we can from there. I've managed to acquire an extra pistol and two rifles; you can have those as well. And I have a Viper mine, too."

"Well." Tyler smiled. "You have been busy. Let me show you what I've been working on for the men who won't have guns."

Tyler walked over to the corner of his shop and Markus followed, still wary of his surroundings. Tyler hunkered down, opened a floor panel, and removed a metal box. He opened the box and Markus could see what looked like homemade grenades. Tyler removed one of the golf ball-sized spheres and tossed it to Markus.

"Not bad, eh?" Tyler asked.

"What kind of fuse?" Markus inquired.

"It's a Martian-style standard frag fuse. It's been pre-set to three seconds, to keep the men from messing with them. I had to use a homemade mixture of plastic, which seems to have a fast enough burn rate to deliver a good blast. What do you think?"

"They look good. You formed ball bearings around the core and coated them with something to hold them together?"

"Yep, should work well enough. I made them a little smaller than normal, so they wouldn't have such a powerful blast and coated them with clear resin to hold them together."

Markus and Tyler spoke for several more hours, setting rally points and working out the details of when, how, and where they would make their move. Markus was putting a lot of trust in this man he had only just met, but that was a necessity in guerilla warfare. Still, you never showed anyone all your cards. The conversation was wrapping up, and they had arranged a drop point for Markus to leave the weapons he had taken from the mercenaries. Tyler gave him a few grenades and went back to the floor panel to deposit the rest of them. The clang of the floor panel was the perfect cover sound for the light rattle of the ventilation grate.

Tyler turned around and Markus had disappeared as stealthily as he had arrived. Tyler let out a slight chuckle, turned off some of the shop equipment, and went home for the night. *It has been a good day,* he thought. *There is still hope for people who refuse to give up freedom. Maybe I'm not so impartial to the Martians after all…*

Katherine had spent all day glued to the multi-screen control panel watching the docks. An hour ago, about eight hours after a few other crews had arrived, three others boarded their ships and left. About fifteen minutes after that, four other ships arrived and offloaded. *It is strange behavior,* Katherine thought, *because the pirates and mercenaries usually work twelve-hour shifts. It is also odd that they would have that many ships out at one time; they have not had any kind of outside patrols before. Why start now? Unless they're searching for Jonas,* she reasoned. *He must have sent his message!*

That presented another problem, though. If they were looking for him, then she would have a much tougher time finding him.

Katherine was lost in deep thought when the slightest noise brought her to the surface with a start. She could feel the hair on the back of her neck stand up and, without moving, she scanned the immediate area for some kind of weapon; there were none. Her heart was pumping furiously and felt like it moved to her throat. She decided confront her fear rather than keep her back to it and hope it would go away. Besides, she tried to convince herself, it might be nothing anyway, right? Katherine turned to face the phantom, pirate, or whatever other horror she was trying not to think of just as Markus stepped around the corner. Kat rolled her eyes and exhaled in relief.

"Taking a break?" asked Markus.

"Yeah, I guess," Kat responded, shaking off the adrenaline. "How'd your meeting go?"

"It went well. So far, my good suspicions about Tyler have been right and the bad ones wrong."

"So." Kat leaned forward in her chair. "Do we have a revolution or what?"

"We're planning one. Whether or not it succeeds is another thing entirely."

"Great!" Katherine stood up and moved toward the tiny pack stove Markus had sitting on a crate. "How about dinner? I'm starving."

"I thought you didn't like food pellets?"

"Oh, no pellets tonight." Kat smiled. "I found an MRE buried in the bottom of your rucksack." Markus raised an eyebrow. "I know, I know, I shouldn't have been snooping around your stuff. But I was so sick of those pellets after lunch that I had to see if there was anything else around. I thought if there was, it would be in your pack," Katherine said, shaking the small black bag.

"How does spaghetti sound?" She asked, hoping to assuage the irritation on Markus face.

Markus was really glad he was not married. *It must be a lot of work,* he thought. *I much prefer to not have to worry about keeping someone happy and remain a grouchy old man.*

"Sure, Katherine," he said with a sigh of resignation. "Spaghetti sounds great."

Kat's smile widened, and she filled a pot with water from one of the irrigation pipes and put it on the pack stove.

"What did you learn about the ships?" Markus asked, sitting himself on a crate in front of the stove.

"I narrowed the possibilities down to three ships that give me the best chance of taking one without raising the alarm." Kat pulled the locations up on her handheld and showed them to Markus.

"Good, that's what we want. The old east wing is the only place to safely dock and not have *Manta* discovered. There's a maintenance port right here." Markus gave Katherine the schematic. "If you can find him, I can meet you there and we can make our way back here. There's only room for one ship to dock at a time. So, even though I hate the idea, the best thing to do is couple the ships, you transfer to *Manta*. Then send the other on a loud and distracting excursion in the opposite direction. Understand?" Markus said gravely. "I'll take you to your drop point and leave you there." Markus could see Katherine stiffen.

He explained, "So I can make it to the dock in time to meet you two there and guide you back through the mines. Okay?"

"Okay." Kat relaxed a little. "How long do I wait before I go?"

"You'll wait four hours. After that, take your time and move when you're ready, all right?"

Katherine nodded.

"There is no hurry. You only get one chance," Markus emphasized. "Wait for the best opportunity, and take it. Don't balk, *move.*" Markus's features hardened. "Sometimes you have to stop and think things through before you act; sometimes you have to act and don't have time to think. Experience teaches you when to do which. When you make a decision, stick to it. Be flexible. You may need to adjust your plan in mid-stride, but do not cease to move forward with your plan of action. Hesitation is death. Do you understand?"

"Yeah." Katherine said, wide-eyed and motionless.

"The water's boiling." Markus interrupted the mood.

"Oh!" She snapped out of it and refocused on her task.

"That's how you must focus in combat, Katherine. Be aware of your surroundings, but don't be so distracted by them that you cannot accomplish your task. I know it's a lot to try and learn in such a short time, but we don't really have a choice."

"I know." Katherine sighed as she carefully poured the boiling water into the expanding bag of freeze-dried spaghetti. "Anything else I need to know?"

"Yes, a lot. But that's enough for now. Besides, the smell of that spaghetti's making me hungry. Do you know how to shoot?"

"Sort of…Jonas and James were always trying to get me to play war simulations with them. But they were really gory, and I never liked them much."

"It's a good start. I'm giving a few weapons to Tyler, but I'm saving two spare pistols: one for you, and one as a backup for myself. I'll teach you some of the basics after dinner."

"All right," she said with zest. "I was a pretty good shot in the simulator." Kat handed him a large plate of spaghetti.

Markus chuckled. "We'll see."

Markus knew when Matthew only gave him one of his two prized pistols that he must have heeded his advice and sent the other with Jonas.

Jonas had slept for twelve hours when he awoke to the creaking and rumbling of ice thunder. He went aft to get a food pellet and his second-to-last instant coffee packet. He was running low on supplies. He went back to the bridge and checked the sonar. There were fewer ships, but they were expanding their search pattern and were nearly on top of him.

Jonas quietly typed on the keyboard and asked Manta if turning off the heat would help reduce their thermal signature. She said only by a tenth of a percent. Jonas did not want to tarry. However, he knew if they had already reduced the number of ships searching for him, they would probably reduce that number further within a day or two. So, he loaded a copy of *The Count of Monte Cristo* onto his handheld, set a fireplace simulation on the screen next to the sonar, and settled down to read.

Three of O'Connor's men walked the nameless drunk to the central hub. He was still smashed and had no inkling of what was going on. His only objections were his offensive effluvium and the fact they were keeping him from important business. Another twenty of the pirates had formed a defensive circle in the center. Passersby looked on curiously but did not really take note. The three men brought the man to the center of the circle. They had not been there for more than ten seconds when there was a speaker reverberation throughout the entire colony.

"Citizens of Europa." O'Connor's voice rang through the emergency notification system. "Several of my men have been murdered by an unknown assassin. Attempts to catch this man have been thwarted by assistance from other citizens. If this man or anyone who knows him is listening, *you* are responsible for this." Every terminal in the colony, public and private, was filled with an image of the group of pirates standing around the man in central hub. The picture zoomed in on the unknown man. The pirate standing behind the man raised his rifle and shot the man in the head. There were screams from several surrounding citizens and then silence.

"This man had no family and probably no friends." O'Connor stated coldly. "The next person will be someone you know. We have already taken eleven people hostage. If someone you know was taken or is missing, now you know what fate awaits them. One person will die every day at the same time and place until someone turns in the person or people responsible for the death of my men." The screens went blank.

All the pirates in the hub withdrew, leaving the dead man where he lay.

"Well." O'Connor exhaled, turning away from his office terminal and looking across the desk at Doyle. "Now we see what happens."

Katherine's face was white as she stared at the terminal screen. It too had switched to the execution, like all the other terminals in the colony, and had since resumed its previous function. Markus and Kat had moved to the screen when O'Connor's voice had come over the speakers. Markus turned, walked back to his seat, sat down, and sighed. Then he picked up his plate and began finishing his spaghetti as Kat looked on in disbelief.

"I guess you're used to it?" She said with a tone of both confusion and anger.

"Nope; you never get used to it. You just focus on what you're doing at the moment and do it. Right now I'm focusing on eating a nice dinner. You should too. You need to keep up your strength," Markus answered without looking up.

"Fine." She stood up and marched over to her plate. She sat down to eat, despite feeling sick to her stomach. She ate about half as much as she was capable of and put down her plate, just as Markus was finishing his.

"I don't understand how you can eat after seeing that. Don't you feel anything?" Katherine asked angrily.

"You ate after seeing that." Markus cast a glance at her plate.

Katherine just gave him a haughty look, stood up in a huff, and stomped back over to the terminal.

Markus shook his head and laughed to himself. He let her cool off for a while, busying himself cleaning his weapon and the one he was going to teach Katherine to use. He set up a target down the corridor and dialed her weapon down to a setting of about three hundred feet per second. The lesson went well; she did have some skill, but she needed practice. They would get plenty over the next two days, while they waited for the patrols to thin out and for the work of Tyler's false rendezvous points to flag any potential traitors.

Markus taught Katherine how to break down, clean, and service her weapon. He taught her the basic rules of cover and concealment, and the difference between the two. He told her stories of his battles, his victories, and his mistakes.

In the meantime one more person was executed, just as O'Connor had said they would be. The latest one: a waitress at one of the miner's favorite watering holes. She did not have any family, but was well known. Her death sent ripples of anger and hatred through the miners. Still, everyone did nothing. O'Connor then went for effect by announcing who would be killed next. The third victim was to be a man who was married and had three children.

T hat same evening, Tyler waited at the dead end of a maintenance tunnel for about five minutes before being startled by Markus's hand on his shoulder.

"Sheez, Markus!" Tyler turned and whispered loudly. "Don't do that!"

"Sorry."

"Why the meeting? It's the executions, isn't it?" Tyler answered his own question.

"Yes. We can't let this continue any longer than absolutely necessary. We have to get the men together and set a day soon."

"I agree, but I still need at least two more days. Maybe three or four to get all of the locations, weapons, and plans to the men. And besides, I don't think it's been long enough for your fake rendezvous points to leak." Markus handed him a piece of paper with two names on it. "Oh, I guess they have."

"I'd like to start sooner, but I know how long these things take to put together. Let's make it three days," Markus urged. Tyler gave him a grim look.

"I know, three more executions. But we have to make sure we

give ourselves the best chance of succeeding, otherwise there will be a lot more than three executions."

"You're right, of course. Let's make if four," Tyler conceded. "I guess I've forgotten war is a nasty business. No matter how you play it, people are going to die. All you can do is try to make it so you lose as few of yours as possible."

"Agreed," Markus responded resolutely. "Let's plan on meeting at the assembly point with your squad leaders one hour before the execution in four days."

"If something changes, send word, and I'll do the same."

"Agreed." Markus nodded and disappeared around a corner.

Tyler looked at the names of two of his men Markus had written on the paper, took out his mini-torch, and burned it. He had hoped Markus's plan would not uncover any spies in his group, thus saving him from a difficult decision. Should he simply exclude those men from further information? Even if he did that, some of the other men might not be inclined to believe one of their own was a traitor and may tell him what was going on anyway. Or if they did not, and the traitors realized they were no longer in the loop, they would know something was going on and tell their contact. Either way, the enemy would be alerted, and surprise was one on a short list of very small advantages they had at the moment.

Tyler sighed, keyed his com, and began making his way back to the shop. He called one of his best friends, whom he had also designated as a squad leader, and asked him to meet him at the shop to help with a repair. The other knew that meant there was business to discuss under the cover of shop racket.

FOURTEEN

Katherine could hit a moving target from twenty yards with three quick shots, and she could put a full magazine in a ten-inch group on the target at twenty-five yards. She was good for the average person who knew how to shoot; *really* good for an amateur. Markus taught her all he could in the last day and a half. He just wished she had more time.

But there was not. They picked her ship thirty minutes ago and were nearly ready to leave. Markus had a knot in his stomach, because he knew how dangerous this was for her. If he could, he would steal the ship and find Jonas himself, but he could not. He had to clear a path, cover them when they arrived, and get to the east wing to get the water pumped out of there before she found him and they docked.

Kat took one last look at her data pad after she shouldered her backpack. Markus had laid out her primary route in green, marked several alternate routes in yellow, and put multiple pathways in red that he had confirmed hostile. She had watched the patrols dwindle over the last thirty-six hours. With Markus's help she began to see signs of the crews beginning to become nonchalant and bored with their routine.

Regarding the executions, Markus explained to Katherine the cost of war and that while it was essential to do the right thing; it was often necessary to do it at the right time. He said, "Even in a fight you have ultimately won you may still have to suffer a bloody nose and put up with the humiliation of a black eye."

"I'm ready." Katherine looked at the time on her data pad.

"Remember; never panic. A cool head is often the only difference between victory and defeat." Markus checked his watch. "We're out of time. Go." Markus nodded and they departed in opposite directions.

Markus estimated that it would take him almost four hours to get back to the old east wing, *if* they had not planted any new surprises. Markus feared the large power draw needed to pump the water out of it might attract unwanted attention. That was why he wanted to roughly time it to Katherine's heist. Hopefully if either of their actions were noticed, he would draw attention away from her, or she from him.

Katherine reached her target destination in just under two hours. She quietly moved up to the ventilation grate. There were some steel crates sitting in a short row about five feet in front of her, offering a bit of cover, but not high enough to block her view. All she could do now was wait and hope that the pirates held to their current shift schedule. If so, shift change was in just under two hours.

Markus inadvertently came across a Viper mine from behind and was able to switch it off, much to his relief. He deduced that the direction he had come from was the direction the pirates would come to check the status of their trap. So he first broke out the only two lights that dimly lit the passageway and gingerly picked up the mine, then turned it one hundred and eighty degrees. As he stepped around the corner to continue on to his destination, he could not help but grin to himself in the darkness.

He reached the pressure door to the east wing and checked the timer on his data pad. Katherine had made, or was just about to make, her move for the ship. Markus felt a slight pang of guilt at having sent the girl on such a dangerous mission. He knew he should not; he had sent troops into battle who were only months older than her. The difference was that they were soldiers; she was not. He fixed his mind on the control panel ten feet to the left of the door. It was the junction panel from the central computer to the east wing: the only place to reinitiate the safety protocols he had previously disabled in order to pump the water out of the wing.

D uring the long wait, Katherine busied herself by trying to keep her feet from falling asleep in the cramped airshaft, and with the immensely tedious task of slowly loosening the clamps that held the intake vent grid in place. Once she dropped her pliers and barely caught them before they hit the floor. Their clanging would have brought the guards straight to her. Katherine's adrenaline began to surge as she saw one of the two guards look at his watch, say something to the other, and motion with his head toward the door. It was shift change. She drew her pistol and readied herself to move.

She watched as the two guards left the dock, the pressure door closing behind them. A firm push on the ventilation grate freed it with a slight groan from its hinges. Katherine extruded her head from the opening and took a quick look around before she completely emerged from her hiding place. She quickly placed the grid back into place and lightly secured it before running for the ship. She opened the hatch, threw herself through it, and closed it behind her. Not pausing to catch her breath, she rapidly walked to the pilot's seat and began the startup sequence.

The ship was already on standby, which greatly increased

her odds of success. Within thirty seconds the main drives were online and she had begun to submerge. She watched the pressure door, anxiously hoping the guards did not return until the ship was below the surface and they could no longer see it or its tell-tale ripples. As the cockpit of the ship dipped below the surface, she could not know whether or not they would see her leaving. She held her breath as she engaged the sonar and eased out of the dock.

Katherine cleared the innermost mining operations and made her way toward one of the more remote ones. She was to time her transmission with Markus's initiation of the east wing's purge. Given the depth capabilities of *Manta*, it was most likely he would hide somewhere in the southern trench. Unfortunately, she was still four miles from it and her time was up.

She inserted a data cube and sent an encrypted message that only *Manta* could decipher. The pirates could detect it, but it would take them a while to find its source.

"Come on, answer," she said aloud, her knee involuntarily bouncing up and down. She repeated the message again; nothing.

*M*anta sat silently on a shelf on the north wall of the southern trench when she began receiving a broken transmission and decided to wake Jonas.

"Captain?" She waited for him to stir and raised the volume on her voice to get his attention. "There is an incoming message for you from Katherine Shaw using my encryption code. Her voice pattern indicates she is in distress."

"Katherine?" Jonas said with tired disbelief. "Let me hear it."

Static. "…Katherine. I'm in a ship four miles north of the southern trench at the Hobart mine…link ships…and transfer to *Manta* so we can dock and meet Markus at the…the colony…we have to be in one ship…Jonas?…there?"

The transmission was cluttered, but he got the gist of it.

"Manta, get the reactor to full power," Jonas ordered. "Load the last two probes, set them to match our sonar signature and power. Set one to go north and the other to go south of whatever position they're fired from."

"Yes, Captain. Shall I open a channel to Miss Shaw on the same encryption code?"

"Yes. Dust yourself off and let's go."

Manta was still powering up to full capacity, which would only take a couple more minutes. In the meantime, she began sending ripples through her skin, causing her to smoothly lift from her resting place and send clouds of silt billowing up in every direction.

"Probes are programmed and loaded, Captain. Full power ... now," she stated coolly.

Jonas did not answer, but gunned the throttle and headed straight up for the edge of the canyon.

"M, can you trace the transmission when we reach the top of the canyon? So we know what ship she's in?"

"Negative, Captain. I can only determine the direction from which it came."

"Good enough."

Manta shot out of the canyon, banked, and leveled off, heading in the direction of the Hobart mine.

"Katherine," Jonas yelled into his mic. "Are you there?"

"Jonas?" Kat answered hopefully.

"It's me; I'm heading your way. How will I know what ship you're in?"

"Uh ... " She hadn't thought of that. "I'll vent some atmosphere when you get close. I can see you on sonar. Hurry, the patrols were north of the colony. But I'm guessing they started heading this way after I started transmitting." She began moving toward him to close the distance.

"Great! What are you doing out here, Kat?" Jonas asked with exasperation.

"When we got your message we thought you might need help getting back to the colony. We weren't actually going to try anything until James was taken by the pirates and I escaped and found Markus," she said hurriedly.

"What?" Jonas asked. "No, forget it. We don't have time for this now, Kat. Start venting atmosphere. Manta, fire the first probe."

"Yes, Captain," she replied. The probe launched a second later.

"Captain, there are three ships approaching from the north. At current speed, the first will intercept in eleven minutes."

"Understood, Manta. Alter the first probe to go west by northwest. You hear that, Katherine?"

"Yes, I'm venting air, and my engines are shut down. Hurry."

"I see you. Extend your docking coupler. And orient your ship nose up; it will make it easier to dock when I get there." Jonas reached over, flipped the switch, and opened *Manta*'s outer door. "Manta, can you establish a remote link with Katherine's ship?"

"Not unless she disengages its safety protocols, Captain."

"Kat ... ?"

"Already on it ... "

"Good. Starting link up maneuver now."

"Incoming ships are ten minutes out, Captain. However, the first appears to be altering course to intercept the probe. If it continues on its current course it will no longer lead the other two, and they are twelve minutes out," Manta reported coolly.

"Thanks, M," Jonas replied inattentively.

"Pressure seal established, Captain. Equalizing," Manta stated.

Jonas was already at the air lock, throwing the handle to the open position. The air hissed as the seal broke and the inner door swung open. Water dripped to the floor and Jonas held his breath for an incessant two seconds before the door of the other ship hissed and opened. Katherine came into view not three feet from him, her eyes wide with adrenaline as she cast him a quick look and turned her back to him to close the door to her ship. She crawled across the docking coupler to *Manta*. Katherine was stunned when Jonas put his arms around her and pulled her to him, squeezing her tightly.

"I missed you," Jonas whispered into her ear, as he pressed his cheek to hers.

"I missed you too." She returned the embrace.

Jonas held her for about five seconds; at least, he hoped it was only that long. He wanted to tell her everything that had happened to him and everything he was starting to feel for her. But they had to escape almost certain death first.

Jonas put his hands on Katherine's shoulders and gently pushed her away.

"We have to go."

"I know." She nodded.

He looked into her eyes, gave her shoulders one last squeeze, and turned, quickly running out of the air lock. Kat followed, closing *Manta*'s inner pressure door.

"Manta," Katherine ordered. "Disengage the pressure seal and secure the outer door."

"Yes, Miss Katherine Shaw. And welcome aboard," Manta responded.

"Glad to be here." Kat could hear the seal break and the outer door closing just in time to be thrown to the floor by *Manta*'s sudden acceleration.

"Hang on!" Jonas yelled from the bridge.

"A little late!" Kat yelled.

Katherine made her way to the front and harnessed herself into a chair.

"Go to the old east wing. There's a maintenance dock on the bottom side that has enough open area to accommodate *Manta*'s wings."

"M," Jonas addressed Manta. "Pull up the colony map for Katherine and feed me a course to where she indicates."

"Yes, Captain." The map appeared on the holo-display in front of Kat. "The two trailing ships are now nine minutes out and closing. If you maintain your current course, they will intercept you before you reach the docking point."

"Great!" Jonas said irritably to the blip on the sonar. "Let's head for that ditch to the east. M, program the last probe to follow the southern trench south."

Manta responded affirmatively as Jonas banked right and headed east toward the shallow valley that ran north from the southern trench, nearly to the east wing. He skimmed the floor, leaving a thick cloud of silt in his wake. It would at least give the enemy ships a little bit of fuzz on their sonar screens. The interceptors matched his depth and course as they continued their futile attempt to catch up with him. Jonas abruptly changed course and headed south before diving into the valley. The enemy ships were seven minutes behind them now.

"Manta, fire the last probe. Stop active sonar, take the controls, and spin us one hundred and eighty degrees to face north."

"Yes, Captain. Hold on."

Katherine heard the probe launch and then thought her neck was going to break as she felt *Manta* come about one hundred-eighty degrees. Then her head was slammed into the back of her chair as Manta gunned the throttle.

Manta relinquished the controls and Jonas continued on a northward course, this time not so close to the floor so he would not leave a silt trail in their wake.

"M, can you still hear those ships?" Jonas asked quietly.

"Yes, Captain, they appear to be altering course to follow the false sonar signature on the probe. The ship that went after the first probe appears to be actively pinging, Captain...The first ship is altering course and appears to be heading to our previous position, where we launched the last decoy. The other two ships are coming about and heading this way, and decreasing their depth."

Katherine looked at Jonas.

"I know." He glanced at the sonar. Another fifty-foot decrease in depth and the other ship would reach a sufficient "altitude" to see over the edge of their shallow valley. Jonas was committed; they were in the middle of the hornet's nest with no place to hide. There was no time for *Manta* to bury herself, and he was out of probes and torpedoes. There was nothing left to do but run for it.

"How long before they catch us when we stop, M?"

"Six minutes, Captain. Two for torpedoes."

"Katherine." Jonas kept his eyes glued to the display. "Go aft and get all the food packets I have left and stuff them in my backpack."

"Okay." Katherine started unbuckling herself. "Anything else?"

"Everything else is in there. Hurry, thirty seconds to dock," Jonas urged.

"M?" he paused.

"Yes, Captain?"

"The second we are clear, you close the hatch and take evasive action. Go hide in the trench until I call you, understand?"

"Yes, Captain. But interstellar law forbids an A.I. from … "

"Forget about that right now!" Jonas scolded. "Just do whatever it takes to get away from these guys, okay?"

"Yes, Captain. I will."

He threaded *Manta* through the piling under the new east wing and held tight to the central hub as he brought her up under the old docking coupler on the ventral side of the old east wing. He stalled her out as best he could in the tight space and reversed thrust.

"M, take the controls and dock us. When you reach fifty percent equalization, open the hatch." He had just finished the sentence when there was a sharp jolt.

"Clamps engaged, Captain. Equalization in ten seconds. Good luck. Farewell."

"No … " Jonas pushed back a swell of emotion at the thought of losing his ship, and friend. "Just see you later."

"See you later. Pressure equalized."

Katherine was next to him, and they were up the ladder and into the air lock in less than twenty seconds. They could hear *Manta* closing her inner, then outer doors as they closed theirs and the lock flooded. Jonas knew she was away. He held his ear to the door and listened. Twenty seconds later he heard the gut-wrenching sound of torpedoes passing, then two more, then three more. *Manta* could elude a group of them, but spaced as they were, some of them would eventually catch her. He continued to listen, his stomach tight, barely breathing, for two minutes. He started as the sound of an explosion rang through his head. He pressed his com button and attempted to establish a link. Nothing. She was gone. He turned and looked blankly at Katherine, who already had a tear rolling down her cheek. He stood up feeling numb, pulling her up with him. His grief was interrupted by a harsh yell from a familiar voice.

"Jonas!" It was Markus. He stepped through the door. "I'm glad you two made it." Markus walked up to him, grabbed his hand, and shook it. "But no time for reunions, we have to go. It won't take them long to figure out what we're up to." He started to turn away, when he realized he had misinterpreted Jonas and Katherine's teary-eyed gaze on each other. There was only one thing of importance that could have been lost if both of them were here safely: Jonas's ship.

"Your ship?" Markus asked Jonas. He did not respond. He had the look of a man who just had to shoot his own dog. Markus put his hand on Jonas's shoulder.

"Come on you two, we have to go," he implored. "Jonas, do you have the pistol your father gave you?"

"Yes," Jonas picked up his backpack from the deck Katherine had brought at his behest. Jonas pulled the weapon out, wrapped the holster around his waist, and buckled it. As he did so, he became aware for the first time that Katherine was also wearing a holstered pistol around her waist.

The three headed out at a half jog toward the auxiliary pressure door to the central hub one hundred and fifty yards to the west. They made it through and, knowing the safety protocols were still overridden, Markus closed it behind them. They made their way down the hallway and into one of the maintenance corridors, and moved up a half dozen levels before entering the ventilation system and beginning a meandering course back to the arboretum. They heard the sound of bullets ricocheting through the vents and Markus held up a hand for them to stop. They moved forward slowly and came to a junction. Markus quickly glanced around the corner and then rounded it. He appeared seconds later and motioned for them to follow.

Jonas found the corridor riddled with bullet holes and observed two recently dead mercenaries lying on the floor. Markus was stripping them of their weapons.

"Jonas, grab that mine," Markus ordered. "It's off, but unload it before you shoulder it."

"Got it." Jonas briskly stepped over and unloaded the Viper mine. He already knew how to do so from the war simulation games he and James were always playing. The real thing had a much more substantive feel to it. He adjusted the strap on the mine and slung it over his shoulder. "What happened?" he whispered.

"Just a little turning of the tables, so to speak." Markus winked mischievously. "But we need to keep moving. They'll send a group to check it out when these two don't report in."

They had to pause ten minutes later and wait for a distant patrol to pass by, no doubt headed to the shooting site, but the rest of the journey to the hideout was quiet.

Katherine sighed as she fell into a seated position on a crate. Jonas groaned as he set the mine on the floor. The strap had been digging into his shoulder. Markus passed some food pellets around. Kat rolled her eyes but took one and ate it anyway.

"Jonas." Markus sighed. "In all the commotion Katherine probably didn't get a chance to tell you ..." Katherine shot him a panicked look. Markus didn't want to be so blunt, but there was not a good way to bring up the subject.

"What?" Jonas looked at Katherine.

She opened her mouth, but could not speak.

"Your parents, Jonas. O'Connor killed them." Jonas's face went pale. "Presumably because he somehow found out about your father helping me and the message they sent you. They captured James and tried to take Katherine, because they assumed they were helping too, but she was lucky enough to escape … I'm sorry to have to tell you this way, but there wasn't really a good way to say it."

"How?" Jonas whispered.

Markus hesitated.

"O'Connor and his men torpedoed your home. Katherine told me about the message drone you sent. It must have gotten there shortly after it happened. James, Katherine, and Tyler found it hours later when they went to see your parents. I'm sorry Jonas … your parents …" Markus shook his head. "They were my only friends …"

Tears streamed down Jonas's face as he stood up and walked over to Markus, putting his hand firmly on his shoulder.

"Not any more …" He meant to say he would take their place as his friend, but could not get it out before choking up again.

"Thanks." Markus understood, and inclined his head slightly in acceptance.

Jonas nodded, turned, and slowly walked away.

Katherine looked helplessly at Markus, who threw his head in the direction Jonas had gone, indicating she should follow. She walked up the stairs leading into the adjacent room, which was a half-level higher and had another viewing window into the waterfall pool. Jonas was standing in front of the window, leaning heavily on the sill. She walked up beside him, putting her arm around his waist. Jonas put his arm around her shoulder and they stood there in silence staring into the water for many minutes before Katherine spoke.

She told Jonas about everything that had happened since he had been gone: about the takeover and Markus killing the pirates. She recounted how she escaped the mercenaries, that she did not know whether James was still alive, Mr. Tyler, and their plans for rebellion. She spoke, not giving him the opportunity to respond, so he did not feel he had to.

FIFTEEN

Jonas lay in the darkness on his bedroll, wide awake. He checked his watch for the fiftieth time: eight eleven a.m. They had brought him back to the hideout and told him about his parents, and he had stood listening to Kat for an hour. He looked at his watch when he lay down: five thirty a.m. He had yet to close his eyes. He had lost everything he had known and loved today. *Not Mom and Dad, I guess,* he thought bitterly. *They were killed days ago, but I didn't find out about it until today!* Even though he had planned to go into hiding, he had expected to go home after all of this. Now his ship was gone, they were gone, and he didn't have a home to go back to.

He thought about getting up and making something to eat, but he didn't want to wake up Katherine or Markus. He tried again to sleep, the darkness enveloping him like a visual representation of his suffocating grief. He checked his watch again and fought the urge to drown his grief with hatred for the men that killed his parents and his ship. He knew his father or his mother would not have wanted him to do that. But it was difficult. As his father had told him, " ... anger is an excellent panacea for a broken heart. However, it doesn't heal the hurt; it only covers the feelings of pain and vulnerability with bitterness and hatred. It makes one feel that by hating that person, they have power over them. But hatred begins to take on a life of its own and will consume a person from the inside out."

His father had taught him to not act in anger when fighting, but also not to live his life in anger either. It was not of The Way. A follower of The Light did his best to live at peace with all. However, there was a time for peace, and there was also a time for war. But one never fought for vengeance, only for protection, justice, and freedom. Before the Federation had been formed, the ancient founders of the Great American Republic had understood this, as did the rebels that ultimately won freedom for the Republic of Mars. Liberty was a concept and subject in history that Jonas would not have learned if schooled on a Federation colony.

He knew everything happened for a reason; that if you followed The Way there were no coincidences. And that those who followed were guided along the difficult path. Words Jonas knew were true, but words bring little comfort during grief. Worse, he could not afford the luxury of grieving right now. He tried for what seemed like hours to push back the pain before finally losing consciousness.

Jonas was awakened by the low mumbling of voices and the smell of coffee, which he had not had the luxury of drinking for three days. Opening his eyes and remembering where he was and what had transpired, his heart was instantly heavy again. He turned his head and looked at Katherine, who was sitting about twenty feet away. She was talking with Markus and did not notice Jonas looking at her. In his despair, he had forgotten how much he had begun to miss her while he was gone and the fear he felt when he first heard her message and thought she was in danger. When there was a break in the conversation, she glanced in his direction and noticed him looking at her.

"Hi," she mouthed silently, smiling with her eyes.

He smiled back and winked. Markus saw her talking and looking past him. When she noticed, she blushed slightly. Jonas realized, looking at her then, that he had not lost everything he cared about.

Markus turned to see Jonas sitting up.

"It's about time," Markus said lightly. "I was getting tired of whispering. We didn't think you were ever going to wake up."

Jonas half-grinned politely as he put his boots on and stood up. He walked over to where they were sitting and stood. Katherine handed him a cup of coffee.

"Feeling any better?" Markus asked. He merely wanted to make conversation, but he realized the second he said it that it was a stupid thing to ask.

Not really, Jonas thought. "A little ... " He looked at Kat and held a gaze with her for a long three seconds. Not only did he realize in that brief time how much he enjoyed looking into her big brown eyes, but that he was suddenly so concerned about her worrying about him that he had momentarily forgotten his own pain.

"No, actually I don't." He looked back at Markus. "And I probably won't for a while. I thought I'd lost everything I loved." He turned back to Katherine and looked into her eyes. "But I haven't. Maybe sometimes you can't see what you're missing until everything you had before is gone."

"Character is born of adversity," Markus quietly recited and smiled.

Daniels sighed and fell back into his chair. He had assuaged the captain of the nearest Martian battle cruiser and convinced him that there was no need to investigate. Daniels assured him that the beacon was merely a malfunctioning relic that someone had accidentally set off. The commander probably would not have been convinced if he had not happened to see that the transponder code on the beacon was dated just after the start of the war for independence ... a lucky break. He checked the message indicator on his terminal and found a video communiqué from O'Connor. Daniels smiled when he got to the part about finding and destroying the idiot who had caused him all this grief by sending that stupid beacon. However, his shoulders dropped slightly when O'Connor stated that it was Jonas's ship they had destroyed.

Daniels poured himself a glass of black port, turned away from his desk, and looked out across the gasless horizon into space. He tired of this. Only a couple more weeks; he would have his ship, and he could retire.

Markus watched the two kids, as he referred to them inside his head. Of course Katherine and Jonas would have austere objections to being referred to as "kids." They had, for the last day and a half, been steadily falling head over heels for each other. They were virtually inseparable, and only stopped talking when they slept. It was kind of cute, in a ridiculous sort of way. Markus rolled his eyes, something he had done a lot lately. *I guess I am getting old,* he thought. *That, and I suppose I missed out on the whole "falling in love" thing when I was younger.* He looked at the little black book Matthew had given him. *If I only knew then what I know now... No... It doesn't matter. The past is gone and whatever I've done has been erased, and "is as far as the east is from the west." I am beginning to understand that my past, however horrible, brought me here. I was allowed to live when I should have died and have made it thus far to fulfill a purpose. I'm not sure what that is exactly, but for now, I'm going to try and keep these two alive so they can have a life together. That, and get rid of Daniels and his stinking pirates.*

Jonas and Katherine had gotten quiet, for a change. Markus looked over and saw them looking at the computer terminal. There was another execution taking place. Markus checked his watch.

Right on schedule, he thought with loathing for Daniels and O'Connor. He stood and walked over to see some old bald fat guy Markus thought he should know. Katherine, holding Jonas's hand, looked up at Markus.

"It's Mr. Giovanni." Her eyes teared up.

"He owns a restaurant we used to go to … he's harmless," Jonas looked at Markus pleadingly.

"I know …" Markus whispered, reaching over to turn off the monitor.

Kat and Jonas both looked at him with a surprised and slightly irritated expression.

"Do we really need to watch it? We already know what's going to happen, and there's nothing we can do about it right now." They could all still hear the audio, unfortunately. After the deed was done, O'Connor began to speak.

"Undoubtedly, everyone who is missing a friend or loved one has probably figured out that we have them. The following people are in our custody, and one will be executed every day in the order I announce, starting tomorrow with Alissa Grayson, followed the next day with James Shaw …"

Katherine gasped and squeezed Jonas's hand tightly. None of them heard the remaining names. Now they knew … James was alive, but not for long.

"Is Mr. Tyler going to be ready in time, Markus?" Jonas asked anxiously.

"He should be." Katherine looked at him imploringly. "We'll make sure we're ready, Katherine," Markus assured her.

Markus and Tyler's plan was to strike at the execution in two days, if Tyler and his men were ready. However, their plan did not include making the rescue of the hostage a priority. Now they would have to change that. Markus thought for a while and decided it would be best to come up with his own plan to save the kid using as few resources as possible. He did not want to give Tyler something else to think about or risk contacting him again until the scheduled rendezvous. All he could do now was wait until tomorrow morning and check to see if the "go" signal had been set. If not, he would contact Tyler and tell him they had to go regardless.

Markus had been lost in thought for a long time when he realized Jonas and Katherine were no longer in the room. He walked over to the next room and found them sitting side by side each with an arm around the other, as they often did lately, both talking quietly. He hated to interrupt, but it was necessary.

"Hey," Markus interjected from halfway across the room. The two turned and looked in his direction. Katherine was noticeably pale, even in the low light. "It's going to be up to us to save him ... but I have an idea."

Eric had not thought that when he and his family moved to Europa he would have to fight in another war. But he found himself again in a fight for his home. He was on edge and nervously brushed his blond hair from his perspiring brow as he walked to the signal point. He did not know what the signal meant; yet another way of protecting information. All he knew was that it had to be in place by the specified time. It was a weird one too, as signals went, and absurdly obvious. But, he arrived at the location with time to spare and went to work. He was already a maintenance tech, which was a necessary part of his disguise, but this did not fall into his usual repertoire of duties.

He took his laser cutter and had accomplished his task in about ten minutes. Several other men, who were not operatives, had shown up just as he finished clearing away the brush. He had been instructed to cut down one of the trees in the central hub. It was two feet through, over seventy feet tall, and by all appearances perfectly healthy. He did not know how Tyler had pulled it off, but he had gotten approval from somewhere. Given the inordinate nature of the act, it was either an obvious sign that the insurrection was to take place on schedule, or that it was definitely aborted. One thing was certain; it was not a signal that could be missed.

Markus was relieved to see the go signal had been made. Now all that remained was for Jonas, Katherine, and himself to finish planning their mission. And what a task it was! They had been watching footage of all the previous executions to try and determine the mercenaries' deployment strategy and to see if it was consistent; it *was*, which to Markus meant they could formulate a more precise plan. Unfortunately, concise planning was a double edged-sword. If it went right, it could easily go off casualty-free. But if it went wrong, it held a greater chance for disaster. He silently backed away from an intake vent sixty feet above the central plaza. Markus did not know why Tyler had picked such an overt signal. Maybe he thought such an obvious action would not be interpreted as a signal. *Maybe he has some sort of aversion to trees,* Markus quipped to himself.

As he made his way back to the hideout and went over the finer points of the plan in his head, Markus could feel the pre-mission jitters creeping up on him. It was different when it was just himself; if he lived or died it was his victory or defeat to be celebrated or suffered alone. But again he found himself responsible for the lives of others; apparently it was his lot in life. His mind drifted back to the conversation he and Jonas had a few hours ago.

"Will you?" Markus demanded.

"I guess so. I don't see why not." Jonas balked. "How am I supposed to know what I'll feel five or ten years in the future?"

"That's the point, boy!" Markus returned irritability. "What you *feel* doesn't matter. What you *do* does."

"I know. My dad tried to explain it a hundred times, but I guess I just don't get it." Jonas threw his hands out in front of him.

"You said you changed out there, that you chose to follow The Light from now on, right?"

"Yeah." Jonas sounded confused.

"Will you follow the path only when you feel like it? Is that The Way?"

"No. It doesn't matter what you feel like, you have to do what is right; you have to love The Light."

"Exactly, it's a choice. You choose to do what is right in spite of whatever feelings you may have to the contrary at the time. This is the same. It is a choice. You must choose: I will or I won't. It is as simple as that," Markus stated.

"It seems a little more complicated than that."

"It may be. But the basic principle is the same. And no matter how much you may argue one way or another, with things such as this, you must always come back to the basics. I know I don't know nearly as much about this sort of thing as your father and mother did. I don't know much at all, but I was around them enough to pick up on a few things. While I am not in much of a position to explain to you the finer points of committed relationships, I know how I lived my life, and I can tell you what not to do."

" ... A choice, huh?"

"Yes. You said she's had a 'crush' on you for years. Do you think she never felt like punching you in the nose to get your attention? Or just simply giving up and moving on?"

"I guess not ... "

"No. She chose you. And had you not eventually chosen her, she would have had to make herself move on. Again, a choice. Love is a verb. It is an action, *not* a feeling. I can tell you I love you, punch you in the nose; tell you I love you, punch you in the nose and if I keep doing that over and over again ... " Markus raised an eyebrow, wanting Jonas to finish the thought on his own.

" ... I'm not going to believe you," he said with a hint of uncertainty.

"Exactly, my actions do not match my words. You can tell her you love her all day long, but if you don't behave as if you do, the novelty will wear off, and it will eventually mean nothing."

Jonas blushed slightly, not knowing what to say.

"Yes, I know," Markus interjected, saving Jonas from turning a darker shade of red. "You've known each other for years and been inseparable for the last two and a half days. And that's great. But it's different from real love. Trust me son, I know. Most of my past relationships with women have been mere physical ones. And just like getting a new ship, a new gun, or, I'm ashamed to say, a new coat, there's always a new model coming out. It may not be any better than the one you've got, but it's different. And different is always intriguing. The few relationships I had where I genuinely liked spending time with a particular woman were memorable. But, when you live with someone, eventually you find ways to be bothered by them, and they find ways to be bothered by you. It's inevitable. When that happens, well ... " Markus shrugged. "You simply trade in the old model for a new one."

"I don't want to do that." Jonas sounded as if he were doomed.

"You don't have to." Markus paused. He had no idea where all this was coming from. Matthew had spoken to him a few times about the rare arguments he had had with Sarah. But Matthew always ended his venting by coming full circle and telling Markus what a wonderful woman she was and how much he loved her. Over the years, Markus began to realize Matthew and Sarah did not simply put up with each other out of some misguided obligation. Nor did they ever seem to harbor any lingering bitterness toward each other whenever they had a disagreement. What they had was something Markus had never seen before: true love, the kind you only read about in very old books.

But it was not a "happily ever after" love. *No,* Markus now realized, *true love took work. But in the end, it was worth it.* "Your parents," Markus almost whispered, "chose to love each other. Despite their disagreements and the difficulties they faced. They both chose when they married to love each other for the rest of their lives, and they did."

Markus tone lowered at the sudden thought of his lost friends. "They knew each other better and trusted each other more than I ever did, ever could, with anyone. Examine your motives closely. Don't do this out of loneliness, grief from losing your parents, or because you might die tomorrow. If you make this choice, make it with the full intention of the living with it the rest of your life. Sorry, that sounded kind of morbid." Markus grimaced slightly. "What I'm saying is don't make this decision lightly, Jonas. But once you make it, stick to it, and both of you will be the better for it. It's what your parents would have wanted, and it's what The Book says. And for what it's worth, I think it's about time."

Jonas smiled.

"Thanks, Markus. I think understand. You don't think it's too soon, do you? I mean, we've known each other our whole lives, but this is … different."

Markus held his hands up chest level, palms out.

"Hey, predicting the future is not my area of expertise. But I wouldn't worry too much about her answer." Markus could see the look in the young man's face: excitement clouded by fear.

Markus had, in his recalling the conversation, discovered yet another reason to feel anxious. It had been three hours since he left.

K atherine just sat there with a strange look on her face, a look that seemed to keep changing from a combination of shock or maybe fear to almost happy but on the verge of tears. Jonas's stomach was in such a knot; he thought if this went on for any longer he would be sick. Then she suddenly dropped his hand, which she had been holding, and he felt his face start to go pale and his heart begin to fall into his stomach. But before it could, she threw her arms around him and whispered in his ear …

"Yes, I'll marry you." Her tone implied it had been a ridiculous question.

Jonas breathed a sigh of relief and the beginnings of grief turned into joy.

He whispered into her ear.

"I wasn't sure … I mean when you hesitated, I thought you were going to say no."

She pulled away from him slightly so they were face to face. "Nooo, silly!" She lightly kissed him.

"I was just shocked that you asked so soon. That, and it was the last thing I expected today..."

Jonas could see some of the happiness fade from her eyes as it was replaced by worry.

"I know. My timing is probably lousy." He looked downward.

"No," Katherine said firmly. "It's perfect; well, as perfect as I could hope for, given our circumstances." She smiled and looked around.

"I'm glad." Jonas smiled, but then suddenly looked worried again. "What now?"

"One day at a time. Today's almost over, and we already have plans for tomorrow." She broke their embrace and retook his hand.

Jonas's eyes narrowed and went from dreamy to serious as he donned a devious smile. "First we rescue your brother and get rid of the scum infesting our planet." He gently squeezed her hand. "Then we can think about the future. Oh..." Jonas reached into his pocket and removed something. "It wasn't my first choice, but it's all I could come up with, given our circumstances." He smiled and indicated the room with his eyes. "I guessed on the size." Jonas lifted Katherine's hand, and he slipped an elegant but strange-looking ring on her finger. It was a gold-colored titanium hybrid ring with a narrow black wave running around the center of its circumference. Jonas smiled sheepishly.

"It's a corrosion-proof high pressure coolant valve sleeve... they're almost as expensive as a real ring," Jonas added hopefully.

After the ring was firmly on her finger, Katherine lightly punched him in the shoulder and smiled. "You know better than to think I'd care about that!" She held it up in front of her and looked at him earnestly.

"I love it."

When Markus returned to the room beneath the waterfall, he did not have to ask if Jonas had asked Katherine or what the response had been. They both stopped talking and began smiling absurdly when he walked into the room, both looking as though they would burst with excitement.

Katherine started to speak, but all she could manage was to hold up her hand with the ring on it and say, "Look!"

Markus tried to keep a straight face, but they were contagious, and he could not help but smile and shake his head.

"I'm happy for both of you." He sat down, put some water on the heater, and looked back at them. "Are you two going to be ready for tomorrow?"

Jonas and Katherine looked at each other and at then at Markus.

"We're ready," said Jonas.

"Good." Markus's eyes narrowed. "Tomorrow, we take back what's ours."

Jonas awoke in a cold sweat and looked at his watch: 3:00 a.m. He quietly put on his jacket and shoes and picked up his data pad. As he tiptoed past Markus and Katherine, he turned on his data pad and let the light of the screen fall on Katherine. He looked at her, smiling with his eyes, for a few seconds before stepping around the corner into the next room. He reclined himself on the sill of the window. The room was dim, lit only by the filtered blue rippling light of the sun lamps shining through the surface of the water fifty feet above. His hands were shaking, and he was still gripped with fear as he looked upward at the rippling surface of the water and tried to calm himself. *The dream, no it was a nightmare,* he thought, *was so real.* He had felt her blood running over his hands as he held her and watched her face grow pale. It was undoubtedly a dream about tomorrow, a dream where Katherine died.

Jonas's hands were still shaking when someone gently took one, causing him to tense with surprise. It was Kat. He turned to look at her, and there did not have to be much light for him to see she knew something was wrong.

"What is it?" she whispered.

"I can't lose you tomorrow." He gripped her hand tightly.

"You won't." She stepped close and put her other arm around his shoulder.

He looked into her eyes; they shimmered in the refracting blue light. "Dad taught me to only fight with valor and enthusiasm, without fear, hatred, or anger. I had a dream that you are killed, Kat. The thought had crossed my mind, but I had not dwelt on it. But now, I can't seem to find a way to push back the fear of losing you." He put his arm around her waist.

"Do you think I haven't had to deal with the same thoughts too? After we found out O'Connor had gone after you, I wondered every day whether you would come back. And when they came back I thought..." She faltered.

Jonas looked up at her. Her eyes were getting teary. With difficulty he smiled. Squeezing her, he said, "I guess now I know how it feels."

She half smiled back down at him.

"Yeah, lucky you."

Katherine stood beside Jonas for a few more minutes before kissing him and forcing herself to break away and go to bed.

Jonas sat on the windowsill for thirty minutes more, going over the plans on his data pad two more times. He briefly entertained the thought of tying Katherine up in the morning so she could not go with them. But he could not do that to her. James was her brother and she had more right to be there than anyone. *Besides,* Jonas mused, finally breaking his sadness, *if the pirates didn't kill me, she would when I came back and loosed her.*

SIXTEEN

Daniels looked blankly at O'Connor.

"Are you sure this is necessary?"

"He obviously has a connection with the Shaws and the Blacks. That girl had help when she tried to contact the Black kid, which implies that she knew our assassin. And if she knew him, her brother probably knows him." Daniels turned away slightly and sat in silence.

Daniels sighed and fell against the back of his chair, waving his hand in a dismissive manner. "Fine, do whatever you need to." He had not expected to be required to make so many life and death decisions during his short reign on Europa.

"Thank you." O'Connor stood. "Any more inquiries about that beacon?"

"No, I think the incident has been resolved. Just remember, Captain," Daniels said, cajolingly, "people can only be pushed so far before they break. Most will choose not to fight when caught by surprise. But given time, some will begin to observe weaknesses and start to think of ways to exploit them. Such a man is our mysterious patriot."

"So I have learned." O'Connor started to leave but stopped. "All the more reason to eliminate this man, if only to keep more people from getting ideas. Good evening, Commander." He turned, left the room, and headed down the hallway for the lift. O'Connor took out his com link and ordered Magnus to meet him at the brig.

James had been entertaining himself by singing every song he could think of and some that he eventually made up. He imagined traveling to other planets and exploring other solar systems. He had solved logistical problems in the colony's supply lines, and mentally upgraded dozens of mining machines. He knew the number of alloy panels, and that there were exactly one hundred and twenty-two shared four-corner panel joints in his cell. He endured Katherine's ridicule whenever she caught him talking to himself in the past. But he had begun to do it with increasing frequency. He tried to keep track of time. But with no watch, and the lights in the corridor continually shining through the transparent door, it had been a futile effort. It seemed to become increasingly difficult to maintain the now-strange feeling of sanity that kept threatening to evaporate from his mind. His diet was comprised of nothing but food pellets and water, which were automatically dispensed into the cell whenever he hit the button on the wall.

There was a sound outside his door, and James stood and moved to the back of the room. Magnus stepped into view outside the door. James felt his stomach tighten as the memories of the pain Magnus had inflicted on him came flooding into consciousness. He gathered his courage as the door slid open and the monster stepped through. As Magnus approached, O'Connor stepped into the doorway.

"Good evening, James. I hope you have enjoyed your stay with us."

Magnus punched him square in the face. There was sharp pain, colored sparks, and darkness. James awoke in another cell, his head throbbing and his entire face feeling like it was broken. He could feel what could only be dried blood on his lips and across his right cheek. Magnus must have broken his nose. He found his way to the water dispenser, punctiliously washed his face and took a long cool drink. *Well,* he thought, *here I am again.* He sat down on the floor and began counting the panel joints in his new cell.

D oyle was getting irate. "I'm telling you, Captain, there is something going on!"
"I understand your concerns, but you don't have anything other than a hunch, Doyle! I fail to see the significance of someone cutting down a tree." Dwight raised his hand, gesturing to Doyle to stay quiet. "And if you want to continue this conversation, you will lower your tone, Lieutenant." O'Connor emphasized the lower-ranking title.

Doyle took a deep breath.

"Yes sir." He paused for a moment. "The hydroponics bay on our ship produces enough oxygen to sustain us during long voyages. It is the same here, sir."

"Understandable, but I thought the Arboretum produced all of the oxygen necessary for the colony," O'Connor inquired.

"It does. However, all of the other vegetation here also produces oxygen. They stockpile the extra for refilling the life support systems on their mining ships as well as selling it to the ore freighters or any other ships that may pass by." Doyle could see. "I checked, and there was nothing in the work order about the tree being diseased. They destroyed a valuable asset for no apparent reason, except for the fact that it also happens to be one of the trees that surrounds the central plaza where we conduct our executions." Doyle leaned forward in his chair for emphasis.

O'Connor's eyes flinched. He got it. He touched the screen on his terminal and pulled up a schematic of the plaza in the central hub. Indirectly across from the missing tree there was … nothing significant. Just a wall; no businesses, and no air vents.

"All right," O'Connor relented. "Put a couple of extra men here." He pointed at the map to the area beside the wall. "And here." He pointed to an upper walkway that crossed the now-open area about forty feet above the main plaza floor. "What do you think?"

"That should work. Thank you, sir."

The crowd present for the executions had dwindled since the first. Now there was only a distant passerby and perhaps a few closet sadists who purposefully timed their passing. But with the exception of O'Connor's men, the plaza was clear for a hundred yards in any direction. The event was still broadcast on every audio and visual channel throughout the colony.

The door to James's cell slid open. *Great,* he thought wryly, *another punch in the face.* Magnus stepped into the cell and slammed him into the wall, placing handcuffs on him. He grabbed James by the back of the shirt and half pushed, half carried him out of the cell. James then realized he was back in the colony, and that his new cell had been one of Constable Askuru's detention cells. He always knew where they were, but had never seen inside one. *Why,* James wondered, *have they brought me back here?*

He was escorted toward the central plaza. He could think of no reason for them to take him out of his cell other than for interrogation, and the fact that he was being taken out into public was even more confounding.

He was led into the central plaza, where a large circle of mercenaries were positioned. He could see others, as well as many of O'Connor's pirates, dispersed throughout the area. As people passed by him and his guards, they stared, but looked away as soon as he looked back at them. When he arrived at the circle, there was a small group of citizens looking at him with strangely horrific looks on their faces. Doyle was standing in the center of the circle, holding a pistol in his hand. Suddenly it hit him like Magnus's fist. The people staring, the extra guards, the public place, and O'Connor's man standing in the circle of armed men he was about to enter? He was about to be executed. James could feel his adrenaline surge and began looking for a way to escape, but there was not one.

James decided he would not go down without a fight. There was no way he could win, but maybe he could leave them something to remember him by. His hands were bound behind him, so all he had left were his feet. He was walked into the center of the circle so that he stood face-to-face with Doyle, who seemed jumpy. There was a pause, as if they were waiting for something, but nothing happened. Doyle relaxed, and the psychotic gleam in his eye returned as he raised his weapon towards James's head. James knew he was about to die anyway, so he figured he might as well strike at the most convenient target. And he did.

Eric cursed as the round grazed the head of the man about to shoot James Shaw and winged the mercenary behind him. *Why did he do that!* He screamed in his mind as the shot missed because of the kid's action. He quickly picked his next target and fired, dropping one of the riflemen on the catwalk above the plaza. The second one tried to hide behind the railing, but it only offered a couple of inches of hard cover from Eric's higher position. Another quick shot and he was done. Now he could focus on the men in the plaza, which was erupting into chaos.

The main group of Tyler's rebels converged onto the plaza, firing on the pirates and taking up their positions. Large power cables trailed behind about ten of them as they moved into their designated positions. Eric could see the horror on the face of one of the mercenaries as one of the colonists cut through his comrade with the unseen beam of an industrial cutting laser, along with the tree trunk he was taking cover behind. The air crackled as if small thunder pierced the atmosphere. The smell of ozone began to burn the nostrils of some of the pirates, and they realized what was happening. Red, blue, and green beams of light began to appear as the first invisible laser beams began to pass through the wispy battle smoke. *Just one of Tyler's many ideas to provide his rebels with adequate weaponry,* thought Eric.

Jonas was both shocked and amused when James, staring death in the face, kicked Doyle square between the legs, causing him to nearly crumple in half. Unfortunately, the timing could not have been worse; it caused Tyler's sniper to miss taking him out. O'Connor had relieved the security droids of their duties, keeping weapons out of the colony. He probably thought it easier than reprogramming all of them. *Big mistake,* Jonas thought as he opened his jacket, un-holstered his father's JLM and shot one of the guards surrounding James. Two more fell; one was Katherine's target, the other Markus's.

After James kicked Doyle where it mattered most with every bit of strength he had left, he stood stunned for about two seconds after, expecting to be dead already. He saw two of the mercenaries around him fall over, but it was not until all of the rest of them began firing out into the plaza that he realized what was going on. Someone was trying to save him! He could run, or he could hit the deck. He opted for the second, since running could get him caught by friendly fire just as easily as it could from the enemy. *Plus, when all I can do is spit at people who have guns,* James thought, *playing dead isn't such a bad idea.* The lights in the plaza dimmed and flickered momentarily, James noticed, but he did not really care. It was strange, though; he had never seen that happen before.

Katherine fired into the left flank of the circle from her perch on the balcony two levels up. Just as her first magazine was empty, she saw at least one of the mercenaries spot her. She ducked behind the corner just as a hail of bullets sparked on the wall where her face had been. She was going to fire her second magazine as planned, but even though the flurry of bullets thinned, it continued sporadically for another ten seconds. Her designated time expired, and she quickly scurried through the doorway and into the adjoining corridor.

She ran fifty yards down the hallway and out onto the next balcony, where she took up position across the plaza from a man she met that morning, named Quinn. She could not see him, but he was there, because there were six pirates firing at his position. Katherine took careful aim and began firing. The third shot winged its target, and three of the now five capable fighting men turned. They quickly spotted her, and again, she had to duck behind the corner as a barrage of metal rained down on her position.

Markus hit Magnus square in the chest with three rounds, with absolutely no affect. *Armor,* Markus chided himself. Magnus was already withdrawing behind the main group. He was probably moving to protect O'Connor. Markus took out three of the guards in the circle as the main group of rebels rounded the corner across the plaza and began firing on their flank. Markus wanted to cut off the head of the snake and take O'Connor out. But first they had to get James. Markus threw a grenade in the general direction Magnus had disappeared, and went back to laying down cover fire for James.

Jonas felt the concussion of Markus's grenade and looked that direction. They were both crouched behind two large tree planters about twenty feet apart. Markus gave the go sign, and Jonas made a short, low lunge before he began low-crawling to James. He had cover at the moment, but it was about to run out. He rounded the last tree planter and brought himself up to a crouch; he quick-peeked around the corner and could see James lying motionless beside one of the dead mercenaries. *Did they get him?* Jonas thought. He took a longer look around the corner and could not see any pirates in his line of sight.

Jonas took a chance and yelled, "James!"

James's head stayed down, but turned toward Jonas enough so he could see where he was. When James saw Jonas, he winked, telling Jonas he was all right. Jonas could see that James's hands were still bound behind him, making it nearly impossible for him to crawl. Jonas looked further around the planter, and there were still about six mercenaries behind solid cover firing back at the colonists. The backs of three were exposed to Jonas, and they weren't looking in his direction. But if he started shooting at them, it would likely destroy his chances of bringing James to safety. The mercenaries were at least twenty feet beyond the maximum distance he thought he could throw a grenade for effect; plus, it would have to be a left-handed throw. *So much for that option,* he thought.

Wait a second, Jonas thought, *I don't need to hit them, just give myself a distraction.* He backed about three feet away from the planter and took out one of his grenades. He lined up his throw, punched the detonator, and began counting. He blindly threw the grenade as hard as he could in the direction of the exposed flank of the mercenaries. As soon as it left his hand, he made a break for James. About halfway across the nearly fifty feet he had to traverse, the grenade detonated. He made it to James (who was starting to sit up), grabbed him by the arm, and yanked him to his feet. They ran back toward cover. Jonas heard two rounds strike at his feet and felt the air blast of another as it passed behind his head. They still had thirty feet to go.

Katherine arrived at her new position in time to see James and Jonas running toward Markus. A half second later, she noticed two pirates shooting at them from a balcony. She brought her pistol to the handrail and rested it there as she began firing in the direction of the pirates. The cover fire worked, and they dove behind a planter as she fired the last round from her magazine. She retreated back through the doorway and around the corner again, just as another rain of bullets buffeted her position. James was out of the plaza and under cover, which meant it was time for Kat to move to the rendezvous point.

She rounded the corner and stepped into the hallway as she was seating a fresh magazine in her pistol. There was a pirate standing right in front of her, looking just as astounded as she was. She tried to bring her pistol up to fire and thought she got two rounds off before seeing a rifle butt coming up on her left. She shifted her head to the right, but it was too late for her to move out of the way. She saw sparks and felt a crushing weight on her chest as she fell to the floor. Darkness overtook her.

Jonas removed a laser cutter from his jacket and carefully cut the cuffs off of James.

"Whew! It's good to have those off." James breathed, rubbing his wrists. "I can't believe you guys pulled this off!" he said, slapping Jonas on the shoulder in greeting.

"Neither can I, but this is just part of it. No offense, buddy, but to everyone except Kat, Markus, and me, you weren't even a part of the plan."

"Markus who? I thought..."

Jonas pointed behind them, and James could see Markus firing narrowly past them toward the pirates. "He's the one who's been killing all the pirates."

"*Old* Markus?" James said, shaking his head in disbelief, "I never would have guessed."

Jonas handed James the rifle he had pulled off one of the pirates during the rescue.

"Me neither, but we don't have time for that now. You have to meet Katherine over there, in the alley behind the grocery store." Jonas briefly pulled out his data pad and could see Katherine's locator beacon nearly where it should be. "She'll be waiting to take you to your next position. Markus and me will try and meet you there in about an hour."

James was checking the rifle's magazine and power pack. "She's okay? They told me they had her too!"

"They almost did. She said it was pure happenstance that she got away. We have to split up now and try to cut off their reinforcements. Take care of her."

"Like you have to ask, she's my sister … Ohhhh!" James could see the concern in Jonas's eyes. James, grinning, slapped Jonas on the shoulder again and raised himself to a crouch. "You and Markus watch each other's backs; I'll take care of her." He took a quick look around the planter. "See you in an hour." James made a low bound for the next planter back and safely slid behind it. He looked back at Jonas and nodded that he was ready.

Jonas turned and began firing on the few remaining mercenaries from the original group that had been in the plaza as Markus began firing at the only visible pirate left on one of the walkways. The attack had gone according to plan. The colonists had come in right after the first shots and pulled the pirates' attention from the rescue group, who were now at their back right flank. That would not last long, though; reinforcements would come from Markus's and Jonas's left flank to back up the remaining mercenary forces, putting him and Markus in a no-win crossfire position.

Another look and Jonas saw that James was gone. It was time to move. Markus had not taken out the pirate he was shooting at, but had at least forced him to move into a position not threatening to Jonas.

"Markus!" Jonas yelled over his shoulder. Markus's head appeared from behind his cover. "Cover me!" Markus gave him the go sign and disappeared. Jonas waited two seconds and lunged for a large tree planter, re-securing himself adjacent to Markus.

James's adrenaline was raging as he made it to the relative safety of the alley. He slowed to a jog and began looking for his sister. He emerged from the other side of the alley directly between the two battlefronts. Ducking back inside, he backtracked, looking for anything that he could have missed along the way. There were half a dozen doors, but they were all locked. He even checked the trash chute, but no Katherine. He knocked open the grate to an airshaft, stepped inside the tunnel, and yelled for Katherine. No answer. There was nothing to do now but wait. He had no way of knowing she lay unconscious only two levels above him.

O'Connor watched from relative safety as the mercenaries, along with a couple of his own men, were expeditiously picked off. He quickly moved in the direction of his men, when his way was suddenly blocked by Magnus.

"Too many," Magnus grunted.

O'Connor looked around the hulk for a second and could see that the mercenaries were quickly being overwhelmed, and that there was now a large group of colonists moving toward them.

"Fine." O'Connor relented. He immediately keyed his com and began ordering reinforcements. Several hundred yards down the corridor they met a group of his men who were already on their way.

"You're with me," O'Connor ordered as he pointed at the men. They turned right down the next hall and took the lift up to the next level. He switched com channels. "Daniels!"

"Commander Daniels is unavailable at the moment, Captain O'Connor," the formal voice of the com lieutenant answered.

"Well, tell him to make himself available, you little toad," Dwight snarled. "We've got a full-blown revolt down here and I need the rest of my mercs, now!"

A few seconds passed. "Captain, I've dispatched your men. *What* is going on down there?" Daniels impatiently replied.

"They're rebelling, that's what's happening! I told you we shouldn't have stayed here longer than planned! They've obviously been planning this for some time, they're too well organized."

"Yes, you did tell me that. Can you handle the situation?"

"We'll see, won't we!?" O'Connor cut the signal. "Pencil-pushing twit!"

Magnus grunted in agreement as he jogged behind him.

"Doyle!" O'Connor barked into the com.

A second later Doyle answered.

"Yes, sir?"

"Access the central computer and start using the surveillance systems to locate all of the colonists; I want to know where they are and what they're doing."

"Already trying, Captain, but I can't seem to access the core right now."

"What do you mean, you 'can't?'" O'Connor snapped.

"I mean it looks like all remote access to the colony's core has been cut."

"Then try a hard access point!"

"Tried that too, but none of the terminals are working either. Someone must have cut all access to the core, probably literally."

O'Connor cursed loudly. "... Do whatever you can ... Out."

Markus removed his rucksack from the shrubs as he trotted behind Jonas toward the direction they reckoned reinforcements would come from. They entered the large corridor that led to the main dock. Mercenaries from the surface would likely come from that direction. Jonas covered Markus from two directions as best he could, while Markus set up multiple grenades with motion-sensing triggers and tripwires, as well as the reloaded Viper mine he had recovered. Tyler and his group would be setting similar surprises elsewhere. With the charges set, Jonas and Markus set off down the adjoining hallway.

The apartment section that the mercenaries were living in began stirring like a hive of angry bees as men emerged from their quarters and roused others who were between shifts. They quickly formed several squads and moved in the direction of the central plaza. Just as thirty of them emerged from the end of the corridor, the lead man in the group noticed something out of place. Too many trash cans. Disaster struck, as it seemed hell itself rained in on them from all directions.

Tyler and his best men were waiting about eighty yards from the end of the corridor in case their trap failed. If this group of mercenaries were to successfully deploy, they would easily flank and overrun the main group of colonists with superior skill and firepower. The charges worked as they had hoped; an entire group of the enemy entered the zone before the point man unwittingly set off the trap, ensuring the destruction of himself and everyone around him.

Tyler and Quinn quickly moved toward the smoldering destruction while their group covered them. They placed several grenade traps to slow any more mercenaries that may appear. They could not afford to stay and cover the corridor. They had to get back to the colonists to ensure progress and reinforce their numbers. Tyler left two men behind to cover the corridor and report if the situation changed.

The colonists had half the plaza secure. Some were taking up defensive positions to hold their line, and two other groups were beginning to break off, flank, and advance. O'Connor was wondering where his reinforcements were when he heard a combination of small concurrent blasts that to the untrained would have sounded like a single thunderous eruption. The sound came from the direction of the housing wing, and he knew none of his men had any explosives. That meant the colonists had used them on someone or something, most likely his men. Magnus looked at him, his huge jaw muscles visibly tightening as he had the same thought.

There were mercenaries and some of his crewmen converging on the location from their scattered positions throughout the colony. They took up positions as O'Connor instructed. Four more joined him and the small group he had gathered on the plaza's secondary level. Dwight involuntarily winced as an unseen laser scorched the wall and burned an arching pattern about six feet above his head.

O'Connor took Magnus and two other men and moved toward the docks. As they neared the docks, O'Connor heard a muffled concussion. He cursed to himself and increased his pace.

James moved back down the alley from the direction he came and rounded the corner to see a group of mercenaries coming straight for him. He looked where Jonas and Markus had been, but they were gone. If the mercenaries used this alley to bypass the plaza, they could flank the colonists on the other side. He had to slow them. He stepped around the corner, firing a quick spray of rounds in the direction of the mercs, then sidestepped back to cover. He saw them split and jump for cover. He was fairly sure he winged one of them. *That should keep them occupied for a few minutes,* he thought, as he sprinted for the other end of the alley.

James stopped short of the exit, not wanting to come running out like a madman and get shot. He pulled the empty magazine from his rifle and put in a fresh one. He then made a careful throw and tossed the empty magazine at the nearest colonist. James unconsciously put body English on the projectile as it nearly hit the target colonist in the head. The man ducked, then whipped his head and his rifle around in the direction from which the mysterious projectile had come. James slung his rifle behind him, in an effort to look as harmless as possible, and waved his other arm. The man appeared to relax when he saw him.

The man shrugged his shoulders and mouthed, "What?"

James tried to give crude hand signals to the man indicating that the enemy was about to come through the alley. The colonist finally appeared to get it and relayed the message to the next man over. After about ten seconds, the man signaled James to come over to them. James berated the man to the air as he ran across to the colonist's position. His distraction would not last much longer.

"There's a group of mercenaries about to come through the alley any second!" James yelled breathlessly.

"We appreciate the warning." A familiar voice came from behind.

James turned.

"Mr. Tyler." James reached out and shook his hand. "It's good to see you." James threw a confused look at the alley and back to Tyler. "Everyone's looking the wrong direction."

Tyler pointed at the alley.

"Just watch," he said with a hint of anticipation, as they remained crouched behind cover.

Two mercs emerged from the alley, their rifles ready to fire on colonists' flank. Tyler quickly removed a data pad from his jacket. He touched the screen, and the alley burst forth with flames and several mercenaries. They watched the alley to make sure no one else emerged, and, when satisfied, everyone went back to their previous positions.

James turned immediately back to Tyler. "Is Katherine here?"

"No. Were you supposed to meet her?"

"I was, but she wasn't there. I was waiting for her in that alley when the mercenaries started my way." James face turned worried. "We've got to find her."

"We'll keep our eyes open, son, but we've got our hands full. And I can't spare any men to go looking around. You can stay with us or, and I wouldn't recommend this, go try and find her."

"I have to find her. She's my sister."

"You should wait until we move before running back over there."

"All right…" James shifted his attention to the front line. Tyler yelled at one of the men further down the line, a man with uncommonly dark skin. The man acknowledged, then moved to the end of the line and joined six or seven others. The group threw several small objects. Soon half the plaza was filled with smoke, and the colonists started to move.

James crept over to the edge of cover and made a mad dash back to the alley. He glanced around the corner for a quick look and could see that the colony's climate system was already clearing the smoke from the area. But it was apparently all they needed, for no one remained at the location James had just come from. He could hear the sounds of battle re-erupt past the center of the plaza. He had no idea where to go from here. He opted for the maintenance opening further up the alley, hoping he would stumble across Katherine along the way.

K atherine awakened, feeling like she could not breathe. As she opened her eyes she tried to scream, but all she did was squeak. She forced herself to take another laborious breath and realized during the second that elapsed that the man lying on top of her was dead. She remembered firing two shots before she felt everything go black and sparkly.

"Great!" She balked, as she tried again, unsuccessfully, to push the dead weight off of her. She had no idea how long she had been unconscious. She finally got one of her arms out from under the man, then used it to squirm out from under him. She freed her other arm, which increased her rate of progress, and in a few more seconds she was free. She holstered her pistol, unclipped the man's rifle, and stripped him of his spare magazines. She gave the rifle a quick examination and was pleased to find it similar to a gun she had used during one of her rare episodes of playing war simulations with Jonas and James. She threw the strap over her neck and shoulder and began running down the hallway as she removed her data pad with her free hand and checked the time. Nearly thirty minutes had passed!

Katherine frantically ran down the corridor and down the access stairs that led to the alley below. She was slightly out of breath when she cautiously opened the locked stairway door and stepped into the alley.

"James!" she whispered loudly. No answer.

She ran to both ends of the alley and saw no sign of him. It appeared the battle had moved and was now raging at the other end of the plaza. *Which means the colonists must be winning!* she thought. Time was growing short, and if she waited for James much longer, she would be late.

SEVENTEEN

They cautiously moved down a small corridor that paralleled the larger one leading to the main docks. Their pace was interrupted when Markus's data pad vibrated in his jacket pocket. He removed it and observed a green number one blinking on his screen. He hit the reply button and sent the same message back to Tyler. Jonas gave him an inquisitive look and Markus responded with a thumbs-up.

The main force of colonists was trying to push the mercenaries away from the main docks and cut them off. Markus and Jonas were tasked with doing whatever they could to hold the main dock. They arrived just in time to see a ship breaking the surface of the water.

Markus knew a grenade could not sink a ship, and that was all he and Jonas had. He did not have time to come up with a good plan, so he just ran straight for the ship with Jonas on his heels. The ship locked onto the dock, and he could hear its hatch hiss open on the far side as he rounded the bow. As the hatch came into view, he flipped the detonator on one of his grenades and threw it through the opening. He heard a yell before flames bellowed out of the hatchway. Jonas was on his flank, weapon ready. Markus took point and they entered the ship before the smoke could clear, denying anyone the chance to recover from the shock of the blast. They entered the small ship and found no survivors. More ships would come, and they had to get ready for them.

Jonas opened the cockpit shield on the ship and heard the faint sound of an explosion. He turned to see Markus running out the door. Jonas quit tinkering with the ship and followed. As he ran down the dock after Markus, he could see the doorway where one of their traps had gone off. They took positions behind crates on either side of the doorway and waited. They waited for several minutes, but there were no mercenaries or pirates bursting through the doorway.

O'Connor's anger flared as he cautiously walked up and kicked one of the dead men and launched into a tirade of flamboyantly foul language.

"I told all of you to slow down!" Dwight turned toward Magnus, who had been a few feet ahead of him and was still recovering from the stun of the concussion. "*You* know better!" Magnus just shrugged his shoulders before shaking his head again, trying to recover from the stun. *That's how they're getting the drop on us,* thought Dwight, *with booby traps!*

O'Connor did not know how many, if any, colonists were inside the docks. There was a good chance that the rest of the entrances would be similarly trapped. He took the rifle off one of the dead men, removed its magazine, and started down the corridor. Magnus followed close behind him, still looking woozy. When he reached the next doorway, about a hundred feet from the first, O'Connor stood to the side of the door and hit the keypad to open it. Fire erupted from the door as it opened and tripped another device. When the door was fully open, he reached around the corner and threw the rifle through the opening, causing another explosion. He and Magnus quickly entered the doorway and could see two colonists ducking for cover at the first entrance where they had been waiting to ambush any intruders.

Jonas's body jerked with surprise as one of their traps went off at the doorway behind him. He turned to look and another mine went off. Jonas stood, leaped over his cover, and fell into a crouch on the other side. Just as he popped his head back up for a look, two men came through the doorway and immediately spotted him. Markus loosed a three round burst at them from his rifle, and the two pirates began firing as they ducked behind the cover of the crates.

"Time for us to go," Markus yelled to Jonas.

"What about the ship?" Jonas dropped his head behind the crates as the pirates' next volley of bullets struck them.

"Forget it. You locked the controls, right?" Jonas nodded. "Then we've done all we can do here. There'll probably be more of them soon, and we can't win on two fronts."

"To the rendezvous point?" Jonas more suggested than asked. Markus nodded.

"On three, retreat to my position. One … two … three!" Markus stood and fired a series of bursts at the pirates, effectively making them drop behind cover long enough for Jonas to move through the open and back to his cover position. Markus then turned and fired on the dock control panel behind them. Sparks flew as the controls shorted out. The dock entered emergency mode, and the exterior ship doors began to close. It would take hours to override the emergency protocols and reopen the doors. They ran for the only exit that lay behind them.

Jonas removed his last grenade and armed it.

"Ready?" he asked Markus.

Markus nodded.

Jonas already knew where to throw it and about how far. He stayed behind cover and let it fly. He heard it strike the floor and detonate just after they had taken their second steps. Jonas reached the doorway first and hit the control pad to open the door. They were through it before the pirates could get a bead on them. Jonas knew where the rendezvous point was and immediately began moving for it, with Markus close behind.

James felt like he was wasting time looking for Katherine. One, because he had no idea where to look, and two, there was a battle raging that he should be in the middle of. He did not want to stop looking for his sister, but he could wander aimlessly for hours and never be any closer to finding her than when he started. He decided to head toward the fray, opting to stay in the maintenance shafts and use a more stealthy approach.

Katherine decided not to wait for James any longer and started for the rendezvous point. She knew Jonas and Markus had successfully rescued him, but had no idea where he was. *Perhaps he had to stay with Jonas and Markus,* she thought. She heard the distant clash and moved through the vacant battlefield quickly and cautiously.

Dwight and Magnus hit the deck when they heard the distinctive clanging and rolling of a grenade. Their cover of crates was rocked and slightly pushed back by the blast. "Gone," Magnus said after a quick look.

Magnus followed as Dwight stood and ran through the door. O'Connor caught a glimpse of the two fleeing saboteurs as they rounded a corner further down the corridor and took off at a full sprint after them.

Jonas glanced over his shoulder just as they rounded a wide curve. Two of the pirates were chasing them. He did not know if it was the same two they left at the docks, but he was fairly sure they were the same two he had run from at the abandoned base.

"They're chasing us." Jonas glanced over his shoulder, but they were lost around the corner. "I think it's O'Connor and Magnus."

Markus increased pace and took the lead. They probably could not win a firefight with O'Connor and Magnus. O'Connor was likely wearing armor, and Markus knew his one-man goon squad was. Markus was wearing his, but his old armor would not stop a direct hit from accelerator rifle.

As they came to the end of the corner, Markus suddenly stopped, brought his rifle to his shoulder, and fired as he took two steps back and jumped into a hallway to his left. Jonas was too far to Markus's right to risk following him across the corridor as the squad of mercenaries in front of them brought their weapons to bear. Jonas dove to the right, into the opposing hallway across from Markus, as bullets ricocheted through the corridor. Markus activated his last grenade and hurled it toward the wall in front of Jonas. The grenade bounced off the wall and once off the floor before it detonated.

"Get to the rendezvous point and warn Tyler that they're trying to flank him," Markus yelled across the corridor. He was effectively cut off.

"What about you?" Jonas yelled back.

"I'll survive! Go … *now!*" Markus ordered harshly.

Jonas hesitated and stared at Markus for a second before he turned and took off at a dead run down the hallway.

When Jonas was out of sight, Markus retreated down his hallway. They would be coming soon, and he had to put some distance between them to have any chance of eluding them.

O'Connor heard the gunfire and the grenade.
"This is O'Connor," he barked into his com-link. "We're on level one at junction 457. What unit has engaged the enemy?"

A few seconds passed.

"This is Mosby, Captain. We've engaged two rebels at junction 456. I have two down and two dead; orders, sir?"

"Hold your position and we'll join you from your twelve o'clock. Instruct your men not to fire."

"Aye, aye sir."

O'Connor rounded the corner to see four men, rifles pointed at the two adjacent hallway openings. Mosby signaled that the two rebels had each gone into opposite sides of the intersection. O'Connor acknowledged and indicated that two men should stay with the wounded, one would follow him to his right, and the other should follow Magnus to his left. At O'Connor's signal, they all moved for their respective hallway entrances and rounded the corners at the same time, each providing their counterparts behind them with cover. They proceeded in opposite directions.

Jonas reached the rendezvous point on level two within five minutes. His heart fell into his stomach ... no Katherine or James. They should have been here at least twenty minutes ago. It got worse; he thought he heard something echo down the corridor from the direction he had just come. It could be James and Kat, but it was more likely O'Connor and his men. Tactics dictated that they would not run after him, and they could not know exactly where he had gone. That would give him a little time to find a defensive position or hide.

"Why don't you put those goggles to good use?" O'Connor snapped as he and his mercenary came to an intersection.

The man was wearing a sensor mask on his helmet, but was apparently unaccustomed to using it. After a brief befuddled look, he flipped down his visor and switched to infrared. After a moment, he detected a faint glow of lingering heat through a doorway ahead. The man pointed silently and quickly moved that direction. O'Connor followed. They reached the source of the glow. It was the residual heat of a handprint on the rung of a maintenance ladder leading upward. The man pointed and started climbing.

Dwight reached the top of the ladder and found the merc crouching and looking down the second of two corridors. He heard O'Connor behind him, tapped the side of his helmet, and started toward the otherwise inaudible noise the mercenary's audio-enhancing gear descried.

Jonas removed an air intake grate from the wall, but the opening was blocked by a tangle of pipes. He turned and caught the edge of the grate with his knee. He cringed as he tried to catch it, but it was too late. The grate crashed to the floor with a clang that sounded like it echoed through the entire colony. *So much for not giving away my position,* he thought. He opted for the only available cover: a small maintenance alcove like a thousand others throughout the colony.

Thumbing the switch on his JLM to full auto, he waited. Finally he heard a sound different from the auricular hallucinations his imagination had been creating. Jonas's heart rate doubled, and he tried to quiet his breathing as he leaned his head out past the edge of the alcove. His weapon raised and pointed in the direction of the sound. His shoulders were beginning to burn. Straining his ears, he tried to get a fix on their distance. *If they get too close,* he thought, *they might move on me before I can attack. If I emerge too soon they will not be close enough to ...* there they were!

Jonas emerged from the alcove, squeezed the trigger of his pistol, and emptied his thirty-round magazine in two quick bursts. Both men went down, as Jonas released the empty magazine. One man began to move. Jonas recognized him as Captain O'Connor, and began fumbling for a full magazine. O'Connor was facing the wall to Jonas's left as he began to rise, still dazed from the impact. Jonas tried to remain calm as O'Connor began to turn from a kneeling posture and reestablish the grip on his weapon. Jonas could see that O'Connor's left arm was bleeding profusely, and Jonas could see ten impact marks on the front of his body armor.

O'Connor was muttering a torrent of indiscernible curses as he turned his head toward Jonas, his rifle following not far behind his gaze. Jonas had nearly dropped his fresh magazine and was only now sliding it into his pistol. After that it would take four tenths of a second for the first round to chamber before the pistol could fire. Everything was moving in slow motion. Jonas knew he would not make it in time. Even so, he set his weapon sights directly on O'Connor's head as the magazine locked in place. As O'Connor's rifle was brought to bear, his facial expression changed from anger to arrogant triumph.

Jonas could hear his pistol chambering the round as O'Connor's look of triumph turned to one of confusion and fear. He lurched forward and the burst of bullets intended to kill Jonas sprayed past, close enough to nick one of his ears. Jonas did not know what happened, but could see in his peripheral vision the silhouette of someone in the shadows behind O'Connor. Jonas did not hesitate and fired at O'Connor's head. Captain Dwight O'Connor was dead.

In the heat of battle, it is sometimes difficult to distinguish friend from foe. Upon seeing O'Connor fall for the last time, Jonas brought his weapon to bear on the figure in the shadows. He glanced down and saw that three shots had impacted O'Connor in the back. Although they did not penetrate his armor, they were what made him fall forward and subsequently miss Jonas. Jonas beheld the specter as it approached and eased the tension on his trigger as Katherine became visible.

"Kat!" Jonas lowered his weapon, ran to her, and embraced her. He leaned back and could see that her eyes were as large as saucers and tearing. She was still looking at O'Connor. Jonas turned her away from the gore.

"Katherine," he questioned soothingly, "are you okay?"

She refocused and looked into his eyes for a second before finally returning his hug.

"Yeah." She sighed. "I couldn't find James..."

Jonas did not ask why as her voice trailed off.

"I got knocked out and stuck, and showed up at the spot too late...I hope he's all right..."

Jonas could see the blood on the side of her head. "It's all right," he comforted. "He can take care of himself. I'm sure he'll show up somewhere." As much as he would have loved to stand there holding her, Jonas pulled away slightly and looked at her.

"He'll be fine, Kat."

She just nodded uncertainly. "We'd better go to the rendezvous point."

Katherine realized that Markus was not with Jonas and gasped. "Markus?"

"We got separated; he was fine when I left." Jonas shook his head slightly. "We have to go." Jonas grabbed her hand and they trotted down the corridor toward the rendezvous coordinates.

James, feeling like he had been wandering aimlessly for hours, emerged from a darkened corridor, moving toward the sounds of battle. As he rounded a corner, his eyes grew wide and he threw himself backward, pressing his back against the wall. It was Magnus. *He has to be the largest human being that ever walked... anywhere*, thought James. He knew he was about to kill his first man, and every second he thought about it more rounds were being thrown at people he knew and who were his friends. He had fired at the group of mercenaries earlier, but somehow this felt different.

James raised his weapon and stepped around the corner, firing four shots directly into Magnus's back. He kept his weapon raised and fixed on target. The man did not go down, but began to stand and turn toward him! He had been in war simulations before, but reality seemed more surreal. What was he supposed to do? James fired another burst, striking him directly in the torso, but nothing happened! His vision began to narrow as his adrenaline surged out of control until all that remained was a small tunnel: black all around with Magnus at the end.

Time slowed as the behemoth of a man continued standing, turning, and bringing his weapon to bear. His tunnel vision began to close and he had to make a conscious effort to reopen it. James knew that mere tenths of a second were passing, and he didn't know what to do. When he finally realized what was happening, he fired two shots from twenty feet away. James saw them leave the barrel of his gun and impact the monster of a man, one in his temple just above his right eye, the second right between the eyes. Time was restored to normal, and then the man fell motionless onto the ground. He approached the fallen giant and discovered he had indeed been wearing a massive coat of armor. That was why his first two volleys did not stop him.

James only pondered what he had done for a moment when the sounds of weapons fire drew his attention. He was now in position on the left side of three pirates positioned behind a large tree pot near the center of the small plaza, and they had not seen him. He put a fresh magazine in his rifle and knelt behind the dead man. He took careful aim and took a deep breath.

He fired a three round burst, striking the man closest to him, causing him to fall, apparently dead. The second man glanced over at his fallen comrade and must have assumed that his compatriot was taken out from the direction they were firing, as he hunkered down and continued firing. James again took careful aim and fired, taking out the second man. The third could see that the second man's wounds were on the left side and well below the level of their cover. He turned and immediately pointed his weapon at James's position. But he was too late. In the three seconds it took him to realize what was going on and react, James had already fired. The man turned in time to take the barrage squarely.

James took a moment to assess the fighting in the small plaza and thought he saw Jonas and Markus. He then concentrated his fire on the high position that seemed to be keeping them pinned down. It was good to see they were still in the fight, but he could not see Katherine with them. He hoped she was all right. He began taking fire and retreated back into the corridor.

Jonas did not know why the pirates at the center of the side plaza suddenly stopped firing. Only a few seconds after that, one of the high positions to their right ceased firing as well. Whatever the reason, it was enough of a lull for Markus to notice and move out of their predicament. They had been pinned down for the last ten minutes. Jonas had not noticed the break in fire until Markus was already moving, and, as soon as he was gone, their position was again pelted with rounds. He was glad he had made Katherine stay with the main group, even though she was cross with him. As a few bits of flying debris cut his face, he decided it was worth it not to have her in the thick of things. Jonas looked to Markus, and he signaled for him to get ready to do the same.

"Tyler," Markus called into his com.

"Yeah, Markus," Tyler answered quickly.

"Can you see me? I'm at your two o'clock."

A few seconds passed. "Got you. We're already moving toward your position."

"Don't!" Markus nearly cut him off. "They have two firing positions in front of and directly above me. They'll be able to pick you off if you come through that narrow area. Use the lasers to give Jonas some cover. Get him out of there."

"Done."

Only seconds expired before three intermittent blue beams crackled through the wispy haze. Jonas scrambled from his position and rejoined Markus. Jonas and Markus coordinated with Eric's group to take out the three remaining snipers, effectively clearing the choke point. The colonists pushed the pirates and their mercenaries back to the maintenance docks, where they had stored many of the ships they had seized. The pirates held the docks until they had nearly all escaped in the waiting ships.

A final push led by Tyler and colonists mopped up what remained of the mercenaries.

Markus and Jonas helped Katherine seal off the entrances so they could not return. They received word that Quinn's group had repelled reinforcements sent from the base at one of the smaller side docks. Markus and Tyler knew they not only had to secure the colony, but the surface base as well. Otherwise Daniels could launch a counterattack at his leisure.

D oyle knew something was wrong the second he stepped out of the ship and onto the deck. There were no base personnel or the usual guards waiting for them beside the air lock doors. When they exited the dock, all was quiet, and red alarm lights were flashing at the ends of all the corridors.

EIGHTEEN

James was reunited with Katherine, Markus, and Jonas after the chaos had briefly subsided. It took fifteen minutes to organize the militia and load them into the remaining ships. They were underway in another five.

As the ships surfaced inside the base docks, the pilots said they could not see any pirates or mercenaries in view.

"That can't be good," Markus remarked wryly to Jonas. Markus stood and stepped up to the first position at the door. *If there are any casualties to be had when the unseen pirates unleash hell on this doorway,* Markus thought, *the old man will be the first.*

Markus is definitely brave to put himself in the line of fire, but he certainly isn't stupid, Jonas thought. As the door opened, Markus launched himself out of it, rolling onto the deck and up into a crouch, weapon ready. It was the best way Jonas could think of to avoid the hail of gunfire ... that still hadn't started. Jonas and the rest of the militia onboard their shuttle quickly piled out after him and took up cover positions on their respective dock. The colonists from the other ships did the same as the last ship surfaced in one of the center pools. Still, there was no resistance. There did not appear to be any enemy presence whatsoever.

Jonas looked at Markus and shrugged. Markus shook his head. Tyler signaled from the next dock over that they were moving forward, and the other groups followed suit. There were two main doors that led to the lower levels of the base. That was the next likely place for an ambush. Tyler and Eric's groups took one door, and Markus and Quinn's took the other. They both signaled they were ready and hit the controls. The unlocked doors slid open. Everyone exchanged looks from the confused to the worried. Markus again led the group through the breach and into the corridor, which was aglow with flashing alarm lights. The colonists took up defensive positions at either end of the corridor and group leaders met in the middle.

"I don't like this one bit," Markus remarked to Tyler.

"Neither do I...What do you make of it?" Tyler asked.

"I have no idea. They just gave up the two places of greatest tactical advantage, which is great, except that Daniels has control of the base and might try to flood us out or something."

"Agreed, we need to move to the upper levels as soon as possible."

"We'll split into two groups. When we reach the upper levels, stay away from the outer corridors. He may be able to close off sections and vent atmosphere."

Tyler nodded, and they rejoined their groups.

Fifteen minutes later the groups met on the surface level, all of them out of breath. The corridor was a T intersection with the militia on both ends and one large corridor in the center that led to the inner base. They moved toward the intersection, checked around the corners, and sparked an explosion of gunfire. From his quick glance, Markus saw that the enemy had positioned themselves behind ballistic barricades just slightly out of grenade range. Markus looked across the intersection at Tyler, who gave him the same grim look.

Jonas looked back to the center of their group at Katherine. He had tried to convince her to stay, but she refused. Jonas had no delusions of trying to change her; she was stubborn … "strong willed," she called it. It was one of her best and worst qualities.

They began to return fire, and lost three men in a matter of minutes. Then, although they could still hear weapons fire and the occasional ricochet, only a few bullets seemed to be bouncing in their direction. Markus could not see but heard what sounded like chaotic fighting behind the barricades. They held position as the noise dwindled, and finally stopped.

"You there," a voice yelled from behind the barricade. "Are you colonists from the mining operation below?"

Markus shrugged, held his hands palms up at Tyler, and then answered, "Yes!"

He yelled, "I'm Constable Askuru. Who are you?"

"Colonel Mons of the Republic Marines. Are you friend or foe?"

Markus was as shocked as everyone else looked.

"Friend! But we don't know if we can trust you. Commander Daniels is Martian too."

"Our other group is after the *Commander*," the colonel said the word with disdain, "as we speak. Send one man out meet me. I'll prove we're the good guys. Just make sure your weapon is slung."

"I'll go," Markus told Jonas and looked at Tyler, pointing to himself.

"I'm coming out!" Markus yelled. He stepped out into the open with his rifle slung in front of him; his pistol holstered; his hands low, open, and out to his sides; his stomach in a knot. He could see helmets and rifles lined up along the barricades further down the corridor. It was probably a trick, but on the off chance it was not … he had to risk it. His heart pounded and his mouth was dry as he made the long walk down the corridor toward the unknown, unaware of what had transpired days before …

F our days prior to what would come to be known as "The Europa Incident," there had been another incident: a disruption of the Martian satellite network that resulted in a four-minute loss of all planetary media and communication transmissions. The entire plexus had been corrupted when a fragmented program imbedded itself in various nodes, then began to coalesce. The program did not match normal viral parameters, and the countermeasures could not lock it into one system node and eliminate it. So it did the only thing it could to eliminate the problem: a hard reboot before the unknown program could initiate.

This, of course, caught the attention of *everyone* when the entire Mars communication network blacked out. Just as everyone's curiosity piqued and anyone who was not watching a broadcast or talking on a com device when it happened also began to notice, the system flashed to life. Every com device and every broadcast receiver on every channel, from the handheld to the in-home to the public theatre showed the same image. It was as if a comic book storyline had come to life and the super villain was about to announce to the entire world his evil plot to destroy it. Katherine, however, did *not* look like a villain of any sort. Her large brown eyes, which seemed to be pleading before she even spoke, and sharp features immediately seized the attention of anyone who was watching. The light from the camera she had used combined with the ambient light behind her made her look almost ethereal. She did not speak for several long seconds, as if unsure what she wanted to say and not certain if anyone would actually listen.

"Hello. I am Katherine Shaw of the Europa mining colony that orbits Jupiter." Her voice seemed to crackle with tension. "Europa is currently being occupied by a mercenary and pirate force led by Captain O'Connor, who is working in concert with Commander Daniels. I don't know why they are here or what they hope to gain, but dozens of people have already been killed. More probably will be when we attempt to send this message. If this actually works, I'm sorry. I know it's illegal to send a transmission this way, but I don't know what else to do. Whoever receives this transmission … please help us and relay it to the Republic military. Please help us …" She paused for a second, then cut the recording.

The communications network nearly crashed again as citizens the world over called the authorities. This was entirely unnecessary, since most of the police and several of the unsecured military channels had also intercepted the recording. It only took two hours to cut through the red tape and contact generals, an admiral, and the president. One of the generals alleviated doubts about the validity of the message when he relayed the story of how an old marine distress beacon had been activated just over a week before, and how Commander Daniels convinced them that it was merely some sort of equipment malfunction. They, of course, had no reason to doubt his word at the time. Many of the companies operating on Europa contacted the government and informed them that there had been strange shipping delays, several of their ships had disappeared, and they had been out of contact with the moon for over two months, allegedly due to some sort of communications glitch at the base. They had also spoken with Commander Daniels.

The *Olympus* was the oldest Martian battle cruiser in the fleet, stolen from the Federation when the war of independence started. The *Chugiak* was the newest, commissioned three months earlier, and still on its first tour with the *Olympus* along, in case it ran into trouble. They received orders to proceed with celerity to Europa and eliminate the hostile occupying force that had taken over the colony and its mining operation. They were to consider any of their own forces that may be present as hostile. They were four days away at top speed. The captains gleaned a few more details from Mars once they were underway, but their knowledge regarding the situation was limited.

Colonel Mons conveyed the short version of the story to Markus in about two minutes. After seeing the Colonel's credentials and speaking with some of the men, Markus was convinced that these were real Martian Marines. Another five minutes of Mons interrogating him, and the colonel was convinced that they too were the good guys. Markus stepped from behind the barricade and waved for Tyler to come forward. Tyler warily came forward and met with Markus and Mons in the middle of the corridor. A few minutes later, Tyler and Markus motioned for the colonists to come out. After several tense moments, everyone began to be at ease. The next order of business was to finish the liberation of the colony. Colonel Mons stated that they had deployed their forces through the cargo docks, and also had another squad outside in power-suits, ensuring that anyone attempting to leave by way of the main hangar would be promptly shot down. Three other marine groups were moving through the colony, but they still had not secured all hostiles in and around the main space docks. The colonel quickly briefed them, displaying a base holo-schematic from his computer armband. He showed them where he wanted them to take up positions to provide support fire. Tyler started to argue, wanting to more actively participate.

Colonel Mons held up his hand.

"I know you and your people want to finish this, Mr. Tyler. But you have already suffered more casualties during this entire event than I find acceptable. We are here to prevent the deaths of any more colonists. Please, let us do our job." Mons gripped Tyler's shoulder and looked firmly at him. "*You* and your people have already achieved victory today, not us." The colonel spoke loudly enough for all of the colonists to hear. "Let us help you finish this without further loss."

"As you say, Colonel," Tyler conceded.

"Good." Mons gave a quick look to his lieutenants, who had been watching, and without a word they were rejoining and moving their squads. "I look forward to celebrating your freedom with you all tonight." The colonel saluted, turned, and jogged back to his men, who were already leaving.

Daniels had set the base's self-destruct sequence and fled to his ship when he heard the rebels had taken back the colony. He thought he would escape until he noticed movement on the moon's surface just outside of the hangar. It was an entire squad of soldiers in power suits bearing Martian Marine markings. He watched in horror as they quickly took up defensive positions outside the hangar and deployed two mobile anti-aircraft turrets. If he tried to take his ship out of here, they would blow him out of the sky before his engines were warm. He ran over to a terminal and ordered a mercenary group to man the base defense turrets and wipe them out. But they stated they were already attempting to repel at least two other marine groups that had entered the base.

If the fiercely patriotic marines didn't shoot him on sight, he would certainly be tried and found guilty of treason, as there were hundreds of colonists that would gladly witness against him. Meaning he would still die, just later. He needed a distraction … He entered his security code, bypassed the safety protocols, and began venting the atmosphere from the brig where the remaining Republic base personnel were being held prisoner. He interfaced with the com-center and saw that the sensors had just picked up two battle cruisers positioning themselves directly overhead. Once they were in place, they could blast anything that tried to take to the sky into dust. His only chance was to get rid of that marine squad outside the hangar.

Daniels sprinted out of the hangar toward the nearest gun turret. The marines had intentionally positioned themselves at the edge of the gun turret's range. Still, with luck, he could wreak enough havoc to give him an escape window. Running through corridors and making a few turns, he rounded the final corner and found himself face to face with a squad of marines. He froze, feeling himself going pale.

"… Am I g-glad to see you guys," he finally managed. They were glaring at him, weapons aimed at his head. "Pirates have taken over the colony, and took everyone prisoner. I …"

A young soldier stepped forward, removed Daniels' weapon, and motioned for him to walk to the back of the unit. Daniels, being both a coward and shrewd enough to pick his battles, did as he was told.

Tyler held the colonists back, using them only as support troops as the marines initiated an assault on the base's com center. The Com was not the best place to make a last stand, but it was where the majority of the mercenary forces had somehow ended up. Several marines were killed and a half dozen were wounded during the short two-minute battle. Martian Marines usually opted for speed and stealth as opposed to entrenching themselves and attacking from fixed positions. They were the fierce masters of mobility, and that was the main reason they were feared.

Colonel Mons walked out of the smoke toward Markus. "Constable." His face and tone were grave. "Good news and bad. Commander Daniels was just captured attempting to escape. However, he managed to begin venting the atmosphere from the brig, where we believe there are friendly Republic personnel. My computer guys say they're working on something more important at the moment, we still have to secure the Com, and there's some minor mopping up to do. Are any of your people capable of helping the prisoners?"

"We'll do our best, Colonel." Markus turned and motioned for his and two other colonist groups to follow him. They all acknowledged and followed, looking a bit confused.

Jonas was on Markus's heels in seconds. *For an old guy,* Jonas thought, *he sure can run.* Markus gave him the quick version of where they were going and why. Jonas dropped back to Quinn and gave him the information, and he relayed it to his and Eric's men. There was no need to tell Katherine, who had been keeping pace with him and heard everything twice. They were both fatigued from hours of physical exertion and adrenaline dumps.

"Do you think…" Jonas took a breath. "You can do anything with the…" Another breath. "Terminal once we get there?"

Katherine started to speak, but was breathing too hard. She simply nodded with a slightly worried look.

Jonas rounded the last corner with Markus to see a marine standing casually with a rifle pointed at Daniels. The squad behind him lowered their weapons when they recognized the group as the one described by Colonel Mons a few minutes prior. The control terminal beside the door showed the atmosphere level quickly dropping below life-supporting levels. The pressure doors were covered with dents, blackened and warm from the soldier's attempts to blow them open.

"Which one of your people is the best hacker?" The marine lieutenant asked curtly.

Katherine stepped forward, feeling as though the marines were somehow looking at her with slight awe. When the lieutenant spoke she realized why.

"Miss Shaw!" He gave a low and respectful head nod. "Just about every man here was hoping to get to meet *you*."

"Why?" she asked, feeling more self-conscious. She stepped past the lieutenant. The marines parted, clearing a path for her to the terminal.

Lieutenant Barov looked slightly amused.

"Because of your message, of course. That's why we're here." Several of the other Marines nodded in agreement. "Nearly everyone on Mars saw your message when it broadcast, and everyone else has seen it on the news since then. Every citizen in the Republic is anxiously awaiting news of whether our operation is a success, and how you've faired throughout the ordeal."

Jonas looked at Markus. Markus just shrugged.

"Oh," said Katherine, noticeably blushing as she tried to work and ignore the fact that she was now the center of so much attention. She was trying to bypass the need for a password by simply restarting the safety protocols, which would normally not allow the atmosphere to be vented if there were people present. Her concentration was broken by a scuffle behind her; she reflexively crouched down when she heard gunfire.

She turned to see Markus and Jonas, with a group of marines and colonists in tow, running around the corner. What were they were doing? *Daniels!* Her mind screamed as she realized he was no longer in sight.

James initially started off with them, but realized he would be leaving Katherine, so he turned back and stayed with her and the remaining marines.

The *Chugiak* stayed in place over the base as the *Olympus* launched her Merlin fighters and began lumbering after a fleeing Corvette. Judging from its trajectory, the ship had launched from the dark side of the base, away from the hangars. The ship stayed close to the surface, heading toward the opposite side of the moon. Before the fighters could catch it, the Corvette broke orbit, and its powerful engines pushed it out of weapons range.

Markus caught up with Daniels. He shoved the former commander from behind, sending him sliding and sprawling onto the metal floor. Markus was upon him when Daniels turned and slashed at him with a previously hidden knife. The gash in his arm did not cause him any pain, but revealed a secret that few knew: the circuitry of the artificial replacement arm he received during his time with the Federation. Markus grabbed the blade of the knife with his inhuman arm and wrenched it from Daniels, tossing it behind him.

Using his synthetic arm, he took Daniels by the throat, lifted him off the floor, and slammed him against the wall with a hollow thud.

"What is the password!" Markus spit through his teeth.

Daniels gasped for air and started to speak, but instead spat in Markus's face.

Markus slammed Daniels' head into the wall again. This time it sounded like a melon being dropped.

Everyone present was stunned by Markus's sudden miraculous strength. Jonas stepped up to Markus to try and convince him to take it easy and could hear crackling sounds in Daniels throat as Markus tightened his robotic vice grip.

"Tell me the code!" Markus demanded again.

Daniels just gurgled.

"Markus!" Jonas grabbed Markus's synthetic arm. It felt like a piece of steel.

Markus ignored him and slammed Daniels' head into the wall again.

"Tell me!" Markus visibly relaxed his grip slightly.

Daniels coughed and choked. He glanced at Jonas. His eyes grew cold and he gurgled an answer.

Jonas could not make out exactly what he said, but it was heavily seasoned with profanity. He could deduce some of the statement from Markus's answer...

"Well," Markus again tightened his grip. "I'm new to *their kind*, and their ways are new to me. But I am what I am, and right now..." There was a snap as Markus's grip tightened and Daniels quit breathing. "I'm the man who killed the most hated man on the planet."

The body of Commander Daniels fell to the floor, as Markus turned away without looking back. Jonas was shocked to see that his face was calm as he stopped, inhaled, and released a deep breath before stating flatly, "He refused to give up the password necessary to save the lives of the prisoners trapped in the brig. Commander Daniels was regrettably killed during intense interrogation." Markus walked past several colonists who were staring, still shocked at Markus's arm, and at what he had done. Markus had been the easy-going, sometimes almost pushover, constable at the colony for over a decade. No one thought him capable of such savageness.

Jonas could not help but jump as Markus put his synthetic arm on his shoulder. But it did not feel like the cold, iron-hard robotic vise that had just squeezed the life out of a man. It was the warm right hand Jonas had shaken dozens of times since the first time he met Markus as a child. It felt human.

"Come on." Markus cocked his head back in the direction they had just come from and smiled. "We should get back and help Katherine and the others."

Jonas smiled and nodded back.

The doors hissed, then screamed like a banshee as air from the base poured into the lower pressure of the brig. Two marines wedged a breach bar between the doors to prevent them from closing again as the rest surged past them into the main hallway.

Katherine took a series of deep breaths and let her arms drop wearily to her sides.

"You did it!" Jonas came running up and hugged her unexpectedly as she turned around, causing her to jump. "Are they alive?"

"I don't know yet, they just went in."

Marines started emerging with coughing former captives over their shoulders. Some were half walking with the help of a soldier.

Lieutenant Barov was yelling at his men inside the brig, telling them to make sure they had everyone and double-time it to the hangar. He emerged a few seconds later.

"We have to get out of here, constable; the base is set to self-destruct. *That's* why our computer guys were tied up. They were trying to stop it. Apparently they can't. We have thirty minutes to evacuate." He checked his watch. "Twenty-eight."

Everyone assisted the former captives to the nearest lift. Some began to feel better and ran under their own power. They made it to the lift and began the ascent to the hangar level.

"What about everyone in the colony?" Katherine asked the lieutenant.

"We will have to re-establish the surface base and rescue them as soon as possible. Until then, they're going to be on their own."

"Isn't there something we can do?" she pleaded.

"Our best men have tried everything. They don't have time to hack the system; they probably couldn't do it if they had a week. They succeeded in opening the blast doors to the computer core, but destroying it would not stop the sequence. We can't use an EMP blast from a battle cruiser, because that section of the base is shielded to protect the core from EMP." He did not have to say that using an EMP weapon to fry the computer core was a last ditch effort anyway. While it would fry the circuitry and prevent the self-destruct, it was still a gamble whether or not the reactor would shut down automatically, as it should, or if they could manage a manual shut down, if that too failed.

"We have to tell everyone so they can evacuate," Katherine demanded.

"They will not have time to reach the base, get to a hangar, board a ship, and clear the base before it blows. The safest place for them to be is down there. But you're right, Miss Shaw. We should warn them." Barov nodded to his communications man, who began relaying the message.

Jonas stood in silence, racking his brain for some elusive answer he could feel somewhere in the back of his memory.

"*Manta*," he mumbled.

Katherine looked at him and started to take his hand, thinking he was grieving his lost ship.

"Wait, wait!" Jonas held his hands up. "When I was inside the Federation base, I found a device. It was some kind of computer wiping device." The lieutenant was looking at him sideways with an eyebrow raised. Jonas knew what he must be thinking... he was nuts. "There used to be a Federation outpost here, about eighty or ninety years ago. I found it while I was trying to circumnavigate the ocean. But there's no time to explain all of that right now. Inside the base there was a device that had been left to wipe the computer core. That base had been set to self-destruct too, but this device wiped the core while still allowing it to reboot and restore its basic functions."

Lieutenant Barov looked more than a little hopeful. "Where is it?"

"It was on my ship ... that the pirates sunk. I thought maybe you guys might have something like it." They were quickly moving down the corridor to meet with Colonel Mons.

They reached the computer core where Colonel Mons appeared calm, although his voice was edged.

"Colonel." The lieutenant saluted. "I need every man here to gather some materials for me. I have a plan that might still allow us to stop the self-destruct sequence."

"You're well aware, Lieutenant, that we only have about twenty-five minutes until meltdown."

"Yes, sir. If it does not appear we can stop it, we will retreat in time to avoid the radiation plume."

"Do it."

"I need every available man to listen up!" Lieutenant Barov raised his voice. "I need a two-foot aluminum pipe, an explosive shaped to fit inside the pipe, a lot of fine conductive wire, and a thin sheet of copper, gold, or platinum that is at least two feet square. Go!" Marines scrambled in every direction in search of the strange list of components.

Lieutenant Barov ordered his men to move their equipment to the evacuation point. Two men inside the computer core's housing room emerged. They had finished removing the core's secondary layer of shielding, leaving its circuitry exposed. He ordered all remaining personnel to evacuate to the hangar.

Barov had placed plastic explosives inside the aluminum pipe and rigged it with a timer. Several of his men had painstakingly wrapped a large amount of fine electrical wiring around the pipe and then wrapped a piece of platinum sheeting around it. He placed the entire contraption into a carbon fiber cylinder and set the timer to detonate one minute before the self-destruct sequence finalized. That gave him six minutes to get out of the base. Everyone else was already about two minutes ahead of him.

Jonas reached the marine drop ship and looked around the corner one last time as the hangar doors began to close.

"Wait!" he yelled, holding up his hand for Markus to hold the door.

"Thanks!" Barov said breathlessly as he ran through the ship's door. The doors closed as the last few marines filed into the last transport. The other squads had already evacuated. Atmosphere shook the ship as it rushed out of the opening hangar doors. They did not have time to wait for the air to be pumped out of the hangar. If plan B did not work, they had three minutes to get clear of the base. The urgency of the situation made the ship feel slow and cumbersome as it lumbered out of the hangar and sluggishly accelerated.

Less than two minutes remained, but they would not know if it worked until the countdown was up. Barov was deep in thought, trying to make sure he had not forgotten anything, although he knew it was too late if he had. He had never actually built an improvised EMP device, but he had studied their construction after reading about them in an old military handbook. The EMP would fry the computer core, stop the self-destruct charges, and shut down the reactor controls. The reactor's failsafes should engage and shut down the reaction.

The pilot announced they were clear.

Jonas and Katherine held each other's hand tightly. Markus was the only one who appeared to have any semblance of calmness, although Jonas could not figure out why. The transport ship gained altitude as it approached one of the battle cruisers.

Ten seconds remained … Five, four, three, two, one, zero …

NINETEEN

Jonas knew they could not hear the detonation in space, but he thought the pilot would tell them when the base was destroyed. Everyone was looking at each other uneasily, not wanting to be the first to ask if Barov's device had worked, and somehow jinx it. It had only been three seconds since the countdown would have finalized ... it could have been slightly delayed, or they may have synchronized their watches improperly. Jonas stood and stiffly walked over to a portal that was oriented in the direction of the base. He had the appearance of a man walking to what he knew would be the remains of a fallen comrade. He peered out the portal for several long seconds. His face dropped, and his shoulders slumped.

Jonas mumbled something under his breath. He turned to face everyone. "It's still there," he said, almost inaudibly in disbelief. Still not quite believing it himself, he looked again.

"It's still there!" he yelled excitedly.

The marines looked at each other for a split second, then the entire ship erupted in a collective cheer as they clamored to look out the portal.

Markus stood and shook Lieutenant Barov's hand. "Well done, Lieutenant. Well done."

"Thank you, Constable," he just managed to say, before he was mobbed with shoulder slaps, hugs, and handshakes.

Katherine stood and threw her arms around Jonas, squeezing him tightly. Jonas held her strongly and nodded over her shoulder at Markus, who was looking at them both and smiling.

They maneuvered into a hangar on the underside of the battle cruiser *Chugiak*, where they offloaded.

"Colonel Mons!" Jonas yelled across the hangar as they were being escorted in a different direction from the group of marines they had arrived with. Colonel Mons turned and held a hand up, indicating for them to wait. After a moment he briskly walked over.

"Jonas," he said properly, "what can I do for you?"

"We were wondering when we would be allowed to return home, sir."

The colonel smiled.

"Soon, of course. We've already sent an engineering group down to the base to assess the damage to the computer core and make sure the reactor is actually shut down. They will need to reinitiate the reaction before we can allow you to return and descend below the surface."

"How long will that take?" Jonas asked.

"Probably several days. But right now I have to debrief my men. The captain has invited all of you," Colonel Mons indicated the entire group of colonists, "to rest and have lunch with him in the mess hall. I will see you in a few hours." With that, Colonel Mons turned and walked away.

They followed their escort to the mess hall, where they met Captain William Riley of the *Chugiak*. He greeted them warmly but at no more than thirty seemed too young to be captain of a battle cruiser. Captain Riley congratulated the colonists on their victory and listened attentively to Markus, Katherine, and Tyler's accounts of what transpired at the colony. He then turned to Jonas and began inquiring about the hidden Federation base he had found in the unexplored depths of the ocean. Apparently, Lieutenant Barov had taken note of Jonas's comment in the lift earlier and reported it.

Jonas told the captain all about what he had found there regarding the human experiments, and the Federation's attempts to destroy the facility to cover them up. He slipped and mentioned the ships he had found, realizing too late that if a Republic cataloging expedition were able to enter the base and explore it, they would realize one was missing. He decided to tell the captain about recovering one of the ships, erasing the memory and uploading *Manta*'s A.I. to it. He stated that he placed the ship in orbit, leaving out the part about the *M2* piloting herself out of the facility. He did not have to say it for everyone to assume he had simply piloted the ship out of the hangar remotely.

Jonas finished, and the captain sat silent for a few seconds.

"Intersystem salvage law dictates that you must be allowed to keep your new ship, Jonas. And even if it did not, since the owners of the facility, the Federation, no longer have standing to protest, it would still be yours. As for the facility itself, I would imagine the Republic would want me to seize it for research. Given the experiments you've described, we could use it for ammo to condemn the Federation with, even though you have stated most of the records have been erased." Jonas began to draw a breath to protest, and Captain Riley held up his hand. "However, they will also likely reimburse you for the other ship and all of the salvageable equipment contained therein. Does that seem a fair enough agreement?"

Jonas looked at Markus, who nodded.

"Yes, sir. That seems fair. Thank you."

"Good! We will be staying on until a new base commander is assigned. If you wish to bring your ship here, I will have my mechanics give it a thorough going over and see to it she is fully refueled and equipped. If you wish, you are welcome to stay on board until they are finished. It's the least we can do. Your rebellion spared the lives of many of my marines, and I realize it was at great cost. For that, I am indebted to you all. Besides." Captain Riley winked. "I'd like to have my men take a look at that cloaking skin your ship has. I've read of early experiments with the technology. The research was allegedly abandoned by the Federation about sixty years ago. You may use one of our remote fighter stations to establish a link and bring her in whenever you want."

"Okay. How about now?"

"Certainly." Captain Riley signaled the commander and instructed him to bring Jonas to a remote station so he could bring his orbiting ship in.

It took Jonas about thirty minutes to establish a link with *M2* and bring her up to the *Chugiak*. She had been doing an excellent job of hiding, mostly thanks to her optic camouflage. The *M2* materialized just over the horizon of Europa, much to the chagrin of the *Chugiak*'s commander, who was standing beside Jonas at the remote piloting station. *M2* did her best to make covert corrections to his piloting errors as he brought her into the hangar. When she had safely touched down, Jonas hurried down to the hangar to inspect her. He was still a little anxious about the captain being so accommodating, and was afraid he might take his ship from him. Jonas knew the salvage laws; pretty much everyone who flew or dreamed of space flight did. But governments, even the Republic, could usually find a reason to do what they wanted in the end. And until now, his only experience with the Republic government had been through the late Commander Daniels. *Not much of a basis for trust,* Jonas thought as he reached the hangar and was reunited with his new ship.

The ship mechanics walked around it, staring like art connoisseurs admiring a fine creation. She was an even more beautiful ship than he had remembered.

"Hey M," Jonas greeted, slightly out of breath as he approached. He was still adapting to the thinner air onboard the *Chugiak*, equivalent to a 15,000' increase in altitude.

"Hello, Captain," M coolly answered on an external speaker for all to hear. "I am happy to see you returned safely from your journey. Why are there Republic warships here?"

"It's a long story, and I have a headache. I'll fill you in later. In the meantime, would you allow these men access to all but your core systems? They would like to download your schematics and details about your camouflage system."

"As you wish," M2 opened her hatch and activated her interior lighting. She sent a text communiqué to his com device. "Your headache is likely due to the decreased atmospheric pressure. Some people are susceptible to headaches during rapid barometric pressure changes. Your body will eventually adjust. I suggest a mild sedative in the meantime."

Katherine joined Jonas in the hangar and seemed unusually clingy, but he liked it. It was probably because of all the attention she was getting from the crewmen and marines onboard. She was probably the most famous person in the Republic right now. While not an introvert by any means, she was not used to being a celebrity. Although still very young, and a little too thin by most men's standards, Katherine was very attractive and had obviously caught the eye of many of the soldiers. Jonas had to admit, he was a little jealous. But the feeling was eased by Kat's nearly ridiculous efforts to make it clear to everyone they were engaged.

A s Jonas gave Katherine the tour of M2, he seemed distracted and even a little anxious. When they were alone on the bridge, she asked him.
"Jonas, what's bothering you? You seem worried."

"Oh." He waved his hand irritably to brush away the thought and indicate the ship. "I'm just worried they're going to try and come up with some excuse to take her from me."

Katherine squeezed her lips together and started not to answer, but decided to anyway. "The Republic helped us, rescued us if the base would have been destroyed, and saved the colony. They have been nothing but kind so far, and haven't given us any reason to doubt their intentions." Her voice was slightly raised by now. "I don't think the people of the Republic will soon forget the reasons we broke away from the Federation: one of them being the government taking what it wanted, when it wanted, and simply changing the law if it got in their way. Everyone we've met up here so far has been nice; so don't start getting paranoid. The battle is over. Let it go." She set her jaw and looked defiantly at him.

Jonas's first feeling was anger. It hurt and caught him off-guard to be corrected by Katherine. He listened until she was finished and took a deep breath. He was silent for a moment, and looked into her eyes, which softened soon after.

"You're right." He sighed, hugged her, and kissed her on the forehead.

"I know," she said smugly and smiled up at him.

"Let's stay up here until they're done with her. It will give us a chance to get a good look at a real battle cruiser. In all the excitement, I'd forgotten I've wanted to see one of these ever since I can remember."

"All right." Katherine took a quick breath. "It will be like a vacation!"

The next two days flew by as the captain's steward, various chiefs, and sometimes even the captain gave them thorough tours of every part of the massive cruiser. Before Jonas knew it, *M2* was ready to launch. As he walked onto the hangar deck, he felt a slight pang of nervousness at the thought of flying a spaceship for the first time. So far, he had only flown simulations.

The deck chief approached Jonas. His jumpsuit was a fresh one, but it already had oil smudges on it. He was a well-aged man who had seen battle on Federation ships before defecting at the beginning of the Mars Revolution, where he had enlisted with the Republic. He had a haggard appearance, but his eyes were bright and filled with life. He was a man who, despite thirty years of hard work, still loved his job, and it showed in the morale of every man on the flight deck working for him.

"Doctor Black. Good to see you!" The chief shook Jonas's hand.

When the commander conducted security checks on Jonas

and Katherine, he discovered Jonas's newly acquired academic rank, and the captain and crew had taken to calling him Doctor Black.

"*M2* is a beautiful ship. I wish I could spend more time with her…" The chief winked at Katherine. "Don't tell my wife, she'd be jealous…but I'm afraid she's ready to go." He indicated for them to follow him as he walked around the ship. "We checked all her guns and they seem to be in top shape, although you're going to need to take her a few kilometers away and test fire them, just to make sure. We refueled her reactor too. She was obviously built for extended reconnaissance missions; she holds enough matter in reserve for over a year at full power. Her skin was intact, but needed a good polishing, which we gave her. Her camouflage is amazing! And if she's as old as you say, I don't know how they did it. The Federation was stupid to leave her there, but that's why we left them, right?" He turned and winked as he stepped inside and proceeded to the bridge.

Jonas was amazed at how different the bridge looked; it was beautiful, aglow with holo-displays, lights, and polished alloy.

"What happened?"

"You like that?" The chief beamed. "We got all of her systems running and fully functioning, with a little help of course. Right M?"

"Yes, Chief," M2 responded coolly. "Good evening, Captain; and how are you, Miss Shaw?"

"Fine, thank you," Kat answered.

"Hey M," Jonas replied. "You look great!"

"Thank you."

"Okay M, show him," the chief said, nearly giddy with excitement.

The deck, ceiling, and walls forward of the aft wall seemed to vanish, and all that remained of the bridge were the rails, seats, and control consoles. Jonas and Katherine both let out a simultaneous gasp. It appeared the entire ship had vaporized around them, leaving them suddenly standing on glass in the middle of the hangar. Jonas started to smile uncontrollably as the shock faded.

"Thought you'd like that," the chief replied before Jonas could speak. "It's a common feature in newer vessels, but this one was sixty years ahead of her time."

"I've never seen anything like it…," Jonas said, still unable to suppress his involuntary smile. "How can I ever thank you, Chief?"

"No need. I'm just doing my job. Besides, getting the opportunity to work on this, I mean her (sorry, M), is thanks enough. And it gets even better, for me at least. The captain has put me in to head up the project for installing optical camouflage on all our ships. It means I get a permanent job back home on Mars. The captain's been trying to get me to take a cushy old man job for years… I never thought I'd be excited about it."

"I thought the military already had optical camouflage?" Katherine asked.

"We do, but it's more of a color and pattern-shifting sort of thing. But this! This is a perfect representation of the exact background the ship is in front of from every visible angle. It doesn't get any better than this. But, enough of my babbling. You have a test flight to go on. Are you two ready? I mean three; sorry, M."

Katherine nodded at Jonas.

"We're ready to go," Jonas said. The chief started to walk away when Jonas spoke up.

"Hey, Chief?"

"Yes, *Captain?*" He smiled.

"What's with all the apologizing to M?"

"Oh, that." He looked up sheepishly. "She said I had to call her M, and not 'it,' and be polite to her… or she would, uh…"

M2 cut his sentence short.

"I would cause him no end of grief."

"That's it." He smiled and pointed upward.

"M! Why did you do that?" Jonas scolded.

"I don't know, Captain… I believe it is a developing subroutine in my basic programming. Perhaps you should ask Miss Shaw, since she was my primary programmer."

Katherine was looking away, trying to appear innocent and ignore the conversation. Jonas looked at her accusingly.

"What?" Katherine turned and answered shrugging her shoulders. "I was trying to make her more human."

"Great." Jonas rolled his eyes. "M, apologize to the chief for causing him trouble."

"I regret if I have caused you any inconvenience, Chief. I truly enjoyed working with you, and thank you for all the repairs you conducted."

"Why, thank you. The feeling is mutual. I'll miss you, M."

"I will miss you too."

The chief smiled and nodded to Jonas and Katherine before he turned and walked down the corridor and exited, sealing the hatch behind him. Jonas sat in the captain's chair of his newly refurbished ship. The simuleather felt cool and soft as it conformed to his body weight. The controls were just as he had left them. He smiled at Katherine as she took the navigator's seat to his right.

Jonas keyed the com.

"*Chugiak*, this is Captain Black of the *M Two* requesting permission to depart," Jonas said in his coolest pilot's voice, already smirking at Katherine as she turned to roll her eyes.

"*M Two*, this is *Chugiak* control. You are clear for departure. Please proceed along the coordinates we are sending to conduct your engine and weapons tests."

"Copy that, *Chugiak*. Flight plan received."

"Inform us when you have successfully executed your maneuvers. Good luck. *Chugiak* out."

Jonas powered up the engines and brought M to a hover over the hangar deck, swinging her nose around and pointing her at the launch bay. The *M2*'s engines roared as she gently glided into the launch bay. Jonas was still unaccustomed to certain aspects of hangar etiquette. A pilot was only supposed to use landing thrusters to lift off the flight deck, as there was no need to power up primary engines for lift off in the near zero gravity of a battle cruiser. The deafening noise in the hangar bay was abruptly cut off as the massive pressure doors sealed her into the launch bay. The air was drawn from the air lock, and the outer doors opened.

Jonas eased the ship clear of the *Chugiak* and turned in the direction of his flight plan.

He eased forward on the throttle and the ship surged forward, firmly pressing him into his seat. The *M2* quickly pulled away from the *Chugiak* as Jonas dipped closer to the surface of Europa. He kept a prudent altitude of a hundred kilometers swinging around the moon in close orbit. Io was passing close to Europa, and they could see many of that moon's details on the display. They reached the designated coordinates for the weapons test. Jonas manually targeted an ice upheaval on the surface. A rapid shot from each of the rail guns impacted the surface seconds later in, at such a distance, a tiny blast of ice and debris. He fired an invisible burst from the laser turret at the same point, producing plume of steam as ice vaporized.

Jonas activated the com. "*Chugiak*, this is the *M Two*. Weapons test successful, all systems operating perfectly. Proceeding to the far side of the moon."

"Jonas, this is Captain Riley. Good luck on the rest of the test. You will be out of contact for about fifteen minutes. Let us know when you are back in range."

"Will do, Captain. *M Two* out."

Commander Burke gave Captain Riley a sideways glance as the transmission was cut. They had, only minutes before, ended a heated discussion regarding the use of unsecured transmissions between the *M2* and *Chugiak* during this "test flight." Commander Burke knew from what the chief had told him that Jonas's ship did not need a test flight, but Captain Riley ordered it anyway. The captain had then instructed the Com officer to use an unsecured channel during the flight. It was reckless, and the captain knew it. Two days before, one of their scouts had intercepted an encrypted transmission from the far side of Io. The transmission had been decrypted only this morning, which was when the captain disappeared to speak with the captain of the *Olympus* in private. Shortly after that, the *Olympus* was recalled by Republic command and broke orbit. This, in and of itself, was not unusual, since ship's captains were often given missions that required operating with autonomy and secrecy from the rest of the fleet.

Only twenty minutes ago, Captain Riley had briefed Commander Burke on the contents of the decrypted message, and what he and the captain of the *Olympus* intended to do with it. Burke opposed Riley's nearly complete disregard of most of their ethical philosophy as officers. He argued that if they had simply asked him, Doctor Black would have volunteered. Captain Riley stated he had considered that, but they could not do it because Jonas was a civilian and, therefore, deemed a security risk. Captain Riley declared the discussion over at that point.

Jonas and Katherine were amazed at the views afforded them by the M2's 180 x 180 degree monitor. Jonas had never seen Europa from the outside before, and Katherine had not seen it since she was five, when she and her family had moved there. Now it seemed they were propelled through space in a glass ship. Jupiter took up the entire left half of the bridge view, with its incredible mass of swirling storms. Io hung in front of it, looking very close, but insignificant with the gas giant looming behind it. The entire scene was mesmerizing.

"What's that?" Katherine asked, pointing at a black spot that had just appeared on Io.

Jonas strained to see it.

"I don't know, but it looks like it's getting bigger. I don't remember Io having any activity on it. Do you?"

"No … it's getting bigger. Is it a ship?"

"It could be, or maybe an asteroid. M, is there any way to magnify an image on the view screen?"

"Yes, Captain. The most precise method is to use the selector console on the arm of your chair to highlight the area and then roll the edge to magnify. Or you can point at what you want to look at and say "Magnify.""

"Magnify." Katherine pointed at the spot while Jonas was still fiddling with the manual controls.

"It's a ship," Katherine said.

"Captain, we are being scanned," M stated coolly.

"Is it a Republic ship?"

"Commencing scan...No, Captain, it is not one of the Republic ships I have seen. The ships I have encountered to date are the only ones in my database."

"Well, I guess we continue. M, what is it doing?"

"It is rapidly closing and is on an intercept course."

"Have they tried to contact us?"

"Negative. Shall I try to hail them?"

"Yes."

Several moments passed.

"They do not respond, Captain. They have accelerated and are still closing. I have conducted a secondary scan. The ship appears to be heavily armed, and they are nearing weapons range."

"I don't like this...engage cloak. We're getting out of here." Jonas increased engine power and made a minor course change. "That should throw them off. Maybe we can make it back to the *Chugiak* and figure out what's going on."

"Captain, they have altered course to intercept."

"What? I thought they couldn't see us with our camouflage engaged?"

"They cannot. However, they can probably detect the thermal signature of my engines. And I just detected a laser scan from them. They are powering weapons."

Jonas rolled the ship in an attempt to evade and dodged the first volley. Katherine had only just strapped herself into her chair, narrowly avoiding being thrown across the bridge. He changed course and increased power to maximum. *M2* lurched and accelerated faster than he thought possible for a ship of that size.

"This is the *M Two*," Jonas yelled into the com. "We are under attack, requesting any Republic ship in the area to come to our aid. Please respond."

He dove toward the surface to gain more speed and try and

get the horizon between him and the hostile ship. He knew their time was rapidly running out. They would fire again at any second and would likely fry his engines. Then they could pick them apart at their leisure.

He had an idea.

Jonas quickly changed course again and shot back up at a low angle, away from the surface of the moon. If his engines were disabled with their next shot, he should be propelled away from the moon and, if he was lucky, far enough away to exit their radio blackout and call for help.

"They have weapons lock, Captain," M stated.

TWENTY

They waited to see if Daniels had escaped, not out of concern for his welfare, but out of concern for their paychecks. Doyle had assumed command of *The Venutian Witch* and held position behind Io. They had sent a scout probe out the day before to check the status of the two behemoth cruisers and found them still hovering over Europa base. The next day, one of the cruisers broke orbit and left. Doyle decided to stay put while he and the crew assessed their situation and planned their next course of action. He was also hoping the other cruiser would withdraw so they could leave unnoticed.

The following day they had intercepted a transmission from the area of Europa. O'Connor had not been one to hold a grudge, but Doyle was. With the only battle cruiser on the far side of Europa, they rounded Io and rapidly accelerated toward the ice moon, taking care to stay behind it in what should be the cruiser's blind spot.

Doyle relished the idea of blowing that little punk out of the sky. He had surmised from an injured group of mercenaries that had escaped with him, that the kid had somehow killed Captain O'Connor. He intended to settle the score, and the crew were all for it. He had the magnified image of the tiny Corvette on the main view screen.

They continued to close, and Doyle began to smile as they closed to weapons range. "What!" he shrieked as the entire ship vanished.

"Where did they go?" he demanded.

The sensors operator spoke up. "Maybe the ship has some kind of camouflage. Switching to thermal imaging... there! It's just a hot spot, and it's moving pretty fast. I'll bet it's their engines."

"Lock weapons and fire!"

"We can only get a full lock on the engines, sir, not the rest of the ship."

"Fire anyway!" Doyle snapped.

The *Witch*'s forward laser cannons and two rail guns fired. But it was a clean miss. The auto-targeting program had targeted the heat of the engine wash, not the actual engines.

"Flank speed. Target manually," Doyle yelled.

The tiny thermal image took evasive action and dipped toward the surface of the moon. It *was* a fast ship, and it was starting to pull away. It changed course again and headed back toward open space, going against all logical evasive tactics. *The Venutian Witch* adjusted its angle to narrow the distance between them and the invisible Corvette. The pirate gunners had their gunlocks recalibrated to target in front of the engine heat on the ship. Suddenly their sensors were overloaded with targets.

A larms screeched, and Jonas almost failed to act quick enough to avoid a collision with the second ship. Fighters blurred past him as he dove under the massive battle cruiser. "Captain Black." Jonas's com chirped. "This is Captain Frederick of the *Olympus*. Fall in behind us and stay there. We'll take care of the *Witch*." He cut the transmission before Jonas could respond.

Jonas flew close enough under the belly of the *Olympus* that

he could see the various dents and scratches left from tiny asteroid strikes on her hull. It took less than a second to fly beneath
the ship; he flinched as he passed through the wash of the battle
cruiser's immense engines.

The shiny black surface of *The Venutian Witch* reflected the
images of the stars and the Republic fighters closing on it as
it turned. Its camouflage was perfect for hiding against the
background of open space, but it stood out like a fresh black eye
against the backdrop of Jupiter.

Three squadrons of Republic Merlin fighters coalesced into a
three-pronged claw formation and fired a quick burst from their
guns, followed by their first of two missiles. They immediately
broke formation and formed pairs, continuing their approach in
a loose, random formation. The auto defense turrets on the pirate
ship took out about three quarters of the missiles, but there were
too many for it to handle. The pilots could see, from the still-
distant view, the infamous pirate ship covered with tiny flashes
of fire as the missiles impacted.

The Merlins fired their laser cannons in focused bursts until
they drained their capacitor banks. Some of the laser barrage was
deflected by the *Witch*'s reflective camouflage, which doubled as
laser armor. They were within a kilometer when they launched
their last missiles and began a fusillade with their quad 20mm
accelerator cannons. One, then another Merlin succumbed to
turret fire from the *Witch*. Three of the defense turrets exploded
as missiles struck their intended targets. Another missile slightly
missed its turret and struck near its base, dislodging the turret
from the ship and sending it and its gunner careening through
space. The *Witch* was venting atmosphere from two places, and
one of her engines blacked out.

The pirates launched six fighters and two small Corvettes. A
pair of Merlins alerted the rest of the attack force to the opening
hangar doors, and four of the six fighters were destroyed as they
exited the *Witch* by an awaiting Republic fighter squadron. A pair

of Merlins from the same squadron came around on the tails of the two remaining pirate fighters, quickly dispatching them. The Corvettes were tougher. Built to raze fighters, they succeeded in destroying two of the Merlins and sending three more limping back to the *Olympus*. Since one of *The Venutian Witch's* engines had been disabled, the *Olympus* had been slowly closing the gap between them.

Two of the Republic fighter squadrons had broken off their attack of the *Witch* and focused on the two Corvettes. One Republic pilot ejected from his fighter as a blast from one of the pirate Corvettes tore the wing off of his Merlin. His wingman placed his ship between the pilot and the pirates as his seat rocketed clear of the battle. The pirate Corvette spotted the single ship and the helpless pilot and arched toward them for an easy kill. It began taking evasive action for no apparent reason before it burst into a flaming ball of gas and metal. The *Olympus* had closed within firing range and destroyed the comparably tiny Corvette with a single salvo from its guns. The other Corvette was being pummeled by a squadron of Merlins as it tumbled slowly away from the battle, its engines destroyed.

"They just destroyed two and three...only number one engine is working, sir! There's no way we're going to outrun them..." The sensor officer on *The Venutian Witch* looked at Doyle, hoping he had a plan to get them out of there.

Doyle stared at the view screen, looking more pale than usual, before keying the shipboard com.

"Attention crew of *The Venutian Witch*. I am going to fire all but three of our remaining missiles at the Republic battle cruiser. Then I am going to detonate the remaining three onboard and destroy the *Witch*. Anyone wishing to abandon ship has approximately five minutes to do so. That is all."

The bridge crew stopped what they were doing and stared

at Doyle. Two of them began to stand up and leave. The Com officer spoke up. "Sir, Captain O'Connor…"

"Is dead!" Doyle screamed. Doyle slumped into his seat; O'Connor's seat.

"But," he said flatly, "he wouldn't have gotten us into this mess in the first place. Do whatever you want." Doyle waved his hand in dismissal. "You can die here, or use an escape pod, get captured, and executed in two months. I don't care." Doyle targeted the Republic ship and began launching their remaining missiles at the *Olympus*.

A fusillade of missiles erupted from *The Venutian Witch*, all targeting the Olympus. The Olympus' auto guns caused most of the missiles to burst harmlessly a safe distance away. However, two got through the defenses. One struck the bow, causing minimal damage, while the other struck and disabled one of the forward gun turrets. The Merlins withdrew back to the protective hangar of the *Olympus*. Several dozen escape pods began bursting away from the pirate ship like sparking metal spores.

An inferno erupted from the hull of the *Witch* as the *Olympus* began pummeling the pirate ship. She was engulfed in smoke and debris as various levels were breached and subjected to decompression. Then, much sooner than expected, *The Venutian Witch* burst into a ball of fire, sending deadly debris rocketing every direction. The wreckage caused little damage to the armored hull of the *Olympus*. Had the Merlin squadrons not withdrawn when they did, they would have all been destroyed.

The *Chugiak* came into view around the other side of the moon. Had the pirates not already been disintegrated, the combined force of two battle cruisers would have made even shorter work of them. Secondary explosions erupted from the various remains of the former pirate ship's hull for almost twenty minutes. The captain of the *Olympus* graciously rescued the occupants of the escape pods, subsequently placing them under arrest.

The *M2* hung in space, looking like a tiny pilot fish next to the hulking mass of the *Olympus*. Jonas and Katherine stood for a long time at the front of the bridge, his arm around her shoulder and hers around his waist, staring at the burning wreckage and the mopping up of the pirate escape pods. With the 180 degree-entire-bridge view screen activated, it felt as though they were floating in the middle of it all with nothing between them and the infinite vastness of space. Confident that the last vestige of the pirates had been destroyed, they both felt freer than they had ever been.

M's com tone sounded and Jonas keyed it; it was the *Chugiak*.

"Doctor Black, are you and Miss Shaw all right?" Captain Riley sounded tense.

"Yes," Jonas replied. "We're fine. I'm glad you guys were still around. I thought the *Olympus* left this morning?"

"Well, that requires a little explaining. If you will return to the *Chugiak* for a bit, we will check out your ship, and I'll debrief you."

"Okay … We're on our way." Jonas thought something sounded strange.

" … Why didn't you just ask?!" Jonas stood, knocking his chair to the floor. He was not upset at first, but then he realized that they had endangered Katherine and lost it.

The commander raised an eyebrow at Captain Riley.

"I am very sorry, Jonas, but you have to understand … "

Jonas interrupted.

"I can understand putting me and my ship at risk. I would have done that if you asked me to! But I will *not* forgive putting Katherine in danger! If you or anyone ever does that again, I'll kill him!" Jonas hissed through his teeth. He could not ever remember losing his temper to the point of rage. He knew he was traveling down a precarious path, and started to calm down when he realized what he had said.

"You have to ..." Katherine quietly started.

"What?" Jonas and Riley both interrupted. Riley was surprised that she suggest Jonas actually kill him. Jonas was irritated because she had interrupted his tirade.

"You have to forgive him, Jonas." He started to demand why, but she did not let him. "Remember what your father taught you about harboring anger and giving darkness a foothold. You have to let it go. Captain Riley did what he was supposed to do. He did what he thought was best; he did his duty. Now it's your turn to do yours." She stared at Jonas calmly, her eyes pleading with him to calm down and listen.

Jonas tried to force his anger to subside, but no one likes being rebuked, and his first instinct was to lash out again. He stared at Katherine for two long seconds as her pleading and beautiful stare calmed him. He was right to be angry; he was wrong to lose control and become enraged. He was wrong to threaten Captain Riley, who had done his duty and had been nothing but helpful and kind to both of them. He closed his eyes for a second and sighed. He took Katherine's hand and turned back to Captain Riley.

"I apologize for my outburst, Captain." Jonas spoke calmly and formally. "I should not have threatened you, and ask your forgiveness. You were wrong not to trust me, and to put Katherine in danger. However, I understand that you have only known us three days and did what you thought was right. Please do not let my immaturity affect what small amount of comradeship we may have started." Jonas held his hand out over Captain Riley's desk.

Captain Riley ignored it, walked around his desk and up to Jonas, looking at him critically.

"*You*," he said harshly, "Jonas Black, are an honorable man. Yes, Miss Shaw, I *was* doing my duty, but sometimes," Riley looked at the commander, "doing what is right is more important. And I apologize to both of you." He turned back to Jonas, still regarding him with military bearing. He continued. "I have met few men twice your age that have shown to possess half the character you do. And I would be honored to be considered the friend of the good and soon to be famous Mr. and Mrs. Black."

He slightly smiled and thrust his hand out.

TWENTY-ONE

It had been almost three weeks, and at the same time it had only felt like the blink of an eye. Captain Riley had graciously sent Jonas's registration request for *M2* to Mars and streamlined the process. Her new official designation was *Em II*, and she was registered as a yacht/light freighter. It was an unusual classification, but would sidestep certain jump gate and docking taxes, depending on where he went and what he was doing at the time.

The doctors aboard the *Chugiak* had successfully repaired Markus's artificial arm, allowing him to resume his position as the colony's constable. Mining operations had slowed to a snail's pace as cleanup efforts around the colony took precedence. The colony was almost back to normal. But it would take much longer to repair all of the unseen damage than it did to fix the all of the obvious mechanical problems. Over two hundred Europans had lost their lives either during the occupation or during the revolution. On a colony with a population of just under five thousand, that meant almost everyone knew someone who had died. Whether by kinship, friendship, association, or merely remembering a familiar face, everyone felt the loss of such a significant number of people.

Jonas had felt the loss of his parents more since things had slowed. Keeping himself busy helped, but Katherine helped even more. They had been nearly inseparable since the fighting had ended, and they both agreed they wanted to keep it that way. Jonas received a significant amount of money from an insurance policy his mother had taken out on herself and Matthew. In addition, the Republic had already sent a team of specialists to inspect the abandoned Federation base. They had listed the contents in their report and the Republic deposited what they deemed an appropriate amount from the salvage therein in his bank account. They also included the bounty that the Republic had posted for Captain O'Connor. He had just received notice that morning and checked the balance. After almost bursting to tears with glee, he showed it to Katherine, who did.

It was mid-afternoon, and he had to hurry back to the colony. *Manta* had been recovered several days ago. Jonas stepped out of *Manta*'s hatch to unplug the optic wire from the outlet that connected her to *Em II*, which was docked in the base hangar half a mile above.

Markus was finishing the first section of *Manta*'s skin repairs. She would not be ready to have her A.I. reactivated for another week. When she had been sunk, her core remained intact. However, many of her peripheral circuits had been shorted or corroded by seawater and needed replaced before she could be rebooted.

"You're going to be late if you don't quit hanging around with the old guy and go," Markus called to him from the atop *Manta*'s far wing.

"After finding out that the old guy can outrun me and probably curl ten times what I weigh with his *bad* arm, I think I'll try to keep on his good side." Jonas smiled as he stepped into view.

"Right now, I'm not one who's good side you need to worry about keeping on." Markus pointed at the clock on the wall.

"I know…" Jonas smiled sheepishly. "Are you going to be there?"

Markus feigned injury. "You have to ask?" Then he smiled. "I wouldn't miss it for anything. Now get out of here."

Jonas sat in silence and thought of his parents as he was shuttled down to the colony. He smiled to himself. *Dad,* he thought, *would be happy but have that serious look and be disseminating all sorts of advice as it randomly came to him. Mom would be ecstatic, probably going from crying to laughing and back again. Whatever their actions, they would have been joyous today.*

Captain Riley rehearsed his lines at least three dozen times. It was not that they were difficult; he just did not want to make a mistake. It had been a tradition for ship's captains to perform weddings since the time of wooden sailing vessels on Earth. It had been decided in 2107, with the Martian Odyssey cruise ship incident, that the captains of spacefaring ships be legally included in that ancient rite. However, since he would not be doing so on his ship, he needed the approval of the justice of the peace, which of course Markus gave.

A t least half the colony filled the central hub. The story of Jonas's trip and discovery of the secret Federation base had been spread by the colonial militia members. Markus conducted a full investigation of all of the murders committed by the pirates, as well as all of the "murders" of the pirates by the colonists. All of this was public record, and it was soon discovered that Jonas killed the famous pirate Captain O'Connor. Between Katherine accidentally shutting down the entire Martian communications network and Jonas's killing of the galaxy's most wanted and uncovering the Federation's secret genetic experiments (the details of which were still classified), he and Katherine had become involuntary celebrities throughout the entire Republic.

Jonas wanted to simply get married aboard the *Chugiak* with only her family and their friends present. But she insisted on a traditional ceremony. She wanted more time to plan everything. However, he had to leave within the week if he was to take his position at the university. Katherine's parents had refused to allow her to go with him unless they were married, and if she waited, the earliest she could have gone to Mars was nearly six months away. Neither of them wanted to be away from each other for a week, and six months was out of the question.

So now a massive crowd of people gathered outside Markus's office, with only a glass wall separating the wedding party from thousands of eyes and hundreds of cameras peering up into the second story room.

Katherine could barely breathe as she stepped into Markus's office and walked up to Jonas. She felt overwhelmed, thinking of everything that had happened in the past months. Now she was standing here completing the biggest decision of her life with thousands of people watching. That did not even include the millions who might be watching, as the whole event was being broadcast to Mars via dozens of cameras outside; a fact she had successfully forgotten until now. But when Jonas took her hands, all of that disappeared.

Jonas was keeping his hands firmly clasped behind his back as Katherine walked into the room. He had tried keeping them at his sides, as instructed, but this was the only way he could keep them from shaking. Doubt flooded his mind when he saw her; *why would a woman as beautiful as her want me?* On a scale of 1–10, he figured himself a six; smarter and in better shape than average, but not in Katherine's league. And she was the type of woman that would get even more attractive with age. When he took her hands she looked up at him and smiled and his insecurity melted away.

Markus had to muffle a snicker when Jonas and Katherine were pronounced married by Captain Riley. They both wore such large smiles that they had to pause to get rid of them before they could kiss each other. The eight-hundred-pound glass panel walls of his office rattled as the colonists in the plaza erupted in thunderous cheer. *Who would have thought three months ago,* he furtively shook his head, *these two kids would be here today.* He could not have imagined that he would have finally found redemption: that they would be heroes.

Jonas and Katherine turned and hugged James, who was Jonas's best man. Then they simultaneously embraced Markus, squeezing him so hard he thought they might actually hurt him. He felt a tear fall from his eye as he realized they would be leaving tomorrow, and that he would be losing his newest and best friends. Worse than that, they were more like family. He did not want them to let go, but was relieved to breathe again when they did, quickly making Captain Riley their next "victim."

Tyler shook Jonas's hand and kissed Katherine on the cheek. Eric and Quinn were there with their wives and children, offering congratulations too. When they had concluded with their friends and family, they turned toward the crowd and waved to everyone, causing the glass walls to rattle again.

The next morning, Jonas and Katherine ascended to the surface base with Markus. Jonas handed him *Manta's* override codes so she would accept him as her new owner.

"I'm sure going to miss you two," said Markus.

"We'll miss you too," Jonas said, shaking Markus's hand.

Katherine hugged him.

"Come and visit us as soon as you can. Jonas won't be able to get away long enough to make the trip out here until the end of the year."

"I will. I'm thinking of retiring in a couple of more years anyway. Maybe I'll settle on Mars."

"Good. We'll be expecting you." Jonas smiled before turning and stepping into the doorway of *Em II.*

"Thanks for everything, Markus." Katherine was getting teary-eyed. "Will you stay in touch with us?"

"You don't even have to ask. Now you two get out of here, or

Jonas will be late for his new job." Markus winked and made a shooing motion with his hand. *Besides,* he thought, *if they stick around any longer I'm going to get misty-eyed.*

Katherine waved and closed the hatch. Markus backed away as *Em II*'s engines powered up. Jonas and Katherine waved one last time through the simulated window before it dissolved back into the skin of the ship. A few seconds later, the black ship, her designation and registration code displayed via her camouflage system, lifted off and gently glided into the air lock.

Markus looked out the view port of the hangar as the ship lifted away from Europa and slowly shrunk into what looked like just another star. Markus felt lonely for the first time in ten years. He remembered why it was so easy not to get close to people. Eventually you would have to part ways, and it hurt. He would go visit them soon. He looked at his watch and snorted, smiling slightly. It would be a long time before he would see his two favorite people again, but he was supposed to meet Tyler, Quinn, and Eric at the Scotsman in an hour. He had made more new friends in the last few weeks than he had in the last twenty years. *I guess I won't be that lonely after all,* Markus thought, smiling as he headed back down to the colony.

The trip to Mars took nearly two weeks. The legendary red planet had grown increasingly beautiful as the decades passed. Mars was now spotted with blue crater lakes and striped with green and blue valleys framed with red walls. Jonas requested permission to land at Olympus Mons spaceport shortly after entering orbit.

"This is Captain Black of the Europan ship *Em II*, requesting permission to land at Olympus spaceport."

"Captain *Jonas* Black?" A female traffic controller asked.

"Yes."

Her image appeared on the view screen. "Captain Black, you are granted permission. I'm transmitting the flight path to hangar three forty-three. Please proceed immediately."

A virtual flight path appeared on screen. "Thank you."

"Anything for Jonas and Katherine Black; I'm so glad I got to meet you. I watched your wedding on TV. We've been expecting you all day."

"You have?"

"Of course, media representatives are waiting for you both in the hangar. Everyone is anxious to get the whole story of what happened at the Europa mines."

Jonas made a conscious effort not to groan. "Is there any way you could get us a different hangar?"

The traffic controller giggled. "Of course not, silly. Three forty-three is the one I was told to give you. Besides, they're a determined lot, so you're going to have to meet them sooner or later." She glanced from side-to-side. "At least this time you have fair warning." She winked, seeing his apprehension.

"Thanks for the warning," Jonas said wryly, forcing a smile.

"Certainly; good luck with the cameras." Her image faded.

"Great." Jonas looked at Katherine.

She shrugged. "I guess we might as well get it over with. They'll probably get bored with us once they have their story anyway."

"I hope so..."

Jonas followed the designated flight path into the Martian atmosphere. Gas machines had been churning out atmosphere for over two hundred years in an effort to produce one with a similar density to Earth's. After two centuries, terraforming was still as much an experiment as it was in the beginning. The Martian atmosphere, while still being cultivated, was stable with no indications of degradation. The climate was similar to the high mountain areas of Earth, and slightly more temperate in Valles Marineris, now simply referred to as "The Valley," where the air was denser.

As they descended below forty thousand feet and passed through a thin cloud layer, the massive plateau of Olympus Mons loomed before them. The flight plan led Jonas directly into the side of the sixteen-mile-high wall of the dead volcano.

He felt strange as he rapidly closed on the hangar door, especially since neither the flight plan nor Em had instructed him to reduce speed. They were still at Mach five and only forty miles away before the indicator prompted him to decrease speed to Mach two. In the few seconds it took him to react and the ship to decelerate, they were less than thirty miles away with an ETA of one minute.

Jonas slowed his ship the fourth and last time as he passed through the massive steel hangar doors and brought the *Em II* to a hover. Katherine walked over and stood behind him as he brought the ship gently to rest on deck. He released the controls, realizing his knuckles were white. Not only was it only his third real landing, he could see through the bridge display the hundreds of people watching him do it. He let out a sigh and turned to look at Katherine. Although she smiled at him reassuringly, he could see she still had a death grip on the back of his chair.

Jonas put his hand on Katherine's.

"I don't want to go out there." she quietly shook her head.

"Me neither, but better to get it out of way now. You know from watching the news how reporters are, they won't leave us alone until we give them something. And I don't know about you, but the longer I sit here and think about it, the more nervous I'm going to get. We might as well do it now."

She released her grip on the chair and transferred it to his hand.

"All right, what do we tell them?"

"The truth. Everything from start to finish; that way they won't have anything to bother us about later … At least I hope so." Jonas shrugged.

Katherine stood on the tips of her toes, kissed him, and smiled.

"It should be enough to keep them occupied for awhile."

They donned their jackets. Em already checked and found the ambient temperature a cool forty-eight degrees. Jonas was already wearing his father's pistol and decided to leave it on. Katherine saw that it was still on his hip and turned away, smirking and rolling her eyes.

"I don't think most professors pack heat," she remarked as innocently as she could.

Jonas smiled crookedly.

"Just giving the media what they want. Besides, I'm not like most professors, am I?" he replied smugly, then wrapped his arms around her from behind and gently squeezed her.

"That's for sure. I'm glad I didn't marry someone who was boring, old, and wrinkly. In fifty years I won't mind, except you'd still better not be boring," she teasingly scolded him.

"I promise I won't be a boring old guy. Are you ready to go out there?"

She turned toward him.

"Ready as I'll ever be."

They turned to stand before the hatch, looked at each other once more, and took a deep breath.

Em's door hissed open as air escaped into the lower pressure of the atmosphere. The Martian air felt cold, thin, and dry. Every member of the crowd, clamoring to be the first in front of them, fell silent as the two stepped from their ship, shocked that the man who had killed the galaxy's most wanted criminal and that the greatest hacker in recent history were barely old enough to be married, much less anything else. Most of them had already seen Jonas and Katherine in the limited footage available, but they looked much younger in person. The silence only lasted seconds before the crowd burst into a torrent of questions.

Jonas ignored them for a moment as he watched his previously petrified wife smile and field questions like a pro. Moreover, she was calm, articulate, and gracious. In a few months, she had changed from his cute but slightly goofy and clumsy friend to the most graceful and beautiful woman in the known worlds; the one he loved more than he ever thought it possible for one human being to love another. She turned slightly and saw him staring at her, causing her to smile coyly before going back to her reporters.

Only four months ago I was… It seems like a lifetime ago, Jonas thought, *and I feel more mature, but not a day older.* He looked around at the reporters and cameramen, who all looked like they had at least ten years on him and Kat. *I guess to everyone else, we probably do look like kids.*

Markus had said, "You're only as old as you feel."

Markus said something else one time too, something his dad used to say...

In an instant, memories of Jonas's life rushed through his mind. He thought of growing up on a sheltered but alien moon, building his ship with his dad, being an explorer of a largely unknown world, finding the secret base, flying and owning his own ship, and fighting pirates hand to hand, in space, and underwater. Losing his parents, getting this great job, moving to another world, finding The Light, and, best of all, meeting the girl of his dreams... the one he already knew. Jonas suddenly realized he had done more in his short lifetime than most people did in three. He had been through the fire, tempered, and finally knew who he was; who he really was. For the third time in his life, he felt his fears melted away by a peaceful confidence. He pointed at the first reporter he made eye contact with, who quickly launched into a string of questions. When she was finished, he smiled confidently and answered each one concisely.

As he was hit with the next barrage of questions, he looked over the crowd and out the hangar doors into the dark blue sky. He drew a deep breath of the crisp air. He would miss Europa, but Mars was going to be a good home.